PENGUIN CLASSICS

THE GENEALOGY OF KINGS

Prof. Muhammad Haji Salleh is one of the Malaysian writers who has been awarded the National Literary Award in 1991. He also won the SEA Writers Award in 1997. In 2008, he was named National Scholar of Excellence.

He was the President of the Malaysian Translators Association (1978-1982) and meanwhile many of his poems have been translated into English, German, Chinese, Dutch, Thai, Russian and Portuguese. He also serves on the editorial board of the Southeast Asian Literary Journal, *Tenggara*, a member of the Board of Directors of the Language and Library Council, and a member of the National Literary Awards Panel.

His career began as a teacher at the Butterworth Trade School in 1960 and then continued his teaching career in several schools as a tutor, lecturer, senior lecturer and subsequently held several academic positions at local and international universities. He also made history as the youngest professor who was appointed to the post in 1979 at the age of 37.

Upon returning to Malaysia, he served at the National University of Malaysia and the University of Science Malaysia. For 42 years, he has worked at USM, UKM and UM . He has been invited to teach in the United States, Brunei, Germany and the Netherlands as a visiting professor and has received fellowships from several universities in the United States, Japan and the Netherlands.

He was previously a Guest Professor under the Fulbright-Hays program (1977) and taught at North Carolina State University, Raleigh , USA (1977–1978); lecturer in the Department of Malay Literature; Deputy Dean of the Faculty of Social Sciences and Humanities, UKM; Director of the Institute of Language, Culture Malay Literature. Then became Professor of Literature at the age of 36 (1978). Muhammad is an 'Asian Scholar in Residence' at the University of Michigan. In 1992-1993, he was elected Fullbright Visiting Reseacher, at the University of California, Berkeley; bears the Chair of Malay Studies at the University of Leiden, Netherlands (1993-1994).

In June 1996, he participated in the National Association (Moscow) seminar on 'National Construction and the Literature / Cultural Development in Southeast Asia', in which he presented the paper 'Audience on the Staircase'. The effects of a visit to Moscow, including the performance of 'The Queen of Spades' directed by Peter Fomenko, in the theater of E. Vakhtangov, are reflected in some of his poems.

بسم الله الرحمن الرحيم

الحمد لله رب العالمين والصلاة والسلام على رسول الـ...

The first page of Raffles MSS 18

THE GENEALOGY OF KINGS

SULALAT AL-SALATIN

TUN SERI LANANG
TRANSLATED BY
PROF MUHAMMAD HAJI SALLEH

PENGUIN BOOKS
An imprint of Penguin Random House

PENGUIN BOOKS

USA | Canada | UK | Ireland | Australia
New Zealand | India | South Africa | China | Southeast Asia

Penguin Books is part of the Penguin Random House group of companies
whose addresses can be found at global.penguinrandomhouse.com

Published by Penguin Random House SEA Pte Ltd
9, Changi South Street 3, Level 08-01,
Singapore 486361

First published in Penguin Classics by Penguin Random House SEA 2020

10 9 8 7 6 5 4

ISBN 9789814914185

Typeset in Adobe Garamond Pro by Manipal Technologies Limited, Manipal
Printed at Markono Print Media Pte Ltd, Singapore

www.penguin.sg

A LITERARY BACKGROUND

The *Sulalat al-Salatin*
(*Genealogy of Kings* or *Sejarah Melayu*)

The *Sulalat al-Salatin* (*Genealogy of Kings*), often translated as *Malay Annals*, is a very central text to the history of the states of the Malay Archipelago. It was written at the behest of the Raja di Hilir, Lord of the Upper Reaches:

> We request that My Lord, the Vizier, to inscribe for us a genealogy of all the Malay kings and their customs, together with all the ceremonies of the palace, so that they may be made known and observed by all our descendants who come after us and from them derive some benefit.

Feeling the burden of the request on his shoulders, the Bendahara, Vizier, set to plan his genealogy. He collected stories of the old chiefs and lords of the past and named it *Sulalat al-Salatin*, that is the 'Entire Genealogy of Kings.'

Moreover, it is also 'literary' in its widest sense of the term (*kesusasteraan*). The Malays learn not to measure all their history through written notes and documents, for they were a people who celebrated the sophisticated instruments of oral expression and its musical qualities. The sounds of the language echo throughout their literature, even in what we consider as 'post-traditional' times. The more modern documents, from the eighteenth and nineteenth centuries, however, were written but they are important only as part of a bigger scope of the narration of happenings and their interpretation. Thus, truth may not only be sought in the written pages but also in the words spoken by the bards and singers.

Malay historical time is measured against the wide flow of events of birth, death and reigns and abdication of its various kings. More often than not they were used as time markers. We are invited to estimate the years and the decades from their reigns.

The *Sulalat al-Salatin* is, without doubt, the single most important literary-historical text in the Malay language. It traces the history of what is now Palembang, Bentan, Aceh, Singapore (Temasik), Brunei and Malaysia, and many of its colonies, like Siak and Kampar. Along the way it describes for us the literary art and concept of what is considered history or *sejarah* among the Malays of the pre-modern era.

This text is thus a history of the Malays of Sumatra, the Riau Archipelago and the Malay Peninsula, most probably conceived while Melaka was at its height. Thus, we can feel the exuberance of a people in its flush of success and how their pride is deeply etched into its language. Furthermore, and pre-eminently, it is also a moral history, in the sense that events and time are allowed to flow through its pages, but the author always draws a moral lesson and conclusion at the end of each chapter and finally at the end of the *Sulalat al-Salatin* itself, as an emphasis to the meaning of history itself. The good, the just and the generous are praised, while the selfish and unjust are punished, either in the same chapter or during their lifetimes.

The Melaka (and Johor) points of view and their historical approaches are thus, quite obvious, though the writer or editor at certain times and situations did allow his reflection and criticism.

As has been noted, Melaka was an exceptionally cosmopolitan capital in the fifteenth century in Southeast Asian history. It saw the arrival of numerous Persians, Arabs, Chinese and Indian residents along with other Southeast Asians, especially the Javanese, Acehnese, and various groups of Sumatranese (among whom were the inhabitants of the colonies of Melaka), Ambonese and Kampucheans. They lived in the city, sharing space, business and cultural activities with the local inhabitants.

A TIME FRAME

The Melaka of the *Sulalat al-Salatin* began with the Malay kingdom of Palembang, around the seventh century through Bentan and Temasik; and Melaka, in the thirteenth century. When it fell in 1511, Melaka's history continued its troubled journey in Pahang, Johor and Bentan, and Kampar, across the straits to Sumatra. It ended with the fall of Melaka. This is the latitude of time as described in the MSS Raffles 18, the earliest manuscript of the *Genealogy*, written between 1612 and 1614. This manuscript is now in the Royal Asiatic Society, dated 1812.

In some other versions the description of life and administration in the other Malay states were updated to the post-Dutch era. The author of the *Sulalat al-Salatin*, in one version, is purported to be Raja Bongsu, alias Raja Abdullah of Johor. This early version was taken to Goa, in Sulawesi, before or during the fall of Melaka. However, when it was returned to Johor, the Vizier at that time, Tun Seri Lanang, was instructed to improve it with due ceremony, so that 'our descendants who may come after us may derive some benefit' from it.

Like the *Hikayat Hang Tuah*, an epic based on the popular hero of the same name, it is perhaps the most popular of Malay literary or historical texts. There are more than thirty copies (of the different versions) in Malaysia, Indonesia and Europe.

In Malaysia, the Dewan Bahasa dan Pustaka has three copies (MS93, MS86, MS86a).

The Royal Asiatic Society, in London, has seven manuscripts in all,

1) Farquhar 5 *Sejarah Melayu*
2) Raffles Malay 18 *Sejarah Melayu*
3) Raffles Malay 35 *Sejarah Melayu*
4) Raffles Malay 68 *Sejarah Melayu*
5) Raffles Malay 76 *Sejarah Melayu*
6) Raffles Malay 80 *Sejarah Melayu*
7) Maxwell 26 *Sejarah Melayu.*

The School of Oriental and African Studies, University of London, has three manuscripts,

1) MS 36495
2) MS 36499
3) MS 297496

Cambridge University Library has one manuscript, Or. 459, while John Rylands has another, Malay 1.

Finally, the Leiden University Library has thirteen manuscripts,

1) Cod. Or. 1703, 17
2) Cod. Or. 1704, 17 (copied by Muhammad Sulaiman)
3) Cod. Or. 1716, 18 (copied by Muhammad Cheng),
4) Cod. Or. 1736. 19 (copied in Riau)
5) Cod. Or. 1760. 21
6) Cod. Or. 3210, 31 (copied in Riau)
7) Cod. Or. 12026, 64
8) Cod. Or. 12027, 64
9) Cod. Or. 14319 A. 65
10) Kl. 5
11) SED. 902 (556, 75)
12) Cod. Or. 63 (I) 2
13) Cod. Or. 64 (II) 2.

The beginning chapters of *Sulalat al-Salatin* were possibly drafted and written in 1612 in Pasir Raja, when the town was the capital of the Johor Empire. However, in 1613, the Acehnese attacked Johor and the writer, Tun Seri Lanang, was captured. Fortunately, he was saved, brought to Aceh and was installed as a minor raja in Samalanga, in central Aceh, and probably finished the work there, in 1614.

The earliest manuscript of the *Sulalat* (Raffles 18) in the Royal Asiatic Society has been transcribed by Winstedt, 1939, and Muhammad Haji Salleh, 1997. Incidentally, Cod. Or. 1704 in the Library was copied by Muhammad Sulaiman and is a work of the finest calligraphy and illumination.

This work has been translated into English, French and German.

A MORALISTIC BENT

It is a belief and practice in Malay society that literature should be composed by its most enlightened and erudite members. Though it was often stressed that literary works were to entertain, in fact, beneath the texts themselves was a consideration that they should be socially and morally beneficial. There are thus numerous references made, on the different levels, consciously or unconsciously, directly or tangentially, to the problems present in a society at a certain time. Some of these problems may describe the nature and quality of conflicts in their various forms. Society must survive and therefore its authors (oral and written)—noble sages and thinkers of their times—were exhorted to provide certain solutions, which they could follow and act upon.

Although literature was written for the society as a whole, many of the works of the past were composed especially for kings and administrators. For example, the *Taj us-Salatin* (Crown of Kings) which specially set out to teach values and principles, was to act as a guide to good governance. The title of the works itself suggests that the crown must possess a deep knowledge of its duties and functions, so that as a 'shadow of God on earth' he may be able to fulfil his task professionally and satisfactorily. Works in this genre have been the staple reading material of kings in the Malay Archipelago for some centuries.

I would include the *Sulalat* in this cluster of works that help to guide the ruling Sultans, for there are many episodes and chapters that describe events and actions initiated by the rulers, and their attendant good or evil consequences.

Though the contemporary definition of literature would not include such works that speak of good governance and administration, Malay historical works and religious treatises, these writings often include fiction and poetry and share many common qualities with the prevalent literary style. In the traditional definition and meaning of literature, *kesusasteraan* is invariably wider and more all-encompassing than its modern one. In this designation, literature also includes the *mantera*, incantation, the proverbs, the poems: *pantuns, gurindam* and the *syair*. All of them share a certain aspiration to be 'instructive', often enough also having the qualities of the didactic.

In several interviews with Malay and Sumatran storytellers, puppeteers and members of the audience of traditional performances (Muhammad Haji Salleh, 1989), it was found that good literature or good works seem to be those that bring over *pengajaran* (teaching) or *pelajaran* (knowledge). This definition demands that good works guide, advise or teach, directly or indirectly. The directly didactic have been as popular as the subtler ones, as they have been accepted as products of the best minds, contributing to a communal pool of knowledge and wisdom.

In the villages of the unlettered society of pre-nineteenth century, only a few were able to master the formidable art of reading and writing. However, literature, in all its forms, especially the oral performances, were the most popular (and inordinately more entertaining), as a source of this kind of teaching and knowledge. It was also the most available. Stories were told on the verandas and in the outer rooms of village houses, under the trees of the yard, to the children to whom these stories later became the reference points in their lives.

From the *wayang kulit* (puppet theatre), *menora* (the dance-drama) and the rich *lipur lara* oral narratives, they gained knowledge of the modes of behaviour of the good protagonists and their subsidiary characters.

And into these presentations were also sown popular proverbs, poems (*syair* and *pantun*), and religious texts.

It is also interesting to note that stories like *Hikayat Isma Yatim* even provided practical pointers on how to choose a wife, a husband, plan a park and so on, besides its exemplary teaching on how to be an ideal writer/man/woman.

The range of themes of literature is as wide as the experience of the people themselves. Malay literature describes *la condition humaine*—its suffering and sorrow, its laughter and smiles, its fragile existence on the surface of the great oceans and land, the pride of the kingdoms and their colonies, their fall, and consequently, the collapse of the states themselves.

Their natural backdrop is the sea, lakes, rivers, forests, hills, and caves. We meet human characters in their dilapidated huts, the great palaces with magical furnishings, great ships, orchards, and paddy fields that sustain them through the seasons. Between this backdrop and events, we again find a collection of various subjects dealing with knowledge, ethics, religion, morality, and the ideal life.

History, as we noted earlier, was written for the benefit of the reader (the audience)—the descendants of the king and the author. Clearly the *Sulalat al-Salatin* was arranged to be a didactic collection of episodes. It set out to teach by example and commentary, directly or tangentially. A clear case in point is the story of the unjust King of Singapore, who sentenced to death his wife, a senior minister's daughter after accusing her of adultery, without due investigation. As an act of rebellion, the minister opened the gates of the city to his Javanese enemies, resulting in its sacking, and his exile. Another very didactic scene of events is to be seen in the last episodes of the *Genealogy*, which parallel those of Singapura, where favouritism, negligence and injustice brought about division among the Melakans, finally making them vulnerable to the attack of the Portuguese.

What I would like to establish at this juncture is that Malay literature, especially the traditional, was and is in fact, very close to its society. It dealt with its real problems and also its dreams and ideals. It dealt not only with the pain of separation of lovers but also pleasure of their reunion.

It also deliberated on the division among people, on how to police the streets at night to keep the thieves at bay. On a higher moral ground, it described the nobility of humility, magnanimity and courtesy. It also helped to define the arc of authority and responsibility for those in power. More than anything else these moral and religious spaces were accorded a special eminence, for they were seen to be the saviour not only of the person, but also the village and the state.

Besides being the products of the intellectual elite, these works were also seen as the words of the *sahibul hikayat* (the author of the narrative), *orang tua-tua* (the older generation), *orang dahulu kala* (those from the ancient times) who were seen as the wisest in their societies. These composers were also looked upon as being closer to the source of truth and wisdom. Their words were likewise seen as sacred, for they were the teachings of their forefathers, and especially recorded for their descendants.

With this preliminary sketch of the didactic nature of Malay literary works vis-à-vis its moral and social functions, I would like to refer the reader to translations of the work, firstly, John Leyden's (1821 and republished in 2012), and C. C. Brown's (1970) and my own transliteration (1997).

The chosen version, as noted earlier, is Raffles MSS 18, the oldest extant manuscript. I have made a new transliteration (1997) of this text. This manuscript is among the best that is kept in the libraries worldwide.

A CONTEMPORARY RELEVANCE

But, why, one asks, the *Sulalat al-Salatin*, from the thousand-odd titles? The answer is quite simple. It is recognized as the greatest Malay literary work and spans the early period of Malay history, providing numerous episodes that help us interpret the different phases of their history, their successes and failures. In it too we find various themes that describe the mind of the villagers and their rulers. It is the only text that deals with Malay history since the beginnings of the Malay rajas and their states.

It still speaks to them, to their present reality, for it describes for them as Malaysians, Bruneians, Singaporeans and Indonesians, the very roots of their identity, thoughts, ideals, the philosophy of governance, the responsibility of the ruler and the rights of the *rakyat,* subjects.

This *Genealogy* brings the lessons and wisdom of the past for the generations of the future. These selected lessons and thoughts of the past seem to be as relevant then as they are now, for they consider life and history in the states of the Archipelago, their achievements and failures, the various kings and their successes or otherwise, their personae and impact on the people of the land. Their values and concepts of justice and ethics are described for our consideration and verdict. And so, to their idea of *sopan santun* and *budi Bahasa*—intricate courtesy and expression of interpersonal relationship.

We are also shown the exemplary literary style of the author, Tun Seri Lanang, (considered to be one of the finest) who negotiated through a web of classical language to tell the truth and define the idea of justice. Tun Seri Lanang's use of metaphor, turns of succinct phrases, subtle allegories and symbols belong to those of a genius. To this student of his works and his translator, he was indeed a literary genius.

Many too are the description of the nobles and administrators, the princes and the princesses, the serious and the humorous. These are their history, and our story.

For those who would study the Malays and Malaysia, this work is a valuable historical and intellectual introduction.

In terms of style and linguistic achievement, the *Sulalat al-Salatin* is an exemplary work. This is attested to by Abdullah Munshi, an author writing in the nineteenth century.

THIS TRANSLATION

There have been two translations into English before this present one, and one would ask: What need is there for another one?

The earlier versions were for readers of the twentieth century, which try to imitate the original language of Tun Seri Lanang. However, as times changed along with the English language itself, there is a dire need for another one that is more accessible to those of the present generation, to their taste and idea of the work of literature.

This is my aim. Thus, this rendering is generally in an English that is closer to the speech of the twenty-first century. As this translation is for a general readership, I have tried to keep the historiographical and linguistic references to a minimum. Should a reader be interested in greater detail and explanation I would like to refer him/her to my transliteration of the MSS Raffles 18, published in 1997. He/she is also welcome to compare them with C.C. Brown's.

I am always entranced by the fine poetic qualities of the narrative, and have done my utmost to retain its metaphors, turns of phrases and their wonderfully precise terms, and not to forget, the music of his sophisticated Malay.

I

Bismillahirrahmanirrahim.

In the name of Allah, most Merciful, and most Compassionate. Praise be to Him, Lord of the Universe; and prayers of peace unto His Messenger and all His Companions.

In the Du al-awal, 1021st year of the Hijrah of Muhammad, the Messenger of God, (peace be upon him), on the twelfth day of the month of Rabiul Awal, on a Sunday, at the time of the midday prayer, during the reign of the Paduka Seri Sultan, Alauddin Ri'ayat Shah, the shadow of the lord on earth, *zilalullah fil alam*, who was on the throne in Pasir Raja, there came My Lord, Seri Nara Wangsa, by the name of Tun Bambang, the son of Sheri Agar, the King of Fatani, to seek His Majesty's audience.

His lordship carried the word of the Yang Pertuan di Hilir, the Lord of the Downstream Territories, he who was honourable in place and time, and truly a jewel among all true believers, for he shed light on every point of faith and welfare—may Allah bestow on him all the exemplary qualities of character and generosity, and may he rule with justice in all the states that he reigns over.

So said his lordship, 'We request that My Lord, the Vizier, inscribe for us a genealogy[1] of all the Malay kings and their customs, together

---

[1]   *Peteturun*, genealogy, this is a rare use for *turun*, but describes well the line of descendants.

1

with all the ceremonies of the palace, so that they may be known and observed by all our descendants who will come after us, so that they may know the words and the history of our people, and from them derive some benefit.'

After your humble servant, who is duly conscious of his own inadequacies and his insufficient knowledge, one who is mindful of his own ignorance, has listened to the words of his most honourable lordship, thus the burden of the task has fallen on your humble servant's shoulders to bear.

So, your humble servant bestirred himself to the task. He then requested the blessings of God, the Creator of the World, and the Prophet's, the foremost among humankind. Thus, your servant duly composed this *hikayat*,[2] and assembled stories of the old chiefs and lords of the past so that they may entertain Your Majesty. Your servant named it *Sulalat al-Salatin*, that is, *The Entire Genealogy of Kings*. If one should read it, one should not deliberate on it with a pure discourse, for as the Prophet, (peace be upon on him), has said, *tafkirufi ala'i Llahi wa la tafkirufi dzati 'Llahi*, that is, you shall discourse on the greatness of Allah, and think not of His essence.

Thus, begin the words of this *hikayat*, as told by the original author of the narrative.

* * *

During his times, Alexander the Great, the son of the King of Darab,[3] (from the tribe of Rome; Macedonia was the name of his country), journeyed to the east to observe the rising sun. He soon arrived at the

---

[2] *Hikayat*, Arabic. A tale, a history, or narrative.

[3] *Iskandar Zulkarnain, Iskandar Dua Tanduk, anak Raja Darab atau Macedonia* (Maqaduniah), born in 356 (according to the *Genealogy*), known in the Malay Archipelago through the *Hikayat Iskandar Zulkarnain*, an early narrative of the conquest of the Persian Empire. He was said to have invaded much of the Middle East and crossed over to India. From there his descendants reappeared on Bukit Siguntang, in Palembang, to initiate the beginnings of the genealogy of Malay Sultans in the Archipelago.

borders of the country of the Hindus. There was once in this country a great king, and equally great was his kingdom, as half of India was under his authority. His name was Raja Kida Hindi.

When he became aware of the arrival of Alexander, His Majesty commanded his Vizier to assemble all the people of the land. When they had gathered, he began the task to expel King Alexander. Presently the two sides met and began to battle, as is described in the *Hikayat Iskandar*,[4] the Epic of Alexander.

Raja Kida Hindi was defeated and taken prisoner by Alexander, and was asked by Alexander to embrace his religion. After that Raja Kida Hindi became a Muslim in the religion of the Prophet Abraham. Soon, King Alexander commanded him to return to his country.

In the intervening time, it was narrated that Raja Kida Hindi had a daughter; she was extremely fine-looking, none was her compare in those days—the light of her face shone like the rays of the sun. The princess was wise, both in her deeds and demeanour. Shahr al-Bariyah was her name. Once King Kida Hindi called his Vizier aside, to a quiet place.

He said to his Vizier, 'We have summoned My Lord here because we should like to ask your view—my daughter is a woman who has no comparison in her beauty and demeanour in these times; we should like to present her to King Alexander. What is My Lord's advice?'

The Vizier bowed in obeisance, 'What Your Majesty has proposed is the best of possible offerings. If God should will it, on the morrow I will go, My Lord, to Prophet Khidir, and inform to him all that Your Majesty has reflected here.'

So, the minister rode into the hills to seek Prophet Khidir. In the meantime, when he had departed, Raja Kida Hindi decreed that the name of Alexander be imprinted on all the coins, on all the tall standards and banners of the land.

When the Vizier greeted the prophet of God, he welcomed him and invited him to take a seat.

---

[4]   *Hikayat Iskandar Zulkarnain* was known quite early in the Archipelago, the latest by the seventeenth century.

Said the Vizier to Prophet Khidir, 'Be it known, My Lord, that His Majesty Raja Kida Hindi has much love for King Alexander, almost to distraction. My words are unable to describe it. It is also well known that His Majesty has a daughter whose beauty is incomparable in these times—her face shines like the sun, she is wise, gracious and kind. In our times, no one is her compare, in these lands where the sun rises and sets. Her beauty and demeanour are likewise without equal. It is the wish of my master to present her to King Alexander as his consort.'

The author of the story related that the Prophet Khidir soon departed to seek an audience with King Alexander and he relayed all that had transpired between himself and the vizier.

In due time, King Alexander entered the audience hall, where all the rajas, religious scholars and officers of state took their seats, while the chiefs and knights spread around his throne, and behind them were his chosen and trusted servants.

At that same instant, Raja Kida Hindi was also present in the hall, sitting on a golden chair, coated with jewels. Soon the Prophet Khidir stood up and paid his respects to King Alexander. He began his words with the name of Allah *Subhanahu wa Ta'ala*, and praised the Prophet Abraham, *khalilullah,* and all the ancient prophets who preceded him. Soon, he pronounced the articles of marriage before King Alexander and he repeated them to Raja Kida Hindi.

Thus said Nabi Khidir, 'Be it known to Your Majesty, oh Raja Kida Hindi, that to this king of ours Allah has bestowed the lordship of all the kingdoms on earth, from the east to the west, from the north to the south. Now it has come to our knowledge that Your Majesty has a daughter of incomparable beauty. It is His Majesty's wish that you shall love her and on his part he will take My Lord as his son-in-law, so that all the descendants of Raja Kida Hindi and those of King Alexander shall forever be interwoven. What says you, My Lord?'

The author of the *hikayat* narrated that when Raja Kida Hindi heard the words of Prophet Khidir, he stepped down from his royal throne and stood on the ground and subsequently made obeisance towards King Alexander.

He said, 'Be it known to Your Majesty, the Prophet of God and all those who are now assembled, that I am truly a servant of King Alexander, and be it also known that all the lords and our descendants are likewise servants to His Majesty. Now let it be known to all those present that Nabi Khidir is my own representative and my daughter's, Princess Shahr al-Bariyah.

When the Prophet heard the words of Raja Kida Hindi, he turned to look upon King Alexander, and said, 'I have joined in marriage the daughter of Raja Kida Hindi, Princess Shahr al-Bariyah, to King Alexander; her dowry is three hundred thousand golden dinars. Does Your Majesty approve?'

When King Alexander has made known his consent, the daughter of Raja Kida Hindi was ritually married to King Alexander, before all those present, according to the decree of the Prophet Abraham.

Thereupon all the rajas, chief officers of the state and all the prime ministers, knights, scholars, priests and judges began to scatter gold, silver, jewels and gems at the feet of King Alexander. Thus, there grew before His Majesty two or three piles of gold, gems and jewels.

These were presently given away as alms to the poor and the needy. When night had fallen, Raja Kida Hindi accompanied his daughter to King Alexander's, bringing with them all her possessions, all the jewels bequeathed by her ancestors, and those worn by her to enhance her beauty.

That night, King Alexander became her husband. He was amazed to gaze upon her countenance—words may not describe his feelings.

On the morrow, His Majesty commanded that Princess Shahr al-Bariyah be dressed in the most magnificent royal costumes, and he bequeathed her innumerable gifts. To the rajas he gave noble costumes, all of them beaded with exotic gems. To these were added a hundred chosen steeds, and all their saddles too were of gold, and similarly inlaid with gems. And all those who saw them were full of awe and wonder.

* * *

On the morrow, King Alexander presented Princess Shahr al-Bariyah
with a complete wardrobe of royal costume and gave her innumerable
gifts. And then King Alexander presented sets of noble fabrics to
all the rajas, which were decorated with gems and jewels. Three godowns were opened. And Raja Kida Hindi himself was presented with
royal costumes, a hundred golden bowls containing jewels and noble
varieties of gems, and a hundred specially chosen horses, and all their
accessories, also decorated with gold, jewels and gems. And those who
watched them were filled with wonder.

After his wedding King Alexander remained for ten days in
Hindustan. On the eleventh, he departed, as was the custom of the
days of old, and the princess, the daughter of Raja Kida Hindi, followed
her husband. So, King Alexander rode to the east, as was described
in the renowned *hikayat*. In time, King Alexander returned from the
country where the sun rose; he remained for some time in Hindustan.
Raja Kida Hindi duly came out to greet him with presents and gifts of
precious jewels and magnificent gems.

Raja Kida Hindi greeted King Alexander and related how he
missed his very presence. Neither could he put his yearning into
words, or express his great longing for his daughter, Princess Shahr
al-Bariyah. He requested his daughter from her husband, who readily
fulfilled his father-in-law's request. Soon after that Raja Kida Hindi
presented him and his daughter a hundred noble costumes, and gave
both of them gold, silver, jewels, and beautiful objects all—they were
innumerable. Raja Kida Hindi then bowed in obeisance. He then
presented King Alexander with a hundred ceremonial costumes from
his own wardrobe.

The drums were then beaten to signal the entrance of the kings, the
nafiri[5] royal trumpets were then blown, to mark the departure of King
Alexander, all in accordance with the rites of old. His Majesty's intent
was to conquer all the rajas who had not come under his authority, as
was now well known.

---

[5] *Nafiri*: a trumpet used as one of the appurtenances of royalty.

It was narrated that Princess Shahr al-Bariyah, the daughter of Raja Kida Hindi, in time, was with child. However, King Alexander knew not that she was with child. It was only a month later that she became aware that she was carrying the child of King Alexander, for her menses had ceased.

Soon Princess Shahr al-Bariyah informed her father, 'Be it known, my father, that I have not had my menses for the past two months.'

When Raja Kida Hindi heard his daughter's words he was extremely delighted that his daughter was carrying King Alexander's offspring, and accordingly nursed her as was the custom of the royal house. When the gestation months were complete, Princess Shahr al-Bariyah gave birth to a boy.

Raja Kida Hindi named his grandson Raja Arashthun Shah, (Child of a Great King). Great was his affection for him. In time, Arashthun Shah grew, his looks were magnificent, quite identical to his father's, King Alexander Zulkarnain. In time, Raja Kida Hindi requested the hand of Raja Turkistan's daughter for his grandson. Soon Raja Arashthun Shah begot a boy, his name was Raja Afdhus.

Forty-five years after King Alexander's return to Macedonia, Raja Kida Hindi himself returned to the blessings of the Lord. Raja Arashthun Shah succeeded him to the throne of India; His Majesty reigned for three hundred and fifty years. After which he departed for the eternal realm. Raja Afdhus' son ascended the throne after him, reigning[6] for a hundred and twenty years. When he departed this earth, Raja Ashkainat replaced him on the throne; he was king for three years, and was succeeded by Raja Kasdas, who reigned for twelve years. When he in turn departed for the eternal world, his brother, Raja Amtabus, became king; he was on the throne for thirteen years. When he in turn departed, Raja Kharuaskainat became the ruler in the land for a period of thirty years. After him Raja Arhad Ashkainat was crowned, he was the ruler of the land for nine years. His son, Kudar Zakuhan, ascended

---

[6] *Pemerintahan, kerajaan*, reign, the period during which a monarch is the official ruler of a country.

the throne, ruling for seventy years. He was in turn succeeded by Raja
Nikabus, who ruled for the next forty years.

In time, it came to Raja Arusiribikan's turn to become king—he
was the son of Raja Kudar Zakuhan. He took to himself a wife, the
daughter of Raja Nushirwan Adil, the King of the east and the west.
With his Queen, the daughter of Raja Nushirwan, Raja Arusiribikan
begot a boy by the name of Raja Dariya Nusa. When Arussiribikan
reached the ripe old age of a hundred, he passed on. His son Raja
Dariya Nusa subsequently succeeded him, reining for ninety years.
When he died Raja Kastih was installed ruler; his reign was only for
four months. He was followed by Raja Ramji, who ruled for twenty
years and nine months. After His Majesty came Raja Shah Taramsi.
He was the scion[7] of Raja Dariya Nusa; reigning a total of twenty years.
Raja Teja succeeded him, ruling for seventy years. After him came Raja
Ijqar, who was on the throne for ten years.

The son of Raja Shahi Tarsi, Raja Uramzad, was then crowned
and he ruled for a hundred and sixty years. He was followed by Raja
Yazdikarda, who was on the throne for sixty-four years and four
months. In time, he was succeeded by Raja Kofi Kudar. His Majesty
reigned for sixty-three years.

Next in line was Raja Tarsi Bardaras, the son of Raja Uramzad,
the grandson of Raja Shahi Tarsi, the great grandson of Raja Dariya
Nusa, the great grandson of Raja Arusiribikan, who was the son of Raja
Kudar Zakuhan, the grandson of Raja Amtabus, the great grandson of
Raja Sabur, the great-great grandson of Raja Afdhus, the son of Raja
Arashtun Shah, who was the son of King Alexander. Tarsi Bardaras
took the daughter of Raja Amand Nakana as his Queen. They begot
two sons, Kudar Shah Jahan, and Raja Suran Padshah—both of them
were extremely good looking.

Allah knows the truth; to Him shall we return.

---

[7] *Keturunan*, scion, a descendant, heir, or young member of a family.

II

The words of the narrative now turn to describe a *negeri* in the country of the Kelings, in the southern slice of the sub-continent of Hindi. It was known as Naga Patam, while its King was Raja Shulan.

Raja Shulan descended from the grandson of Raja Nurshirwan Adil, the son of Raja Kobad Shahriar, the King of the east and the west. No one knew the extent of his country. He was indeed a great king, for all the kings of Sindi and Hindi were under his authority.

Once upon a time, he commanded that his innumerable armies and soldiers be gathered. Soon all the kings from the numerous states assembled, with all their subjects, complete with their instruments of war and weapons. When everyone was armed, Raja Shulan rode on, his intention was to conquer all the *negeris* in the east. His soldiers and subjects soon advanced, following their king. Forests and jungles were turned to flat land, all the highlands became level, and the stones were all a-strewn, from the feet of so many subjects walking on them. In time, all the states which fought against His Majesty were defeated. All the rajas in the east were subjugated.

Before long, Raja Shulan arrived at a *negeri*, Gangga Shah Nagara was its name. It was located on a hill. If one were to look at it from its base, it appeared to be extremely elevated; however, from behind, it looked less so. One can see the fortress even now near Dinding, in Perak. Its king was Raja Linggi Shah.

When word reached His Majesty that Raja Shulan has arrived, he commanded that all his subjects be gathered, the gates of the fortresses be secured and the moats filled with water for their needs, and all the buildings be guarded. In the meantime, all the subjects of Raja Shulan advanced and blockaded Raja Linggi Shah Johan's fortifications. Raja Linggi's forces fought in retaliation.

After surveying the situation Raja Shulan advanced, on his elephant. Though he was constantly attacked with arrows and spears from the fort above, he continued to march towards the gates of Gangga Nagara, oblivious to their weapons, and finally pounded on the gates with his mace. Soon the gates gave way. Raja Shulan presently entered the fort with all his warriors. When Raja Linggi Shah Johan noticed Raja Shulan approaching, he arose, holding his bow. Immediately he shot an arrow which pierced the elephant's forehead, causing it to collapse. Raja Shulan quickly jumped away while striking at Raja Linggi Shah Johan's neck, decapitating him. His head fell, rebounded and rolled away. Raja Linggi Shah Johan died. When the subjects of Gangga Nagara saw that their king has been slain, they fled the field of battle.

Raja Shulan presently departed after Gangga Nagara had been defeated. In due time, he arrived at the borders of a state known as Langkawi. In the days of old, Langkawi was a large state, its fort was of granite, and you may still see its ruins now. Its original name, however, was Kelangkui, meaning a treasure house of jewels. As we are not able to pronounce its name well, it finally became Langkawi. Its king was Raja Chulin, a grand monarch. All the kings to the east were under his rule.

As soon as Raja Chulin received word that Raja Shulan has arrived he commanded that all his subjects be gathered and all the rajas under him be summoned. When all the rajas had assembled Raja Chulin led his people to defeat Raja Shulan.

Innumerable were they, like the sea at high tide; the elephants and horses looked like islands, the banners and standards like trees in the forest. Their weapons were precisely arranged, spears with ornamental pendants appearing like the flowers of the *lalang* weeds. They marched for a full four *keruh*[1] before they met and began to battle. The din of war was beyond one's imagination—the clamour of the elephants battling each other, of horses biting at each other, and all the soldiers clicking their bows. And all those carrying spears spiked at each other, all those carrying lances pierced each other and those with swords wounding each other. All the weapons that descended on the plain seemed like a heavy rain falling. Though there was thunder in the skies it could not be heard for all battle cries of the warriors; and along with them the deafening clash of the weapons.

From the field of battle rose clouds of dust, and the day became frenzied as though there was an eclipse of the sun. Both the armies fused into each other; they were unrecognizable to their enemies. Those who ran amok were in turn attacked, some even slashed at their own friends.

As the war wore on, many perished on both sides; and so too, many elephants and horses. Much blood flowed into the dust that rose no more into the air, being thick with blood. When at last it settled those battling each other could then be seen. However, neither would give way. Subsequently Raja Chulin charged his elephant into Raja Shulan's numerous subjects. Where it charged many died, and they were piled in towering heaps. Many were the dead among the Kelings, so they subsequently retreated.

When Raja Shulan observed the state of the battle he advanced and again charged to expel Raja Chulin. His mount was an elephant eight spans tall, but Raja Chulin's elephant was extremely brave. So the two met and battled. The din that they made was like endless thunder and their clashing trunks like lightning splitting the hills. Neither would surrender. Raja Chulin stood on his elephant, weighing his spear, and soon hurled it at Raja Shulan. It penetrated through the elephant's

---

[1]   *Keruh*, a Persian measurement of distance, about three kilometres according to Dr Bukhari Lubis.

howdah,[2] piercing a span deep into its side. Immediately Raja Shulan
retaliated, with his arrow directed at Raja Chulin; it struck his chest,
penetrating it. Raja Chulin fell from his ride and died.

When his subjects perceived the tragic turn of events, they broke
ranks and ran for their lives. They were followed by the Kelings, who
killed everyone they could lay their hands on. Subsequently the Kelings
rushed into the fort and plundered it. Great was their loot, of many
kinds and riches.

Raja Chulin had a daughter, Princess Onangkiau was her name,
and she was a beauty without compare. It was she who was presented
to Raja Shulan, who took her as his wife.

Raja Shulan returned victorious. When he arrived in Benua
Keling he built an extremely large *negeri*. Its fort was of black
granite, seven-span thick, and nine spans tall. So skilful were the
stone workers that the joints between the slabs were quite invisible,
looking as though they were cast. Its great doors were of steel, inlaid
with gold and jewels.

The fort enclosed seven mountains within it. In its exact centre was
a lake, so wide was it that it looked like the sea. If an elephant were to
stand on the opposite beach, it would not be visible from this side of
the lake. Several species of fish were released into it.

In the middle of it there was an extremely tall mountain, forever
enveloped in the clouds, as though touched lightly by the dew. Many
were the species of wood, flowers and fruits that were planted on the
island; every specie to be found on earth grew here. When Raja Shulan
wanted to be with his subjects it was to this place that he came.

On the edge of the lake he planted a great forest. He released all
the wild animals there and when he wanted to go hunting or to snare
the elephants it was to this forest that he would go. He named the state
Bencha Nagara; you may still see it in the country of the Kelings. If one
were to narrate the entire story of Raja Shulan, its book would be as
thick as the epical narrative of the *Hikayat Amir Hamzah*.

---

[2] *Baluan*, howdah.

In due time Raja Shulan's consort, Princess Onangkiau, the daughter of Raja Chulin, gave birth to a beautiful girl. In those times, none was her compare. His father named her Princess Cenandi Wasis. When she grew into a young maiden, Raja Suran Padshah married the princess. Raja Suran Padshah and the Princess bore three children: a boy, by the name of Raja Chiran—he became the King of Chenderagiri Nagara; another, also a boy, Raja Chulan; and the last one, Raja Pandaian, who was brought up by his grandmother. It was he who sat on the throne of Naga Patam.

In time Raja Shulan died. It was his grandson, Raja Chulan who succeeded him, extending the borders of the *negeri* beyond those of his grandfather. All the *negeris* of Hindi and Sindi came under his authority. All the rajas of the east and west similarly came under his sovereignty.

As time passed Raja Chulan deliberated on a strategy to defeat China. He soon commanded that all his soldiers and armies be assembled. With them also came his innumerable subjects. All the kings under him came along too, also with their subjects there were one thousand and two hundred kings in all. When all of them were finally assembled, Raja Chulan led them to defeat the Great Chinese Nation. So many were the subjects who marched that jungles and forests became fields, the earth trembled as in a quake, the mountains moved, their peaks tumbled into the plains. Thus, all the tall hills became flatlands, and all the great river plains became dry fields. The armies and subjects of the king marched for six months, without breaking ranks. If they had arrived on a dark night their presence would light up their surroundings as a moon during its fourteenth night, from the shimmer[3] and sheen[4] of all the weapons; and even if there was thunder in the sky it would not be heard for the clamour and yells of all the warriors.

---

[3] *Bergermelapan*, shimmer, to shine with a glistening or tremulous light.
[4] *Kilauan*, sheen, a gleaming or glistening brightness, lustre.

Within a few weeks, they arrived in Temasik. News was received in China that, 'Raja Chulan is coming to attack us, bringing with him an innumerable number of soldiers and subjects. He is now in Temasik.'

The Raja of China was full of awe listening to the news.

His Majesty enquired of all his minsters and officers, 'What are your views on how to expel this evil fortune, for if he were to arrive on our shores, China will be defeated?'

The Prime Minister of China enjoined, 'Lord of the World, the task to find a solution falls upon your humble servant's shoulders. Yes, oh Lord of the World, earnestly, it falls on me to deal with it.'

The King commanded, 'My Lord, do deliberate on it.'

The Prime Minister commanded that a ship be constructed. Into it were laden fine needles, and on to the vessel he also transplanted full-grown persimmon and jujuba trees—all of them had already borne fruits. He selected from among the oldest of people, all of them toothless, to sail to Temasik.

When they have arrived in Temasik it was reported to Raja Chulan, 'There is a vessel from China that has docked.'

Raja Chulan ordered his man, 'Go and ask the Chinese man how far his country is from here.'

So, the man went to enquire of the man from the vessel.

He answered, 'When we weighed anchor in China, we were all quite young, only twelve years old then, and we were the ones who planted these trees. Now we are old, our teeth have fallen, all the trees have borne fruits; it's only now that we have arrived here.'

He took a few needles and showed them to the Keling, saying, 'When we set sail from China these needles were like iron rods, as big as our lower arms. Now they are all rusted out. That is how long it takes to arrive here. We do not know how many years it took.'

As soon as he heard the words of the Chinese sailor, the Keling sought his master. He repeated to His Majesty all that he had heard. When Raja Chulan understood his messenger's report, he said, 'If as reported by the man, this country of China is indeed very far away, when shall we be able to ever reach it? It's better to turn around.'

All the warriors replied, 'What Your Majesty has said is indeed true.'

Raja Chulan then fell to thinking, 'All the contents of the land I have now known. But the contents of the seas, what does that look like? In that case, let me now journey into the sea, so that I may know of it.'

After thus thinking Raja Chulan commanded that all carpenters and craftsmen be gathered. He instructed them to fashion a glass cage that could be opened or closed from the inside. So, the carpenters and craftsmen set to building a cage as desired by His Majesty. Finally, they fitted it with a golden chain and brought it before His Majesty. On sighting the singular box, Raja Chulan was extremely glad. He gave gifts to all the carpenters and craftsmen—innumerable were they.

Soon Raja Chulan entered the cage. He could see all from inside it. His Majesty secured it. And the men soon eased him into the sea and the cage sank to the bottom. His Majesty observed the wonders of Allah *Subhanahu wa Ta'ala*. By the power of Allah, the cage beached on an undersea world named Dika.

Raja Chulan then left the cage; he began to inspect the surroundings and take pleasure in all that was beautiful around him. He found the underworld, a comely and handsome place, an extensive one and well-built.

He entered the fort to meet the tribesmen of Barsam, who were innumerable; no one knew how many they were altogether, except Allah *Subhanahu wa Ta'ala*. They were both Muslim and heathen by the half. When they set their eyes on the countenance of Raja Chulan and his costume they were amazed and were full of wonder. The people brought him to their King, Raja Aftab al-Ard.

When His Majesty came face to face with Raja Chulan, he enquired of him, 'Where do you hail from?'

A subject of the King answered, 'Oh My Lord, he has just arrived. Of his origins none of us knows.'

So, Raja Aftab al-Ard enquired of Raja Chulan, 'Where are you from, and from where did you depart to come here?'

Raja Chulan replied, 'I am from within the world. I am King to all human beings. I am Raja Chulan.'

Raja Aftab al-Ard was astonished to hear his answer.

He asked, 'Are there other worlds besides our own?'

Raja Chulan presently replied, 'There are indeed many worlds, and many kinds of inhabitants within them.'

Raja Aftab al-Ard was captivated by Raja Chulan's words and praised Allah the Perfect, the Omnipotent, and then invited His Majesty to take his place beside him on the throne.

Raja Aftab al-Ard had a daughter, Princess Mathab al-Bahri was her name. Presently Raja Aftab al-Ard gave his daughter to Raja Chulan. In the three years that he was married to her, she bore him three boys. However, when he looked at them, he was extremely concerned about their future.

He said, 'What will happen to me here in this undersea world? What might be the ways to bring my children to the world beyond?'

Before long Raja Chulan went to see Raja Aftab al-Ard.

To him Raja Chulan said, 'When my children have grown into adults, it would please My Lord to send them to the world above the sea, so that the lineage of King Alexander, the Two-Horned, will never be broken, but will continue till the end of time.'

Raja Aftab al-Ard agreed to his son-in-law's request.

Soon Raja Chulan sought Raja Aftab al-Ard, to take his leave to return to the world above the sea. He and his wife, Princess Mathab al-Bahr, wept at the prospect of leaving their sons.

Instantly, Raja Aftab al-Ard ordered that the winged horse be fetched, Faras al-Bahri was its name. He presented it to Raja Chulan, who quickly mounted it. It took them out of the undersea world, and then flew towards the sky. Then it strode in the middle of the sea. When all the subjects of Raja Chulan noticed that the person riding the steed was Raja Chulan, one of his minsters fetched a good mare and brought it to the Bentiris beach.

As soon as Faras al-Bahri saw the mare it instantly touched land and approached the female horse. Raja Chulan then dismounted and stepped on hard earth. A little later, Faras al-Bahri returned to the world below.

Said Raja Chulan to all the carpenters and craftsmen, 'You must now fashion a memorial to mark our descent into the sea. It is our wish that it shall be permanent, till the end of the world and that you shall write on it so that our descendants who come after us may be knowledgeable of their lineage and heed these words of ours.'

All the craftsmen and the wise men listened carefully to His Majesty's words. Then they split a rock and carved on it His Majesty's ancestry in the Hindi language. When this was accomplished, His Majesty commanded that they inlay their writing with gold, silver and marvellous gemstones as well as jewels.

Said Raja Chulan, 'At the end of time there will be a king who is a descendant of mine. He shall inherit these possessions, and he will be the one to conquer all the countries in the east, in the lands below the wind.'

Soon after that Raja Chulan set sail for the Country of the Kelings. When he beached in Bencha Nagara, he took to wife the daughter of Raja Kudar Shah Jahan, who was the son of Raja Tarshi Bardaras, the King of Hindustan. Here he bore a son by the name of Adiraja Rama Mendeliar.

In due time, he returned to Benua Keling and died there. It was Adiraja Rama Mendeliar who succeeded him on the throne in Bencha Nagara. This royal line of Bencha Nagara is still composed of the descendants of Adiraja Rama Mendeliar, till the present.

Allah knows the truth; to Him shall we return.

III

The words of the narrative now turn to a *negeri* in the Kingdom of Andalas. Palembang was its name, its king, Demang Lebar Daun. He was a descendant of Raja Chulan. The river that flowed through it is its tributary, now known as Muara Tatang. In the upper reaches of Muara Tatang is another river, Melayu is its name. By the bank of the river, there is a hill, known as Seguntang Mahameru.

On the hill, there lived two women who had recently made it their home. One was called Uwan Empuk and the other Uwan Malini; they both farmed on the hill. Their farm was extensive, and the *padi* bountiful, beyond words of description. One night, when the *padi* was about to ripen, from afar they saw before them a spectacle, as if their house was on fire.

Uwan Empuk and Uwan Malini both wondered, 'What is the light that burns like a fire? I am afraid to look at it.'

Uwan Malini comforted her sister, 'Be not afraid, it may be the luminous bezoar of the great dragon.'

Full of apprehension, they both remained quiet, and finally fell asleep.

When they awoke in the morning, they went to bathe their faces. Said Uwan Empuk to Uwan Malini, 'Let's go and see what was shining in the dark, last night.'

'Let's go,' replied Uwan Malini.

So, they both trudged up the Seguntang Hill, only to discover that their *padi* grains had turned to gold, the leaves to silver and the stalks to bronze. They were extremely fascinated by the sight.

Uwan Empuk said, 'This was the spectacle we saw last night,' and continued to climb to the top of the hill.

They found that the peak too was coloured gold. One of the anecdotes told after that, even to this very day, is that the summit of the hill, is in fact, golden.

There they noticed three extremely good-looking young men. All of them were robed in royal costumes, complete with crowns of gold, and inlaid with jewels and gems. All of them were astride an albino elephant. Uwan Empuk and Uwan Malini were amazed.

They marvelled at the spectacle of the young men, who were exceptionally striking in their looks and manners, and moreover their costumes were similarly conspicuous. In their hearts, they thought, 'Perhaps it was because of these three young men that our rice has turned to gold, the leaves to silver and the stalks to bronze, and indeed the earth itself is golden.'

Uwan Empuk and Uwan Malini enquired of the three young men, 'Where do my young lords hail from? Are you the descendants of genies or fairies? We have lived here for a while now, but have never set eyes on a human being, until this very day, when we saw you.'

The young men answered, 'We are not from the race of genies or fairies. We are the descendants of King Iskandar Zulkarnain, Alexander the Great. Our ancestor is Raja Nushirwan, King of the east and the west, our ancestry begins with Raja Sulaiman *'alaihissalam*, King Solomon. We are Mancitram, Paladutani and Nila Tanam.'

Uwan Empuk and Uwan Malini enquired of them, 'If My Lords are their descendants, what brings you here to this distant hill?'

To answer the sisters they began to narrate the story of how King Alexander of the Two Horns took as his wife the daughter of Raja Kida Hindi and the legend of Raja Chulan descending into the ocean—they recounted them all to Uwan Empuk and Uwan Malini. Uwan Empuk and Uwan Malini were charmed, 'What is the proof to what My Lords have been saying?'

The three replied, 'These crowns are the signs that we are the descendants of King Alexander. Hai aunties, if you do not believe us, these are the signs, we have descended on your farm and have caused your rice to turn to gold, its leaves to silver and its stalks to bronze, and the peak is also golden now.'

Uwan Empuk and Uwan Malini believed the three princes. They were enormously happy and brought them to their home. Soon they harvested the padi and became wealthy because they had found the three princes.

It was narrated that the Palembang in the legend is the same city of Palembang that we see now. In the days of old it was a great empire; none in the Island of Andalas was its compare.

When the Raja of Palembang heard the news of Empuk and Malini finding the princes who descended from the heavens, Demang Lebar Daun paid them a visit. On his return, he brought all of them to his *negeri*. Soon the news of the three princes, the descendants of King Alexander, who descended on the Seguntang Mahameru Hill, spread far and wide. All the rajas from every corner of the state came to pay homage. The eldest was fetched by the people of Andalas, to be crowned as their King in Minangkabau. His official royal title was Sang Seperba. Then came the people of Tanjung Pura. They fetched the middle one to be King of Tanjung Pura. His royal title was Sang Maniaka. The youngest remained in Palembang, with Demang Lebar Daun. Soon, Demang Lebar Daun installed the prince on the throne there. His royal title as King was Sang Uratama. Demang Lebar Daun willingly stepped down to become his Vizier.

* * *

Once there was an albino cow of Uwan Empuk and Uwan Malini, silver was its colour. By the will of Allah *Ta'ala*, the cow spewed up foam, and from it emerged a boy. Bat was his name. He stood erect and spoke:

Aho susati Paduka Sri Maharaja srimat srispst suran bumi buji bal pekerma sklng krt makota rana muka tri buana prsang sakrit bna tngk derma rana syaran kt rana besinggahasana rana wikerma wdt rtt plawik sdid dewi di perabudi kala muli malik sri derma raja-raja permawasuri.[1]

Bat gave the King the title of Seri Teri Buana. It is now well-known that the descendants of Bat are the original readers of the ancient formula in the ceremonial installation of kings.

In time, the kingdom of Seri Teri Buana grew in fame. All his subjects, men and women, from all corners of the state came to pay him homage[2] and brought him numerous gifts. On his part, Seri Teri Buana presented to all those who sought his audience a set of fine costumes each. He gave the titles of Awang[3] to all the men and Dara to all the women. That was the beginning of the titles of Awang and Dara.

When he had been installed King, Seri Teri Buana wished to take a wife. If he found a beautiful princess, he would marry her. However, when he slept with her in the night, on the morrow, the princess suffered from a skin discolouration, for he had touched her body. As the princess suffered from such a disease His Majesty left her. Forty women but one suffered the same fate.

It was related that Demang Lebar Daun had a daughter, she was extremely good-looking, and no one was her compare in those times. Her name was Princess Uwan Sundari. Seri Teri Buana requested the permission of Demang Lebar Daun to take his daughter as his consort.

---

[1]   In ancient Sanskrit.

[2]   *Penghormatan,* homage, an official show of respect or honour towards a king or dignitary.

[3]   *Awang/Dara,* these are titles given to young men and women initiated into the service of the palace as young heralds.

Demang Lebar Daun raised his hands in obeisance, 'If Your Majesty marries my daughter, she will suffer the same fate as the other princesses. However, if My Lord chooses my daughter, you must enter into a contract with your humble servant, only then would I offer my daughter to your Lordship.'

It is now well known that it was Demang Lebar Daun who first employed the phrases *Yang Dipertuan* (He who is made the Lord) and *patik* (your very humble servant).

Seri Teri Buana enquired, 'What is the contract that my uncle would wish me to enter into?'

Demang Lebar Daun replied, 'My Lord, all my descendants are prepared to be servants to Your Majesty. They should be improved in the days to come by all Your Majesty's descendants. However, should my descendants commit the biggest of sins, they should not be put to shame or disgraced in any manner of abuse or slur. If their sins are too great, then they should be put to death, that too in accordance with the laws of the Syariah.'

His Majesty replied, 'We consent to this covenant with my uncle, Demang Lebar Daun. But we would ask a promise of My Lord.'

Demang Lebar Daun bowed in obeisance, 'What promise, My Lord?'

Seri Teri Buana continued, 'To the end of time, your descendants shall not rise against my descendants, in acts of treason, though they be cruel and evil in their conduct.'

Demang Lebar Daun replied, 'I give my consent, My Lord. But should your descendants be the first to alter it, then my descendants would accordingly be released from the contract.'

Seri Teri Buana said, 'I give my word to this covenant.'

They both took an oath that if any one of them should alter the covenant his house would be overturned by the will of Allah *Subhanahu wa Ta'ala,* its roof downwards and the supporting poles upwards. That was the reason why Allah *Subhanahu wa Ta'ala* bestowed a distinctive quality on Malay rajas—that they never put to shame their Malay subjects, even though their sins be great—they are never bound, hanged, or disgraced with evil words. Should there be a raja who gives shame to his subjects, it was a sign that his *negeri* shall be destroyed by Allah *Subhanahu wa Ta'ala*. Thus, all Malay servants of the raja are bestowed with a trait of never being treasonous, or turning away from their king, though he is evil in his person and unjust in his ways.

After the covenant, and an oath-taking that accompanied it, Princess Uwan Sundari was presented to Seri Teri Buana. Thus, Seri Teri Buana wedded the princess, the daughter of Demang Lebar Daun.

When night had fallen, His Majesty slept with the princess. When it was morning again, Seri Teri Buana noticed that Princess Uwan Sundari did not suffer a discoloration to her skin. His Majesty was extremely pleased and asked that the good news be brought to Demang Lebar Daun. The Vizier presently came. He saw that his daughter was safe; there was no danger to herself. He was extremely happy.

In the meantime, Demang Lebar Daun made preparations to initiate a ceremonial bath for Seri Teri Buana. He instructed that a tower of seven tiers be constructed. When the edifice was completed, Demang Lebar Daun presided over the ceremony, along with a feast that lasted for forty days and forty nights—with banquets and entertainment for all the rajas, the prime ministers, eunuchs, courtiers, military chiefs and all of His Majesty's subjects. As they were celebrating, the music resounded throughout the kingdom.

Several horses, cattle and sheep were slaughtered for the feast. The overcooked and discarded part of the rice was piled as high as small hills. Foam from the pots was like those from oceans and the heads of cattle and buffaloes like islands. When the forty days and forty nights were complete, the water for the ceremonial bath was paraded throughout the *negeri*, with accompanying music. Thus, Seri Teri Buana and his consort, Princess Uwan Sundari, were carried in a procession to circle the tower. They were then bathed in the tower by Bat. When this was concluded, they were then dressed in costumes from the *darmini*[4]

---

[4] *Darmini, Dimani, Berdimani*, does not seem to be Malay in origin. Brown's Telugu scholars think this word might have originated from that language: *dermai* and *berudai-*

chest, while Princess Uwan Sundari wore the fine *berdimani* fabric, both of them in their full royal regalia. They then took their seats on the golden throne.

Soon the ritual *nasi adap-adap*, meal for newly betrothed, was carried forward and placed before them. They then partook in the rice, facing each other, for the first time after their nuptials.[5] When that ritual had been completed, the banners of the coronation were raised high and paraded around the *negeri*. Bat then placed crowns on the heads of the royal couple.

Soon, Seri Teri Buana departed to bestow presents of garments on all the officers of state. When this was duly completed, he re-entered the palace and all who had come to witness the ceremony returned to their respective homes.

Time passed. After some years on the throne of Palembang, Seri Teri Buana longed to have a view of the sea. He thus summoned Demang Lebar Daun. Soon after, the old Vizier appeared before His Majesty.

The monarch enquired, 'What does my uncle think of our plans to sail out to sea to find a good place to build a *negeri*?'

Demang Lebar Daun replied, 'I am in full agreement, My Lord. I shall be your escort, for I may not be separated from Your Majesty.'

Seri Teri Buana said, 'If that is the case, my uncle should then make the necessary preparations.'

So Demang Lebar Daun took his leave and instructed that preparations be made. When they were all ready, Demang Lebar Daun left his *negeri* in the care of his brother.

He said to him, 'Please take great care of this *negeri* because I am now accompanying His Majesty. Wherever he goes I shall follow him.'

His brother replied, 'Very well then, I shall not go against your wishes.'

---

mani. Darapata is a dhoti-like apparel from silk and decorated with gems, while *dermai* originates from *dharma,* meaning good. *Berudai* on the other hand a women's apparel like a sari. Thus *berudai-mani* is a burudai decorated with gems.

[5]   *Perkahwinan*, nuptial, relating to marriage, conjugal nuptial vows.

His Majesty's royal silver vessel weighed anchor. His ship was trailed by the prime minister's, then the military chief's, each in his own vessel. The boats were numerous—so many that they were countless. Their masts rose like trees, and their banners like the clouds moving in the skies, and the umbrellas of all the rajas as the vapours. The sea seemed full of ships accompanying His Majesty's. As they sailed down the Palembang River, they crossed the Sepat Straits and from there proceeded to the Sambar Straits.

News of their departure was heard in Bentan, 'The Raja from Seguntang Hill, who is descended from Iskandar Zulkarnain, is now in the Sambar Straits.'

The Raja of Bentan was a lady, Uwan Seri Bini[6] was her name; in one version of a chronicle her name was Permaisuri Sakidar Shah. She was a great Queen, for in those times it was she who journeyed to Syria. The Queen, Sakidar Shah, was the first monarch to be installed with full royal honours in a coronation, and it was only after that that other rajas followed her precedent.

After she heard the news, she commanded the Viziers, Indera Bokala and Aria Bokala, to welcome Seri Teri Buana, who promptly came to greet Seri Teri Buana, in a fleet of four hundred vessels.

Uwan Seri Bini instructed Indera Bokala, 'If the Raja is older than us, say to him: "Your younger sister pays her obeisance" and if he is younger than us, say: "Your auntie sends her greetings."

So, Indera Bokala and Aria Bokala set sail from Cape Rungas, in the direction of the Sambar Straits. The sea was full of vessels of those who had come to welcome His Majesty.

When they met him, Indera Bokala and Aria Bokala found him to be too young.

So, they said, 'Your auntie sends her greetings, she welcomes Your Majesty to Bentan.'

So, Seri Teri Buana sailed to Bentan and approached the palace, to greet Uwan Seri Bini. It was her intention to take him as her husband.

---

[6] Prof. Asmah Haji Omar is of the opinion that the term should be Bini and not Beni.

However, when she saw him standing before her as a young man, she took him for her son. She loved him with all her heart, and in time installed him on the throne to succeed her.

As time passed, Seri Teri Buana expressed a wish to go to Cape Bemayan, with his entourage and friends, and therefore sought permission from Uwan Seri Bini.

'Why does my son wish to sail to Bemayam? Aren't there game in their pens here? Aren't there all species of deer and porcupines in their enclosures? Aren't there fishes in the pond and also the many kinds of fruits? All kinds of flowers grow in our garden. Why does my son desire to find his amusement in places far away?'

Seri Teri Buana replied, 'If my auntie does not permit me to go, I shall die here, sitting or standing, dead in all ways.'

Uwan Seri Bini replied, 'Rather than let my son die, it is better that we let you go.'

Presently, Indera Bokala and Aria Bokala were ordered to fit the vessels and make all the essential preparations. When all was ready, Seri Teri Buana weighed anchor and sailed with his Queen, accompanied by all the royal vessels—boats for the menfolk, cargo barges, sleepers, row boats, house boats with platforms, a pantry junk, and dugouts for fishing. The boats accompanying His Majesty's were innumerable.

When they have arrived in Bemban, His Majesty disembarked and sported in the sand. The Queen went ashore with all the wives of the officials and nobles, and amused themselves on the beach, picking corals.

The Queen sat under a pandanus tree, holding court to all the wives of the officers. His Majesty was extremely happy seeing her palace maids at play, doing things they enjoyed. Some were picking shells, some digging for lingula, others collecting mangrove blooms to string them, yet others were picking beautiful flowers from the *teruntum* shrubs and fashioning them into decorations for their hair. Some were harvesting bananas and cooking them. Some were collecting the *butun*[7]

---

[7] *Butun*, possibly related to the other mangrove species. '*Butung*', according to *Kamus Dewan* is barringtonia asiatica.

leaves, while others gathered beautiful corals as toys and souvenirs, yet others took *latuh*[8] leaves and mixed them into a vegetable dish, while some others picked the agar-agar seaweeds for their sweet *pincuk* salad. Everyone was in their highest spirits. All of them were jubilant.

In the meantime, Seri Teri Buana went on a hunt with all the men and returned with much game.

It happened that a deer crossed Seri Teri Buana's path. He struck it with a spear, piercing its back, but the deer was able to escape. Seri Teri Buana gave chase and speared it again on its side; this time it was unable to run and soon died.

Promptly he climbed over the rocky lookout, and from there could see a great boulder, tall and gigantic. Seri Teri Buana looked towards the island beyond. He saw a stretch of sand; it was silky white, like a fine fabric known as *kain buka mafar*.[9]

So, he enquired of Indera Bokala, 'What coast is it that we are beholding now? What land?'

Indera Bokala spoke, 'That, My Lord, is the island of Temasik.'

Seri Teri Buana ordered, 'Let's set sail there.'

'Your words are our command,' Indera Bokala replied.

So, Seri Teri Buana climbed into a boat and was rowed across the narrow straits. However, when they were in the middle of the sea, a storm descended, and their boat was under water. The crew began to bail, but there was too much water in the vessel. Soon they started to cast their valuable possessions overboard. That too did not help. Fortunately, the vessel was quite close to Teluk Belanga, the Belanga Cape.

The captain spoke, 'Your Majesty, in my humble opinion, it is possible that the crown is reason why the boat is sinking, for all the other valuables have all been cast into the water. If it is not given to the sea, then the boat might not be saved.'

---

[8] *Latuh*, an edible specie of sea grass. Also known *as jerangau laut.*

[9] *Kain buka mafar*, exact meaning is unknown, but seems to generally refer to a fine cloth, usually white in colour.

Seri Teri Buana consented, 'In that case, please cast off the crown.'

So the crown was duly cast into the sea. Immediately the storm died down and the vessel rose to the surface. The crew could now row it ashore. As soon as the boat beached, it was moored[10] alongside the jetty. Seri Teri Buana disembarked with all his followers and stepped on the sand. They then began to sport on the beach and collect fine-looking corals. Then His Majesty climbed to the sandy bank and walked into the interior. He amused himself in the meadow by the estuary of the Temasik River.

Then, all of a sudden, his followers spotted an extremely fast-moving animal; its body was reddish brown, its head black and its chest white. Its movement was extremely rapid and its mien courageous; it was a little larger than a billygoat. As soon as it sighted the many men, it galloped away and disappeared.

Seri Teri Buana enquired of those who accompanied him, 'What animal was that, and what is it called?' But not a soul could answer him.

Demang Lebar Daun bowed in obeisance, 'My Lord, I have heard it told of old that it's the lion which has such features. In my opinion, it is indeed a lion.'

Seri Teri Buana summoned Indera Bokala, 'If it pleases My Lord, do return to Bentan now. However, please convey to Her Majesty that we shall not be returning. If she has any love for us, please send us some subjects, elephants and horses. We wish to establish a *negeri* here in Temasik.'

Soon Indera Bokala returned to Bentan. On his arrival he entered the audience hall to greet Her Majesty, Uwan Seri Bini. To her he related all the words of Seri Teri Buana.

Uwan Seri Bini replied, 'Fine, we shall not go against our son's wishes.' She soon sent him several of her subjects, along with numerous horses, so many were they that they were countless. Thus, Seri Teri Buana founded a *negeri* in Temasik. He named it, Singa Pura, the Lion City.

---

[10] *Berlabuh*, moor, to secure (a vessel, etc.) with cables, ropes, or anchors, or (of vessel, etc.) to be secured in this way.

After he had ruled for several years in Singa Pura, Seri Teri Buana's consort, the daughter of Demang Lebar Daun, Uwan Sundari, bore him two princes.

At the time of her death, Uwan Seri Bini had two granddaughters. The two princes of Raja Bentan were then bethrothed to them.

And when His Majesty was on the throne for forty-eight years Seri Teri Buana and Demang Lebar Daun passed on. Seri Teri Buana was buried on the hill in the Lion City. And while His Majesty was on the throne, the wheels of time had turned for twenty-five years.

His eldest son was in time crowned King, to succeed his father. His royal title was Paduka Seri Pikrama Wira, while Tun Patih Putih Permuka Berjajar became the Bendahara.[11] Whenever Paduka Seri Pikrama Wira was indisposed it was Tun Perpatih Permuka Berjajar who entered the audience hall as His Majesty's representative.

It was narrated that when Tun Perpatih Permuka Berjajar held court, he would not descend to the floor, except to greet those who would become kings. When Tun Perpatih Permuka Berjajar came to pay obeisance in the audience hall, a carpet would be spread for him. If the King arrived, he would depart. All the nobles and chiefs would accompany Tun Perpatih Putih Permuka Berjajar to his residence.

Now the chronicle turns to the account of Demang Lebar Daun. His lordship had a son; he was appointed prime minister by the Paduka Seri Pikrama Wira, with an official title of Tun Perpatih Permuka Sekalar. His seat was by the side of the Bendahara (whose official title was Tun Jana Buga Dendang) and held court to the Temenggung, who was known as Tun Jana Putera Yul, and the army chief under the Temenggung (his title was Tun Tempurung Gemeratukan). In those days, all the prime ministers, chiefs, warriors, eunuchs and courtiers would be present, carefully observing the customs and traditional hierarchy; it was indeed a beautiful and grand spectacle to behold.

---

[11] *Bendahara*, the title of a very high official in a Malay state, vizier, higher than a Perdana Menteri (Prime Minister).

Paduka Seri Pikrama Wira had a son; he was known as Raja Muda, the Crown Prince, in the *negeri* of Singa Pura. In time, Singa Pura developed into an extensive state. All the merchants would gather there in great numbers. And the *negeri* became famous throughout the world.

Allah knows the Truth; to Him shall we return.

IV

The words of the narrative now turn to the Betara of Maja Pahit, who descended from the gods of the heavens. He took the daughter of the Raja of Tanjung Pura, a scion of the kings of Bukit Seguntang, as his wife. They begot two boys. He crowned his elder son in Maja Pahit. It was related that the Kings of Maja Pahit were all descended from Princess Semangangrat and were titled as The Betara. His kingdom was extremely large. All the Rajas of Java and Pustar had come under his authority.

When the Betara of Maja Pahit heard that Singa Pura had grown into a prosperous state, and its raja did not acknowledge his authority, His Majesty was enraged and presently commanded that a mission be sent there. His dispatch was a wood-shaving, seven spans of the arms long, continuous and unpolished. It was as thin as paper and was rolled like an earring.

So, the envoy of the Betara sailed to Singa Pura. In due time, he arrived, and was received by a representative of Paduka Seri Pikrama Wira, who took him up the hill to pay His Majesty his obeisance and present him the Betara's letter and gifts. The letter was read by Paduka Seri Pikrama Wira.

It said: 'May it please the Paduka Seri Pikrama Wira, my younger brother, to take pleasure in the work of our Javanese carver. Does Singa Pura possess such a craftsman?'

The gift was then unwrapped by Paduka Seri Pikrama Wira. He saw a wood shaving rolled like an earplug.

His Majesty smiled, understanding its implication and the demands of the Betara of Maja Pahit.

His Majesty said, 'He mocks our manliness, so he sends us an earplug!'

The envoy bowed, and spoke, 'My Lord, that is not the message of your brother, the Betara of Maja Pahit. What His Majesty meant is, "Are there any craftsmen in Your Majesty's kingdom who can shave wood as fine as this?"

After Paduka Seri Pikrama Wira had heard the words of the envoy, he said, 'Even finer ones are found here in Temasik.'

Hence Paduka Seri Pikrama Wira summoned a craftsman, Sang Bentan was his name. As soon as he arrived, His Majesty asked that a child be brought into the palace and ordered that the boy be shaved before the envoy. So, the craftsman shaved the boy's hair, who cried as his head was moved from left to right. Though he was crying, Sang Bentan continued with his task. In a moment it was finished and he was without his hair. The Javanese envoy was amazed to see such an accomplishment.

Paduka Seri Pikrama Wira said to the envoy, 'See how fine is the work of our craftsman. He could even shave the head of a boy, what is to him shaving a mere piece of wood? Take this axe to Maja Pahit, as a gift to our brother.'

He was surprised to see the axe, and soon took leave and made preparations to return to Java, bearing the axe as a gift. His vessel soon set sail from Singa Pura.

In due time, he arrived in Java. The envoy approached the throne and bowed in obeisance before His Majesty, the Betara of Maja Pahit, and presented to him the letter and the gift. He described how the craftsman had shaved the boy's head and relayed all the words of Seri Paduka Pikrama. Upon hearing his report, the Betara of Maja Pahit was full of fury.

His Majesty said, 'This is a metaphor to say that if we came to Singa Pura our heads will be shaven thus, like the boy's!'

Instantly the Betara of Maja Pahit commanded his warriors to prepare their vessels to invade Singa Pura. A hundred vessels and besides these, a beamy, flat-bottomed boat[1] as well as a Javanese galley and a dug-out[2]—so many were they that they were countless. The Betara of Maja Pahit appointed his most senior general as its war chief to lead the mission to Singa Pura.

In due time, they arrived. As soon as they reached the harbour, the Javanese began to battle with the people of Singa Pura. Many were on the battlefield; the clank of weapons rose to the skies, along with the deafening din of the warriors' yells. On both sides much blood was spilt, many died. When night had fallen the Javanese retreated to their ships. The account of the war between Singa Pura and Java is indeed a long one; if we were to describe it all, it would bore our listeners, so we have chosen to describe only the important events, for lengthy descriptions are not preferred by the judicious. When Singa Pura was not defeated, the Javanese returned to Maja Pahit.

Allah knows the truth; to Him shall we return.

---

[1] *Melambang,* according to Wilkinson is a flat-bottomed boat.
[2] *Cerucuh,* dug-out, or small boat.

V

Now the words of the narrative turn to Adiraja Rama Mendeliar, the son of Raja Chulan, the King of Bencha Nagara. He had a son, Jambuga Rama Mendeliar was his name. When Adiraja Rama Mendeliar died, his son succeeded him on the throne.

His Majesty had a daughter, Princess Talla Punchadi was her name; she was a most beautiful princess. Words of her beauty travelled far and wide, and soon many rajas came to seek her hand in marriage. But Raja Jambuga Rama Mendeliar would not consent to any of their proposals.

He said, 'Not from a descent like mine.'

In due time, the news of the princess's beauty reached Singa Pura. Presently, Paduka Seri Pikrama Wira ordered Maha Indera Bahukala to sail to the country of the Kelings to ask her hand for his son, the Crown Prince. Soon Maha Indera Bahukala set sail for Benua Keling, accompanied by several ships.

When they arrived in Bencha Nagara, Rama Mendeliar instructed that the letter and gifts be fetched and ceremonially received in a procession, with a great display of reverence and honour. When the letter has been read and His Majesty understood its intent, he was extremely happy.

He addressed Maha Indera Bahukala, 'We happily give our consent to your proposal, but please do not trouble yourself to send your son here, let us accompany our daughter to Singa Pura.'

Soon Maha Indera Bahukala sought leave of Raja Jambuga Rama Mendeliar. The King sent a letter and gifts to the Raja of Singa Pura. Thus, Maha Indera Bahukala departed from Benua Keling.

After several days at sea they arrived in Singa Pura. His Majesty Paduka Seri Pikrama Wira duly instructed that the letter be received in a procession appropriate for all great kings. When it arrived at the audience hall, it was acknowledged by a senior courtier[1] and presented to Paduka Seri Pikrama Wira. His Majesty instructed that it be read for all to hear. When he understood its content, he was extremely glad.

Soon after, Maha Indera Bahukala approached the throne to impart the message of Raja Jambuga Rama Mendeliar, upon hearing which his heart became gladder still.

When the favourable winds began to blow, Raja Jambuga Rama Mendeliar instructed that ships be fitted and prepared. When they were ready for the ocean, his daughter, Princess Talla Punchadi, was accompanied by a knight.[2] Soon she boarded the vessel along with five hundred others, who would be her escort, assisted by her maids of honour. The vessel soon set sail. Several ships were in attendance, besides some dinghies[3] and batelas.[4]

On their arrival in Singa Pura, they were welcomed by His Majesty, Seri Pikrama Wira, at Tanjung Buras[5] with full honours. When they had finally arrived in the city of Singa Pura, His Majesty, Paduka Seri Pikrama Wira began the wedding celebrations of his son to the daughter of the King of the Kelings. The celebrations went on day and night, for a full three months.

On his part, Raja Pikrama Wira gave his official consent for his son to marry Talla Punchadi. After the ceremonies were over, the Keling knight sought permission to return. His Majesty, Pikrama Wira

---

[1]   *Bentara*, senior herald.
[2]   *Hulubalang*, knight.
[3]   *Sambuk*, dinghies.
[4]   *Perahu bertiang dua, batil*, batela.
[5]   Tanjung Buras, according to Winstedt and Brown this is 'Burus'.

furnished him with letters and gifts for the Raja of the Kelings. Thus, the mission weighed anchor and returned.

His Majesty Paduka Seri Pikrama Wira ruled for fifteen years. The wheel of time turned and His Majesty passed on. His son, the Crown Prince, succeeded him; his official title was Seri Rana Wikrama. It was he who bore, with Princess Talla Punchadi, the daughter of the King of the Kelings, two offspring, one a boy and the other a girl. The boy was named Dam Raja.

Tun Perpatih Permuka Berjajar too was deceased. His son became the Bendahara; his official title was Tun Perpatih Tulus. He himself bore two children, a boy and a girl. The girl was Demi Princess.

His Majesty Seri Rana Pikrama chose her for his son, Dam Raja, and His Majesty married her to his son Dam Raja, while the son of Tun Perpatih Tulus was betrothed to His Majesty's daughter. Now Tun Perpatih Permuka Berjajar had also died and was succeeded as Bendahara by his son. He was titled Tun Perpatih Tulus.

Meanwhile, Tun Perpatih Tulus had two children—a son and a daughter whose name was Demi Puteri. She was chosen by Seri Rana Wikrama for his son, while the son of Tun Perpatih Tulus was married to the King's daughter.

* * *

His Majesty, Seri Rana Wikrama, had a warrior; his name was Badang, who was exceptionally robust and strong. Badang hailed from the province of Sayung and was the servant of a Sayung chief. He was regularly tasked with clearing the jungle.

One day, he positioned fish traps in the Besisik River. However, after a while he noticed that not even one of them had caught any fish. But there was a deposit of fish scales and bones. Each day it was the same story. He regularly discarded the fish scales into the water—that was the reason why the river was named Sungai Besisik, a River of Scales.

On seeing this, Badang thought, 'Whatever is eating the fish in my traps? Let me hide and spy on the perpetrator that has eaten the fish?'

Thinking so, he spied from behind the shrubbery of the marshes. What he saw was a demon—it was the culprit. Its eyes were like flames of fire, its hair like the twines of a basket, while its beard reached its navel. Badang reached for his machete and sought to embolden himself. He chased after it and seized its beard.

Badang said, 'So it's you who has devoured my fish! Now you are dead!'

As soon as it heard Badang's words, it began shaking with fear and struggled to free itself from his clutches. But it was to no avail.

The demon implored, 'Do not kill me; I shall fulfil all your wishes. If you desire to be rich or to be brave and strong, or if you wish to be invisible, that too I shall give you, but please do not kill me.'

Thus, Badang reasoned in his heart, 'If I were to ask for riches, then my master will take them from me. If I were to become invisible, I would end my days being killed by others. As this is how things are, let me request for physical power and strength so that I will be strong enough to carry out my master's tasks.'

Arriving thus at his conclusion, Badang answered the demon, 'Make me strong and robust so I may break huge trunks, that are one or two cross-folds of the arms in circumference,[6] and the trees that are one or two cross-folds wide I may uproot with merely one hand.'

The demon answered, 'That shall be done. If you want strength, I shall give it to you, but first you must swallow my vomit.'

Badang answered, 'I agree. Throw up so that I may eat your vomit.'

So, the demon threw up; much was his vomit. But Badang consumed it all. All the while, he held on to the demon's beard, not letting it go. After he had finished consuming all the vomit, he tried his hand at uprooting the big trees. Indeed, he could easily break all of them. And so, the trees that were as large as one or two cross-folds in girth were easily felled. Then he let go of the demon's beard and walked towards his master's clearing. There he uprooted all the big trees. Even the great ones he could simply pull out of the earth with merely one

---

6   *Lilitan bulatan*, circumference.

hand, along with their roots—they broke easily under his boundless strength, while the smaller trees he could just fan with his hands and they went flying in all directions. And at that moment, the tall grasses were flattened too and the place became a clean field, unexpectedly large in its width and breadth.

When his master saw what he had done, he asked, 'Who cleared our field? It has become clear so soon.'

Badang replied, 'It was I who did it.'

His master enquired, 'How did you do it, clearing it so fast, and as far as the eye can see?'

So Badang related the whole story to his master. Soon his master made him a free man.[7]

When news of Badang reached His Majesty's ears, he asked that Badang be summoned, and made him a warrior. It was he who was commanded to lay the chain that marked the sea roads in Singa Pura.

When the King was about to dine, he would ask Badang to pick the *kuras*[8] shoots for his salad, from the forest in Kuala Sayung. Badang went alone; his vessel was eight metres long. His pole was a *kempas* tree trunk.

As he arrived at Kuala Sayung, he climbed the *kuras* tree, however its branch broke under his weight. Badang fell to the ground, his head hitting a rock. The rock was riven, but his head was intact. You can see it even now in Kuala Sayung. The pole and the vessel are also still there.

Badang returned on the same day; he loaded his vessel with bananas and yams, only after that did he journey downstream to Johor. However, he consumed all the bananas and tubers as he went down the river.

One day, His Majesty, Seri Rana Wikrama built a trading vessel. When it was completed even two hundred people could not push

---

[7]   There is some confusion in the original text. He was indeed made a free man ; *dimerdehekakan*. However, we can presume that he was a slave before being freed and after that made a servant and a warrior.

[8]   *Kuras*, salad from the shoot of the forest species of *kapur* or *keladau*.

it down to the water. But when Badang arrived, he single-handedly launched it and it glided right over to the opposite bank.

It came to pass that news of the warrior of Singa Pura reached the shores of the country of the Kelings. It was related that there was a warrior of the King of Singa Pura who was extremely strong. Meanwhile, the King of the Kelings also had a warrior of his own, and likewise, extremely strong. Thus, His Majesty commanded his warrior to sail to Singa Pura in a fleet of seven vessels.

The Raja of Benua Keling commanded him, 'Go to Singa Pura and engage the warrior of Singa Pura in a contest. If you are defeated, the contents of the seven boats are his reward. If he loses, demand that he gives you a reward equal to the contents of the seven boats.'

The warrior replied, 'Your command shall be done, Your Majesty.'

The Keling warrior then sailed to Singa Pura, along with seven other vessels. When they arrived in Singa Pura, news of their arrival was conveyed to Seri Rana Wikrama, 'The warrior from Benua Keling has arrived to duel with Badang. If he loses, all the contents of the seven vessels will be rewarded to his adversary.'

Soon, His Majesty, Seri Rana Wikrama entered the audience hall to hold court. It was then that the Keling warrior came in to pay his respects and make obeisance. Presently, His Majesty ordered that he challenge Badang.

In no time, they were locked in a wrestling match. The Keling warrior was defeated.

In the meantime, there was a rock in front of the audience hall; it was extremely huge.

Said the Keling warrior to Badang, 'Let us gather our strength to lift the rock. The one who is not able to do so, loses.'

Badang replied, 'It's agreed; please, My Lord, after you.'

The Keling warrior gathered all his strength and tried his utmost, but he could only lift it as high as his knees, before he slammed it down hard.

He said to Badang, 'Now it is My Lord's turn.'

Badang replied, 'Very well,' and lifted the rock, threw it into the air and cast it across the Singa Pura estuary. You can see it now, at the end of the Cape of Singa Pura.

At the end of the contest, the Keling warrior surrendered the seven vessels and their contents to Badang and returned home in dejection and shame.

News of Badang, the extremely sturdy warrior of the Raja Singa Pura, reached Perlak[9] in Sumatera. It was narrated by the author of the chronicle that the Raja of Perlak too had a warrior, Bendarang was his name. His strength was renowned. When Badang's name was mentioned, Bendarang entered the great hall to make obeisance.

Said the warrior, 'My Lord, it cannot be that Badang is stronger than your servant! With Your Lordship's blessings I shall sail to Singa Pura and engage him in a contest.'

The Raja of Perlak commanded, 'Go you then to Singa Pura.'

The Raja of Perlak turned to the Vizier, Tun Perpatih Pandak, 'Your lordship must sail to Singa Pura, for we shall ask Bendarang to journey there.'

Tun Perpatih Pandak bowed and replied, 'Your command shall be done, Your Majesty.'

Tun Perpatih Pandak instantly took his leave and ordered that a vessel be equipped. When the preparations were complete, His Majesty repeated his request that Tun Perpatih Pandak sail to Singa Pura to escort Bendarang. The royal epistle was duly carried with full honours to the vessel. Soon Tun Perpatih Pandak's vessel was sailing eastwards to Singa Pura.

A journey of a few days brought them to Singa Pura. News of their arrival was conveyed to the Raja of Singa Pura, 'Your Majesty, Tun Perpatih Pandak, the Vizier of the Raja of Perlak, has come, bringing His Majesty's warrior, Bendarang. His Majesty has requested that he tests his strength against Badang's.'

---

[9]   Perlak, also known as Porolak, to the north of Aru Bay.

When His Majesty heard the messenger's words, he made his way to the audience hall to meet the rajas, the prime minister, eunuchs, marshals, military chiefs, and courtiers, who were already present. Seri Rana Wikrama then commanded Maha Indera Bahupala to receive the Raja of Perlak's letter, and the letter was soon carried into the audience hall in a procession. It was duly read—harmonious and regal was its composition. Consequently, Tun Perpatih Pandak paid his obeisance. His Majesty invited him to take a seat on the same level as Tun Jana Buga Dendang's, while Bendarang took his seat on the same level as Badang.

Seri Rana Wikrama enquired of Tun Perpatih Pandak, 'Why has my brother ordered My Lord to sail here?'

Tun Perpatih Pandak replied, 'Your servant has been ordered by His Majesty to escort his servant, Bendarang, to challenge Badang. If Bendarang loses, then the contents of a godown shall be handed over to Your Majesty. However, if Badang is defeated, the stakes are equal in amount.'

Seri Rana Wikrama said, 'It is agreed then; tomorrow we shall witness them in a contest.'

After a conversation lasting a few short moments, His Majesty departed for his chambers, and those who came to pay him obeisance returned to their respective homes.

In the meantime, His Majesty requested that Badang be summoned. Badang hurried to be in His Majesty's presence.

Badang raised his hands in obeisance.

'It's tomorrow then, we will match you with Bendarang.'

Badang bowed low and said, 'My Lord, Bendarang is indeed a strong warrior in these times, his strength is renowned in all the lands. If I were to be defeated, would not Your Majesty be embarrassed? In my mind, if Your Majesty still wants me to challenge him, it is wise that he be summoned tonight, and served with a meal, so that I may read his comportment. If I am able to fight him, I shall do it; if I am not able to, then Your Majesty must forbid me; do not let me challenge him.'

His Majesty agreed, 'It's true what you have just said.'

When evening fell, His Majesty ordered that Tun Perpatih Pandak, Bendarang and all his escorts be summoned. When they have arrived, they were bestowed with victuals, special fare and drinks, accompanied by music.

In the hall, Bendarang sat beside Badang. Badang then jostled him, and in turn Bendarang placed his thigh over Badang's. He pressed it down with all his might. In turn Badang summoned all strength and was able to lift Bendarang's. Now Badang pressed hard on Bendarang's. Bendarang tried to lift it but was unable to.

What transpired between the two warriors no one present did see; only the two of them knew what happened between them. Within an hour, all the guests were drunk. They duly requested to return to their vessel.

After the guests had departed, His Majesty enquired of Badang, 'Were you able to defeat Benderang?'

'With Your Majesty's sovereign eminence, sire, I shall be able to defeat him. Do let me challenge him tomorrow.

'Very well then,' said His Majesty. Soon after that His Majesty returned to his palace. And all those in attendance returned to their respective homes.

* * *

When they had arrived at their vessel, Bendarang said, 'If it is possible, let not me be matched with Badang, for I may not be able to defeat him. In my observation he is indeed extremely robust.'

Tun Perpatih Pandak replied, 'Very well then, it shall be easily done.'

On the morrow, from the early hours of the morning, His Majesty Seri Rana Wikrama held court for all his subjects. Soon Tun Perpatih Pandak too was present in the hall.

Seri Rana Wikrama began, 'Now we shall watch a match between Bendarang and Badang.'

Tun Perpatih Pandak raised his hands in obeisance, 'Your Majesty, let's not pit them in a contest, for fear that if one should be defeated, then it would begin another between Your Majesty and Your Majesty's brother.'

His Majesty smiled listening to the words of Tun Perpatih Pandak. He replied, 'Very well then, we shall not go against your words.'

And soon, Tun Perpatih Pandak sought permission to return to his lodgings.

In the meantime, His Majesty gave him a letter to be delivered to the Raja of Perlak. Before long, Tun Pepatih Pandak was on his journey home to Perlak.

There was a story that was being told—that it was Bedarang who broke the rocks placed as a border to ships' lanes.

When they had arrived, the letter was carried on an elephant in a procession, which was later secured by the hall. It was then read by His Majesty. He was extremely pleased to hear its contents.

He asked Tun Perpatih Putih, 'Why was the contest between Bendarang and Badang not being carried out?'

Tun Perpatih Putih relayed to His Majesty all that transpired when they were having their drinks in the audience hall.

After he heard Tun Perpatih Pandak's explanation, His Majesty remained quiet, not saying a word.

* * *

As time passed, Badang died. He was buried in Buru.[10] When news of his death was heard in the country of the Kelings, the King sent a gravestone as a mark of reverence. That gravestone may still be seen there at present.

* * *

After a reign of thirteen years, His Majesty, Seri Rana Wikrama, was deceased. His son, Dam Raja, was crowned after him. His title on the

---

[10] Buru, an island in the Karimun Archipelago.

throne was Paduka Seri Maharaja. In time, His Majesty's consort was with child. When the months were complete, she gave birth to a boy. As he came into the world, the midwife put her foot on his head, as was the custom of old. It became a recognizable symbol for it was right in the middle of his forehead. Paduka Seri Maharaja named his son Sultan Iskandar Zulkarnain.

Allah knows the truth; to Him shall we return.

VI

The page of the chronicle now turns to the Raja of Pasai,[1] as told by the author of old.

There lived two Marah brothers close to Pasangan, though their origins were from the Sanggung Mountain. The older was called Marah Jaga,[2] and the younger, Marah Silu. Marah Silu was often laying his trap for fishes in the river, but what he caught were only galley worms. As this continued for many days, he took the worms, placed them in a pot and boiled them. It turned out that the worms became gold and the foam, silver. Marah Silu went again to the river and repeatedly boiled the worms, which turned to gold as before.

When it became known that he had collected much gold, it was reported to Marah Jaga that his brother had consumed the galley worms. Upon hearing this, he became annoyed with him, and wanted to kill him. Thus Marah Silu fled to Jeran. The spot that Marah Silu caught the galley worms was called the Galley Worm Field, Padang Gelang-Gelang.

---

[1] Pasai, in Acheh, North Sumatra, to the south of the Jambu Ayer river.
[2] Marah Jaga, this form of name is still to be found in Minangkabau and used in *Hikayat Raja-Raja Barus*.

Words are now narrated regarding Marah Silu who lived in the Jeran Jungle. He gave much gold to the folks of the forest, and they obeyed all his words and orders.

One day Marah Silu went hunting. His hound, Pasai, began to bark, and when he examined what the dog was barking at, he noticed a mound, as though it was piled with earth. Curious, he climbed over the mound; from there he could see a large ant, it was as big as a cat. Marah Silu picked up the ant and ate it. He made the mound his abode of residence and called it Samudera,[3] meaning: a Large Ant.

* * *

The chronicle now turns to the episode of the Messenger of God (peace be upon on him) reminding his friend, 'At the end of time, there will be a *negeri* where the sun rises, Samudera is its name. When you have news of the *negeri,* go you presently to the place. Bring its population into the religion of Islam, for in that *negeri* many saints will arise. But you should bring along with you a mendicant scholar from next *negeri* of Ma'abri.'

After the Prophet had spoken thus, news of Samudera reached the inhabitants of Makkah. In time, the Governor of Makkah ordered that a ship sail there, bringing with it all the insignia of state, and also to call at Ma'abri. The captain of the vessel was Ismail.

Thus, the vessel sailed east, making a stop at Ma'abri. There the ship cast anchor.

The King of the *negeri* was Sultan Muhammad. It was he who asked, 'Where does this ship hail from?'

An answer came from the ship, 'We are from Makkah, on our way to Samudera.'

In the meantime, it was related that Sultan Muhammad was descended from Abu Bakar bin al-Siddik, the Truthful, may the Lord be content with him. He was a faithful companion of the Prophet.

---

[3] Samudera, in North Sumatra, on the north side of the Jambu Ayer river.

'We are making this journey on the orders of the holy Prophet, (peace be upon him).'

The Sultan subsequently crowned his oldest son to succeed him in Ma'abri. He soon departed with his youngest son, leaving his palace, wearing only the garbs of the *fakir*.

He ordered the sailors in the vessel, 'Take me to Samudera.'

Those in the ship thought, 'This is indeed the *fakir* that the Prophet, (peace be upon him), has referred to in the Sultan's dream.'

Thus, the *fakir* embarked, and the ship soon set sail.

After a few weeks into their journey, the vessel arrived in a *negeri*, Fansuri[4] was its name. Soon all the inhabitants of Fansuri became Muslims.

On the morrow, the *fakir* landed and brought with him the *Quran*. He requested that they read the book of God. However, not one of them could read it.

The *fakir* thought, 'This is not the country referred to by our Prophet, peace be on him.'

The ship, commanded by Captain Ismail, continued on its journey east. In time, they arrived in the *negeri* of Thobri. And the population of that *negeri* subsequently became Muslim. And the *fakir* soon came on shore. He asked that they read the *Quran*. However, no one was able to.

So, the *fakir* boarded the vessel and sailed southwards. After a span of weeks, they arrived in Haru. In Haru too all the inhabitants of the *negeri* became Muslims. The *fakir* fetched the *Quran* and asked that it be read. There too no one could.

So, he asked, 'Where is this *negeri* called Samudera?'

The people of Haru responded, 'You have already passed it.'

So, the *fakir* again boarded the ship and set sail. They then came to the *negeri* of Perlak, and the population was similarly converted to Islam. The ship then continued on its journey to Samudera.

On their arrival, the *fakir* disembarked. He met Marah Silu who was picking corals on the beach.

---

4   Fansuri, in North West Sumatra.

He asked Marah Silu, 'What is the name of this *negeri*?'

Marah Silu replied, 'This *negeri* is called Samudera.'

'Who is the governor of this *negeri*?'

'I am its governor,' said Marah Silu.

Soon, he converted all the inhabitants of Samudera and taught them the articles of faith. When he had become a Muslim, Marah Silu returned home, and the *fakir* likewise, to his boat. In the evening, he dreamt of conversing with the Prophet, (peace be upon on him).

The Prophet said, 'Hai Marah Silu, open your mouth wide.'

So, Marah Silu opened his mouth. Into it the Prophet spat. And when he awoke from his sleep, he could smell a sweet fragrance in the air, quite similar to spikenard.

When the day had dawned, the *fakir* brought the *Quran* ashore. He requested that it be read by Marah Silu, and he was able to read it.

The *fakir* said to Captain Ismail, 'This is the *negeri* that the Prophet referred to in his command.'

In time, all the articles of the state regalia were downloaded and brought ashore. He then crowned Marah Silu and named him Sultan Malik al-Salleh.

In the *negeri* there were two chiefs; one was called Seri Kaya and the other Bawa Kaya. Both of them embraced the religion of Islam. Seri Kaya was titled as Sidi Ali Ghiatuddin, and Bawa Kaya, as Sidi Samayuddin.

After a few days, Captain Ismail sailed back to Makkah, leaving the *fakir* to reinforce further the religion in Samudera.

In the meantime, Sultan Malik al-Salleh ordered that Sidi Ali Ghiatuddin sail to Perlak to ask for the hand of the Raja of Perlak's daughter. The Raja of Perlak had three daughters, two of them from his royal wives and the other from his concubine, her name was Princess Genggang.

When Sidi Ali Ghiatuddin arrived in the palace, Sultan Malik al-Salleh introduced his three daughters. The two royal princesses were seated at a lower level, while the daughter of his concubine was on a higher one. There she sat, splitting the areca nut for the betel preparations. Her other siblings were dressed in pink sarongs, wearing palm-leaf ear-plugs and holding the *jengekelenar* flower; all of them were exceptionally beautiful.

Sidi Ghiatuddin said, 'I did not know that Princess Genggang is the daughter of the Raja of Perlak's concubine.'

The Raja of Perlak laughed, 'Very well, it's your choice, My Lord.'

His Majesty then ordered that a ship be readied for the return journey. Tun Perpatih Pandak was requested to escort Princess Genggang to Samudera.

On their arrival in Samudera, Sultan Malik al-Salleh came to welcome them in Jambu Air, and subsequently took them to his palace, showering them with numerous honours and much respect. In Samudera itself he had ordered that the observance of their wedding be celebrated over a period of several nights. When these were over, Sultan Malik al-Salleh was wedded to Princess Genggang.

After His Majesty had married Princess Genggang, he offered gifts to all the military chiefs, and similarly to Tun Perpatih Pandak. He gave alms of gold and silver to all the poor people in Samudera.

Time passed. After they had been married for some time, Tun Perpatih Pandak sought leave to return to Perlak. His Majesty and Princess Genggang bore two children, both of them boys. He named the elder boy, Sultan Malik al-Zahir, and the younger Sultan Malik al-Mansur. The older prince was sent to be tutored by Sidi Ali Ghiatuddin, and his younger brother, by Sidi Samayuddin.

In time, Sultan Malik al-Zahir and Sultan Malik al-Mansur grew into young men, in the *negeri* of Perlak, but in the meanwhile, Perlak was defeated by forces from over the Straits. Many of the inhabitants of Perlak found refuge in Samudera. Thus, Sultan Malik al-Salleh thought of establishing a *negeri* for his sons there.

So, His Majesty addressed all the lords and officers, 'Tomorrow we shall go hunting.'

His Majesty departed early in the morning, riding his elephant, Parmada Buana, with a jungle beyond the river as his destination. As soon as they had arrived on the beach, His Majesty's hound,[5] Pasai was his name, started to bark. Curious, His Majesty came to see what Pasai was barking at and he found that it was a hill the size of four palaces, including all its buildings and gardens. It was so appropriate, looking as though it was already mounded. Immediately, His Majesty ordered that the place be cleared. And he commanded that a *negeri* be built on the hill and a palace be erected. He named it Pasai, after the hound.

His elder son, Sultan Malik al-Zahir was crowned King there, while Sidi Ali Ghiatuddin was made the Vizier. Then His Majesty divided all the subjects, the state regalia and apparatuses into two sets, one was for his older son, Sultan Malik al-Zahir, and the other for his younger one, Malik al-Mansur.

As time passed, Sultan Malik al-Salleh became unwell. He soon ordered that all the lords and officers of state of Samudera, along with his sons, be assembled.

When they had all gathered, His Majesty said to them, 'Oh my two sons and all my friends, you are all my captains. My time has come. If I die, preserve well the *negeri* after I am gone. And my sons, covet not the possessions of others, and crave not the wives of your subjects, and preserve the brotherhood between the two of you.'

And to Ali Ghiatuddin and Sidi Samayuddin he said, 'My brothers, please continue to support my two sons, and keep conflict at bay between the two of you, change not your loyalty towards them, and serve not other rajas.'

Both of them fell on their knees and wept.

They answered him, 'My Lord, the beacon of our lives, in the name of Allah *Ta'ala*, who has created the universe, we promise that we shall never serve other masters.'

Presently, Sultan Malik al-Salleh crowned his son, Malik al-Mansur of Samudera. After three days, His Majesty departed this earth. He was buried by his palace, and was known as 'Marhum di Samudera', and remembered as a past King of Samudera.

---

5   *Anjing pemburu*, hunting dog, hound.

After their father had departed this earth, Sultan Malik al-Zahir and Sultan Malik al-Mansur ordered that all the military chiefs[6] and subjects be assembled, complete with the elephants and all the instruments of state.

And through the passage of time, Pasai grew into a populous state.

* * *

The chronicle now turns to the Raja of Shahr Nuwi, who reigned over a large kingdom; numerous were its military chiefs and soldiers—its population was innumerable. It came to the ears of His Majesty that Samudera too was well-populated; many were the merchants and traders who resided there while the Raja reigned over a vast kingdom.

The Raja of Shahr Nuwi enquired of his military chiefs, 'Who among you can seize the Raja of Samudera?''

There was a military chief, he was robust and brave, Awi Dichu was his name.

He raised his palms in obeisance, and said, 'Your Majesty, with your lordship's blessings, and a force of four thousand soldiers, I may capture the Raja of Samudera and bring him back alive.'

Soon, the Raja of Shahr Nuwi gathered four thousand soldiers and a hundred *pilu* vessels and gave them to Awi Dichu to command. When all the preparations were complete, he ordered that they sail to Samudera, pretending to be merchants. Awi Dichu followed them, claiming that he was an envoy of the Raja of Shahr Nuwi.

As the news of their arrival reached the Raja of Samudera His Majesty instructed that they be welcomed by all his military officers. When they disembarked, the royal letter was received and duly borne to the palace.

In the meantime, Awi Dichu decorated four chests, which he ordered to be borne by four strong soldiers.

---

[6]   *Hulubalang*, military chief, a military officer.

Awi Dichu said to the four military officers who were inside the chests,[7] 'When you have come before the Raja of Samudera, the four of you must open the chests, rush out and seize the Raja of Samudera.'

Thus, the chests were secured from inside and were carried to the Raja, claiming that they were gifts from the Raja of Shahr Nuwi.

When they arrived before the Raja, the letter was duly read. And the chests were carried into His Majesty's presence. Instantly each of the four military officers rushed out and seized the Raja of Samudera. Upon seeing this, all the military chiefs of Samudera drew their weapons, ready to battle with those from Shahr Nuwi.

Said the soldier of Shahr Nuwi, 'If you challenge us, we will kill your King!'

Thus, all the Pasai warriors remained motionless at their stations, not being able to retaliate. Instantly, all the soldiers of Shahr Nuwi made haste to board their junk, carrying the Raja of Pasai, and sailed home.

When they had arrived in Shahr Nuwi, Awi Dichu presented the Raja of Pasai to his master. His Majesty was extremely pleased, presenting all those who had gone to Pasai with royal robes.

In the meantime, the Raja of Pasai was ordered to tend to His Majesty's fowls.[8]

* * *

Now the words of the narrative turn to Sidi 'Ali Ghiatuddin deliberating in Pasai with all his senior ministers. He built a vessel and bought Arabian products, for all the Pasaians of old could converse in Arabic. Sidi 'Ali Ghiatuddin and all the chosen soldiers in the vessel were dressed in Arabian costumes. Soon Sidi 'Ali Ghiatuddin boarded his ship, and when all the preparations were ready, he sailed to Shahr Nuwi. After a journey of several days they arrived. Sidi 'Ali Ghiatuddin

---

[7]   *Peti*, chest, a box.

[8]   *Ayam*, fowls.

landed and sought the audience of the Raja of Shahr Nuwi, laden with gifts and fruits. He fashioned a tree of gold with its fruits shaped from various gems—its price was equivalent to a *bahara*[9] of gold.

When His Majesty saw Sidi 'Ali Ghiatuddin's gifts, he wondered, and said, 'What do you seek of us?'

Sidi 'Ali Ghiatuddin and all in his mission replied, 'We seek nothing, My Lord.'

Thus, His Majesty continued to be extremely curious, as he was looking at their gifts.

The Raja of Shahr Nuwi thought, 'Whatever is their wish that they had given us such a valuable set of presents?'

Soon they all returned to the vessel.

After the lapse of a few days, the captain of the ship sought the audience of the Raja of Shahr Nuwi, bringing other gifts—a chess set of gold, its pieces of jewels; its value was also equivalent to a *bahara* of gold.

The Raja of Shahr Nuwi enquired, 'What is your wish? Say, so that we may give it to you?'

They replied, 'We wish for nothing, My Lord.'

Soon they returned to their ship.

After the lapse of some time, the season to return to Samudera blew with the north-eastern winds. So, Sidi 'Ali Ghiatuddin made the necessary repairs to his ship and was about to set sail.

They then sought leave of His Majesty, coming before him and bringing gifts—this time a pair of golden geese inlaid with jewels—also the value equivalent to a *bahara* of gold. Along with them was a golden vase, filled with water to the brim. Next, the geese were released into the golden vase. Soon they were swimming, diving and chasing each other. The Raja of Shahr Nuwi was in awe of the workmanship of the magical geese.

The Raja of Shahr Nuwi said, 'Speak your mind, all of you. What is your wish? In the name of God that I worship, all that you ask will be given to you.'

---

[9] *Bahara*, a measure of 180-270 kg of gold.

Sidi 'Ali Ghiatuddin replied, 'Your Majesty, if you would
bestow on us a request, we would like to ask for the person who
tends your fowls.'

The Raja of Shahr Nuwi replied, 'He is the Raja of Pasai. However,
now that you have requested for him, we will give him to you.'

The Pasaians replied, 'As he is a Muslim, so we request him from
Your Majesty.'

Thus, Sultan Malik al-Zahir was given to Sidi Ghiatuddin, who
presently brought him to the vessel. When he had boarded the ship, he
was cleansed and attired in royal robes.

As the winds blew, they weighed anchor and sailed for several days
in the open sea.

* * *

The words of the narrative now turn to Raja Malik al-Mansur in
Samudera. One day, he asked of Sidi Samayuddin, 'I would like to visit
my brother, can My Lord arrange it?'

Samayuddin bowed and warned him, 'Do not depart, should there
be a malicious hidden plan. '

Though he repeated his warning, Sultan Malik al-Mansur would
not hear of it, so he remained quiet.

Then the gongs were beaten to relay the message: 'Sultan
Malik al-Mansur is departing to visit his brother's *negeri*. However,
Sidi Samayuddin, the senior minister who is conversant in the
administration of the state, does not agree with his departure, for he
foresees evil.'

On his part, Sultan Malik al-Mansur convinced himself and
departed for Pasai, and then entered Sultan Malik al-Zahir's palace.
Soon however, he was overcome with desire for one of the palace maids
and brought her back to his palace.

He said to Sidi Samayuddin, 'My revered uncle, I was overcome with
desire, and my work is ruined for my desire was exceptionally demanding.'

Sidi Samayuddin replied, 'The justice of Allah has been done.'

Soon it was heard that Sultan Malik al-Zahir had already arrived in Jambu Air. In his heart Sultan Malik al-Zahir was aggrieved about a wrong done against him, though he did not divulge it to anyone. However, Sultan Malik al-Zahir ordered that Sultan Malik al-Mansur be welcomed, as befitting a royal visitor. In the meantime, Sultan Malik al-Mansur departed from Samudera, sailing downstream to the estuary. At that moment Sultan Malik al-Zahir came by the Keteri River and proceeded to his brother's palace.

In the meantime, Sultan Malik al-Mansur returned to Samudera. As he had not heeded Sidi Samayuddin's advice, there was no need for any regret on his part. However, Sultan Malik al-Zahir nursed a plan of vengeance against him.

It was narrated that Sultan Malik al-Zahir had a son, Sultan Ahmad was his name. When Sultan Malik al- Zahir was captured, his son was but a small boy. When Sultan Malik al-Zahir had returned from Shahr Nuwi, Raja Ahmad was already an adult. In the meantime, Sidi 'Ali Ghiatuddin had resigned from his post.

There was a new minister for His Majesty, Tun Perpatih Tulus Tukang Segara, who would succeed his father-in-law.

One day, Sultan Malik al-Zahir enquired, 'Tun Perpatih Tulus Tukang Segara, what is My Lord's opinion on the deed of Sultan Malik al-Mansur?'

Tun Perpatih Tulus Tukang Segara replied, 'We have a plan.'

Sultan Malik al-Zahir continued, 'If Sultan Malik al-Mansur were dead . . .'

Tun Perpatih Tulus Tukang Segara continued, 'If Sultan Malik al-Mansur is dead then there is no art to it. Let us assemble for a ceremony at Sultan Ahmad's circumcision,[10] and invite Sultan Malik al-Mansur. It is then that we execute our plan.'

In order to prepare for the ceremony, Sultan Malik al-Zahir instructed that the state and the audience hall be decorated. When all was ready, His Majesty ordered that the ceremony be commenced.

---

[10] *Berkhatan*, circumcision.

Before long, Sultan Malik al-Mansur arrived in Samudera. Sultan Malik al-Zahir invited his brother and Sidi Samayuddin into the palace, but their retinue of soldiers remained outside. Then Sultan Malik al-Zahir ordered his military chief to seize Sultan Malik al-Mansur and Sidi Samayuddin and bring them to Manjung.

His Majesty then instructed Sidi Samayuddin, 'You stay here, do not accompany Sultan Malik al-Mansur. If you still want to follow him, I shall ask that you be beheaded.'

Sidi Samayuddin replied, 'It's better that the head be separated from the body, and not from its master.'

So, Sultan Malik al-Zahir ordered that Sidi Samayuddin be beheaded and his head thrown into the sea, while his body was impaled in Kuala Paya.

Thus, Sultan Malik al-Mansur was brought in a boat to the east. When they arrived at Jambu Air, he noticed a head caught in his rudder. Sultan Malik al-Mansur was duly informed. As His Majesty picked up the head, he realized it was Sidi Samayuddin's. He then turned to look landward.

His Majesty asked, 'What field is this?'

To this day it is called Padang Maya.

Sultan Malik al-Mansur disembarked and requested Sidi Samayuddin's corpse from Sultan Malik al-Zahir. The body was duly given to him. Presently, Sultan Malik al-Mansur buried Sidi Samayuddin's body and head in Padang Maya.

In the meantime, His Majesty travelled to Manjung. Soon after the departure of Sultan Malik al-Mansur, Sultan Ahmad was circumcised.

Some three years passed; Sultan Malik al-Zahir remembered his brother in Manjung.

Said he, 'Wah, so mean was I; just because of a woman I dethroned my brother and killed his minister.'

His Majesty was overcome with remorse and ordered his soldiers to go in several boats to fetch him. So Sultan Malik al-Mansur was accompanied back with due royal honours. When they arrived at

Padang Maya, Sultan Malik al-Mansur made a stop to visit the grave of Sidi Samayuddin.

He called out his greetings, 'Assalamu'alaikum, my uncle. Please remain here, for now I am being fetched by my elder brother.'

Sidi Samayuddin answered from his grave, 'Where is Your Majesty headed? It is better for us to stay here.'

After hearing him, Sultan Malik al-Mansur cleansed himself and made a prayer of two genuflections. When the prayer was over, he laid himself by the grave. There his life ended.

It was relayed to His Majesty that his brother had died in Padang Maya, beside the grave of Sidi Samayuddin. Consequently, His Majesty hastened to Padang Maya. After his arrival he ordered that his brother be buried according to the rites of great s.

Soon after that he returned to Pasai full of repentance and grief. To make amends, he abdicated his throne and crowned his son, Sultan Ahmad.

In time, Sultan Malik al-Zahir fell ill. He reminded his son, Sultan Ahmad, 'Hai my son, the jewel of my eye, never go against the loyalty of your servants. In every task you must deliberate with all your ministers and do not, do not, hurt their feelings. Be forever vigilant in the tasks that are dishonourable and do not take lightly in the practice of your worship of Allah *Subhanahu wa Ta'ala* and take not the possessions that do not belong to you.'

Sultan Ahmad wept on hearing his father's last words. After a few days His Majesty departed for the next world. He was buried by his son close to the mosque, while Sultan Ahmad reigned Samudera after his father's demise.

* * *

There was a man of Pasai, Tun Jana Khatib was his name. He travelled to Singa Pura. On his arrival, he walked across the town. He once befriended the Lords of Bunguran and Selangor. It happened that while he was walking besides the palace of the Raja of Singapura, the princess was looking out of the window and caught sight of Tun Jana Khatib.

There grew an areca palm besides the palace. Tun Jana Khatib put a spell on the palm and it split into two. When the Paduka Seri Maharaja saw what he thought was happening, he was greatly angered.

Said he, 'Look at Tun Jana Khatib, as he knew that our wife was looking, he was showing off his skill.'

His Majesty ordered that he be slain. Soon the executioner brought him to the gallows. Incidentally, Tun Jana Khatib was stabbed close to a place where a woman was making the *bikang* cake. His blood dripped to the ground, but his body disappeared and landed in Langkawi. The cake maker placed the cover of her food on a clod of Tun Jana Khatib's blood. It became stone and may be seen even now.

After a lapse of some years, swordfishes began to overrun Singa Pura. People who were standing on the beaches were struck: if it was on their chest, then their beaks would penetrate through it; if it was through the neck, then the head was severed, and they died instantly; if it was through the hips, they too soon died. Many were killed by the swordfishes. There was pandemonium. People went around shouting, 'The swordfishes are attacking us, and many are already dead!'

Paduka Seri Maharaja mounted his elephant and, accompanied by his prime minister, military chiefs and eunuchs went out to the beaches to review the situation. His Majesty was surprised at how many of his subjects had been killed by the swordfishes. Whoever was pierced by the fishes would die with their teeth clenched. More and more people came to be killed. So, His Majesty ordered that they form a bastion with their legs. However, when they were pierced many died. The fishes came as in a rain. The dead on the beach were innumerable.

In the meantime, there was a boy who suggested, 'Why are we making a bastion of our legs and making ourselves easy targets? Wouldn't it be better if we erected a bastion of banana trunks?'

When Paduka Seri Maharaja heard his suggestion, he said, 'It's true what the boy has said.'

Thus, His Majesty commanded that all his subjects erect a bastion of banana trunks. When the fishes flew towards the beach, they hit their beaks on the stems. The people then slashed at them. Thus, countless swordfishes lay dead. Soon none came to beach anymore.

His Majesty then returned to his palace. His senior officers of state came to protest, 'My Lord, this boy, as he grows older will be having a mind of his own. It's better that we do away with him right now.'

The Raja agreed, 'It's true what My Lords have said.'

So, His Majesty ordered that they boy be slain. When he was killed, the right to his life was borne by the whole *negeri* of Singa Pura.

After reigning for twelve years, Paduka Seri Maharaja died. His son, Seri Sultan Iskandar Shah, was crowned King.

He married the daughter of Tun Perpatih Tulus, and they bore a boy, Raja Kecil Besar. His Majesty had a Bendahara, who was originally from Singa Pura. Sang Rajuna Tapa was his title. He begot a girl, who was extremely lovely, and was chosen as His Majesty's concubine, whom he loved profoundly.

One day, an accusation was spread by all the palace maids that she was having an affair. Sultan Iskandar Shah became extremely irate. He ordered that she be impaled with her legs apart at the end of the market. Her father, Sang Rajuna Tapa was deeply humiliated seeing what was done to his daughter.

Said he, 'If it was true that my daughter was involved in an affair, then just slay her. What need is there to humiliate her in such a manner?'

Subsequently Sang Rajuna Tapa sent a letter to Java, saying:

If the Betara of Maja Pahit wishes to invade Singa Pura, now is an appropriate time, for I shall assist from inside the fort.

When the Betara of Maja Pahit heard the words of the Bendahara of Singa Pura, he immediately ordered that an armada of three hundred vessels be readied, made up of numerous ships of various kinds and sizes. Two hundred thousand of his Javanese subjects set sail on this armada. When they had arrived on the shores of Singa Pura, they began to battle with the defenders of the *negeri*. After a few days into the battle, Sultan Iskandar Shah ordered the Bendahara to release the rice rations for the people of the *negeri*.

Sang Rajuna Tapa replied, 'There is no more rice left in the godowns,' for he wished to help the enemy. In the early dawn the next day, Sang Rajuna Tapa opened the gates of the fort. The Javanese rushed in and battled with the people of Singa Pura inside the fort. Many were killed on both sides; their blood flowed as in a clogged drain, overflowing into the fort near the beach. That is the very blood that may still be seen on the field in Singa Pura. Singa Pura was defeated. Sultan Iskandar Shah fled to Muar.

By the will of Allah *Ta'ala*, Sang Rajuna Tapa's house, along with his wife's were turned into stone. These are still there by the canal.

After Singapura was defeated, the Javanese returned to Maja Pahit. In the meantime, Sultan Iskandar Shah arrived in Muar. He stayed in a place where he noticed that at night there came numerous iguanas, and during the day they filled the whole area. So, his people began to kill them, some were consumed. The rest were thrown into the river. On the following night as well, numerous iguanas crawled up from the river. During the day they were killed and thrown into the river, thus causing the water to exude a foul smell. In time, it came to be known as Biawak Busuk, the Stinking Iguana.

Sultan Iskandar Shah soon moved from that place and proceeded to walk to another, close by. It was there that he built a fort.

During the day it was built, however, in the night it began to rot. Thus, it is now known as Kota Buruk, the Rotten Fort. Again, His Majesty moved from there, and set up camp in another place. After that, he and his people walked to a place called Setang Ujung. His Majesty found it to be a good location, so he retained a minister there. It is that place where ministers paid their visits, and continue to pay, even to this day.

Then Sultan Iskandar Shah returned and walked to the beach by a river; Bertam was its name. His Majesty stood under a tree and began to hunt. There under the tree his hunting dog was kicked by a white mousedeer.

Said Sultan Iskandar Shah, 'This is a propitious place. Even the mousedeer is daring. Let's build a *negeri* here.'

The senior officers of state agreed, 'It's true what Your Majesty has said.' So, he ordered that houses and buildings be erected there.

His Majesty enquired, 'What is the name of this tree under which we are standing?'

'Melaka,' replied an officer.

Sultan Iskandar Shah decided, 'In that case "Melaka" shall be the name of this *negeri*.'

Thus, the Sultan remained in Melaka, built and extended it. He initiated the ceremonies. It was His Majesty who first ordered that the four ministers be seated in the audience hall to deliberate on the rules of conduct, with the heralds standing in the gallery—forty on either side—to convey each and every one of the King's commands and to appoint the sons of the aristocrats as young pages to carry the insignia of the state.

Sultan Iskandar Shah's reign in Singa Pura lasted for only three years before it was defeated by the Javanese. After that he moved to Melaka. He reigned for twenty years in all, thus making his rule altogether twenty-three years.

The wheel of time turned, and the Sultan departed for the eternal world. His son, Raja Kecil Besar, succeeded him. His royal title was Sultan Makota.

In the meanwhile, Tun Perpatih Tulus too was deceased, his son succeeded him as Bendahara.

His Majesty, Sultan Makota, married the daughter of the Bendahara. They bore three children, a boy by the name of Raden Bagus, and another boy by the name of Raja Tengah, and finally, Raden Anum.

However, after two years on the throne, His Majesty departed this world. It was his son, Raja Tengah who replaced him. He married the daughter of Tun Perpatih Muka Berjajar, and had a son with her, by the name of Raja Kecil Bambang.

Raja Tengah ruled for many years and was extremely just and very caring towards the welfare of his subjects. Not even one of the rajas in the world was his compare during these times.

* * *

It came to pass that one night, His Majesty dreamt of beholding the magnificence of our Prophet's visage (peace be upon on him).

The Prophet spoke to him, 'Repeat after me, "There is no god but Allah; Muhammad is his Messenger."' So, His Majesty repeated the words of the Prophet.

The Prophet continued, 'Your name shall be Muhammad. On the morrow, in the afternoon, a vessel from Jeddah shall cast anchor, and some men will disembark. Your Majesty shall follow their instructions.'

Raja Tengah replied, 'It shall be done.'

In an instant, the Prophet of Allah vanished from his sight.

At dawn, Raja Tengah was woken from his sleep. He noticed that his manhood has been circumcised and his lips did not stop from repeating the articles of Muslim belief.

All the palace maids were full of disbelief listening to what was said by the Sultan.

Said one of his ministers, 'I fear that His Majesty is possessed by the devil or he has become insane? Let us quickly inform the Bendahara.'

So, the maids promptly relayed the news to the Bendahara, who soon came into the palace. He too observed that the Sultan did not stop repeating the articles of the Muslim faith.

The Bendahara enquired, 'In what language is His Majesty speaking?'

The raja replied, 'Last night we dreamt of seeing the magnificence of Prophet Muhammad, (peace be upon on him).'

And so, His Majesty narrated it all to the Bendahara.

The Bendahara enquired, 'Is there any proof of the dream that Your Majesty dreamt of last night?'

Raja Tengah replied, 'My manhood looks as though it has been circumcised. This is the proof that we have dreamt of the Prophet, (peace be upon him). Furthermore, he said to us, "In the afternoon a vessel from Jeddah shall cast anchor, and a man will disembark, who will perform their prayers on our beach. Follow all his instructions."'

Said the Bendahara, 'If a vessel does come at the time of the afternoon prayer then it is true what His Majesty has dreamt; if not, he is possessed by the devil.'

Answered the King, 'It is true what My Lord has said.'

The Bendahara then returned home.

Soon the afternoon turned to the time of prayer. There came a vessel from Jeddah and cast its anchor. Sidi 'Abdul 'Aziz was the name of the man who duly performed his prayers on the sand. Everyone was surprised to see his gestures and genuflections.

They asked, 'Why was the man's head nodding up and down?'

The crowd jostled to have a look at him; they were packed tight, without any space between them. The noise that rose was a clamour of confusion, and the commotion soon reached the ears of the monarch. Instantly, the Raja mounted his elephant and departed, accompanied by his chief officers. On arrival, he could see that pundit's gestures which were indeed identical to those which he saw in his dream.

The Raja said to the chief officers, 'It is true what we have dreamt last night.'

After Makhdum Sidi 'Abdul 'Aziz had performed his prayers, the Raja ordered his elephant to kneel down, and he brought him to the palace. Soon the Bendahara and all the aristocrats and officers of state became Muslims. After that, everyone in the *negeri* was asked to follow the new religion.

In time, the raja was tutored by Makhdum Sidi 'Abdul 'Aziz.

His Majesty's new designation was Sultan Muhammad Shah. And the Bendahara became known as Seri Amar Diraja. Then Tun Perpatih Besar was appointed as chief of the treasury, with the title of Seri Nara al-Diraja. It was he who fathered a girl, by the name of Princess Ratna Sundari.

Subsequently, Sultan Muhammad Shah prepared to reorganize his administration. It was His Majesty who was to proclaim that the colour yellow be restricted only to the royalty and may not be used for a handkerchief, or the fringes of curtains, or ends of bolsters or as a sheet for mattresses, and no one may use it to string things as an ornament for one's house, or for other purposes other than material for a suit of the Malay coat and headgear—only these were permitted.

It was also forbidden to build a house with a balcony with suspended posts that did not reach the ground, or with posts that were connected from the roof down to the ground, and the kiosque. It was forbidden to build boats with windows. And in the audience halls as well, windows were similarly forbidden.

As for umbrellas, the forbidden colour was more white than yellow, for the white umbrellas were for royal use, and yellow ones were for the princes.

In the meantime, no one not of royal blood was permitted to use the *keris* with a hollowed blade in a metal sheath, and neither was it allowed for any offspring of His Majesty's subjects to wear golden anklets; even if they were of gold with a head of silver, that too was forbidden to all except Malay rajas. If one transgressed these prerogatives of the Raja, the punishment was death.

As for the use of gold, no one was allowed, however rich he may be; on the other hand, if it was a gift from the Raja, he or she may use it at any time.

However, if anyone entered the palace and did not don a long dress and a *keris*[11] with a *sebai*[12] shawl he was not allowed in—this was a requirement for one and all. If one came with a *keris* inserted on his back—it would be confiscated by the palace guards; anyone who went against this regulation would pay for it with his life.

---

[11] *Keris*, the well-known Malay dagger.
[12] *Sebai*, a scarf worn by both men and women.

When the Raja was holding court in the audience hall, the senior ministers, military chiefs and eunuchs[13] sat on the right gallery. All the princes would sit on the left gallery, all the sons of military chiefs on the right side of the veranda, while all the heralds and young warriors would stand on the dais, bearing swords. The heralds[14] on the left were descendants of ministers who were eligible to be appointed the Bendahara or the Temenggung. The Chief of the Heralds on the right was a descendant of military chiefs who may be eligible to be appointed the Laksamana, the admiral or Seri Bija al-Diraja. Whoever had been titled Sang Guna may become the Laksamana; whoever had been titled Sang Setia may become the Seri Bija al-Diraja, and whoever had been titled Tun Pikrama may become the Bendahara.

And in the ceremony of obeisance it was the chief of the four or five heralds who first make their first bow, that is, before the eunuchs who sat in the *seri balai*, place of honour. Except the senior ministers, the chosen Champa captains, Nakhoda Jemu, and the sons of the lords sat along the gallery's veranda. All the heralds holding royal implements like the spittoon, water goblet, fan, shield, bow and arrows were positioned alternately, except for the betel bowl which was placed inside the gallery. As for the sword of state, it was the Laksamana, or the son of Seri Bija al-Diraja, who bore it and sat on the left-side gallery.

In the ceremony of receiving missions from abroad, the one who greeted the letter in the audience hall was the chief herald on the right; and the one who transmitted the words of the Raja was the chief herald on the left. The letter of the arriving or departing mission would be placed on a silver saucer and metal salver, borne by the servant from within. The silver saucer would then be received by the marshal on the right, placed at the level of the Bendahara. And moreover, the shawl and tray would be given to the bearer of the letter. If it was a letter from Pasai, it would be received with full state honours—with the *nafiri*[15]

---

[13] *Sida-sida*, eunuch.

[14] *Abintara*, herald.

[15] *Nafiri*, a trumpet, a royal instrument in official ceremonies.

trumpets, royal *nagara* kettledrums, and twin white umbrellas, side by side. The elephants would be herded side by side to the end of the gallery, for the Kings of these two states were of equal status, though they might be older or younger—they merely conveyed greetings. However, if it was a letter from other states, the reception would be on a reduced scale, and only accompanied by drums, flutes and a yellow umbrella. If it deserved an elephant then it would be borne on an elephant, if it deserved a horse, then it would be received at the outer door. If it was a raja of a higher status, he would be then accompanied with a flute and two umbrellas, one yellow and one white; the elephant would kneel down outside the inner door.

If he was of a lower rank, then it would be a person of lower or the middle rank who would invite him in. If he deserved to be received on an elephant then an elephant would be brought forth, if he deserved to be carried on a horse, then it was a horse that would be brought forth. However, if he did not deserve a horse, he walked along with an umbrella and a trumpeter, but his umbrella would be green in colour, or blue or red, as befitted his status. The largest of the yellow umbrellas were for the princes and senior officers of state, and the red and purple were designated for the eunuchs, heralds and military chiefs. The blue ones were for all titled lords. As the titled lords arrived, they would pause. The formula of installation would be read before the Raja. When this was completed, the person would be escorted out of the Hall.

As concerns the reception of the formula of installation—the officers were also from the titled families and presented with the accompanying official shawls. The official reader of the formula at the installation of the Sultan would be the same officer who addressed the titled person. He would be escorted into the hall, and a ceremonial mat would be spread at a special place chosen by the Raja, and that would be the place that he would sit at later.

This was followed with the gift of a suit of costumes. For the Bendahara it was five salvers of costumes—a salver of coats, a salver of head bands, a salver of shawl, a salver of waist band and a salver of sarong. However, if it was for the princes and ministers or military chiefs then it was four salvers of costumes—the waist band was not included. If it was for the military chiefs, heralds and eunuchs, it was three salvers—a salver of sarong, a salver of coat and another for the headdress and shawl—both in one tray. If he was deserving of two salvers—the sarong was on one salver, while the coat and the headgear in another. There were instances when all of these were presented on just one salver; while in some cases without any salver, the articles of clothing—the sarong, the coat and the headdress—were ceremonially folded and borne by the Raja's servant, who carried them. In the case of a titled guest, in addition to presenting the gifts, the Raja's servant also helped carry the gifts out of the hall [to the guest's travelling coach].

When the costumes were being presented, the chiefs and officials to be honoured stepped out to change their old costumes for the new ones. When they were ready, they returned to the audience hall, where they would be presented with the frontlets and armlets. All those who were bestowed with titles wore armlets, but each according to his status—some wore dragon armlets, with supports, some with bejewelled armbands, and some merely with supports. Some with designs of the *birah* palm, some however were in silver. When this was completed, they then made an obeisance, after which they departed, accompanied by officials befitting their status; or the one who fetched them would be the one who accompanied them home.

Thus the individuals honoured by the King moved in a procession, some accompanied by only the kettledrums and flutes, some with the royal long trumpets, some with the royal kettledrums and white umbrellas, but all of these were rare articles, for they were heirlooms of old, like the white umbrellas and *nagara* kettledrums; while the yellow umbrellas and trumpets were especially uncommon, for they were few in number.

However, when His Majesty departed for the Aidilfitri prayers, he would be carried in a sedan chair, the chief treasurer holding the front, on the right the Temenggung, and to the left would be the Laksamana, at the rear the two senior courtiers. The one near the chains, by the Raja's knee, on the right side, the Laksamana, while on the left would be the Seri Bija al-Diraja. All the courtiers and military chiefs walked before the Raja, each according to his rank. The state insignia would be carried in front, the royal lances would be borne, one on the right, and the other on the left. In this manner, the royal regalia would be carried in front.

Those who carried the lances walked before the courtiers who carried the spears. The state emblems were to be in front of the Raja, and before them were the state drums, the kettledrums on the right of the Raja, the *nafiri* trumpets on the left. However, while in formation they would be more to the right than to the left; but while sitting they would be more to the left than to the right. This was also the case for the ceremony of obeisance—officers walked in front of the Raja, but the smaller instruments were carried at the head of the procession. The lances and spears were in the forefront. And so were all the various types of musical instruments. The Bendahara walked behind the Raja with all the senior ministers and the *kadi*.[16]

To begin with, if the Raja were to arrive on an elephant, the Temenggung sat at its head, the Laksamana or Bija al-Diraja at its rear, bearing the sword of state. However, at a royal *nobat*[17] ceremony, all the senior officers were placed to the left of the drums, and the junior ones to the right.

Those who were eligible to be granted the *nobat* betel were, firstly, the royal princes and the Bendahara, the chief treasurer, and the senior eunuchs and courtier—that is, if the Bendahara was present at the ceremony, he was then offered the betel. However, if he was not present, then no *nobat* betel was offered, even if there were royal princes in the hall.

Now, on the subject of the Raja at his duties. It was the Chief of the Treasury[18] who took command within and ordered that the mats be laid in the gallery, and the audience hall be adorned, the decorative

[16] Religious minister especially having authority in matters of marriage.
[17] *Nobat*, 'a large hemispherical kettle drum.' Used in official ceremonies including the coronation and marriage.
[18] *Penghulu bendahari*, Chief of the Treasury.

ceiling hangings be hung and the curtains draped. He had to supervise the meal to be served, and order that invitees be bidden and fetched, for all the royal servants and the treasurers were under the command of the chief of the treasury, including the harbour master and all those who collected taxes on behalf of the Raja—all came under his authority. And it was the chief of the treasury who invited guests and arranged their seating in the audience hall.

In the dining hall, it was the practice that each serving was for four officers or guests, and this was also true of the arrangement all the way down. If one was absent, then only the three of them dined in their cluster; if two were absent, then only two. It was not allowed for those of the lower levels to complete the clusters of the upper ones, especially those at the very top. It was the custom of the palace that the Bendahara dined alone, or with the princes. Those were the customs of the Melakan times. There are many more that have not been described besides those already mentioned; however, if we were to relate all of them then they would merely confound those who shall hear them.

Now as concerns the twenty-seventh night of the holy month of Ramadhan—during the day, the prayer mats were carried in a procession to the mosque; it was the Temenggung who led it, walking before the elephant. Then, the royal betel bowl. And all the royal utensils and the drums were also carried to the mosque. When night fell, the Raja departed for the mosque for the evening 'Isya and the Tarawih prayers; after that, His Majesty would return to the palace.

On the morrow, the Laksamana would head a procession to convey the royal turban, for it was the custom of the Malay Raja to go to the mosque wearing a turban; with a robe, which was forbidden to one and all during marriages, except those who have been bestowed them by the Raja. For those intending to be robed in the Keling style during a marriage or Eid ceremony, they were allowed to do so when they were in possession of such apparel.

After the greater or lesser Eid celebrations, the Bendahara and all the senior ministers would enter the palace and then the sedan chair would be carried from the residence of the chief treasurer. When those present had noted the arrival of the sedan chair, they would descend from their seats to the floor. From within the palace, the Raja would then proceed in the procession; he would be mounted on an elephant, to ride to the royal dais. Upon arrival, he ascended it. As he ascended its steps, all those present would take their seats on the floor. The sedan chair would then be positioned beside the palace gallery. Then the Bendahara would promptly ascend the stage to receive the Raja, who would subsequently mount the sedan chair, and depart for the mosque, as had been the practice in the past. These were the customs that needed to be endorsed—if they were corrupt, they should be amended. Those who still retain a recollection of these customs, please do not censure this humble servant.

It was narrated that when Sultan Muhammad Shah was on the throne, he was extremely just in seeing to the welfare of his subjects. Thus, in time, Melaka expanded, and numerous traders made it their main port of call. The colonies of Melaka likewise multiplied—to the west to Beruas Ujung, to the east to Terengganu Ujung Karang. It became known in all the countries under the wind that it was a great *negeri*; and moreover, its Sultan was a descendant of Alexander the Great.

In due time, rajas travelled to Melaka to pay their homage. All those who came were deferentially received and duly honoured by His Majesty, presented with gifts of noble costumes and bestowed with valuable favours, gold and silver—in great quantities.

Allah knows the truth; to Him shall we return.

VII

In the words of the author, there was once a great kingdom, in Benua Keling,[1] the country of the Kelings, Pahili was its name, Nizam al-Muluk Akbar Shah was its Raja. The Raja was a Muslim in the religion of the Prophet Muhammad Rasul 'Allah, (peace be on him). He bore two boys and a girl. The older boy was called Prince Mani Purindan. The middle son was Raja Akbar Muluk Padshah.

In time, when Raja Nizam al-Muluk Akbar Shah was deceased, Akbar Muluk Padshah succeeded him on the throne.

All of His Majesty's assets were divided among the three children, according to the prescriptions of Allah. Then came the golden cuki[2] game board, which was bejewelled, with red gems on one side and green gems on the other.

Mani Purindan suggested to his younger brother, Raja Akbar Muluk Padshah, 'Let's give this cuki board to our sister, for it is not fitting that we use it.'

Raja Akbar Muluk Padshah answered, 'I do not agree with your suggestion. My wish is that we estimate its value. If our sister wishes to own it, then she shall give us its value.'

---

[1] Benua Keling, Kingdom of the Kelings, Kalinga.
[2] *Cuki*, a game quite similar to draughts.

Mani Purindan was embarrassed, for his words were not approved by his brother.

In his mind, he thought, 'If in cases as insignificant as this my brother does not agree with me, how much more so will it be when the issue is much greater? As this is the situation, let me exile myself to some distant place. Though I am here, I am not the King. Where should I exile myself but to the country of the Raja of Melaka, who is a great monarch? It is right that I should pay him homage for he is a descendant of King Alexander.'

He thus ordered that a number of vessels be prepared, and thus began his journey to Melaka. When they arrived at Jambu Air, on the northern tip of Sumatra, a great storm descended and Mani Purindan's vessel sank into the depths. He was cast into the sea, but fortunately fell crosswise on a barracuda,[3] which carried him ashore. When it beached, Mani Purindan raised himself, holding on to a butterfly ginger plant. It was thus that he reached land. That was the reason why Mani Purindan forbade his descendants to consume the barracuda and to use the butterfly ginger flower[4] as decoration.

Mani Purindan then journeyed to Pasai; there the Raja of Pasai wedded him to his daughter—it was their children who became the fountain of all the rajas of the state. Sultan Khamis, the father of Raja Suwat, whom Mani Purindan divorced, was related to the Malays.

After a sojourn of a few days in Pasai, he returned to Benua Keling. When the winds again turned, he ordered that the vessels be prepared to sail to Melaka. He was accompanied by all his soldiers, the military chief, Khoja 'Ali, and another, Tandil Muhammad; they sailed in five boats.

Upon their arrival, his highness was taken by Seri Nara al-Diraja as his son-in-law, a husband to his daughter, Tun Ratna Sundari. They begot two children, a boy by the name of Nina Madi, and a daughter, by the name of Tun Ratna Wati. Tun Ratna Wati was later wedded to Bendahara Seri Amar Diraja, and they bore a boy, Tun 'Ali.

---

[3] *Ikan baluh-baluh*, barracuda.
[4] *Bunga Gandasuli*, butterfly ginger flower.

As the wheel of time turned, the Bendahara, Seri Amar Diraja, returned to the grace of Allah. It was Perpatih Sandang who succeeded him, his official title being Seriwa Raja. In the meantime, Seri Nara al-Diraja too died. Tun 'Ali, the son of the Bendahara Seri Amar Diraja and Tun Ratna Wati, the daughter of his highness Mani Purindan, became the Chief of the Treasury. His official title was Seri Nara al-Diraja.

Sultan Muhammad Shah married the Princess of Rokan; a boy, Raja Ibrahim, was born to them. With his consort, the daughter of the Bendahara, he bore another boy, Raja Kasim was his name.

Raja Kasim was older than Raja Ibrahim. However, it was the wish of the Queen that Raja Ibrahim succeeded his father as King. Sultan Muhammad Shah granted her wish, but he loved Raja Kasim dearly— it was because of his promise and sense of honour towards the Queen that he conceded. He complied with Raja Ibrahim's least behest.

But as for Raja Kasim, if he unintentionally took even a piece of a betel leaf, his father would admonish him. In time, the people of Melaka came to dislike Raja Ibrahim, but loved Raja Kasim.

One day, the Raja of Rokan journeyed to Melaka to pay the King obeisance, and he was much honoured by His Majesty, for the Queen was a relative of his. He was consequently given a place as high as the Bendahara's, although when he dined it was at a lower rank.

All the warriors and soldiers of the Raja of Rokan protested to their King, 'Why are we like the roosting chicken, asleep under the roof, but feeding under the house? Perhaps Your Majesty should request a change.'

Raja Rokan chose to take his seat under the Bendahara. Sultan Muhammad Shah did not object to this choice; and thus, the Raja of Rokan remained below the level of the Bendahara.

After a reign of fifty-seven years, the cycle of time turned. His Majesty moved from this transient world to the eternal one.

After His Majesty was deceased,[5] it was his son, Raja Ibrahim, who replaced him on the throne. His Majesty's official designation was Sultan

---

[5]   *Kematian*, death.

Abu Shahid. It was the Raja of Rokan who represented Sultan Abu Shahid, who was then a young boy, and the state of Melaka seemingly came to be under the Raja of Rokan's authority. It was he who ordered Raja Kasim to live by the sea and become a fisherman. It was as though the Raja of Rokan was the King of Melaka. In time, all the nobles and senior ministers gathered at the Bendahara's to confer with each other.

Said all the ministers and warriors, 'What has happened to Melaka, for now it seems that the Raja of Rokan is our lord and master, and not Raja Abu Shahid?'

The Bendahara, Seriwa Raja, replied in a raised voice, 'What can we do, for the Raja of Rokan is never separated from His Majesty?'

When they heard his answer, they remained silent, and promptly returned to their respective homes. Seri Nara al-Diraja turned in his mind the situation and the possible action that could be implemented. However, Raja Kasim was always summoned and given food, for Raja Kasim was a cousin of Seri Nara al-Diraja.

The days turned into months, and before long a vessel came from above the wind. When it had cast anchor all the fisherfolk gathered around it to sell their catch. Among them was Raja Kasim, who was indistinguishable from the other fisherfolk. It happened that in the vessel was a pious man. Maulana Jalaluddin was his name.

As soon as he set his eyes on Raja Kasim, he invited him on board his vessel, and showed him due respect and honour.

Raja Kasim enquired, 'Why is My Lord offering me such respect, I am but a fisherman trying to sell my catch?'

Maulana Jalaluddin replied, 'You are a prince in this *negeri,* and will in time be the Raja of Melaka.'

Raja Kasim replied, 'How is it possible for me to become the Raja? If it were with My Lord's blessings and fortune to assist me, then I may become one.'

The *maulana* said, 'Your highness, go into the *negeri,* find people who may be able to help you accomplish your wishes, God willing it shall be done. But there is one request I ask of you. The princess who is married to the Raja of Rokan—give her to me.'

Raja Kasim replied, 'It is agreed then—if I become the Raja.'

The *maulana* suggested 'My Lord should hurry to disembark and act tonight. Allah *Subhanahu wa Ta'ala* is with you.'

Soon Raja Kasim disembarked, thinking, 'Where shall I go? In the situation that I am in it is best that I go to the Seri Nara al-Diraja's, for he is my cousin. Perhaps he would like to support my cause.'

Thinking thus, Raja Kasim went to the Seri Nara al-Diraja's. He repeated all the words of the *maulana* to Seri Nara al-Diraja, and asked, 'Would My Lord support us to reclaim the throne?'

Seri Nara al-Diraja replied, 'Yes, I would.'

After making the oath and consolidating their pledge, the Seri Nara al-Diraja made preparations to gather his people. In the meantime, Raja Kasim was mounted on the elephant by the name of Juru Demang; the Seri Nara al-Diraja sat at its head.

Meanwhile, those in the vessel in the harbour disembarked with all their weapons.

Seri Nara al-Diraja said to Raja Kasim, 'What says your highness, in the event that the Bendahara is not with us, should we win?'

Raja Kasim replied, 'What is your opinion, My Lord?'

Seri Nara al-Diraja said, 'Let's go to the Bendahara's.'

Raja Kasim agreed, 'I shall follow My Lord's suggestion.'

Thus, they both made their way to the Bendahara's.

When they had arrived at his gate, the Seri Nara al-Diraja said, 'Quickly send word that His Majesty is waiting at his gate.'

So word was brought to the Bendahara. He promptly descended the stairs of his residence, unarmed, donning his headgear along the way. The night was frenzied. As soon as the Bendahara arrived, the elephant was lowered by the Seri Nara al-Diraja.

Said he, 'My Lord, Bendahara, His Majesty asks that you mount the elephant.'

Thus, the Bendahara mounted the elephant, and proceeded. The Bendahara noticed the shimmer of the numerous weapons, and the Raja was not Sultan Abu Shahid. He was greatly surprised seeing this development.

Seri Nara al-Diraja spoke to the Bendahara, 'What says My Lord: Raja Kasim intends to slay the Raja of Rokan?'

The Bendahara was caught unawares.

He replied, 'I like this development, for Raja Kasim is also my master. For many months it has been my wish to do Raja Rokan in.'

Raja Kasim was extremely pleased to hear the words of the Bendahara, and immediately rushed into the palace. There was much confusion—word went around that Raja Kasim had entered the palace. The nobles, senior officers and the warriors rushed to follow the Bendahara, all of them asking, 'Where is the Bendahara?'

Someone shouted, 'The Bendahara is with Raja Kasim.'

In their hearts they concluded, 'This must be the work of the Bendahara!'

Soon the people found the Bendahara with Raja Kasim. Many of them had already sided with Raja Kasim. Now it came to their ears that the assailants,[6] their colleagues, had overpowered those inside the palace.

In the meantime, however, the Raja of Rokan did not stray from Sultan Abu Shahid's side.

Seri Nara al-Diraja ordered, 'His Majesty has commanded that Sultan Abu Shahid be taken, for fear that he would be slain by the Raja of Rokan.'

Someone shouted that the Raja should not be wounded yet. But no one listened to him, as the situation was extremely chaotic. So, the Raja of Rokan was repeatedly stabbed. As he felt the stab of the *keris* he in turn knifed Sultan Abu Shahid. Thus, His Majesty died a martyr, after being on the throne for a year and five months.

After the death of Sultan Abu Shahid, it was Raja Kasim who succeeded him and was ritually installed. His royal title was Sultan Muzaffar Shah.

In time, the *maulana* came to the new Sultan to demand his part of the promise made to him. His Majesty ordered that a good-looking

[6]   *Menyerang*, to attack.

maid be dressed in a full royal costume, and be taken to the *maulana*, as the Rokan Princess. In the *maulana*'s heart she was indeed the real princess, so he promptly received her and took her to the land above the wind.

When he was on the throne, Sultan Muzaffar Shah was extremely exemplary in his temperament; he was just, generous and fair in all his relations with his subjects. It was His Majesty who ordered that the laws of the land be put in writing so that his ministers need no longer misinterpret them.

The Seri Nara al-Diraja was much loved by the Raja who never went against his words and actions. In time, Sultan Muzaffar Shah took to wife the daughter of Raden Anum, who bore him a boy, a most handsome prince, and they named him Raja 'Abdul.

One day, almost at the end of an extraordinarily long drawn session of court by Sultan Muzaffar Shah, the Bendahara entered to pay his obeisance. However, in the meantime, as Sultan Muzaffar Shah had been long entertaining his subjects, he departed for his chambers,[7] unaware that the Bendahara was coming to see him. The door of the audience hall was slammed shut by a gust of wind just at that very moment. In his heart the Bendahara Seriwa Raja, thought, 'His Majesty is annoyed with me. As I was coming to the hall he ordered that the doors be closed!'

Promptly the Bendahara Seriwa Raja returned to his residence and drank poison. He soon died. Word was carried to His Majesty that the Bendahara had died after consuming poison. Presently all the reasons for him taking the poison were recounted to His Majesty.

His Majesty was extremely disconsolate[8] and promptly went to seek the Bendahara, as was his habit. For seven days and seven nights His Majesty did not hold court. He greatly missed the Bendahara. Soon Seri Nara al-Diraja was appointed the Bendahara in his place.

---

[7] *Ruang balai*, meeting hall.
[8] *Muram, sedih, menderita*, disconsolate, sad.

Bendahara Seriwa Raja had three children, the oldest was a girl, and the younger two were boys. The daughter, Tun Kudu, was extremely good-looking, and was taken as a consort by Sultan Muzaffar Shah. His middle child was Tun Perak, the youngest was Tun Perpatih Putih.

It happened that Tun Perak was not introduced into the service of the palace, so he went to Kelang to find a wife, and stayed on there. In the meanwhile, the people of Kelang had rejected their chief, and requested another. His Majesty, Sultan Muzaffar Shah, enquired, 'Who do you wish to have as your chief?'

The people of Kelang bowed low and answered, 'If it pleases Your Majesty, we request Tun Perak as our chief.'

Sultan Muzaffar Shah replied, 'We are agreeable to your request.' So Tun Perak became the chief of Kelang and its inhabitants.

Allah knows the truth; to Him shall we return.

VIII

The chronicle now recounts the King of Siam. From ancient times, Siam was known as Shahr Nuwi. All the states below the wind were under its authority. Its King was Bubunnya.[1] When it became known to Siam that Melaka was a vast state but did not owe allegiance to it, His Majesty Bubunnya, sent an envoy to demand it.

However, Sultan Muzaffar Shah did not intend to send any proof of Melaka's allegiance to Siam. The Raja of Siam was enraged and promptly commanded that an army be readied to invade Melaka. Awi Cakri was its commander; he brought numerous soldiers and subjects of the King with him.

News of the King of Siam's intention to invade his country was conveyed to Sultan Muzaffar Shah: the Raja of Siam has ordered his commander, Awi Cakri, to bring an army of his soldiers and subjects, and to take an inland route through the upper reaches of Kelantan and Pahang.

When he heard of their intention, Sultan Muzaffar Shah ordered that his subjects be gathered, and those in the distant territories to come to the *negeri*. Soon, they were all assembled in Melaka. In the

---

[1] *Bubunnya*, here he was the King of Shahr Nuwi.

79

meantime, Tun Perak also brought his Kelang folks there, together with their wives and children.

The inhabitants of Kelang came to pay their obeisance and reported their circumstances.

These were their words, 'My Lord, all of your subjects from the other territories, in the bends and reaches of the river, have all come to pay Your Majesty homage, though all of them are composed only of men. But we, from Kelang, have been brought here by Tun Perak along with our wives and children.'

When Sultan Muzaffar Shah heard the appeal of the Kelang people, His Majesty said to one of his courtiers, Seri 'Amarat, 'When Tun Perak comes, do relay the words of the people of Kelang to him.'

It was said that Seri 'Amarat had his origins in Pasai, Patih Semedar was his name. As he was extremely ingenious and eloquent, His Majesty gave him the title of Seri 'Amarat. The position of Mangkubumi was especially created for him, and he was positioned right under His Majesty. It was there that he bore the sword of state and it was he who would transmit His Majesty's commands.

In time, Tun Perak came to pay his obeisance. The courtier, Seri 'Amarat, said to Tun Perak, 'All the folks of Kelang complained of their predicament to His Majesty: only the menfolk from the rest of the country and the hinterland have been sent, but the people of Kelang came along with their wives and children; why is this?'

Tun Perak did not reply. Once again Seri 'Amarat repeated his question. Only after three repetitions did Tun Perak reply, 'Hai Seri 'Amarat, you with your one sword that you must keep in good repair, let it not tarnish, and its blade does not rust. As for us who have come to do His Majesty's command, what do you know of it? His Majesty is here in Melaka with his family and all his possessions. Is it wrong to come from afar with our families? If anything should happen to Melaka who should protect them? That is the reason that the people of Kelang were brought here together with their wives and children—so that they are supported, and will fight their enemies whole-heartedly, and not arguing with His Majesty, but rather attend to defeating their enemies.'

Upon hearing Tun Perak's reply, Sultan Muzaffar Shah smiled and said, 'It's true what Tun Perak has spoken.'

Promptly His Majesty fetched a betel bowl and offered it to him. His Majesty continued, 'Tun Perak should not reside in Kelang. It would be better if he lives in Melaka.'

Soon the people of Siam arrived and began to battle with the Melakans. As the war progressed many of the Siamese suffered casualties and death. Melaka was not defeated. Subsequently the soldiers of Siam returned. As they marched, the rattan that they used to bind their tools were collected in the upper reaches of the Muar River. In time the rattan grew roots, which are still there, and the place is now known as Rotan Siam (Siamese Rattan). The new wooden stumps also put out shoots, likewise, still to be seen in Hulu Muar. Moreover, the wooden stumps for the Siamese kitchen that were used to boil their rice also put down roots, they too are there to be seen now.

As soon as the people of Siam returned, the inhabitants of the hinterland and colonies of Melaka in turn returned to their homes. Meanwhile, Tun Perak was instructed to continue to stay on in Melaka.

* * *

There was once an inhabitant of Kelang, who claimed that he was wronged by Tun Perak. So, he came to the audience hall to complain to His Majesty. Presently His Majesty ordered Seri 'Amarat to relay the man's complaint that he had been unfairly treated by Tun Perak. But Tun Perak did not reply.

It was only after it was repeated thrice that Tun Perak responded, 'My Lord, Seri 'Amarat, as for your single sword, you must continue to cleanse it with the acidic *asam* fruit, let the blade not rust; as to our task of administering the country, what business is it of yours? If it is as small as the coconut shell, it is still a *negeri*, a state. Let me get on with my task, for His Majesty knows when I do it well and when I do not. However, if His Majesty wants to put us on trial, let His Majesty dismiss me from my post in Kelang, then judge me. But, if I am not yet dismissed as a servant how shall I be put on trial?

Upon receiving the report of the answer given by Tun Perak, Sultan Muzaffar Shah was indeed pleased.

His Majesty concluded, 'Tun Perak should not be a mere herald.' He bestowed on him the title of Paduka Raja and asked that he take his position in the gallery, with the same eminence as the Seri Nara al-Diraja.

* * *

During these years the Seri Nara al-Diraja was already advanced in his age, but childless, although he had had a child with a maid, whom he declined to acknowledge publicly. The son was called Tun Shahid Madi. When he became an adult, he married and had children and grandchildren of his own.

One day, when Tun Madi was still a young boy, Seri Nara al-Diraja was holding an audience in his gallery and Tun Shahid Madi passed by. Seri Nara al-Diraja called out to him. When he arrived, he sat him in his lap.

Said the Seri Nara al-Diraja to all those present, 'This is my son.'

The people present all answered him, 'We all know that; but as My Lord does not acknowledge him as your son, we are afraid to say so!'

The Seri Nara al-Diraja smiled at their reply.

It was narrated that in time, His Majesty, Mani Purindan, returned to the blessings of the Lord. He had a son, Nina Madi was his name, and it was he who succeeded his father, using the title of Tun Bijaya Maha Menteri.

When Paduka Raja was promoted, the Malays became divided, some siding with the Paduka Raja and some with Seri Nara al-Diraja, but both sides were people of the same land. The Seri Nara al-Diraja did not agree to find a way to end the discord with Paduka Raja.

In the meantime, Sultan Muzaffar Shah had come to know of their dispute,[2] and His Majesty thought that he should attempt to bring them together again. So Sultan Muzaffar Shah ordered that the Seri Nara al-Diraja be summoned; and he came promptly.

Sultan Muzaffar Shah enquired of Nara al-Diraja, 'Would My Lord like to take a wife?'

Seri Nara al-Diraja lifted his palms to his forehead, 'If as a bestowal from Your Majesty, I would.'

Sultan Muzaffar Shah continued, 'Would My Lord, the Seri Nara al-Diraja, like Tun Kumala?'

Seri Nara al-Diraja bowed, 'Your servant begs for your forgiveness.'

His Majesty continued, 'Would Seri Nara al-Diraja like Tun Bulan, the daughter of Orang Kaya Hitam?'

Seri Nara al-Diraja replied, 'I beg your forgiveness, Your Majesty.'

After many of the daughters of nobles were named by Sultan Muzaffar Shah, the Seri Nara al-Diraja, was still not in favour of any of them. Finally, Sultan Muzaffar Shah said, 'Would Seri Nara al-Diraja prefer Tun Kudu?'

Seri Nara al-Diraja responded, 'Yes, Your Majesty.'

Tun Kudu was the sister of Paduka Raja, and the daughter of the Bendahara Seriwa Raja, now a concubine of His Majesty, Sultan Muzaffar Shah. When His Majesty heard the Seri Nara al-Diraja's answer, that very minute he divorced her and sent her to Paduka Raja's.

Said all the Seri Nara al-Diraja's clansmen, 'How will My Lord take to a young wife, for My Lord is already old, and your eyebrows are all white?'

Seri Nara al-Diraja retorted, 'What do you all know of this matter? If that is so, then the potion my father bought from the country of the Kelings is of no use!'

After her *edah,* the period of abstention from marrying again after her divorce, the Seri Nara al-Diraja was bethrothed to Tun Kudu, the

---

[2] *Bermusuhan,* at odds, discord, feud

Seri Nara al-Diraja and Paduka Raja became warm relatives and the best of friends again.

The Seri Nara al-Diraja soon recommended to Sultan Muzaffar Shah, 'My Lord, it would be good to make Paduka Raja the Bendahara, for he is already a son of the Bendahara himself.'

Sultan Muzaffar Shah said, 'So it shall be.'

Paduka Raja was soon appointed the Bendahara.

It was the Bendahara Paduka Raja who was known as a wise minister, for in these times only in the three countries did he have equals; firstly, Maja Pahit, secondly Pasai, thirdly Melaka. In these three countries were three wise men: in Maja Pahit, Aria Gajah Mada; in Pasai, Orang Kaya Raja Kenayan; and in Melaka, the Bendahara Paduka Raja.

In the meantime, Seri Nara al-Diraja became the chief of the treasury. After a passage of some years, Siam invaded Melaka again. Awi Dichu was its general. The news of their intent reached Melaka. Sultan Muzaffar Shah promptly commanded the Bendahara Paduka Raja to trail the Siamese, along with the Seri Bija al-Diraja, and all the warriors who were ordered to accompany him.

The Seri Bija al-Diraja, it was narrated, was a Malay, whose ancestral origins were from the froth of the sacred cow. It was he who was dubbed Datuk Bongkok, My Lord the Hunchback—for when he walked he was bent and so too when he sat. However, when he heard of the attack of the Siamese, his back straightened up along with his considerable courage; then he was bestowed the title of a great knight, sitting above all the other knights.

When all the preparations to battle the Siamese were completed, the Bendahara proceeded to confront the enemy, along with the Seri Bija al-Diraja, and the numerous warriors. The Siamese were now almost in Batu Pahat.

There was a son of the Seri Bija al-Diraja, Tun 'Umar was his name. His ways were those of the very brave, but he was eccentric in temperament. He was the one asked by the Bendahara to spy on the enemy. So Tun 'Umar rowed a boat alone out to sea, which was rolling from side to side. Whenever he met a Siamese boat, he would crash into it, killing one or two or three of the Siamese. Then he returned once again, this time ramming into others, overcoming some of them. Finally, Tun 'Umar returned to shore, leaving the Siamese wondering what had happened to them.

As night fell, Awi Dichu advanced. In the meantime, the Bendahara Paduka Raja ordered that all the trunks of the mangrove trees—the *nyirih*, the *tumu*, the *api-api*—be tied with fire brands. When the Siamese saw that there were innumerable fires along the shore, the warriors concluded, 'There are too many vessels in the Malay fleet, countless. If they were to attack, what would happen to us? We could not defeat even the single boat just now!'

Awi Dichu, the Siamese general concurred, 'It is true what My Lord has said; let's return.'

So, all the Siamese promptly returned. It was related that the wells in Batu Pahat were carved out from the stone in the place.

Upon seeing them leave, the Bendahara Paduka Raja followed them to Singa Pura. After that, he too returned to Melaka to seek an audience with His Majesty. What happened at sea he recounted to all. Sultan Muzaffar Shah was greatly pleased. He bestowed a rare and noble outfit on the Bendahara and the Seri Bija al-Diraja. All the soldiers who accompanied the Bendahara and Paduka Raja were also bestowed with gifts.

* * *

Now the words of the chronicle turn to the Siamese soldiers returning to their country. When they arrived in Shahr Nuwi, Awi Dichu went into the palace to report to Bubunnya. He duly described all that happened in Melaka.

There was a son of Bubunnya, Chau Pandan was his name. He was the one who was eager to invade Melaka. Thus, His Majesty ordered that preparations be made to accompany him south. This occasion inspired a poet to compose a song:

Chau Pandan anak Bubunnya,
Hendak menyerang ke Melaka;
Ada cincin berwasi bunga,
Bunga berisi si air mata.

Chau Pandan, Bubunnya's youngster,
To Melaka he would forcibly enter;
There's a ring, decked with a flower,
The flower now is dripping with many a tear.

Soon, news of Chau Pandan being commanded to invade Melaka reached the palace. It happened that there was a *sidi*, a religious servant of Allah, who resided in Melaka. The gentleman was forever practising with his bow and arrows; wherever he went he would take them along with him. At that moment, Sultan Muzaffar Shah was in audience with all the lords and chiefs, all were gathered to pay His Majesty their homage. The *sidi* was also in the palace. When he heard of the news of the intended attack, he lifted his bow in the direction of Benua Siam. Said the *sidi* while releasing his arrow, 'You are dead, Chau Pandan!'

Chau Pandan was then in Siam. He felt as though an arrow had pierced his chest. He threw up blood and died. Thus, Siam did not attack Melaka. In the meantime, in Melaka the news that Chau Pandan was dead had been heard—it was reported that he felt his chest was struck by an arrow.

When Sultan Muzaffar Shah heard the news he said, 'It was true what the *sidi* said.' His Majesty showered him with gifts.

Sultan Muzaffar Shah enquired of all his ministers, eunuchs, heralds and military chiefs, 'What do My Lords think; should we send an emissary to Siam; haven't we quarrelled enough with the country?'

The Prime Minister bowed, 'It is true what Your Majesty has said; it is better to have more friends than more enemies.'

Sultan Muzaffar Shah promptly appointed Tun Telanai, the son of the Bendahara Paduka Raja to be his envoy to Siam, and Menteri Jana Putera as his deputy. Thus, Tun Telanai made preparations for the

journey. It was he who was given authority over Syoyar in those times.
He was remembered in a poem:

Lalai mana butan dikelati
Kaka(k) Tun Telanai mana pungutan?
Pungutan lagi di Tanjung Jati.

The sister of Tun Telanai,
Where was she collected from,
In Tanjung Jati she was chosen.

His was given a fleet of twenty three-masted ships.

As the preparations were completed, Sultan Muzaffar Shah said
to the Bendahara Paduka Raja and all the ministers, 'My Lords shall
accompany us to Siam. Our wish is that we shall not make obeisance
nor offer greetings, and neither should the letter show affection.'

Acting upon His Majesty's instruction, the Bendahara Paduka Raja
ordered the officials of state, 'My Lords shall compose a letter as His
Majesty has ordered.'

Not even one official volunteered to compose such a letter. The
Bendahara asked of everyone in the hall, even the herald who carried
the betel container and the water goblet.[3] Not even one of them knew
how to compose such a letter. So, it fell on the Bendahara to write such
an epistle. This was what it said:

Should we engage in war, it is feared that lives may be lost, but in
fighting we are in awe of His Majesty, Bubunnya; it was from a hope
of forgiveness and bestowals that we have commanded Tun Telanai
and Menteri Jana Putera.

After these words were written, there followed other words; His Majesty
was in agreement as to how it sounded. The letter was then borne in a
procession on an elephant, which was secured by the gallery.

---

[3]   *kemendelam*, a type of water goblet.

It was carried by a son of a warrior—the one who sat at the head of the elephant was a herald, and the minister in charge. Thus, the letter was taken in a procession, accompanied by white umbrellas, two drums, a flute, a kettledrum and a *nagara* drum.

Soon Tun Telanai and Menteri Jana Putera raised their hands in obeisance, and both of them were bestowed with a change of costumes each. When this was concluded Tun Telanai and Menteri Jana Putera departed.

On their arrival in Siam, the news of their presence was reported to His Majesty, Bubunnya, 'A mission from Melaka has arrived.'

Bubunnya promptly commanded that the letter be officially received and carried in a procession. When they arrived in the great hall, Bubunnya requested that the letter be read by his minister.

After His Majesty Bubunnya heard the contents of the letter he enquired, 'Who wrote this letter?'

Tun Telanai presently responded, 'The Vizier of His Majesty, the King of Melaka, My Lord.'

Then Bubunnya enquired of Tun Telanai, 'What is the name of the Raja of Melaka?'

Tun Telanai bowed and answered, 'Sultan Muzaffar Shah.'

Bubunnya enquired further, 'What does Muzaffar Shah mean?'

Tun Telanai remained silent.

Menteri Jana Putera answered, 'The meaning of Muzaffar Shah is a Raja aided by Allah against his enemies.'

The Raja of Siam asked, 'Why didn't Melaka fall after being invaded by the Siamese?'

Then Tun Telanai instructed that an old man from Shoyar, who was suffering from elephantiasis, to perform with the spears before the Raja of Siam. The man threw his spear into the air and received it on his back. The spear fell and bounced; he was not in the least hurt.

Tun Telanai bowed and said, 'This, My Lord, is the reason why Melaka did not fall after being attacked by Siam, for the people of Melaka are all invincible.'

In his heart the Raja of Siam reasoned, 'It is true; even the evil ones are invincible, how much stronger then are the good people?'

Before long, His Majesty, Bubunnya, invaded a state neighbouring Siam. Tun Telanai and Menteri Jana Putera and all their men were taken along. In the meantime, the Raja of Siam gave them a tough location, one that faced the setting sun. Not long after that, Tun Telanai conferred with his minister, Jana Putera.

Tun Telanai began, 'How can we choose our position—we are asked to stay in a place with malicious spirits, and moreover there are only a few of us?'

Menteri Jana Putera proposed, 'Let's seek His Majesty's audience.'

Thus, Tun Telanai and Menteri Jana Putera departed to proceed to the palace.

Menteri Jana Putera bowed, 'My Lord, it is the customs of Muslims that if we are to say our prayers, then we face the setting sun; if we are going to war, we must not face the same direction. If it pleases My Lord, give us another location.'

His Majesty Bubunnya said, 'If you cannot face the setting sun, find another place that is suitable.'

So Phra Chau gave them another place, this time facing the rising sun.

The place was less perilous and there they had to confront fewer enemies. Eventually, with the help of Allah Ta'ala the country was defeated. However, it was the Melakans who first trapped the enemy. When it was defeated, His Majesty bestowed gifts on Tun Telanai, Menteri Jana Putera and all their men.

Tun Telanai was presented with a princess by His Majesty, Utang Minang was her name; he subsequently took her as his wife.

Soon Tun Telanai sought leave of the Phra Chau. His Majesty sent a letter along with presents, these were taken in a procession to their vessel. Soon they set sail for Melaka.

After several days at sea, they arrived in Melaka, and the letter was ordered to be received with due custom. When it reached the audience hall, the elephant was commanded to kneel, the letter was presented by the herald and the court preacher read out its contents.

After Sultan Muzaffar Shah heard the full intent of the letter, he was greatly pleased. His Majesty then bestowed gifts on Tun Telanai, Menteri Jana Putera and all those who accompanied them in the mission to Siam.

When the season had turned, the Siamese mission sought leave to return. His Majesty duly presented each of them with a change of costume and replied the letter of His Majesty, the Raja of Siam. Soon they were on their way home.

It was narrated by the author of this chronicle, Tun Telanai and Utang Minang bore boys and girls, one was Tun 'Ali Haru, it was he who was promoted to a Laksamana.

After a reign of forty years on the throne, the cycle of time turned and Sultan Muzaffar was deceased.

His son, Sultan 'Abdul, succeeded him on the throne; his official title was Sultan Mansur Shah. He was then just a young man of seventeen and had married the kin of the Seri Nara Diraja. They had no offspring of their own. However, with his palace maid he bore a daughter, her name was Princess Bakal. During his reign he was exceptionally just and generous.

His Majesty was extremely handsome; in those times there was none his compare.

Allah knows the truth; to Him shall we return.

IX

The words of the narrative now turn to the Betara of Maja Pahit, who was deceased. He had no sons to succeed him. However, he had a daughter, Raden Galuh Awi Kesuma. It was she who was crowned by the Patih Aria Gajah Mada.

There was once a palm tapper, who went fishing with his wife to the sea. As soon as they had arrived by the beach, they found a boy washed up on a plank. They picked him up and took him to their boat. He was apparently unconscious as he had been long at sea and had not eaten or had anything to drink for many days. But as his time had not come, he survived the ordeal. As was said 'Ali radiallahu 'anhu (may God be pleased with him), one does not die except at the appointed time.

The tapper dripped water from the rice broth into the boy's mouth. Soon he opened his eyes to find himself on a boat. The tapper then took him home, and took care of him to the best of his abilities.

After a lapse of a few days the boy mended.

So, the toddy tapper asked the boy, 'Who are you, and why are you afloat on a piece of wood?'

The boy replied, 'I am the son of the King of Tanjung Pura, the descendant of Sang Maniaka, who first descended on the Seguntang Mahameru Hill. My name is Raden Perlangu. We are two siblings, the other also a son. One day, my father, the Raja of Tanjung Pura, went on a picnic on Permain Island. When they were in the middle of the sea, a great storm descended, and the waves were churned into huge surfs. My father's vessel could not be bailed out by his many sailors and subjects and the boat was a total wreck. My father and mother did not manage to climb on, but the rest of them swam to reach another vessel. I myself held on to a plank and was carried by the currents here. For seven long nights I was at sea, without any food or drink. It was fortunate that I met you, my uncle, who has taken such care of me. If you feel any pity for me, please send me back to my father and mother in Tanjung Pura, so that you may be rewarded with great wealth.'

The tapper agreed, 'It is true what you have said, but where shall I find the means to send you back to Tanjung Pura? Stay with us and be our adopted son, for we have no child of our own. Our hearts are greatly charmed by your most handsome countenance.'

Raden Perlangu replied, 'Very well, I shall not go against your wishes, my father.'

The tapper then named the son of the Raja of Tanjung Pura, Ki Mas Jiwa. Both the husband and wife were full of affection for him, and said to him endlessly, 'In future it is you who will be the King of Maja Pahit, betrothed to Princess Naya Kesuma. But should you become the Betara of Maja Pahit, let me be the Patih Aria Gajah Mada.'

Ki Mas Jiwa replied, 'Very well, should we become the Betara of Maja Pahit, we shall appoint my father as the Patih Aria Gajah Mada.'

As time passed, Princess Naya Kesuma, the daughter of the Betara of Maja Pahit was crowned the monarch, but Patih Aria Gajah Mada ruled in her stead.

It was heard that some people spoke in tones of disapproval of the Patih Aria Gajah Mada, that he himself wished to marry the princess.

One day, the Patih Aria Gajah Mada went rowing with his many servants, wearing an old sarong and thus he was not recognized by the villagers.

The boys said, 'If I were in a situation like the Patih Aria Gajah Mada's, I would marry the princess, so that I may become the King. That should be for the best!'

Another suggested, 'It was indeed the Patih Aria Gajah Mada's intention to marry her, for he is a great minister, the likes of a King in this country, who no one may go against.'

Hearing the words of the boys, the Patih Aria Gajah Mada thought, 'If this were so, then all my service and sacrifice are of no consequence.'

On the morrow, the Patih Aria Gajah Mada did obeisance before Princess Naya Kesuma.

He began, 'Your Majesty, in my opinion, Your Majesty has come of age. It is not appropriate for a princess to remain unmarried.'

Princess Naya Kesuma replied, 'If my dear uncle wishes that I be married, you should gather all the inhabitants of the *negeri*. Then, let me make my choice from amongst all of them, and the one chosen shall be my husband.'

The Patih Aria Gajah Mada bowed, 'Very well, Your Majesty, I shall assemble all of them; even though he be a cat or a dog, if it is Your Majesty's choice, he shall be my master.'

Presently the Patih Aria Gajah Mada ordered that the gong be beaten to summon all the subjects of the land to gather in Majapahit— for the princess wished to select a husband.

When the preparations were complete, all the rajas, princess, eunuchs, heralds, military chiefs and all of Her Majesty's subjects— the great and the humble, the bent and the lame—all assembled in Maja Pahit. A small number of them were invited to the occasion; the rest came on their own, after hearing that Princess Naya Kesuma was choosing a husband, for they hoped that they would find a preference in her heart.

When all of them had gathered, Princess Naya Kesuma ascended the viewing tower, and then looked downwards. Those who had gathered were subsequently ordered by the Patih Aria Gajah Mada to parade one by one before Her Majesty. However, when everyone had passed before her, not one of them struck her fancy.

Then, there appeared before her the adopted son of the palm-tapper. When she laid her eyes on him, Princess Naya Kesuma said to the Patih Aria Gajah Mada, 'The son of the palm-tapper is to our liking.'

The Patih Gajah Mada bowed, 'Very well, Your Majesty. Anyone is fine, as long as Your Majesty takes a husband.'

Accordingly the Patih Aria Gajah Mada ordered that the son of the tapper be summoned, and presently taken to his residence. He henceforth took special care of him.

Soon the Patih Aria Gajah Mada commenced the pre-marriage rituals by ordering celebrations of seven days and seven nights long. When the seven days of festivities were complete, the son of the palm-tapper was carried in a procession around the country, and he was duly wedded to Princess Naya Kesuma.

After the ceremonies were over, they became a very affectionate couple. Presently, the son of the tapper was crowned the Betara of Maja Pahit, with the title of Sang Aji Ningrat.

In time, the tapper visited his son in the audience hall.

Said he, 'Where is Your Majesty's promise to make me a Vizier, like the Patih Aria Gajah Mada?'

His Majesty, the Betara of Maja Pahit, replied, 'Do be patient, my father, I am still attending to the matter.'

Hearing his promise, the tapper then returned home.

The Betara of Maja Pahit thought, 'He has done me no wrong, this Patih Aria Gajah Mada. He is but the very support of this *negeri* of Maja Pahit. Without him the country would be ruined. But how shall I repay my father's deeds and thus also fulfil my promise?'

Thus thinking, His Majesty was overcome with anxiety, he did not leave the palace for two or three consecutive days.

When the Patih Aria Gajah Mada noticed His Majesty's demeanour, he entered the audience hall and did obeisance, 'My Lord, what is the reason for Your Majesty staying indoors for such a long while and not holding court?'

The Betara of Maja Pahit replied, 'We have not been well, our body hurts.'

The Patih Aria Gajah Mada bowed, 'As I see it, there is some sorrow that Your Majesty is suffering from. Do tell me, Your Majesty, perhaps I may be of some help in solving the matter.'

The Betara of Maja Pahit replied to the Patih Aria Gajah Mada, 'In truth, my uncle, I am not the son of the tapper. I am the son of the Raja of Tajung Pura, the descendant of the Raja of Bukit Seguntang Mahameru.'

So His Majesty unfolded the story of his father on a pleasure trip and how his vessel was wrecked by a storm. And how he was found by the tapper, who cared for him with kindness. He related all to the Patih Aria Gajah Mada.

'Now my adopted father is seeking a fulfilment of my promise to make him your replacement. This is what is giving me a cause for anxiety.

The Patih Aria Gajah Mada was exceedingly pleased to hear that the Betara of Maja Pahit was the son of the Raja of Tanjung Pura.

He bowed, 'My Lord, do make the tapper my replacement. Let me abdicate, for I am no longer young; age has caught up with me.'

Replied the Betara of Maja Pahit, 'We will never release my uncle, for in my opinion, nothing will be accomplished by doing so.'

The Patih Aria Gajah Mada said, 'In that case, when he comes to seek recompense, Your Majesty should reply him so, "In truth, my father, though the rank of the Patih Aria Gajah Mada is great, great too is its troubles and problems, that you might not be able to shoulder. But there is a greater honour that I can bestow upon you—I give you power over all the tappers in the land. You shall be their chief." He would undoubtedly be pleased with the proposition.'

The Betara of Maja Pahit complimented the Patih Aria Gajah Mada, 'Your proposition is the best possible exit out of this dilemma.'

Subsequently, the Patih Aria Gajah Mada took leave of His Majesty.

On the morrow, the tapper came to make his obeisance. He came to seek His Majesty's promise. The Betara of Maja Pahit repeated the words of the Patih Aria Gajah Mada, and the tapper was delighted to hear them.

In due time, Maja Pahit grew into a great kingdom. All the regions of Java came under its authority.

In the meantime, it came to the ears of the Raja of Tanjung Pura that the Betara of Maja Pahit was his own son. It was decided by the people of Tanjung Pura to send a mission to the Betara of Maja Pahit. They soon set sail. After they had met His Majesty, they promptly sailed home to report to the Raja of Tanjung Pura. It was true that the Betara of Maja Pahit was His Majesty's son. The Raja of Tanjung Pura was extremely delighted to hear this news. The news spread fast across the land of the Javanese.

In the intervening time, the Betara begot a daughter with Princess Naya Kesuma. She was named Raden Galuh Cendera Kirana and was known throughout the land as an extremely beautiful princess. It was even heard of in Melaka.

Sultan Mansur Shah had entertained a desire for Raden Galuh Cendera Kirana. Thus, His Majesty arranged a voyage to Maja Pahit, and duly gave orders to the Bendahara Paduka Raja that the ships be fitted.

Presently, the Bendahara and Paduka Raja ordered that the boatmen prepare the vessels and make the necessary repairs. There were five hundred of the bigger vessels being fitted out, not counting the smaller boats which were innumerable. In these times, the Singa Pura fleet itself was composed of forty three-masted cruisers. However, the Bendahara, the Seri Nara al-Diraja, the Seri Bija al-Diraja, and the chiefs of the warriors remained in Melaka, to attend to the welfare of the *negeri*.

His Majesty then chose forty young men from amongst the sons of the nobles of renown, and also another forty from amongst the high officials of aristocratic descent. Tun Bijaya Sura was appointed as their chief. (Tun Bijaya Sura was the father of Tun Zainal Naina, the Seri Bijaya Diraja, whose name was Tun Sebab).

In the meantime, at sea, Hang Tuah, Hang Jebat, Hang Lekir, Hang Kasturi, Hang Lekiu, Hang Khalambak, Hang 'Ali and Hang Iskandar—they were at the forefront, faster than anyone else in the mission, and no one could trail them.

It was narrated that Hang Tuah was shrewd and courageous in his every single action and deed. In his games he was faster than anyone else, and if he was among his young friends, while responding or being humorous he would roll up his sleeves, declaring, 'Only the Laksamana is my worthy adversary.'

Thus, among his young friends he was dubbed 'the Laksamana' and soon it was by this name that he came to be known.

Sultan Mansur Shah sent a mission to Inderagiri to invite the Maharaja of Merlung, and the Rajas of Palembang, Jambi, Tungkal[1] and Lingga, to accompany him to Maja Pahit.

All the Rajas were glad to escort His Majesty. When all were gathered, Sultan Mansur Shah weighed anchor and departed for Maja Pahit escorted by the Rajas of Palembang, Inderagiri, Jambi, Tungkal and Lingga. Young warriors came in accompaniment. However, the great lords remained to oversee the welfare of Melaka.

In due time, they arrived in Java. The news of their arrival came to the ears of His Majesty, the Betara of Maja Pahit. He therefore promptly ordered that they be welcomed by the Prime Minister, who was accompanied by all the great lords of the land.

It came to pass that at that same moment the Raja of Daha and the Raja of Tanjung Pura, the younger brother to the Betara of Maja Pahit, were having an audience with His Majesty.

When the Raja of Melaka arrived, he was extremely honoured by the Raja of Maja Pahit, who presented him with suits of costumes that were embroidered with precious jewels. After that His Majesty, the Raja of Melaka, was given the highest place of honour and presented with the renowned '*Ganja Larung keris*',[2] and forty other blades to accompany it, all of them had their sheaths broken.

The *kerises* were firstly presented by His Majesty to the Raja of Daha, and so too to the forty accompanying courtiers, who duly

---

[1] Tungkal, located in Jambi, Sumatra.

[2] *Keris Ganja Larung*: A special hollowed keris, Winstedt and Brown transliterated it as 'Ganja kerawang'.

broke their sheaths. The forty blades were then re-sheathed by the
Raja of Daha.

After that, the Raja of Maja Pahit ordered forty rogues to challenge
them, all of whom they successfully overcame.

Then, His Majesty bestowed presents on the Raja of Tanjung Pura,
and requested that he re-sheathed it, which he easily accomplished.
Then the forty rogues were ordered to repeat the same task. This they
did. When it came to the Raja of Melaka's turn, His Majesty instructed
that the task be handled by Tun Bijaya Sura. Promptly Tun Bijaya
Sura ordered that the *kerises* be taken to the craftsmen, to sheathe all
the forty *kerises*. They waited till the task was completed, which was
finished within the day. However, none of the rogues were able to.

The Betara of Maja Pahit remarked, 'How very clever of the Raja
of Melaka, as compared to all the other rajas.'

* * *

The audience hall of the Betara was built high, a flight of three steps led
to it. Beside it, His Majesty tethered a hound[3] with golden chains, so it
sat in front of the Raja of Melaka.

When he observed the situation, Tun Bijaya Sura employed the
art of the warrior—his shield was decorated with bells. He danced and
brandished his *keris* before His Majesty, who ordered him to climb
on to the gallery. Consequently, Tun Bijaya climbed and danced the
various steps and moves of the warrior. Many were his steps and moves;
at times he pounded on his shield. Twice or thrice he pounded it in
front of the hound. The animal broke its chains and escaped into the
forest. After that incident, no longer were dogs secured in the gallery.

The story describes that in the gallery there was a forbidden
chamber, reserved only for royalty, and whoever else entered it would
be struck down by the Javanese guards; thus no one dared to enter it.

---

[3]   *Anjing*, hound, dog used for hunting.

Said Hang Jebat and Hang Kasturi, 'Let's try to enter the forbidden apartment.'

Hang Kasturi replied, 'Yes, let's climb in.'

One day, when His Majesty was holding court for all the Rajas and the chiefs who were assembled there, Hang Jebat and Hang Kasturi stepped into the forbidden apartment. When the Javanese noticed them, they approached and speared the two Malay warriors. With the spears also came a hail of javelins. Quickly Hang Jebat and Hang Kasturi drew their *kerises* and slashed at all the Javanese spears, causing them to fall to pieces; not even one reached them. A load of the broken spearheads was carried away. There was commotion and excitement in the palace.

The Betara of Maja Pahit enquired, 'Why is there such a clamour[4] in the palace?'

Thus, it was described for His Majesty that Hang Jebat and Hang Kasturi had transgressed into the gallery and they have been reprimanded by the guards. The Betara of Maja Pahit said, 'Let them be, don't stop them.'

When they heard his command, they immediately stopped their challenge. Thus, Hang Jebat and Hang Kasturi continued to sit in the gallery each and every day. When the Betara of Maja Pahit was holding court, Hang Jebat and Hang Kasturi would continue to sit in the forbidden apartment.

As for Hang Tuah, wherever he went he would cause much excitement, for the Javanese were in awe of his bearing and style. If he was in the gallery, there was uproar in the gallery, and if he went to the market there was much delight among the people. If he went to the villages there was uproar there too. All the Javanese were full of wonder at the ways of Hang Tuah. They were all surprised to see his style. When Hang Tuah walked past, all the women in the embrace of their husbands became excited and released themselves to attempt to leave their houses to take a look at him.

---

4   *Riuh-rendah*, clamour.

Thus, the Javanese composed a poem:

Onya tanggapana penglipur: saben dina katon parandene onang-uga;
Which means, if it pleases you to receive these betel preparations, to satisfy a day's desire, yet to suffer longing.

Iwer Sang dara kabeh dene Laksamana lumaku-lumaku, penjurit Ratu Melayu,
Meaning, all the wives and all the girls are all excited watching the Laksamana, the knight of Melaka, passing by.

Ayu-ayu anake wong pande wesi: para tan ayua, saben dina dengurinda!
Which means, the young ironsmiths, whenever something was amiss, they would grind it down.

Kaget wong {ing} peken, dene Laksamana tumandang, Laksamana tumandang penjurit ratu ing seberang.
That is, the women in the embrace of their husbands are thrilled to see the Laksamana coming, the Laksamana and warrior from beyond the sea.

Tututana! yen ketemu, patenana karo, ketelu jaruman, mara!
Meaning, follow them! When you find them kill them both, and all who accompany them.

Geger wong pasar dene Laksamana teka, Laksamana penjurit Ratu Malaka.
Which means, the customers in the market were all in an uproar, seeing the Laksamana, the knight of the Raja of Melaka.

Wis laliya kung lagi kungku maning, sumbalinga lipur kung, ati saben gelak kung.
Meaning, though he is forgotten, yet there is much longing, though I try to restrain my memory, my heart harks back to him.

Geger wong paseban dene Laksamana liwat, Laksamana liwat penjurit Ratu Melaka.
That is, there was a noisy excitement in the royal audience hall, when the Laksamana, the warrior of the Raja of Melaka, appeared.

Den urai rambut, den tangwasi: rambute milu tan diremen.
Meaning, let her hair loose, weeping over it.

Those were the exploits of the Laksamana in the land of Maja Pahit; he was an object of desire of the women and the young girls. A poem was composed to remember him by:

Titik embun di daun dasun,
Anak curan di daun birah;
Sedina amboi katon,
Kaya edan rasa manira.

Dew drops on the dasun grove,
Splashing on the birah leaves;
Soon I'll be madly in love,
For if you bathe, you'll certainly get wet.

Busuk[5] enak dene,
Dipangan kelawan bawang;
Besok wasin,
Sirna nanti di laweng.

Disintegrating to become a sea of trails

---

[5] According to Dr Sudibyo, some of the words seem to have been erroneously copied and therefore indecipherable, but the general meaning is: disintegrating to become a sea of trials. Says he: *saya duga baris ke 1 dan ke 3 berawal dengan kata bosok, pada baris ke-3, bacaan dugaan saya adalah 'bosok asin, sirna nganti laweng/h''. Laweng tidak ada dalam kamus Jawa baru dan Jawa kuno. Laweh (jk) = lauk. Terjemahan: Busuk asin musna/ hilang sampai menjadi lauk. Busuk enak dene, Dipangan kelawan bawang; Besok wasin, Sirna nanti di laweng.*

During these times, there was no one that was Laksamana's compare, except Sangkaningrat, the chief of the Daha warriors, who would be able to challenge him. This was etched by the Javanese into their song:

(*Geger*) *wong ing panggungan, dene Sangkaningrat teka, penjurit Ratu ing Daha.*

Meaning, there was uproar among those in the theatre, seeing Sangkaningrat come, Sangkaningrat, the chief of the Daha warriors.

These were the ways of the Melakans who came to Maja Pahit, each with his own style and experience.

Seeing that the Sultan Mansur Shah was such a wise and shrewd King and furthermore his servants were superior in their conduct than those of all the other Kings, the Betara of Maja Pahit concluded, 'Let us take Sultan Mansur Shah as our son-in-law, as husband to our daughter, Raden Galuh Cendera Kirana.'

Presently, the Betara of Maja Pahit ordered that the festivities for forty nights should begin. All kinds of musical instruments—*gong, gendang,*[6] *serunai, nafiri, nagara, gendir, sambian, bheri, sanka, merdangga, prawan, sakati, bonang, ganrang, selukat, celempung, gangsa, suling, gambang, bangbang, ketur, kenong, bende, gong, rebab, kecapi, muri, bangsi, dandi, (salu)udingan, medali,* and *musti kumala,* were sounded, making thunderous music—the noise was unimaginable. There was much play and entertainment. Many were those who partook in them—some clapping their hands, some imitating the call of the peacock, some dancing, some beating the *serama*[7] drums, some putting on the *wayang,* some fighting with the *pupuh,*[8] some putting on the mask play *merakat,*[9] some singing the *kidung* or the *kakawin* verses,

---

[6]   *Gendang,* drums.
[7]   *Bersyerama, bergendang serama* (Sanskrit: syrama), to play the 'gendang serama'.
[8]   *Pupuh,* duelling, fighting.
[9]   *Merekat,* a form of the Javanese shadow play.

some reciting the poems known as *melempang memanjang*,[10] each to his own talent. The audience thoroughly enjoyed themselves, though the crowd was unimaginably large.

* * *

The Betara of Maja Pahit addressed the Raja of Melaka. These were his words, 'As for all the Javanese, they had played to the best of their musical abilities. But the Melakans are as yet to perform.'

Thus, Sultan Mansur Shah repeated the words of the Betara to Tun Bijaya Sura, commanding the Melakans to entertain with dances.

Tun Bijaya Sura replied, 'My Lord, what are our Malay dances? Except the *sapu-sapu ringin*?'[11]

In turn, Sultan Mansur Shah relayed the words of Tun Bijaya Sura to His Majesty.

The Betara of Maja Pahit enquired, 'How does one play the *sapu-sapu ringin*? Order Tun Bijaya Sura to play it; Raden Galuh wishes to see it.'

Presently, Tun Bijaya Sura began by choosing fourteen or fifteen players from among the sons of the aristocrats. He then ordered them to sit with their legs stretched before them, in front of the Betara of Maja Pahit, with their sarongs raised to their knees.

They thus played and danced the *sapu-sapu ringin*. When the Javanese realized that they were stretching their legs before His Majesty, they forbade them from continuing their dance.

Tun Bijaya Sura protested, 'But we were ordered to play by The Betara, so we danced as was instructed. Without His Majesty's command, it would be unthinkable for us to perform it. If My Lord forbids us, we will stop now!'

The Betara interceded, 'Let them play, do not stop them.'

---

[10] *Melempang memanjang*, singing of romances.

[11] *Sapu-sapu ringin*, the name of a children's game. So-called from the first line of a nonsense rhyme sung while playing it.

Thus, Tun Bijaya Sura continued to dance. When their performance was ended, he and his dancers were bestowed with suits of costumes.

The Betara said, 'How clever the Melakans are, more than those from other countries; even at their games they were beaten by the Melakans.'

In the intervening time, the Betara of Maja Pahit requested that the strongest among the warriors be summoned.

The Betara ordered him, 'Steal for us the *keris* of Tun Bijaya Sura, for we see him as the shrewdest.'

The warrior reasoned, 'It is difficult for your servant to steal the *keris* as the Malays wear their weapons in front. Were they at the back, it would indeed be but a simple assignment for me.'

The Betara said, 'Well, so it will be; we will ask him to wear it on his back.'

On the morrow, the Betara was holding court. All the Rajas were present to honour him. Sultan Mansur Shah was also in attendance.

The Betara addressed Tun Bijaya Sura, 'Does My Lord, Tun Bijaya Sura, know how to dress in the Javanese fashion?'

Tun Bijaya Sura replied, 'With your blessings, My Lord, if your servant does not, he is ready to be tutored, please teach me.'

Therefore, His Majesty, the Betara, ordered that a change of costume be readied for Tun Bijaya Sura, who wore it in the Javanese fashion, with the *keris* inserted at the back.

His Majesty then visited those in the cock-fighting ring. Many were those in the audience, and their applause was like thunder in the sky. In the tumult of the match, the Javanese warrior was able to steal Tun Bijaya Sura's *keris*. Thus, when Tun Bijaya Sura turned to look behind him, it was no longer there.

Tun Bijaya Sura exclaimed, 'My *keris* has been taken by the Javanese!' Tun Bijaya Sura then approached His Majesty's page who was carrying his betel. He stole the Betara's *keris*, and promptly wore it on his back.

When the cock fight ended, the Betara sat in the audience hall, while those in the audience sat in their own particular seats.

The Betara took Tun Bijaya Sura's *keris* and placed it under his thigh. Soon Tun Bijaya Sura was ordered to come forward.

The Betara said, 'Do come forward, Tun Bijaya Sura.'

Thus, Tun Bijaya Sura approached the throne and sat under His Majesty. The Betara then retrieved Tun Bijaya Sura's *keris* from under his thigh and showed it to him.

His Majesty began, 'We have just acquired a most well-crafted weapon. Does My Lord Tun Bijaya Sura own such a blade?'

As soon as Tun Bijaya Sura set eyes on the weapon, he immediately recognized it as his own. However, in the meantime, Tun Bijaya Sura promptly unsheathed the *keris* at his back.

He then bowed in obeisance, 'Is this better than my *keris*, Your Majesty?'

As soon as His Majesty laid eyes on it, he immediately recognized the blade that Tun Bijaya Sura was holding, for it was the custom of the reigning King to have a *keris* with all its ornaments. His Majesty's page was also present.

Said the Betara, 'How very clever of Bijaya Sura, we could not deceive him, much as we tried.'

Soon, Tun Bijaya Sura's *keris* was returned to him, and His Majesty's was given to Tun Bijaya Sura as a gift.

Finally, the forty days and forty nights of entertainment came to an end.

On a most auspicious day, Sultan Mansur Shah was wedded to Raden Galuh. After the vows of marriage were spoken, they entered the bridal chamber. There Sultan Mansur Shah and Raden Galuh Cendera Kirana were exceptionally loving towards each other.

On his part, the Betara loved Sultan Mansur very much, and he asked him to sit by his side on the throne. Whenever His Majesty was holding court it was always with Sultan Mansur Shah present, and when they were dining it was also with him.

After a few weeks in Maja Pahit, Sultan Mansur Shah expressed his wish to return to Melaka. Thus he came before the Betara to request leave of His Majesty and also to take Raden Galuh Cendera

Kirana to Melaka. To this request, the Betara of Maja Pahit gave his full consent.

* * *

Soon the ships were fitted and equipped and when they were ready, Sultan Mansur Shah asked Tun Bijaya Sura to request that the *negeri* of Inderagiri be bestowed on His Majesty, and soon Tun Bijaya Sura was present in the audience hall to relay the words of his Sultan.

Tun Bijaya Sura bowed low in obeisance, 'Your Majesty, your son has requested for Inderagiri. Should Your Majesty grant his request he shall collect it, and if not, he shall collect it all the same.'

The Betara turned to his chiefs, 'What do My Lords think—my son has requested for Inderagiri?'

They all replied, 'It is right that Your Majesty bestow it on him so that he may be part of us from now on.'

The Betara replied, 'It is agreed then; we bestow Inderagiri on our son, for in our heart, not only would we give Inderagiri, and the provinces and counties of the whole of the Java, in fact, all of them are the possessions of none other than my son, the Raja of Melaka.'

Soon Tun Bijaya Sura sought permission to depart. When he described all that transpired in the audience hall, Sultan Mansur Shah was extremely pleased.

Then Hang Tuah was subsequently ordered to request the island of Siantan from the Betara. Thus, the Laksamana and Hang Tuah departed to seek an audience with His Majesty to request for Siantan.

When they had arrived at the palace, they bowed in obeisance, 'My Lord, we would like to request Siantan, should Your Majesty approve we shall formally request for it, however, should Your Majesty do not, we will again request for it in all humility.'

The Betara replied, 'Very well, not only would we bestow Siantan, should the Laksamana request even for Palembang, we shall bestow it on My Lord.'

That is the reason why the Laksamana and all his descendants have an authority over Siantan even to this day.

After that Sultan Mansur Shah departed for the return journey to Melaka.

* * *

In due time, they arrived in Melaka. When they had arrived at Ulu Sepantai, the Bendahara journeyed to greet His Majesty, along with the Chief of the Treasury and all the officers of state and nobles— all of them welcoming His Majesty home. They were accompanied by musicians playing the drums, flutes, royal *nafiri* trumpets and the instruments of state.

At sea, there were countless boats. As soon as they came before His Majesty, the officers bowed low and touched Sultan Mansur's feet.

After arriving in the city, they made their way to the palace, together with Raden Galuh Cendera Kirana.

In the meantime, the Maharaja of Merlung Inderagiri was betrothed to His Majesty's oldest daughter, Princess Bakal. In due course, they bore Raja Nara Singa, who was known by his title, Sultan 'Abdul Jalil Shah. In the meanwhile, Sultan Mansur Shah and his consort, Raden Galuh Cendera Kirana, begot a prince, and he was named the Lord of Kelang.

* * *

One day it chanced that His Majesty's stallion,[12] his favourite mount, fell into the cesspool. So many were those who gathered to retrieve it, however, not one amongst them would pledge or volunteer to climb down in order to secure a rope around the horse. Seeing the situation thus, Hang Tuah himself dived in and tied the rope around the animal. It was then that it was slowly drawn up to the surface.

---

[12] *Kuda jantan*, stallion.

When it was safely on land, Hang Tuah took a bath, its water was scented with fragrances.

Some time later, when Sultan Mansur Shah noted that the horse had been retrieved, he was extremely pleased. He was full of praise for Hang Tuah and duly bestowed a new suit of costume on him as was the custom of the palace.

There was once an occasion when a Javanese was laid low with a fever. All the young men laughed at him. The Javanese felt greatly embarrassed, and soon ran amok with a Sundanese machete.[13] Many were killed, no one was able to overcome him. There was great confusion with people running hither and thither.

Soon Hang Tuah arrived at the scene. Upon seeing him, the Javanese pursued and stabbed him. The latter pretended to withdraw and dropped his *keris* on purpose. Seeing this, the Javanese also cast away his machete, but took Hang Tuah's weapon—in his heart guessing that if Hang Tuah were to cast his *keris* aside, and Hang Tuah was a man of great knowledge about *kerises*, then it was indeed a superior blade. However, as soon as Hang Tuah noticed that the machete has been discarded by the Javanese, he quickly picked it up and attacked him. The Javanese stabbed at him with his blade, while Hang Tuah quickly leapt up, foiling his thrust. Hang Tuah instantly lunged at the Javanese with his Sundanese machete, cutting deep into his chest, just below his nipple; the Javanese man died shortly after.

News was brought to His Majesty that the Javanese had died and that it was Hang Tuah who had killed him. Hang Tuah was presently summoned by His Majesty and was bestowed with presents and gifts.

In time, there came upon Hang Tuah *hujjat 'l-baligh*, signs of adulthood. He desired a maid in the Sultan's palace and the news of it came to His Majesty's ears. So, His Majesty ordered that the Seri Nara al-Diraja, slay him.

However, in his heart Seri Nara al-Diraja reasoned, 'Hang Tuah's sins do not compel me to slay him.'

---

[13] *Golok*, machete, a broad heavy knife, slashing and when necessary a weapon.

He therefore asked that Hang Tuah be hidden in his orchard; it was there that he was put in chains. However, news was brought to His Majesty that he had been executed. Sultan Mansur Shah said not a word. A year had lapsed. Rumours spread that Hang Kasturi desired a royal maid in the palace, a favourite of His Majesty. Sultan Mansur Shah and the Queen left the sumptuous palace and moved to another.

Hang Kasturi was then surrounded. One day, Sultan Mansur Shah held court at a small gallery; the Bendahara and Chief of the Treasury and all the senior officers of state were in attendance. Those surrounding Hang Kasturi had gathered in circles, but not one among them was able to break through to confront him. On his part, Hang Kasturi locked all the doors of the palace, only one was left open before him. He had strewn the floor with trays, platters, salvers and trenchers, and it was on these trays and platters that he moved hither and thither. He then slew his mistress, slitting her from her face down to her waist, and stripped her naked.

Sultan Mansur Shah presently commanded that Hang Kasturi be confronted. Unfortunately, not one volunteered to do so.

In these times, Hang Kasturi was a renowned warrior. In such a desperate situation, the Sultan Mansur Shah remembered Hang Tuah.

His Majesty said, 'It's a shame that Tuah is no longer with us. If he were, then he would be able to wipe this shame from our face.'

Seri Nara al-Diraja heard His Majesty but said not a word. However, hearing His Majesty recalling Hang Tuah, twice or thrice, Seri Nara al-Diraja came forward and bowed, 'My Lord, in my observation Your Majesty greatly misses Hang Tuah. If he were alive, would Your Majesty forgive him?'

Sultan Mansur Shah enquired urgently, 'Does My Lord, Seri Nara al-Diraja, hide him away?'

Seri Nara al-Diraja said, 'Would I be so mad as to keep him, Your Majesty? I got rid of him soon after Your Majesty ordered me to do so.'

Sultan Mansur Shah said, with regret in his voice, 'If somehow Tuah is alive, and if his sins were as high as a mountain, we will yet forgive him. In our heart we feel that Seri Nara al-Diraja has him hidden away.'

Seri Nara al-Diraja bowed, 'It is true as Your Majesty has said. However, Your Majesty's order that he be executed, in my mind, was not equal to his sins. So, your servant secured him in chains, for Hang Tuah is no ordinary servant, and I shall have to answer to Your Majesty in future.'

Sultan Mansur Shah was extremely glad to hear Seri Nara al-Diraja's words. His Majesty said, 'In truth, Seri Nara al-Diraja is the quintessence of the ideal servant.' Promptly Seri Nara al-Diraja was bestowed with gifts.

Sultan Mansur Shah ordered, 'Seri Nara al-Diraja, will My Lord please ask that Hang Tuah be brought here.'

So, Seri Nara al-Diraja ordered his man to fetch Hang Tuah.

Hang Tuah was soon standing before Sultan Mansur Shah. However, Hang Tuah's gait, while standing and walking was still weak, he was unsteady from being so long in chains. When he arrived before His Majesty, Sultan Mansur Shah took his *keris* from his belt and gave it to Hang Tuah.

Said Sultan Mansur Shah, 'Take our *keris* and slay Kasturi.'

Hang Tuah replied, 'Very well, My Lord.' He bowed in obeisance.

Hang Tuah promptly departed to seek Hang Kasturi. As he arrived at the foot of the palace's steps, Hang Tuah called out, 'Hang Kasturi, come you down here.'

As soon as Hang Kasturi saw Hang Tuah, he said, 'Are you still alive? I thought that you have died, that was the reason that I embarked on this path. Let us duel with a *keris* each. Come up the stairs now.'

Hang Tuah replied, 'Very well.'

Hang Tuah ascended the stairs. When he had just trodden on two or three steps, Hang Kasturi lunged at him. Hang Tuah fell. Again, he climbed the steps. Again, he was confronted.

After a third attempt and still being attacked, Hang Tuah called out to Hang Kasturi, 'How can I climb the stairs? You continue to stab at me just when I have mounted two or three steps! If you are man enough, come down here so that we may fight man to man, so that we may entertain these people who have come to watch us!'

Hang Kasturi replied, 'How can I come down, there are so many people down there? I duel with you, but others may slay me.'

Hang Tuah replied, 'I shall not let even a single person assist me; we shall fight man to man.'

Hang Kasturi called out, 'How can it be so; if I come down, I will be slain anyway. If you want to kill me, come up here this minute'

Hang Tuah replied, 'If you want me in the palace, make way so that I can come up.'

Hang Kasturi said, 'Very well.' As agreed, Hang Kasturi made way and Hang Tuah climbed up the stairs. As soon as he was in the hall, Hang Tuah noticed that on the wall of the palace was a small shield. He quickly snatched it and began duelling with Kasturi. Thus, Hang Tuah had a shield, while Hang Kasturi was without it.

Around the hall, Hang Tuah noticed that the court maiden who was sought after by Hang Kasturi, had been slain; she was unclothed. Thus, while he was in combat with Kasturi, Hang Tuah was also trying to move her sarong to cover her body, she looked like an impoverished person, insufficiently dressed.

Hang Tuah had just been released from the stocks—he was infirm while standing—and when he duelled he was also unsteady—thus when he was fighting Kasturi he was feeling quite unstable. It happened that once he stabbed at the wooden wall of the palace and the blade of his *keris* was stuck. Kasturi lurched to stab at him.

Hang Tuah complained, 'Is this the way of the knight, to slay in this manner? If you are a man, let me first release my *keris*.'

Hang Kasturi agreed, 'Then free your *keris*, now.'

So Hang Tuah drew his blade from the wall and straightened it. Then they continued to duel. However, Hang Tuah accidentally hit the post, and was also asked by Hang Kasturi to detach his weapon; this was duly done by Tuah. After which they continued to fight for two or three rounds. But Hang Tuah continued to hit the wall and each time Hang Kasturi allowed him to detach his *keris*.

However, as fated by Allah *Ta'ala*, Hang Kasturi himself inadvertently stabbed his blade into the wooden panel, and his *keris* was stuck deep in the wood. At that very moment Hang Tuah stabbed at him, his *keris* penetrating him from his back to his liver.

Hang Kasturi protested, 'Hai Tuah, is this how a gentleman behaves, going back on his words. When your blade was stuck to the wall, I asked you to free it two or three times. But when my *keris* was stuck just once, you stabbed at me.'

Hang Tuah shouted, 'Who enters into a pact[14] with you, for you are a traitor?'

So saying, Tuah stabbed at him, and Hang Kasturi breathed his last soon after that.

Sultan Mansur Shah was very relieved that Kasturi had has been slain, and all of his royal attire was presented to Hang Tuah. Hang Kasturi's body was dragged to the sea and everyone in his family—wife and children—was sentenced to death, and his house, right to the very posts, were dug out of the earth and cast into the sea.

Soon afterwards, Hang Tuah was awarded the title of Laksamana, Admiral, and he was carried in a procession befitting a prince. The new Admiral was placed on the same level as the Seri Bija al-Diraja. Thus, it was Hang Tuah who became the first Laksamana. When Seri Bija al-Diraja was not present in the audience hall, it was the Laksamana who bore the sword of state, for it was the convention of the times that the Seri Bija al-Diraja, carried the sword of state over his shoulder, and stood by the side-gallery. That is the practice followed to this very day.

Sultan Mansur Shah was no longer willing to reside in the palace where Hang Kasturi had died. So His Majesty commanded the Bendahara Paduka Raja to build a new palace. It was the Bendahara himself who supervised the task, for it was the duties of the profession that it had power over the island of Bentan.

The palace had seventeen rooms, each room was three-spans wide by three spans long, its posts the circumference of a man's arms. It

[14] *Persetiaan*, pact.

had seven tiers, with seven summits. In between these were forks. And at each fork was built a penthouse and at each penthouse was built a cross-roof; all of them were fitted with 'sparrow wings' and each of these was intricately carved. Between the windows were angular 'grasshoppers', all of them with loose drapes and images of mountains. Every one of the windows was overlaid with gold leaves, the whole palace was painted in gold. Its summit was of red glass. When the sun shone on it, it seemed as though it was glowing like fire. The walls of the palace were overhung with decorative fringes and were overlaid with large pieces of Chinese glass. When the sun shone on them, they seemed to glow like the sun, radiating a strong glimmer such that it was impossible to look at them with the naked eye.

The crossbeams of the palace were fashioned from the *kulim*[15] wood, two feet wide, a cubit and three fingers thick. The balustrade was two feet thick and two whole feet of it was carved, the door sills were four feet wide, the crossbars of the door were also intricately carved. There were forty main crossbars in all; each one was gilded. It was a wonderfully outstanding article of workmanship. Not even a single palace in the world could compare with it in these times. This was the palace that was named The Grand Palace. Its roof was made of copper shingles.

When the palace was almost complete, Sultan Mansur Shah toured the site to have a look at it. The King entered the main floor while the servants walked underneath it. Sultan Mansur Shah was delighted with its craftsmanship. After that he approached the external kitchen area. His Majesty noticed that one of the crossbeams was dark in colour and smaller than the rest. Sultan Mansur Shah inquired, 'Of what wood was this cross-beam made?'

The workers replied, '*Ibul* wood, My Lord.'

Sultan Mansur Shah, 'Was the Bendahara in a hurry?'

After that, Sultan Mansur Shah returned to his palace, escorted by Tun Indera Segara.

---

[15] *Kulim*, a type of hard wood.

Tun Indera Segara hailed from a family of court eunuchs. It was Tun Indera Segara who reported the Sultan's displeasure to the Bendahara, 'His Majesty was annoyed because one of the crossbeams was smaller than the rest.'

When the Bendahara heard Tun Indera Segara's report, he presently ordered that a new crossbeam of *kulim* wood be harvested from the forest, a cubit wide, and a span and three fingers thick. Almost immediately, the carpenters arrived to seek the precise wood for the crossbeam. The Bendahara Paduka Raja himself went to repair it and he himself chiselled it to its dimensions. The sounds of the carpenters at work reached the ears of His Majesty.

He enquired, 'What is that clatter?'

Tun Indera Segara replied, 'Your Majesty, the Bendahara is hammering the small crossbeam and fitting it himself.'

Instantly, Sultan Mansur Shah ordered that a gift of a full suit of clothes be brought to the Bendahara, who later became known as *Shahmura*.

In due time, the palace was completed. The Sultan was delighted and immediately gave presents to all those who had worked on it. And just as quickly, Sultan Mansur Shah moved into the new palace.

However, after a lapse of some years, by the will of *Allah Ta'ala*, the palace caught fire, which suddenly appeared from its summit. Sultan Mansur Shah, the Queen and all the palace maids fled. All the rajas in the palace left; many came to help, but it was to no consequence. However, all the royal properties were saved from the raging fire.

The tin of the roof melted and it flowed down at the end of the ridge; the palace dripped as though it were in a heavy rain. As it was dripping people rushed in to retrieve the valuable possessions in the palace.

Presently Tun Muhammad, the Speedy, entered to salvage the belongings—each time he went it, he brought out two or three articles—that was the reason he was called 'Tun Muhammad, the Speedy.'

It was related that each time he entered, Tun Muhammad the Speedy brought out two or three chests; and that was also the reason

why he was called by another name, 'Tun Muhammad, the Camel.'
In this manner all the belongings were saved, except a few. The
Grand Palace was entirely burnt to the ground and in due time the
fire died down.

Soon Sultan Mansur Shah presented gifts to all those who rescued
the chattels—those who should receive suits of costume were given
them, those who should receive gold-mounted *kerises* were given *kerises*,
while those who should receive swords were similarly given swords, and
those who should receive titles were subsequently suitably decorated.
In the meanwhile, Sultan Mansur Shah commanded the Bendahara
Paduka Raja to build a new palace and an audience hall. Hence the
Bendahara ordered his men to begin building, as ordered.

The men of Bentan Karangan went into the forest to seek the
wood, and carpenters from Ungaran and Sugal built the palace, those
from Pancar Serapung[16] built the audience hall, and men from Buru
were tasked with the building of the reception hall, while those from
Soyar built the main hall. The double doors on the right of the gallery
were framed by the carpenters from Sudar, while those on the left
were the work of the villagers from Sayung, who sent their carpenters
to build the pen; the Apung folks built the elephant drinking pond,
while those from Merbau assembled the crossbeams. In the meantime,
those from Sawang worked on the baths. The folks from Tungkal built
the mosque's ablution pool, and those from Tentai built the palace
gates, while those from Muar dug the drain around the fort. The new
palace was more beautiful than the old one. When all the work was
completed, Sultan Mansur Shah presented gifts to all the workers. It
was in this new palace that His Majesty resided for the rest of his life.

It was related that with his wife, Tun Kudu, Seri Nara al-Diraja
had three children, the eldest was a boy, Tun Tahir, the middle one,
a girl, Tun Shah, while the youngest was another boy, Tun Mutahir,
who was renowned for his good looks. In due time, Tun Kudu returned
to the blessings of Allah, journeying from this transient world to the

---

[16] Pancar Serapung, a town in a northern part of Lingga Island.

permanent one. Then Seri Nara al-Diraja took as his wife another Malay lady, who bore him two children. The first was a boy, Tun 'Abdul, who was a dandy, and the other, a girl, Tun Naja.

* * *

When news of the boundless reputation of the Raja of Melaka reached China, its King sent a mission to Melaka. Along with it was carried a boatful of needles—only needles were carried in this single vessel. On its arrival, His Majesty ordered that it be received in a procession. When it reached the audience hall, the letter was fetched by the courtier, who handed it to the *khatib* preacher, who read it:

> This is a letter from under the feet of the King of Heaven, to the Raja of Melaka.
>
> Be it known that we have heard of the news that the Raja of Melaka is a great King; thus we wish to forge a friendship with the Raja of Melaka. There is no other greater King than us in this world; nobody has counted the number of our subjects. From each house we have commanded that a needle was collected, that is why the vessel which we have ordered to sail to Melaka is laden with these needles.

After Sultan Mansur Shah heard the intent of the letter His Majesty smiled. His Majesty ordered that the needles be unloaded, and in its place, fried sago to fill it to the brim. Tun Perpatih Putih, the younger brother of the Bendahara Paduka Raja was appointed by Sultan Mansur Shah to be his envoy. Thus, Tun Perpatih Putih sailed to the great country of China.

In due time, he arrived in China, and on his arrival, the Raja of China ordered that the letter be taken in a procession as a mark of respect. It stopped before the Prime Minister's residence, whose name was Li Po. When it was almost dawn, Li Po and all the chiefs and nobles were in the hall, in an audience with the King.

Tun Perpatih Putih entered the hall, while the hovering crow too descended and entered it. When they had arrived at the great outer doors, Li Po and all the officers of state and chiefs paused, while the crow also followed. The gong summoning subjects to assemble, *gong pengerah*,[17] was sounded, thunderous was its boom. Following the signal of the gong, Li Po and the officers of state made their way into the hall, again they were followed by the crow. After they entered, they stopped, again the crow was just behind them. Here the assembly gong was again sounded. They proceeded to make their entrance, going through each of the several doors. It was only when the day had broken that they arrived in the audience hall and took their seats.

There were so many in the audience hall that when they sat down their knees were set against their neighbour's. The crow stretched its wings to shelter all those who had come to pay their homage to the King. It was then that the thunder and lightning broke in the skies, loud and powerful.

That was the signal that the King would arrive in the hall. He was vaguely seen, seemingly shadowy, perceived only from behind the window of the royal sedan, in the mouth of the dragon. Those who were present bowed, never lifting their faces.

Soon the letter from Melaka was read by a courtier. His Majesty, the Raja of China, was very pleased listening to it and the sago gift was duly unloaded. When they arrived before His Majesty, he asked, 'How do you make this?'

Tun Perpatih Putih bowed and answered His Majesty, 'My Lord, we asked that each subject roll one sago pellet. The accumulated amount thus computes the entire population in the country. Nobody knows how many they are.'

The Raja of China was surprised, 'Indeed the Raja of Melaka is a great King, numerous are his subjects, not different from our subjects. Let us take him for a son-in-law.'

---

[17] *Gong Pengerah*, a gong for summoning subjects to assemble.

The Raja of China addressed Li Po, 'The Raja of Melaka has ordered his subjects to roll the sago; what shall be our distinctive mark? From now on the rice that we consume must be peeled by hand and not pounded.'

Li Po bowed, 'Very well, My Lord.'

That was the reason why the Raja of China did not consume rice that was pounded. Even to this day, it is peeled by hand.

It was related that during his audience with His Majesty, Tun Perpatih Putih wore rings on all his fingers. Whoever looked upon any of them and was attracted to it, he would present it to that person. If another person looked at the rings, he again gave one of them to the person. All this happened when Tun Perpatih Putih was having an audience.

One day, the Raja of China inquired of Tun Perpatih Putih, 'What is the favourite food of the Malays?'

Tun Perpatih Putih replied, 'My Lord, our favourite is the water cress, that is uncut, and split along its length.'

On hearing this, the Raja of China ordered water cress to be cooked as described by Tun Perpatih Putih. When it was ready, it was brought before Tun Perpatih Putih, and all the Malays began to eat. They bit at the end of the vegetable and lifted up their faces, that was then Tun Perpatih Putih and all the Malays caught a glimpse of the Raja of China's countenance.

After a few weeks in China, it was time to return. His Majesty then ordered Li Po to make preparations to accompany his daughter to Melaka. Hence Li Po began to make the necessary arrangements. When all were completed, the Raja of China ordered that five hundred young princesses and a senior minister head the mission to escort Princess Hang Liu.

Before long, Tun Perpatih Putih sought permission of the King to return. The official letter was carried in a procession to the vessels and Tun Perpatih Putih sailed back to Melaka.

After a journey of some weeks, they arrived in Melaka. News was brought to Sultan Mansur Shah that Tun Perpatih Putih had returned, bringing with him a princess of China. Sultan Mansur Shah was greatly pleased, commanding that she be greeted by the officers of state, nobles and warriors. When the two parties met and the Chinese mission was being accompanied into the palace, it was done with a great show of deference and esteem. Sultan Mansur Shah was full of curiosity and wonder, beholding Princess Hang Liu, the daughter of the Raja of China.

His Majesty asked that she became a Muslim. As soon as she converted, Sultan Mansur Shah wedded the princess. She bore a boy, named Paduka Mimat. And Paduka Mimat bore Paduka Seri China and Paduka Seri China bore Paduka Ahmad, the father of Paduka Isap. All the five hundred Chinese ministers were requested to make Bukit China their residence; that is the reason why it is called Bukit Cina, the Chinese Hill, even to this day. They were the diggers of the well on the hill, and their descendants came to be known as Biduanda China, the Chinese Royal Pages.

Sultan Mansur Shah honoured the Chinese minister with special gifts. Before long, he sought His Majesty's permission to return. Now it was Telanai and Menteri Jana Putera who were commanded to sail to China. It was only then that Sultan Mansur Shah sent his obeisance, as he had become his son-in-law.

Tun Telanai and Menteri Jana Putera duly sailed to China. By the will of Allah, a storm descended on the path of the vessel and they were diverted to Berunai. On their arrival they disembarked to pay their homage to the Raja of Berunai.

The Raja enquired of Tun Telanai, 'How does the letter of our uncle, His Majesty in Melaka, to the Raja of China sound like?'

Tun Telanai bowed replying, 'This is how it sounds:

I, the Raja of Melaka send obeisance to my father, the Raja of China.'

The Raja of Berunai enquired further, 'Does the Raja of Melaka send obeisance to the Raja of China?'

Menteri Jana Putera interrupted, 'No, Your Majesty. The word "*sahaya*" in Malay means "*hamba*" I or servant. We are the ones sending the letter of obeisance, and not His Majesty.' On hearing his explanation, the Raja of Berunai remained quiet.

When it was the season of the northeast monsoon, Tun Telanai and Menteri Jana Putera sought leave of His Majesty. The Raja of Berunai ordered a letter be composed to be sent to Melaka. This was how it sounds:

I make obeisance to my uncle; this is a letter from a nephew to his uncle.

Soon after that, Tun Telanai and Menteri Jana Putera returned to Melaka. The letter from the Raja of Beruani was duly delivered to Sultan Mansur Shah. And all that happened on the journey was reported to His Majesty. He was extremely pleased listening to it. Subsequently, he bestowed favours on Tun Telanai and Menteri Jana Putera, and showered praises on Menteri Jana Putera.

* * *

The narrative now turns to the state of Pahang, on the east coast of the Peninsula. Sultan Mansur Shah commanded the Bendahara Paduka Raja to invade Pahang. The Bendahara promptly departed, accompanied by Tun Bija al-Diraja, the Laksamana, Sang Setia, Sang Guna, Sang Naya, Sang Jaya Pikrama and all the warriors. Two hundred of the expeditionary vessels sailed in a fleet of big and small boats, all of them armed. After a journey of a few days, they arrived in Pahang. There the two forces met and battled with each other.

In the olden times, the *negeri* of Pahang was a large state, a colony of Siam. Maharaja Sura was the name of its Raja; he was a cousin of His Majesty, Bubunnya. When the Bendahara had landed, a battle between the soldiers of Pahang and Melaka ensued; it involved numerous individuals on both sides. By the grace of Allah *Subhanahu wa Ta'ala*, the Almighty God, Pahang was easily defeated. Its soldiers fled in disarray.[18]

---

[18] *Kekaburan, usai, lari,* in disarray.

Maharaja Sura himself escaped to the upper reaches of the Pahang River. Subsequently the Bendahara ordered Seri Bija al-Diraja, the Laksamana, Seri Akar Raja, Sang Setia, Sang Guna, Sang Naya, Sang Jaya Pikrama, Sang Surana, Sang Aria, Sang Raden, Sang Sura Pahlawan, Sang Sura and all the warriors to follow him. It was related that while Seri Bija al-Diraja was pursuing him, he was at the very same time hunting wild buffaloes and trapping forest fowls; and wherever he found good sandy beaches he would stop to amuse himself.

Seeing this, Seri Bija al-Diraja's men complained, 'How is it with our chief? All of us in the mission have followed Maharaja Sura in all seriousness, but here we are—our chief is still hunting buffaloes and fowls! If it happens that others are to find him first, then they will be rewarded, but there will be nothing for us.'

Seri Bija al-Diraja replied, 'How would you young men know, for Maharaja Sura is never out of my sight. As the fortunes foretell—his name is under mine, his day under mine, and so his time is also under mine. How can he escape my clutches?'

It was related that Maharaja Sura was in the jungle for three nights, he had not eaten or drunk anything during the whole time. But at the end of it, when he arrived at an old woman's house, he requested some rice from her.

The old woman thought in her heart, 'I have heard it told that this Raja is being pursued by Seri Bija al-Diraja. If he knows that Maharaja Sura is here in my compound, what will happen to me? It's better that I report him to the Seri Bija al-Diraja.'

So, the woman spoke to the Seri Maharaja Sura, 'Please stay in my hut, My Lord, I'll go out and look for some vegetables.'

Therefore, the old woman went to the river bank. Her intention was to inform all those following the Seri Maharaja Sura. However, they were already quite far ahead, while Bija al-Diraja was far behind them. So, she informed him of Maharaja Sura's whereabouts. Immediately, Seri Bija Diraja ordered his men to surround him.

Maharaja Sura was subsequently encircled and brought to Seri Bija al-Diraja. Seri Bija al-Diraja then brought him back to the Bendahara

Paduka Raja. However, though he was caught Seri Bija al-Diraja did not put him in the stocks or tie him up but gave Maharaja Sura to his senior minister. The Bendahara too treated him with respect as was the conduct of detention in those days.

Maharaja Sura's elephant was known as Iyu Dikenyang; it was ordered to be brought to Melaka. After all the soldiers and the officers who trailed him had gathered, the Bendahara departed for Melaka, bringing with him Maharaja Sura.

In due time, the Bendahara Paduka Raja arrived home. Soon, he entered the audience hall, bringing with him Maharaja Sura. Sultan Mansur Shah was profoundly delighted and bestowed gifts of exotic and fine cloths on the Bendahara Paduka Raja and along with him all those who accompanied him in the mission. In addition, the Seri Bija al-Diraja was bestowed by Sultan Mansur a ceremonial umbrella, a drum, a flute and the long *nafiri* trumpets, except the *nagara*, the royal kettledrums, for his part in capturing Maharaja Sura.

According to a custom of old that if the Seri Bija al-Diraja travelled beyond Melaka, he was installed a ruler and ordered to reside in Pahang. Thus, when the Seri Bija al-Diraja, afterwards returned to Pahang, he also commenced to govern the state.

It was related that Maharaja Sura was given by Sultan Mansur Shah into the care of the Bendahara Paduka Raja. Even then he was not put in the stocks. The Bendahara in turn put the Seri Nara al-Diraja, to be in charge of his welfare. Seri Nara al-Diraja incarcerated him at the end of the audience hall, where he gave his audience. Though he was imprisoned, Maharaja Sura was given a mattress and pillow, with a shoulder shawl, as was the custom required for a royal.

One day, when the Seri Nara al-Diraja was giving an audience, Maharaja Sura spoke, 'When my *negeri* was defeated and I was captured by Seri Bija al-Diraja, I felt as though I was still in my own country. But after I was surrendered to the Bendahara, so were my feelings, I felt I was in my own country. Only with this old man do I feel that I am really in a prison.'

The Seri Nara al-Diraja, responded, 'Hai Maharaja Sura, though you are a Raja, your manners are less than adequate. The Seri Bija al-Diraja, is a great warrior, did he not defeat your *negeri*? Especially when you were on your own. He had nothing to fear. The Bendahara is an important minister; he is attended to by a great many people and soldiers, how would you be able to escape? I am but a mere servant, if you were to escape, His Majesty will be terribly annoyed with me. That is the reason why you are in jail.'

Maharaja Sura, 'That is why you are the ideal servant.'

After he had been jailed for a time, it happened that his elephant, Iyu Kenyang, was taken to its bath, passing before Maharaja Sura's prison. He called out to him. When it came close, he observed him very carefully, and found that one of its nails was missing.

Maharaja Sura said, 'I have paid little attention to my elephant for much too long, which is also the reason I was defeated.'

In the meantime, there was an elephant, ridden by Sultan Mansur Shah, by the name of Kanchanchi, which became unchained and escaped. Despite all the strategies of Seri Rama, the knight of the elephants, to recover him, he could not be captured. If the elephant were to wander into the marshes or the shrubbery, it would be quite easily retrieved.

In the meantime, the words of Seri Rama were transmitted to Sultan Mansur Shah. Presently His Majesty ordered that it be sought throughout the kingdom. Soon news was brought to Sultan Mansur Shah that Maharaja Sura was very knowledgeable in matters dealing with elephants. So, His Majesty asked that Maharaja Sura retrieve him.

Maharaja Sura said to the man who came to fetch him, 'My obeisance to His Majesty. If I am released from this prison I may be able to recover him.'

So, the man sent to bring the orders of the Raja, returned to present the request of Maharaja Sura. Sultan Mansur Shah, accordingly, directed that he be freed, and soon the elephant was recaptured.

There was much to learn from their captive; thus Sultan Mansur Shah ordered the sons of the chiefs to be tutored by him, for it was a practice of Sultan Mansur Shah that whoever was good with the horses or knowledgeable about elephants or weapons, he would ask the young men to study under him. It was Sultan Mansur Shah himself who paid for the tuition and all the other expenditures.

It was related that Seri Rama was descended from a class of knights and was placed in the gallery to the right side of the palace, his betel set came in a tray with a yellow wrap.

* * *

There was once a female relative of the Seri Nara al-Diraja, who was taken to be his wife by Sultan Mansur Shah. She bore him four children, two boys and two girls. One of the boys was named Raja Ahmad. As time passed, Seri Nara al-Diraja fell ill. When he felt that he was approaching his end, he asked that the Bendahara Paduka Raja be fetched.

Said the Seri Nara al-Diraja to the Bendahara Paduka Raja, 'I feel this illness of mine is my last. However, my offspring are still children. Thus, firstly to Allah *Subhanahu wa Ta'ala* I surrender their fate; then to you, my brother; furthermore, they are your nephews and nieces. I leave them nothing except gold in four brass chests, there will be four servants who will carry them here. That is all I would ask of you, my brother.'

Soon after that, the Seri Nara al-Diraja, returned to the grace of Allah. Subsequently, Sultan Mansur Shah arrived for Seri Nara al-Diraja's burial. On that occasion, His Majesty bestowed an umbrella, a ceremonial drum, a flute, a *nafiri* trumpet and royal kettledrums to accompany the funeral ceremony. When the funeral ended the Raja returned to his palace in grief. Thereupon all the children of the Seri Nara al-Diraja moved to live with the Bendahara Paduka Raja.

In time, the son of the Seri Nara al-Diraja, Tun Tahir, succeeded his father, with the title of Seri Nara al-Diraja, holding the post of chief of the treasury. Seri Nara al-Diraja's younger son, Tun Mutahir, was bestowed the title of Seri Maharaja, and appointed the Temenggung.

Another son of the Seri Nara al-Diraja, Tun 'Abdul, was from a different mother. He was known as a dandy, who took three days to dress himself. If he went riding, he would choose the shadow of trees, and would care for his looks as long as it took to cook a pot of rice.

Allah knows the truth; to Him shall we return.

X

The page of the chronicle now turns to the episode of the King of China. After the mission to accompany His Majesty's daughter, along with Tun Perpatih Putih, had returned, the letter of the Raja of Melaka was carried in a procession. Upon its arrival at the audience hall the King requested the Prime Minister to read it. His Majesty was delighted to hear its contents.

It happened that, at that very moment, His Majesty had fallen ill, and his whole body was afflicted with a skin disease. His Majesty ordered that a doctor be summoned instantly. Although the doctor prescribed certain herbal remedies, His Majesty was not cured. As time passed, hundreds of doctors were summoned, but it was all to no avail.

At last, an old doctor sought His Majesty's audience. Respectfully he raised his hand and said, 'Oh My Lord, it has come to my knowledge that leprosy cannot be cured by any of us, for this disease has a special origin of its own.'

His Majesty inquired, 'What is its origin?'

The old doctor replied, 'My Lord, the wording of the Raja of Melaka says '*sembah*'[1] obeisance—that is the reason for Your Majesty's

---

[1] *Sembah*, a salutation, by a subject, men of lower rank, to his King.

XI

The narrative then turns to the words of Sultan Mansur Shah commanding his armies to invade Siak, for Siak, in the olden times, was a great country. Its Raja was a descendant of the Raja of Pagar Ruyung, a descendant of Sang Seperba, who descended from the Seguntang Mahameru Hill. It refused to demonstrate an allegiance to Melaka; that was the reason that His Majesty ordered that it be overrun.

To accomplish the task, Seri Awadana was ordered to make the journey, along with sixty military chiefs. Sang Jaya Pikrama and Sang Surana were also conscripted into this foray. Seri Awadana was a grandson of the Bendahara Seri Amar Diraja, for the Bendahara had many offspring—the eldest was Tun Hamzah, and Tun Hamzah bore Seri Awadana who was the Prime Minster to Sultan Mansur Shah.

Seri Awadana himself had two children: one was called Tun Abu Saban, the other, Tun Perak. Tun Saban bore Orang Kaya Tun Hasan; and Tun Perak bore a girl, Tun Esah, and a boy, Tun Ahmad. Seri Awadana had an authority over Merbau, for in those days Merbau had a flotilla of thirty swift three-masted *lancaran* vessels. When all was ready, Seri Awadana set sail for Siak. Khoja Baba was in accompaniment.

After a few days at sea, they arrived in Siak. The Raja of Siak then was Maharaja Peri Sura. His Vizier was Tun Jana Muka Bebal. When news of the arrival of the Melaka fleet reached His Majesty's ears, he ordered that the fortress be reinforced and all his subjects assembled. In the meantime, the Melaka fleet sailed upriver.

The Siak fortress was built by the water. So, the Melakans brought their vessels alongside the fortress in pairs. The fortress was then reinforced by armed men, so numerous were they that they appeared as water flowing down from a hill. However, many were the subjects of the Raja of Siak slain in the battle.

It was reported that Maharaja Peri Sura stood at the end of the fortress directing his subjects in the battle. However, when Khoja Baba identified him standing there alone, he drew his bow and shot at him. The arrow penetrated his chest and Maharaja Peri Sura died there. When his subjects saw that their Raja had fallen, they broke ranks and scattered in all directions. The fortress was soon destroyed by the Melakans, who entered it with destruction in mind. They looted the city, carrying away with them much booty.

Megat Kudu, the son of Mahasalini Peri Sura, was captured and taken to Seri Awadana, who brought him to Melaka. Upon arriving in Melaka, Megat Kudu sought the audience of His Majesty, Sultan Mansur Shah. The Sultan was extremely delighted and bestowed gifts on Seri Awadana and Khoja Baba, and all those who accompanied them.

Soon, Megat Kudu was presented with fine clothes, and was married to His Majesty's daughter, and eventually crowned in Siak with the title of Sultan Ibrahim. Tun Jana Muka Bebal was reappointed his Vizier. With his wife, the daughter of Sultan Manshur Shah, he bore a son, Raja 'Abdul.

* * *

Now the narrative turns to the episode of Raja Muhammad and Raja Ahmad, sons of Sultan Mansur Shah. After they both reached adulthood, it was the intention of Sultan Mansur Shah that Raja Muhammad should succeed him on the throne, for Raja Muhammad was a favourite and much adored by His Majesty.

One day, Raja Ahmad and Raja Muhammad went horse-riding. It happened that at that very time of day Tun Besar, the son of Bendahara Paduka Raja was playing the *sepak raga*, rattan ball game, with his friends by the roadside. It was at that very moment that Raja Ahmad and Raja Muhammad rode by. Tun Besar was kicking the ball. On its way down, the ball landed on Raja Muhammad's headgear, causing it to fall to the ground.

Raja Muhammad shouted, 'My headgear has fallen!'

Seeing this, the servant who was carrying his betel container rushed to his side. Raja Muhammad seized his *keris* and stabbed Tun Besar. It penetrated the topmost part of his belly. Tun Besar died instantly. This tragedy was followed by an uproar.

Hearing this, the Bendahara left his gallery to enquire why there was such an outcry.

The young men replied in shrill voices, 'Your son, My Lord, is dead, slain by Raja Muhammad.'

They recounted all that had happened on that fateful afternoon to the Bendahara.

The Bendahara asked, 'So, why are you all armed like this now?'

His clansmen replied, 'We want to avenge our brother's death.'

The Bendahara reasoned, 'It is the custom among Malay servants never to rebel.' And continued, 'Hey, are you rebelling against the Sultan on the hill? Go away all of you, go, for it is not the practice of Malays to go against their masters. But to have this prince as our master, never!'

At these words, his clansmen fell silent. Soon, Tun Besar was buried. All that occurred on that day was brought to His Majesty's attention.

Sultan Mansur Shah enquired, 'What did the Bendahara say?'

So they repeated his words that it was not the custom of the Malay servant to rebel, and that to make him our master, never. The Sultan was red with rage. He demanded that Raja Muhammad be fetched. When he came, His Majesty was angry beyond words.

Sultan Mansur Shah said, 'You are accursed, Muhammad! What can I do when you are rejected by this very earth?'

Sultan Mansur Shah instructed the Seri Bija al-Diraja to journey to Pahang, with Raja Muhammad. In due time, the Minister arrived at his destination and Raja Muhammad was surrendered to the Seri Bija al-Diraja, with instructions to install him as the Sultan of Pahang, with the title of Sultan Muhammad. All the land from Sedili Besar to Terengganu were given to him by His Majesty. And after that, he gave him officers he thought would be suitable as ministers to help him in his new administration—as the Bendahara and the Temenggung. After all the ceremonies were completed, the Seri Nara al-Diraja, returned to Melaka.

In time, Melaka achieved fame as a great state, both in the east and the west. Arab sailors and merchants dubbed it as 'Malaqat'. In these times, no *negeri* could equal Melaka, except Pasai and Haru. Among these three *negeri*, though the Rajas were young or old, in their letters they merely sent their greetings, and not obeisance or allegiance.

Allah knows the truth; to Him shall we return.

XII

The chronicle now turns to the episode of Semerluki, the King of Mengkasar. This is the story as was told by its author.

Once in the country of Mengkasar, Balului became its capital. Its kingdom was extremely large; many were the smaller *negeri* that came under its authority. Mejokok was the name of its King. He married all of the seven daughters of Karaeng Ditandering Jikinik. The youngest, however, was famous for her beauty.

The eldest princess bore a prince, he was named Karaeng Semerluki by His Majesty. In time, Karaeng Semerluki grew into an extremely courageous and robust young man, no one was his compare in the land of Mengkasar. It chanced that Karaeng Semerluki desired his father's youngest wife.

Karaeng Mejokok could read it from Semerluki's behaviour. However, as a father he had to discourage his son's wishes.

Karaeng Mejokok said to Karaeng Semerluki, 'Hai son, if you wish to marry a wife as beautiful as your youngest aunt, go and raid Hujung Tanah, the Land at the End of the Peninsula, and seek a woman as fine looking as she is.'

Thus, Karaeng Semerluki soon prepared a fleet of two hundred vessels of all types. When all was ready, he set sail; his resolve was to defeat all the *negeri* below the wind.

Firstly, he sailed in the direction of Java and soon ordered that all the colonies and dependencies of the Javanese be destroyed. Wherever he went, nobody dared to expel him.

From there, he went by sea to Hujung Tanah, where he plundered the settlements by the river bends, the colonies and hinterland of Melaka.

News of the invasion was reported to Sultan Mansur Shah, 'All our territories—the hinterland and the coastal settlements have been destroyed by the Mengkasarese prince, Semerluki.'

When Sultan Mansur Shah heard of the news, he commanded that the Laksamana halt Semerluki's advance. Thus the Laksamana urgently prepared his vessels.

In the meantime, Karaeng Semerluki, with all his fleet, sailed into the Straits of Melaka. When the two sides met, they were fiercely engaged in a battle at sea, crashing their boats against each other's. Arrows and the darts of the blow pipes rained down heavily. Eventually, the Laksamana came face to face with Karaeng Semerluki. Hastily, Semerluki cast the flying grapnel towards the Laksamana's vessel. When it grabbed hold of the Laksamana's vessel, Semerluki ordered that it be wound in.

However, the Laksamana immediately ordered that it be disengaged. In due time, the Laksamana's fleet had dealt a severe blow on Karaeng's men, many of them lay dead. However, many of the Melaka men too were killed by the blowpipes—for the Melakans had not found an antidote for the potent *ipoh*[1] poison.

Presently Karaeng Semerluki made his way to Pasai. All of Pasai's colonies and protectorates were devastated. The Raja of Pasai immediately commanded Orang Kaya-kaya Raja Kenayan to trail him. Raja Kenayan instantly ordered that his boats be equipped. When they were all fully prepared, he sailed out to sea. It was there that he met Karaeng Semerluki, in the bay of Terli.

---

[1]   *Ipoh*, a poison tree.

The Mengkasar vessels and soldiers battled the Pasaians. Soon, Karaeng Semerluki came face to face with Raja Kenayan. As the vessels drew alongside, he ordered that the grapnel be cast. It landed on Raja Kenayan's and took hold. Then he ordered that the boat be drawn in.

Raja Kenayan shouted, 'Pull hard now, when it comes close, I will jump over and run amok in their boat with my two-handled sword.'

On his part, Karaeng Semerluki commanded his men, 'Instantly cut the cords.' This they did successfully, and the boats came apart.

Karaeng Semerluki sneered, 'This Raja Kenayan is more courageous than the Laksamana!'

In due time, Karaeng Semerluki sailed back in the direction of Celebes, passing the sea of Melaka. The Laksamana pursued him. All the boats trailing behind Semerluki's were destroyed. Thus, many of the Karaeng Semerluki's vessels were wrecked.

Soon he arrived at Ungaran. There he picked his ballast and cast it into the straits of Ungaran, vowing, 'When you float, oh stone, then I shall return to the land at the end of the Peninsula.'

That was how the place received its name—Tanjung Batu (Cape of the Rock). You may see it even now.

So, Karaeng Semerluki sailed home to Mengkasar. And the Laksamana returned to Melaka to seek the Sultan Mansur Shah's audience. His Majesty was pleased and bestowed presents of fine costumes on the Laksamana and all those who had accompanied him.

* * *

After this episode, the story now turns to Maulana Abu Bakar, who had alighted from his boat to bring the book known as *Dur 'al-Manzum*. When the Maulana arrived in Melaka he was greatly honoured by the monarch. His Majesty ordered that the book be carried in a procession to the audience hall. It was from that moment that His Majesty began to study with Maulana Abu Bakar. In turn, the Maulana praised the King, for he was extremely intelligent and consequently absorbed a great deal of his teachings.

Before long, Sultan Mansur Shah ordered that *Dur 'al-Manzum* be brought to Pasai, particularly to Tun Pematakan, so that he may attempt to explicate its meaning. This was successfully done by Tun Pematakan. His answer was duly brought back to Melaka.

Sultan Mansur Shah was exceptionally delighted. His answer was shown to Maulana Abu Bakar, to which the Maulana was agreeable. Much praise was heaped on Tun Pematakan.

Next, Sultan Mansur Shah instructed Tun Bija Wangsa to sail to Pasai to find a clarification on a certain religious issue: Do all those who have gained heaven stay there permanently and those in hell are there forever?

With him he brought seven *tahils*² of loose gold and two women, one Mengkasar-born, Dang Bunga was her name, and another, the daughter of a courtier from Muar, Dang Biba. The letter from Sultan Mansur Shah to the Sultan of Pasai was written on paper of yellow and purple, and adorned with flowers.

Sultan Mansur Shah instructed Tun Bija Wangsa, 'My Lord, please put this question to all the religious scholars in Pasai: "Do all those who have attained heaven stay there permanently, and do all those in hell stay there forever?" Whoever is able to give us the answer, award him with the seven *tahils* of loose gold, along with the two women. Please receive their answer with honour, My Lord, and bring it to us.'

Tun Bija Wangsa bowed in obeisance, 'Your words are my command, Your Majesty.'

Thus, the letter was carried in a procession to the vessel, according to the observances of the state. In time, Tun Bija Wangsa set sail for Pasai.

Upon his arrival, the letter was received by the Raja of Pasai with the utmost ceremony and respect. When it had arrived at the gallery it was instructed to be read. His Majesty was greatly pleased listening to its contents.

His Majesty addressed Tun Bija Wangsa, 'A letter from my brother.'

---

² *Tahils*, a measure of weight, 12 tahils makes *kati*.

Tun Bija Wangsa replied, 'My Lord, His Majesty, your brother, announces that whosoever is able to find a solution to the issue, as is written in this letter, will be rewarded with seven *tahils* of gold and two women. The answer is then to be carried to Melaka.'

The Raja of Pasai presently instructed that Tun Makhdum Mua be summoned. Soon the Makhdum arrived and was invited to sit beside His Majesty.

His Majesty said, 'Sir, the Raja of Melaka has ordered Tun Bija Wangsa to sail to Pasai, with a request to find a solution to a religious issue: "Do all the those who have attained heaven stay there permanently, and do all those in hell also stay there forever?" Please give His Majesty an answer so that we are not embarrassed because of our ignorance.'

Said Tun Makhdum Mua: 'Those in heaven stay there forever, and so do those in hell.'

Tun Bija Wangsa interjected, 'Is there no other interpretation?'

Makhdum Mua replies, 'There is none, for we can check its reference in the *Qur'an*.'

At that moment, Tun Hasan, the student of Tun Makhdum Mua had just taken his seat. He grimaced, not liking his teacher's reading. After His Majesty departed for his chambers, all those who were in attendance returned to their respective homes.

When Tun Makhdum Mua went home, Tun Hasan followed him to his residence.

Tun Hasan said, 'What was your answer to the Melakan envoy, My Lord? If that was the answer, the Melakans too have known it; why should they send a mission here? Perhaps they seek another answer?'

Tun Mua responded, 'How would you respond to the question?'

Tun Hasan, 'To me this is how it should be answered.'

Tun Makhdum Mua said, 'It's true what you have just said. I was mistaken. But what can I do, my answer has been given?'

Tun Hasan answered, 'It's quite simple, sir. Please invite the envoy, and then say to him, 'When you asked me before a gathering of many people that was my answer. Now, in a quiet place, I give you the true one.'

Makhdum Mua replied, 'It's accurate, what you have just said.'

So Makhdum Mua summoned Tun Bija Wangsa. When he has arrived, he served him with a sumptuous meal. Soon after that he was brought to a quiet place.

Tun Makhdum Mua said to him, 'When My Lord asked me before an august audience, with numerous lords and chiefs in attendance, that was my answer. Now, in the quiet of this corner, I give you the true one.'

Tun Bija Wangsa was very pleased hearing the words of Tun Mua. Hence, he gave all the seven *tahils* of gold and the two women to Tun Mua. The words of Tun Mua were officially received and carried to the waiting vessel.

The Raja of Pasai enquired, 'What was the answer brought back by the mission?'

Chief Penghulu Bujang Kari, titled Tun Jana Makhluk Biri-biri, bowed, 'My Lord, Makhdum Mua has been able to find an answer to the question that was raised. He was assisted by Tun Hasan.'

His Majesty was very pleased and spoke many words of praise of Tun Hasan. Soon after that, Tun Bija Wangsa sought leave of the Raja of Pasai.

When His Majesty had written a reply to the issue, it was officially taken in a procession, as was the custom of the times, and Bija Wangsa was bestowed with a gift of a complete set of fine costumes.

Not long after that, he returned to Melaka with the official answer. Upon his arrival, the solution to the issue was carried before a procession, that is, before the letter of the Raja of Pasai.

Sultan Mansur Shah was very pleased to hear the interpretation of the issue and was gracious towards Maulana Abu Bakar. He heaped many praises on Tun Mua.

It was related that in these times, in Melaka, there lived Kadi Yusuf, the great grandson of Makhdum Sayid 'Abdul Aziz, who converted all the Melakans. However, Kadi Yusuf was not tutored by Maulana

Abu Bakar, for he himself was already quite learned. One day, when Kadi Yusuf was walking towards the mosque for his Friday prayers, he passed directly in front of Maulana Abu Bakar's house. At that moment, Maulana Abu Bakar was standing at his door. Kadi Yusuf noticed a light around Maulana Abu Bakar's head, like a halo around a candle. That was how it appeared. Presently, Kadi Yusuf hurried to Maulana Abu Bakar and bowed low at his feet. Maulana Abu Bakar received him with a smile. From then on, Yusuf began to study under Maulana Abu Bakar. However, Kadi Yusuf became distracted and resigned from his post.

His son, Kadi Munawar, succeeded his father, and lived in Melaka.

It was related that in the progress of the years, one day Sultan Mansur Shah was holding court, and the officers of state, chiefs, ministers, eunuchs and military chiefs were in attendance.

The Sultan addressed them, 'We are truly in gratitude to God Almighty for this very extensive kingdom. However, there is one wish of ours—that is—we would request of God Almighty, a wife who is more lovely than the wives of all the Rajas of the world.'

The officers of state bowed, 'Is there a lady lovelier as in Your Majesty requests, for you have wedded the princesses of Java and China? What could be more magnificent than they, for in the times of old, only King Alexander married a princess of China. Now it is Your Majesty who has done so.'

Sultan Mansur Shah replied, 'If it is to marry among the offspring of Rajas, other kings have already done so, but my wish is to marry a lady whose beauty is out of this world.'

The officers replied, 'Your words are our command, My Lord, we shall see it done!'

Sultan Mansur Shah continued, 'We want the hand of the Princess of Mount Ledang. We order the Laksamana and Sang Setia to undertake this mission.'

The Laksamana and Sang Setia bowed low, 'Your words are our command, Your Majesty.'

Tun Mamad was also instructed to accompany them, to bring along the people of Inderagiri, who would clear the path to the top, for Tun Mamad was their chief.

Thus the Laksamana and Sang Setia began their journey along with Tun Mamad. After a few days, they arrived at the foot of the Ledang Mountain and began to climb. About half-way up the mountain, there descended a dreadful storm, and nobody could climb further. Moreover, the slope was extremely difficult.

Said Tun Mamad to the Laksamana and Tun Setia, 'My Lords, do wait for me here, let me go ahead with my assistants.'

The Laksamana agreed. So Tun Mamad went with two or three of his fastest assistants. When they have approached the clump of the singing bamboo they felt as though they would be blown away, as the wind was extremely strong. The clouds were so close that they could touch them, and the sound of the singing bamboo was so melodious that birds would stop to perch and listen, and all the animals of the forest were full of wonder.

Then Tun Mamad came upon a garden into which he duly entered. There he met four women, one was an old lady, very good-looking, with a shawl across her shoulders.

She enquired of Tun Mamad, 'Who are you and where are you from?'

Tun Mamad replied, 'I am a Melakan, my name is Tun Mamad. I am instructed by Sultan Mansur Shah to seek the hand of the Princess of Ledang Mountain as his consort. And you, my lady, what is your name?'

The lady replied, 'My name is Dang Raya Rani. I am the chief handmaiden of the Princess of Ledang Mountain. Please wait for me here. Let me convey your request to her.'

After she spoke these words, Dang Raya Rani and all the women who were with her vanished.

In about a second, there appeared an old lady, her back was extremely bent.

She said to Tun Mamad, 'All your words have been conveyed to the Princess by Dang Raya Rani. In her reply, the Princess said, "If the

Raja of Melaka wishes to marry me, build me a golden bridge, then another, a silver one, from Melaka to Mount Ledang. And as for my dowry: seven trays of the hearts of mosquitoes, seven trays of the hearts of germs, the juice from a young areca plant, a vase of tears, a vase of royal blood, and a third vase of blood from members of the royal family. If he is able to fulfil these requests of mine, I shall submit to the Raja of Melaka's wishes."

As soon as she had finished speaking, she vanished. It was told by the owner of the story that the old woman who was speaking to Tun Mamad was indeed the Princess of Gunung Ledang herself.

Soon after that, Tun Mamad descended from the mountain and returned to the place where Laksamana and Sang Setia were waiting. He relayed to them the words of the Princess.

Not long after that, all the members of the mission descended from Gunung Ledang, and returned to Melaka. In due time, they arrived. The Laksamana, Sang Setia and Tun Mamad sought the audience of Sultan Mansur Shah. To His Majesty they repeated the words of Princess of Gunung Ledang.

His Majesty responded, 'We can fulfil all her requests, but to bleed our children we may not, for we do not have the heart to do so.'

Allah knows the truth; to Him shall we return.

XIII

The words of the story now turn to the Raja of Pasai, Sultan Zainal 'Abidin. His Majesty had a younger brother, who would rebel and wrest the throne from him. When it came to his ears that numerous inhabitants of the *negeri* were planning with the brother to slay him, Sultan Zainal 'Abidin escaped in a small boat, and made his way to Melaka, to request sanctuary from the Sultan. His Majesty, the King of Melaka, commanded that Sultan Zainal 'Abidin be assisted and escorted back to Pasai. When the preparations were completed, the Bendahara Paduka Raja, Seri Bija al-Diraja, the Laksamana and all the military chiefs were instructed to accompany Sultan Zainal 'Abidin to Pasai.

In due course, they arrived. Soon they began to battle; but the Pasai troops were not to be defeated, for while the Melakans were twenty thousand in number, the Pasaians totalled a hundred and twenty thousand, that too if one counts each orchard as contributing one Pasaian into the fray.

The Laksamana and Seri Bija Diraja and all the military chiefs assembled in the orchard where the Bendahara Paduka Raja was stationed. There they discussed matters at hand.

The Bendahara enquired, 'What do you say, My Lords, we have long camped here, and not resolved anything. If this be the case,

142

let's return to Melaka and set His Majesty's mind at rest about our assignment.'

Tun Pikrama, the Bendahara's son protested, 'Why does My Lord want to return? Have we fought our main deciding battle yet? In my opinion, let's attack once more, this time together with the Laksamana, Seri Bija al-Diraja and all the military chiefs.'

The Laksamana and Seri Bija al-Diraja turned to the Bendahara Paduka Raja, 'It's true what My Lord's son has said. Let us all mount a resolute attack as a combined force.'

The Bendahara Paduka Raja agreed, 'Very well. Tomorrow we will all attack together.'

It was in the early morning hours that the chiefs and officers of state assembled around the Bendahara. Soon, he ordered that they be served rice for their early morning meal.

The cooks declared, 'My Lord, the plates are not sufficient for all. There are more than twenty groups to serve!'

The Bendahara spoke to all the chiefs, officers and military officers, 'As we are all going into battle together it would be good to share our food and eat from the same leaves.'

All of them answered, 'Very well, My Lord.'

The Bendahara instructed that large leaves be spread all along the beach as replacement for the insufficient plates, and the rice be served there. So, all the chiefs, high officers of state and military chiefs ate from the same leaves, along with the humble citizens of Melaka who had come along to fight.

When they had completed their meal, the Bendahara Paduka Raja and Seri Bija al-Diraja, the Laksamana, Seri Akar Diraja, Tun Pikrama, Tun Telanai, Tun Bijaya, Tun Maha Menteri, Sang Naya, Sang Setia, Sang Guna, Tun Bijaya Sura, Sang Jaya Pikrama, Sang Suria. Sang Aria, Sang Rana, Sang Sura Pahlawan, Sang Setia Pahlawan, Raja Indera Pahlawan, Seri Raja Pahlawan, Raja Dewa Pahlawan and all the military chiefs disembarked and began to attack the Pasaians. There was a great clamour of battle sounds, the glare of weapons was like wild flashes of lightning. The people of Pasai came as in a full tide, their standards tall as trees.

Soon they were confronting each other, their war cries and yells melded into the noise of the elephants and horses—the din was unimaginably loud, even if the thunder were to rumble now, it would not be heard at all. Many lay dead on both sides and the blood flowed as in a clogged drain, corpses were strewn all over the battlefield. As a result of the extreme push by the Melakans against the soldiers and military chiefs of Pasai, the Melakans were split and dispersed near the water.

The Bendahara stood on the higher part of the beach and looked backwards. He only saw the water. There was a servant, a bearer of spears of the Bendahara, Kerangkang was his name. The Bendahara Paduka Raja ordered him, 'Fetch my spear, though I am old I shall yet attack and cause havoc among them.'

In the meantime, Tun Pikrama was in a defence position, along two others, Hang Wasak and Nina Sahak, their weapons were Pasai bows and arrows. However, the Pasaians were not able to advance, for whoever advanced was slain. So, the Pasaians could only defend their position.

Nina Sahak said to Tun Pikrama, 'My Lord, how can we hold to our ground, there are only three of us? Those who have fled do not know that we are in defence here. You two stay here while I get the others to return.'

Tun Pikrama agreed, 'Very well.'

So, Nina Sahak went to command all those who were on the run to return and gather around Tun Pikrama.

Thus, all of them returned. Then Nina Sahak happened to meet Hang Hamzah, the son-in-law of Tun Pikrama, who was running in panic, trampling things along the way, not looking backwards, and neither was he following the trodden path.

Nina Sahak called out to him, 'Hai, Hang Hamzah, why are you running in such a haste, like an iguana? Aren't you taken as a son-in-law for your good looks and manners and your curly hair; in the eyes of others aren't you are the brave one?'

Hang Hamzah replied, surprised, 'Are you still in Pasai, My Lord?'

Nina Sahak answered, 'Yes, I am.'

Hang Hamzah soon returned, with his jingling shield, and his spear with a shaft of the sturdy handle of *nibung* palm wood. Then he began to yell, jumping up and down, 'I am the Hamzah of the Day of Judgement!'

He then rushed into the multitudes of Pasaians who appeared full and extensive as the sea. After him, the rest of the Melakans made haste to confront the Pasaians, killing all that they encountered.

The Pasaians were dispersed and fled in all directions. Many were those who died. Instantly, all the Melakans approached the Muhammadiyah bridge, all of them entering through the drawbridge *pintu tani*[1] and into the palace. Thus, the Pasai Palace was overcome. Promptly Sultan Zainal 'Abidin was crowned as King by the Bendahara Paduka Raja.

After His Majesty was safely on the throne, the Bendahara Paduka Raja sought leave to return to Melaka.

The Bendahara enquired of Sultan Zainal 'Abidin, 'What is your message for His Majesty in Melaka?'

Sultan Zainal 'Abidin replied, 'That which was said in obeisance in Melaka stays in Melaka.'

The Bendahara Paduka Raja was enraged upon hearing his answer. In anger he said, 'My words of obeisance in Pasai too stay in Pasai,' while he hurried to his vessel.

Thus the Bendahara and all the Melakans departed. Upon arriving at Jambu Air, news reached that Sultan Zainal 'Abidin was again attacked by the Pasaians. The Bendahara Paduka Raja promptly instructed Seri Bija al-Diraja, the Laksamana and all the military chiefs to assemble. When all had gathered, the Bendahara began to consult them.

The Laksamana said, 'Let us return to again install Sultan Zainal 'Abidin on the throne.'

---

[1] *Pintu tani*, the outer gate of the palace.

The Bendahara replied: 'I shall not, for he does not show allegiance to His Majesty, the Yang Dipertuan.'

The others replied, 'Very well, we are in accord with My Lord's decision.'

Thus the Bendahara sailed back to Melaka across the straits. In due time, they arrived and all the chiefs and officers of state went to the palace to seek His Majesty's audience. Sultan Mansur Shah was infuriated because the Bendahara had refused to return to Pasai to reinstate Sultan Zainal 'Abidin on the throne. Sultan Mansur Shah then ordered that the Laksamana be summoned.

When he had arrived, His Majesty enquired of the Laksamana matters concerning the battle in Pasai. The Laksamana paid obeisance, but he spoke ill of the Bendahara. This made Sultan Mansur Shah all the more furious towards his Prime Minister. At that moment all the clansmen of the Bendahara were present in the hall. When the audience ended, Sultan Mansur Shah returned to his palace and all the others to their own homes.

Soon, the clansmen of the Bendahara gathered around him. They repeated the words of the Laksamana speaking ill of him to the Raja. The Bendahara Paduka Raja fell silent.

On the morrow, Sultan Mansur Shah had an audience. All the officers were present, except for the Laksamana. At that moment, Sultan Mansur Shah instructed that the Bendahara Paduka Raja be summoned. Soon the Bendahara Paduka Raja arrived. The Sultan enquired of the Bendahara of the affairs in Pasai. The Bendahara approached the throne, he praised the Laksamana with fine words. The Sultan was full of disbelief. Soon His Majesty gave the Bendahara presents of fine cloths and costumes. At that moment, all the Bendahara's clansmen were also in audience.

When His Majesty had returned to the inner apartments of the palace, all those in the audience hall returned to their own abodes.[2] All of the Laksamana's clansmen returned to his residence. The

---

[2] *Kediaman*, abode.

Bendahara's words of praise for him before the Raja were repeated for his ears. Instantly, the Laksamana went to the Bendahara's. He found him in an audience. The Laksamana came and prostrated at his feet.

Said the Laksamana, 'Indeed, you are truly a great man, My Lord.'

It was related by the people of old that the Laksamana prostrated and bowed before the Bendahara's feet seven times. Soon after that, His Majesty gave gifts to Tun Pikrama and Tun Hamzah in recognition of their contribution in Pasai. Tun Pikrama was bestowed the title of Paduka Tuan and was given authority over Buru, for breaking the defences of the Pasaians.

During these times, his fleet had forty vessels in all. And the son of Tun Pikrama, Tun Ahmad, was awarded the title of Tun Pikrama Wira. Tun Hamzah was conferred the title of Tun Perpatih Kasim. He was the father of the princess, who became the mother of Seri Pikrama, but some sources alleged she was the mother of Tun Utusan. It was also related that the Laksamana, Tun Suria, was also known as the son of Tun Perpatih.

Allah knows the truth; to Him shall we return.

XIV

The narrative now turns to the Raja of Champa.[1] It was related by the author of old that there was a King of Champa, who resided in a *negeri* by the name of Malapatata. Beside his Majesty's palace was an areca[2] palm. At that moment, its spadix was heavy with buds; but however long he waited for it to bloom, it did not.

So, His Majesty ordered his servant, 'Climb the tree and see what the matter is with the spadix!'[3]

Therefore, the servant climbed the tree, plucked the spadix and brought it down. It was soon cut open by the Raja, who saw in it a boy, a very handsome boy. The shell of the spadix became the Jeming state gong, and the shoots became the Beladau sword, which became the sword of state.

His Majesty was extremely pleased to find the boy. He named him Pau Glang and was assigned wet nurses who were the wives of all the rajas and the prime minister. But he would not suckle.

In the meantime, His Majesty had a cow; it had many colours to its hair and had just given birth to a young calf. She was soon lactated, and

---

[1] Champa, an ancient kingdom in Vietnam and Kampuchea.
[2] *Pokok pinang*, areca. The fruit is central in the betel preparations.
[3] *Mayang*, spadix, overflowing flower of the palm.

its milk was given to the boy, who took to it. That is the reason why the Raja of Champa would not drink any milk from a cow.

In time, Pau Glang grew into a young man. By the time His Majesty found the boy, he already had a daughter, Pau Bia was her name. He gave her in marriage to Pau Glang, who emerged from the spadix of the areca palm.

As time passed, the Raja of Champa died, it was Pau Glang who succeeded him to the throne. When he began his reign, His Majesty built a great kingdom, there were seven mountains within its borders and its length was as long as it took to sail a whole day while the winds were blowing. He named the new *negeri* Yak.

In time, Pau Glang begot a son, Pau Tri was his name. When he was an adult his father departed this earth. Pau Tri then succeeded him on his father's throne. He soon married a princess, Bia Suri. With Bia Suri he begot a boy whom they named, Pau Gama. In time, Pau Gama grew into a young man and succeeded his father to the throne.

One fine day, Pau Gama readied his vessels to pay tribute to the Betara of Maja Pahit, and presently sailed there. After a few days into the journey, he arrived at Jepara. News of the ship's arrival reached His Majesty's ears, and also his intention to pay him his obeisance. The Betara of Maja Pahit ordered his high officials to officially welcome him. When they met him, they took him into the *negeri* and welcomed him with great respect and honour.

After his arrival, the Betara gave his daughter, Raden Galuh Ajeng, in marriage to Pau Gama. In time, the princess was with child, and soon Pau Gama requested to return to Champa.

'I agree, but I do not give you leave to take my daughter with you.'

Pau Gama replied, 'Your words are my command, Your Majesty, I shall not go against them. However, if I am still alive, I shall soon return to pay Your Majesty my obeisance.'

Soon Pau Gama requested leave of his wife, Raden Galuh Ajeng. She said, 'What shall we name our child when it is born?'

'Name him Raja Jikanak and when he has grown up, request him to seek his father in Champa.'

His wife agreed, 'Yes, My Lord.'

Soon after that Pau Gama walked to his large *payang*[4] vessel and returned to Champa. Some months after the departure of Pau Gama, Raden Galuh Ajeng gave birth to a boy, he was named Raja Jikanak. When he had grown into a young prince, his mother related all of his father's requests. After hearing his father's instruction, he ordered that wood for several vessels be found. When all was ready, he sought the Betara's permission to sail to see his father.

His Majesty agreed.

Soon Jikanak was on his way to Champa. After several days at sea, he arrived and presently made his way to the palace to make obeisance to Pau Gama. His Majesty was greatly pleased to see his son. He crowned him in Yak. In time Pau Gama died, and it was Raja Jikanak who replaced him on the throne. Jikanak married a lady, by the name of Pu Ji Bat Ji. She bore him a son, Pau Kubah was his name.

When Pau Kubah had grown into an adult, his father died. Pau Kubah replaced him on the throne. He married Pau Mechat; they bore a few boys and girls. His daughter, the princess, was exceptionally good-looking. She was sought in marriage by the Raja of Kuji, but Pau Kubah would not consent to his request. So the Raja of Kuji invaded his kingdom.

Many thousands were on the battlefield. On a good day, the Raja of Kuji ordered his Chief of the Treasury to seek amity. And thus, the gates of the fortress were opened. However, immediately the people of Kuji rushed in and fought with the people of Champa. Some escaped with their families, but some stayed put. Yak was defeated and the Raja of Champa died in battle.

The children of the Raja fled in all directions, hither and thither, and became separated from one another, each trying to save his or her own life. There were two children of the Raja of Champa—Indera Berma Shah and Shah Palembang, by name. Both of them escaped by

---

[4] *Payang,*a type of Malay vessel.

boat. Shah Palembang sailed to Aceh, while Indera Berma Shah, with his family and friends found their way to Melaka.

Upon seeing them, His Majesty Sultan Mansur Shah was greatly pleased. He duly asked them to become Muslims. Thus, Shah Indera Berma and his wife, Kini Mertam, and all their friends became Muslims. He himself was appointed a minister by Sultan Mansur. His Majesty so loved Shah Indera Berma.

These were the beginnings of the Champa community in Melaka, whose ancestry we may trace.

When His Majesty had been on the throne for seventy-three years, the wheel of time turned. His Majesty fell ill. He soon requested that his children, the Bendahara and senior officers of the land be summoned.

When they had gathered, he said, 'Be it known to you all that this world is slipping from my grasp, except the world of the hereafter, which is the only one that I now seek. We entrust our son, Raja Raden to the Bendahara Paduka Raja and My Lords, to succeed me on the throne. If he should make errors you must find it in your hearts to forgive him, for he is yet a young boy, still learning the ways of the palace. It is you who must help teach him its ways.'

Then His Majesty turned to Raja Raden, 'You should take the greatest care of your subjects, if they do commit mistakes you should be generous and compassionate, for Allah Ta'ala has said: *Innalillah ha ma'assobirin*, God is on the side of those who show forbearance. Furthermore, when it comes to choosing your effort and that of Allah, you must choose His over yours. You must entirely surrender yourself to Allah's power and presence for, as the Prophet has reminded us: *man tawakal a'lallaha kafii*, surrender yourself to the will of Allah, my son, follow His example and you will be blessed by the Lord and his Prophet, (peace be upon him).'

After they heard his reminder, all of them wept to their hearts' content.

The Bendahara Paduka Raja and all the ministers responded, 'It's true what My Lord has spoken, but please do not hurt us with such words, for we have gathered here in the hope that Allah *Ta'ala* will give you recovery from this illness. We have given all the wealth of the state, as alms to the poor and the needy. If the grass on Your Majesty's lawn withers, God forbid, then we shall perform all that Your Majesty has ordered us.'

Soon after that, Sultan Mansur Shah was deceased, and was given a burial befitting the Kings of the past.

In time, Raja Raden was crowned king. The Bendahara Paduka Raja gave him the title of Sultan 'Alauddin Ri'ayat Shah. In his times, His Majesty was extremely powerful. However, as time passed Sultan 'Alauddin Ri'ayat Shah became very ill, having to do his toilet twelve times a day. During these times, the Bendahara Paduka Raja and the Laksamana were always by His Majesty's bedside, feeding him ten or twenty times a day, and cleansing him thirty times a day.

Sultan 'Alauddin's grandmother, the mother of Sultan Mansur Shah, known as the Old Queen, had the softest spot in her heart for Sultan Muhammad, the king's son. It was her wish that Sultan 'Alauddin would pass on so that Sultan Muhammad Shah could ascend the throne of Melaka.

After a few days, Sultan 'Alauddin did recover a little. He dined on rice and milk, but then his disease took a turn for the worse, and they almost lost him. The Bendahara Paduka Raja and the Laksamana were immediately informed. They soon came. The wish of the Old Queen was that: 'When I come to visit him and turn him face downwards, he will expire when I turn him over.'

As soon as she arrived, she came close to Sultan 'Alauddin Ri'ayat Shah. However, the Bendahara Paduka Raja and the Laksamana warned her, 'My lady, please do not come close to your grandson.'

The Old Queen asked, 'Why am I not allowed to come close?'

The Bendahara and Laksamana answered, 'If Your Majesty does, then we will run amok.'

The Old Queen replied, 'Well done; the Malays are now intent on rebelling.'

They continued, 'Just this once the Malays are rebelling. If Your Majesty is still intent on coming close, we will run amok.'

Therefore the Old Queen did not dare to approach Sultan 'Alauddin's bedside. In the meantime, the Bendahara Paduka Raja, the Chief of the Treasury and the Laksamana nursed Sultan 'Alauddin, and with His blessings, the Sultan recovered. His Majesty was appreciative of their sacrifices, and bestowed gifts on the Bendahara Paduka Raja and the Laksamana—each was presented with a sedan, and everywhere they went they were carried and accompanied by their clansmen. Whenever the Bendahara Paduka Raja was in attendance he would place a yellow cushion on the seat where he was holding court.

His clansmen would tease him, 'How is it with My Lord, the Bendahara? Just like Pa' Si Bendul, when was presented with a sedan, he kept it out of sight. Look at the Laksamana, when given the honour of a sedan, he would go everywhere accompanied by his clansmen under him! How becoming in the eyes of others! But My Lord, the Bendahara, when he is being carried, not one of us is under him.'

The Bendahara Paduka Raja replied, 'Is it me who is the real Pa' Si Bendul? When the Laksamana is carried in a sedan it's his clansmen who are under it. If strangers would see him they would ask, "Who is being carried in the sedan?" Then his clansmen would answer, "The Laksamana." They would ask further, "Is he an eminent official?" They will answer, "He is too." Then the strangers would say, "Isn't there anybody greater than him?" They would reply, "There are—the Bendahara Paduka Raja is greater than him." If I too were to go around in a sedan, they will ask, "Is he an important man, this Bendahara?" They would reply, "An important man too." Then they would ask again, "Is there anybody more important than him?" They will respond, "None." In the mind of the strangers, I am the King, for the King is still a boy and does not appear in the audience hall. Furthermore, when I am carried, then you are under the sedan, even though I am a Raja. Then I would have done wrong towards the Raja? The Laksamana's clansmen are not involved in royal ceremonies; but you are all members of the royal audience hall.'

After hearing him, the Bendahara's clansmen did not say a word.

It was the habit of the Bendahara Paduka Raja, if he was in possession of a good boat or weapon, he would give it to the Laksamana.

Said the Laksamana, 'Let me have a look at it.'

But he would not show it to him. However, the Laksamana would try to find ways to see it. When the Bendahara saw the Laksamana growing extremely desirous of seeing it, only then would he would show it to him. After he had seen it, the Laksamana would retain it. Those were the ways of old.

The Bendahara's clansmen would complain, 'How is it with My Lord datuk, just like Pa' Si Bendul, when he gets a fine weapon or boat he would give it to the Laksamana, thus his clansmen would get nothing at all?'

The Bendahara Paduka Raja retorted, 'Am I Pa' Si Bendul, or is it you who are Pa' Si Bendul? If I had a good horse or elephant, everyone would ask me for it; but you know nothing about how to use or care for them. The Laksamana is a great knight, that's why I give him the fine weapons. When the enemy is upon us, it is he who will fight them off; and people will say, "He is a great knight, our very own knight." After this last argument, his clansmen remained quiet.

When Sultan 'Alauddin had been on the throne for several years, with his wife, who was the eldest daughter of Seri Nara al-Diraja, and the sibling of Seri Maharaja, he begot with Tun Naja, some boys and some girls. Among the boys were Sultan Ahmad and Sultan 'Abdul Jamal. Sultan 'Alauddin betrothed his eldest daughter to a Raja by the name of Sultan Ahmad.

In the meantime, Sultan 'Alauddin's royal consort bore two boys, one was called Raja Munawar Shah, another, Raja Zainal. Although Raja Munawar Shah was older than Raja Mahmud, it was Sultan 'Alauddin's hope that Raja Mahmud would succeed him.

It happened that burglary was rife[5] in Melaka. Each evening, many were those who would have their possessions stolen. When news of the thefts came to the Sultan's attention, His Majesty was troubled. So,

---

[5]   *Tersebar luas*, rife, widespread.

one night, His Majesty dressed as a thief, and walked with Hang Isak and Hang Siak to investigate the situation. They happened to come to a place where they found five burglars carrying a chest, whom they chased away. They were surprised and soon fled.

Sultan 'Alauddin ordered Hang Isak, 'You wait here by the chest.'

Hang Isak agreed, 'Very well, Your Majesty.'

In the meantime, Sultan 'Alauddin and Hang Isak trailed the five burglars. They caught up with them at the foot of the hill. Sultan 'Alauddin bellowed and slashed at them, striking one on his waist and slicing him in half like a cucumber. The other four fled to the bridge. His Majesty followed them, killing another at the end of the bridge; the other three jumped into the river and swam to the bank yonder.

Soon after that, the Sultan and his party walked back to the place where Hang Isak was waiting.

His Majesty instructed him, 'Take this chest to your house.'

Hang Isak said, 'Very well, My Lord.'

Subsequently, His Majesty returned to the palace. When it was morning Sultan 'Alauddin began to hold court. The Bendahara Paduka Raja and all the senior officers of state, ladies, courtiers, eunuchs and warriors were in attendance.

Sultan 'Alauddin addressed Seri Maharaja, for he was the Temenggung: 'Did My Lord keep watch last night?'

Seri Maharaja replied, 'Yes I did, Your Majesty.'

Sultan 'Alauddin continued, 'We heard that someone was found dead on the top of the hill and another at the end of the bridge. If the news is true, who are their killers?'

Seri Maharaja replied, 'Not to my knowledge, Your Majesty.'

Sultan 'Alauddin said, 'Then your watch has come to naught, for the burglars are having a heyday in the *negeri*.'

Sultan 'Alauddin then instructed that Hang Isak and Hang Siak bring the chest to the palace and place it before all those present.

Sultan 'Alauddin asked Hang Siak and Hang Isak, 'What did you hear last night? Do tell the Bendahara Paduka Raja and all the officers of state.'

Therefore, Hang Isak and Hang Siak narrated all that had happened the previous night. All the officers bowed low, in obeisance and fear of Sultan 'Alauddin. Then Sultan 'Alauddin ordered that they find the owner of the chest. They did as instructed and found a rich merchant by the name of Tirubalam as its owner. Soon Sultan 'Alauddin returned to his chambers and the officers returned to their respective homes.

When night fell, Seri Maharaja mounted a full watch. That night, Seri Maharaja met a burglar; he slashed at him, cutting away his shoulder. His hand was still trapped on the beam of the shop. When it became daylight, the shopkeeper got ready to open his shop. To his shock he saw an arm dangling from the beam of the shop. He yelped.

From that day onwards, there were no more burglars in Melaka. That was how it was during the reign of Sultan 'Alauddin.

And then there was the incident of a man who had wronged Raja Mahmud, the son of Sultan 'Alauddin, who was to succeed him on the throne. However, the fault was not immense.

The Seri Maharaja ordered that he be killed. When the news reached the ears of the Bendahara Paduka Raja, he said, 'Look at Seri Maharaja. If the little tiger is taught to eat meat, soon he himself will be its meal!'

As time passed, the Raja of the Moluccas came to Melaka to pay homage. At that moment, Telanai Terengganu and the Raja of Rokan were in attendance. As were the customs of Melaka of the day, the Raja of the Moluccas was presented with a suit of fine costumes and precious gifts appropriate to his rank.

It was related that the Raja of the Moluccas was a champion in the *sepak raga* ball arena. So many were those nobles who played, but the Raja was at the centre point. When he got the ball, he would kick it up to a hundred and fifty times, only then would he pass it on to another player. To whomever he would like to pass the ball, he would point to him, and it would reach its destination quite accurately. After that he would sit on a chair, to recover his breath, fanned by two assistants. Soon, all the young men began to play. When the ball came to him he would kick it up into the air, making it stay there the length of time it takes to boil rice, except when he wanted to pass it to another player. That was how well he knew the game of *sepak raga*.

It was related that he was also a man of extraordinary strength. If there was a coconut palm with its roots deep into the earth, he could cut it into two with his short, broad *beladau*[6] dagger.

It was also told that the Telanai of Terengganu too could use his spear to skewer a coconut palm that has already sunk its roots into the earth. In the case of Sultan 'Alauddin, however, if he shot an arrow through a coconut palm, the tree would fly into the air.

Sultan 'Alauddin adored the Raja of the Moluccas and the Telanai Terengganu, dearly.

One day, the Raja of the Moluccas borrowed a horse of the maulana, Yusuf. That episode was the kernel of this song:

The Raja of the Moluccas borrowed a horse,
He borrowed it from the maulana,
How wise and astute too he was,
He's the soul of the young, one and all.

After several months in Melaka, the Raja of the Moluccas and the Telanai Terengganu, sought leave of Sultan 'Alauddin, each returning to his *negeri.*

After sometime, it came to the attention of Sultan Muhammad of Pahang that Tun Telanai Terengganu had travelled to Melaka to pay his homage to the Sultan, without first informing him. Consequently, he ordered Seri Akar Raja to Terengganu to slay the Telanai. When Seri Akar Raja arrived in Terengganu, he requested that the Telanai be summoned. But the Telanai would not come. 'Is it not the custom among knights that they are only fetched by other knights?'

So, Seri Akar Raja was ordered by the Raja of Pahang that he be found and killed. Thus, soon Seri Akar Raja returned to Pahang. His Majesty rewarded him with authority over the state of Terengganu.

---

[6] *Beladau*, (*golok*) a broad dagger.

Soon, news of the slaying of the Telanai of Terengganu by the Raja of Pahang reached Melaka. Upon hearing it, Sultan 'Alauddin was enraged.

He said, 'Pahang is provoking us with its arrogance. We should order that it be attacked.'

The Bendahara Paduka Raja responded, 'Your Majesty, I beg of you a thousand pardons. In my opinion, we should not hastily destroy Pahang. If anything should happen, then it is we who shall suffer its effects. It is better that the Laksamana be ordered to go there.'

Sultan 'Alauddin agreed with the Bendahara, 'Very well, My Lord, we will follow your advice.'

Soon, the Laksamana was making preparations. When everything was finalized, the Sultan's letter was taken in a procession to the vessel, and the Laksamana was on his way to Pahang. After a journey of several days, he arrived in Pahang, and news of his arrival was conveyed to Sultan Muhammad, 'The Laksamana has arrived on the orders of His Majesty, the Sultan of Melaka, to seek Your Majesty's audience.'

Before long, His Majesty held court, and ordered Seri Pikrama Raja Pahlawan, the Bendahara of Pahang, to fetch the letter from the court of Melaka. After he had arrived, the letter was received and carried on an elephant and taken in a procession, accompanied by a pair of white umbrellas, drums, and the *nafiri* flutes.

The Laksamana ordered, 'After the letter has been read, make preparations to kill someone from Seri Akar Raja's family.'

The messenger replied, 'Very well.'

As the letter arrived, all the people in the audience climbed down from the high dais to honour it, except for the Raja of Pahang himself. In the meantime, the elephant was secured by the gallery. The letter was consequently received and read. It said,

Greetings and prayers of your younger brother to his elder brother.

After the letter had been read, everyone in the audience took seat. The Laksamana raised his hands in obeisance and sat at his place. At that moment, an uproar emanated from outside the palace.

The Raja of Pahang enquired, 'What is happening outside there?'

The people answered, 'Your Majesty, the Laksamana's men have slain the cousin of Seri Akar Raja.'

The Raja of Pahang repeated it to the Laksamana, 'Your men have killed the cousin of Seri Akar Raja. My Lord, please investigate the matter.'

It was the habit of the Raja of Pahang to address the chiefs of Melaka as 'My Lords'.

Therefore, the Laksamana ordered that the person be brought into the palace. Soon he was detained and restrained.

The Laksamana asked him, 'Is it true that you have killed a relative of Seri Akar Raja?'

The man replied, 'It's true, My Lord.'

The Laksamana relayed his words to the Raja of Pahang: 'It is true that the man has killed the cousin of Seri Akar Raja, but I have not punished him, for Seri Akar Raja has done your brother wrong by killing the Telanai of Terengganu without approval from Melaka.'

The Raja of Pahang said not a word.

After several days in Pahang, the Laksamana sought leave of His Majesty, who subsequently replied to his brother's letter.

Soon, the Laksamana was bestowed with a suit of fine clothes and the letter was taken in a procession to the vessel, as was the custom of old. He then returned to Melaka. On his arrival Sultan 'Alauddin ordered that the letter be received and carried on an elephant, in a procession, accompanied by a white and a royal umbrella. When it had reached the outer doors, the elephant was made to kneel and the letter was borne inside by a courtier. This is how it read:

A letter of obeisance of your elder brother to you,
his younger brother.

It was then received by the Right Courtier, but the drums and flutes remained outside. After the letter had been read, the Laksamana raised his hands in obeisance and took his seat. Sultan 'Alauddin then enquired of the Laksamana. The Laksamana duly related all that happened in Pahang. His Majesty was delighted. Soon, His Majesty bestowed gifts on the Laksamana as was the custom of old.

* * *

The chronicle now turns to Sultan Ibrahim, the Raja of Siak. There was a man of Siak who had done His Majesty wrong. His Majesty then ordered Tun Jana Pakibul to serve him the punishment, and the man was killed. In time, the news of the Raja of Siak ordering a man be put to death without His Majesty's permission reached Melaka. The Laksamana was instructed to journey there. He thus made the necessary preparations and when they were completed, he sailed there.

Upon his arrival in Siak, Sultan Ibrahim ordered that the letter be received according to the customs that were also adhered to in the court of Pahang. Thus, the elephant was secured by the gallery and the letter was officially received and read.

After the letter had been read, the Laksamana said to Tun Jana Pakibul, 'Is it true that My Lord has slain a relative of mine?'

Tun Jana Pakibul replied, 'It's true, on His Majesty's orders.'

The Laksamana turned towards Sultan Ibrahim, facing Tun Jana Pakibul. He pointed the finger on his left hand to Tun Jana Pakibul, saying, 'My Lord is ignorant of the polite manners and conduct of the court. It is true that you are a servant from the forest. Do you think that it is right to put someone to death without first consulting Melaka? Are you taking matters into your own hands?'

Upon hearing his words, Sultan Ibrahim and all the lords remained quiet. After a period of time in Siak, the Laksamana sought leave. Sultan Ibrahim bestowed on him fine clothes and sent a letter of obeisance to Melaka. This is how it sounded:

> The obeisance of your elder brother to my younger brother. Should there have been some errors committed, we hope you will find it in your heart to forgive us.

So, the letter was taken to the vessel, and the Laksamana sailed back to Melaka. On his return the letter was duly read, and the Laksamana raised his palms in obeisance and took his seat.

Sultan 'Alauddin then enquired of the Laksamana, who related to His Majesty all that had happened. The Sultan was delighted and gladly bestowed presents on the Laksamana for his service.

In time, the Bendahara Paduka Raja became very ill. He asked that his children and grandchildren who resided a day or two's journey from Melaka, be summoned.

When they had all gathered, he reminded them, 'Hai, all my grandchildren, exchange not your religion for the world, for the world is but transient. Those who live now, will someday also perish. Keep your heart sincere and serve Allah *Subhanahu wa Ta`ala* and Rasulullah *salallahu `alaihi wasallam* and serve your King. And never forget that the just laws of the kings are concomitant to those of the Prophet, like the jewel and the ring. Furthermore, the Raja is but a representative of Allah. As you serve the Prophet it is like you are serving Allah, as is said in a pronouncement of Allah Ta`ala in the Qur`an: '*ati `ulllah wa `ati urrasul wakwalil miramnikum*, that is: serve the Lord and His Prophet. This is my will and reminder that I would like to leave with all of you. You should never forget this so that you will benefit both from the goodness of this world and the hereafter.'

The Bendahara turned to the Seri Nara al-Diraja and the Seri Maharaja Mutahir, saying, 'Mutahir, you will in time become an important official of state, you may even become more important than me. But speak not from the arrogance of an uncle of the King. If this ever crosses your heart, then you will be slain by your enemies.'

Now, the Bendahara turned to face Tun Zainal 'Abidin.

Said he: 'Hai, Zainal 'Abidin, if you are not involved in any of the Raja's work, you should live in the woods, for the span-long tummy of yours will easily be satisfied by the shoots and sprouts.'

Then the Bendahara addressed Tun Pauh: 'Pauh, remain not in the *negeri*, reside in the heartland, for in such places even trash may be turned into gold.'

Finally, the Bendahara addressed Tun Isak, 'Isak, seek not your earnings in the royal audience hall.'

That was the last will and testament of the Bendahara Paduka Raja to all his children and their children, each to his own, for each received a guidance appropriate to his person and character. When Sultan 'Alauddin Shah heard news of the Bendahara's ailment, His Majesty visited him. The Bendahara Paduka Raja raised his hands in obeisance.

Said the Bendahara, 'My Lord, in my heart I feel that the world is slipping from my grasp, and my only hope is the hereafter. Your Majesty should not listen to the words of the false ones; should Your Majesty do so, Your Majesty will regret it. Do not follow the urges of your desire, for many are the rajas who have been destroyed by Allah because they have followed the paths of their desires.'

Soon after that, the Bendahara Paduka Raja returned to the grace of God. Subsequently Sultan 'Alauddin embarked on appropriate rituals of reverence at the passing of the Bendahara. In time, Tun Perpatih Putih, the brother of the Bendahara Paduka Raja was appointed in his place. He was the one called 'Bendahara Putih'. Bendahara Putih begot a boy who was extremely good-looking, titled Orang Kaya Tun Abu Sait. Orang Kaya Tun Abu Sait himself begot two boys, the elder was known as Seri Amar Bangsa, and the younger, Orang Kaya Tun Muhammad, who begot Orang Kaya Tun Adan, Orang Kaya Tun Sulat, and the mother of Tun Hamzah, also the mother of Datuk Darat. It was related that, among the Malays, Orang Kaya Tun Muhammad was considered as pious, mastering the field of grammar, and having some understanding of Islamic jurisprudence, *fikah*,[7] and the science of faith, *'ilmu usul.*

Allah knows the truth; to Him shall we return.

---

[7] *Fikah*: Arabic grammar and jurisprudence.

XV

Now the words of the narrative turn to Haru, whose ruling monarch was Maharaja al-Diraja, the son of Sultan Sujak, who was descended from Perbata. It was related that Maharaja al-Diraja sent a mission to Pasai, with Raja Pahlawan as His Majesty's envoy. When he arrived in Pasai the royal dispatch was carried in a procession and brought to the audience hall. It was subsequently received by a courtier, who read the letter:

Please accept my greetings, My Lord.

And he read further:

Your younger brother brings his homage to My Lord, our elder · brother.

Raja Pahlawan interrupted, 'What is said is different from what is written in the letter.'
But the courtier continued:

My homage to My Lord, my elder brother.

Again, Raja Pahlawan interrupted, 'What is said is not written in the letter. It were better that I perish in Pasai, and not in Haru. If the letter is chewed by a dog, it will know of each word therein written.'

Yet the Pasaian continued to read. Raja Pahlawan was extremely riled. He ran amok, killing many of the Pasaians. As an act of vengeance,[1] the Pasaians slew Raja Pahlawan and all those who came with him from Haru. That was the reason why Pasai was a rival of Haru.

Soon Maharaja al-Diraja ordered the chief warrior of Pasai, Seri Indera, to ravage the territories of Melaka. In those times, there were villages from Tanjung Tuan to Jugra; those were the villages destroyed by the people of Haru. When news of the incident reached Sultan 'Alauddin Shah, His Majesty commanded that Paduka Tuan, the son of the Bendahara Paduka Raja, along with the Laksamana, Seri Bija al-Diraja, and all the warriors to accompany Paduka Tuan to intercept Haru's fleet. So Paduka Tuan and all the warriors soon departed.

The Melaka's fleet then sailed into the waters of Tanjung Tuan. There they met Haru's vessels, both sides crashing into each other in a din of war noises, sounding like it was the end of the world. But the Haru's armada was much bigger than Melaka's. For each vessel of the Seri Bija al-Diraja's, there were three of Haru's.

The weapons came like rain. Seri Bija al-Diraja's vessels were overwhelmed and sunk, all of their slaves jumped into the sea.

Meanwhile, in Seri Bija al-Diraja's vessel was also Tun Isak Berakah, the son of Tun Pikrama Wira, grandson of Paduka Tuan, and the great-grandson of the Bendahara Paduka Raja. But Tun Isak Berakah and the Seri Bija al-Diraja, were the only the ones who did not jump into the water, and defended their position in the boat. In the intervening time, the people of Haru commandeered half of the bows of their vessel.

Said Tun Isak to the Seri Bija al-Diraja, 'My Lord, let's run amok among the Haruans.'

The Seri Bija al-Diraja, replied, 'Be patient yet.'

---

[1] *Balas dendam*, to avenge, vengeance.

Soon the Haruans reached the main mast.

Tun Isak pleaded, 'Now, let's run amok.'

The Seri Bija al-Diraja, said, 'The time is not come yet.'

So, the Haruans came past the cabin.

Tun Isak again insisted, 'My Lord, let's run amok now.'

Seri Bija al-Diraja replied, 'Be patient yet, My Lord, the time is not appropriate.' Thus saying, the Seri Bija al-Diraja, approached the bridge.

Tun Isak said, '*Cheh* Damn you ! I thought Seri Bija al-Diraja was a man of courage; that is the reason why I chose his boat! Had I known that he is a coward, I would have gone with the Laksamana!'

Soon the Haruans came to the front of the awning. It was only then that Seri Bija al-Diraja appeared from under it.

Now, the Seri Bija al-Diraja, commanded Tun Isak, 'Encik Isak, let's run amok now. Now is the time!'

Tun Isak replied, 'Very well.'

Thus, Seri Bija al-Diraja and Tun Isak ran amok. The Haruans dispersed in different directions—some jumping overboard into the water and some seeking their own boats. They were followed by the Seri Bija al-Diraja, and Tun Isak, who boarded them; soon the Haruans were overcome. In the meantime, Bija al-Diraja's men, who had jumped into the water, returned.

The Seri Bija al-Diraja, and all the Melakan warriors again crashed into the Haruans. Their armada was dispersed and many of the vessels fled. The Melakans gave chase, once in a while crashing into them. Presently, the Haruans were seeking their King. When Maharaja al-Diraja heard that his armada was defeated, he was extremely angry.

Said he: 'If I were mounted on my elephant, Si Betung, and if no moat hinders my path, the whole of Melaka and the whole of Pasai, will I overrun. I will crash against their fortresses with my Si Betung!'

The Haruans were again driven out and they immediately departed. In the meantime, the Melakan armada arrived at the Dungun Port and secured their boats there. They disembarked and made for the river. There they found an old mountain billy goat. Mi Duzul thought it was a man. Caught by surprise he ran helter-skelter and fell. Then he stood up and ran again, breathless, trying to catch up with the many men. They were in an uproar seeing Mi Duzul running so fast.

One of them asked, 'What's happening, Mi Duzul?'

He replied, 'An old Haru man chased me and I ran as fast as I could. I ran and ran, and he kept pursuing me.'

After they heard his explanation, all of them disembarked, fully armed. However, when they arrived there, they only saw a billy goat, not the enemy. All of them had a big laugh.

They said, 'Damn Mi Duzul! We were all deceived by him!'

Soon, all of them returned to their vessel. In time, Haru's armada met Melaka's. They battled with a great din of noise. The arrows fell like heavy rain. The Melakans crashed against their enemies, overpowering them with their wooden spears. Eventually, the Haru's armada was defeated and their soldiers fled to the upper reaches of the river. Paduka Tuan and all the lords and warriors then returned to Melaka.

After a few days into their journey, Paduka Tuan and all the warriors arrived in Melaka and duly sought the audience of Sultan 'Alauddin. His Majesty was extremely pleased on hearing that Melaka had won the war. Subsequently he bestowed gifts on Paduka Tuan, the Laksamana, the Seri Bija al-Diraja and all the warriors, who were presented with suits of fine costumes.

In time the Seri Bija al-Diraja was deceased. He had two children; one was called Tun Kudu, entitled as Seri Bija al-Diraja, the other, Tun Bija al-Diraja, who was the father of Sang Setia.

After sometime, Sultan 'Alauddin ordered that his warriors prepare to invade Kampar; the Seri Nara al-Diraja was appointed its commander. When the preparations were complete, the Seri Nara al-Diraja, departed with Sang Setia, Sang Naya, Sang Guna and all the military chiefs. Ikhtiar Muluk escorted the Seri Nara al-Diraja.

When they arrived in Kampar, the Raja of Kampar, Maharaja Jaya was its King; he was descended from the King of Raja Pagar Ruyung Pekan Tuha.

After Maharaja Jaya received news that the Seri Nara al-Diraja was on his way to invade Kampar, he ordered his Vizier, Tun Damang, to gather all his subjects, and assemble with all their weapons. Thus, Tun Damang departed to gather all the subjects of the *negeri,* and to assemble and arm them. Very soon, the Seri Nara al-Diraja arrived and the Melakans landed. Maharaja Jaya, atop his elephant, expelled them; Tun Damang walked beside the animal, armed with a spear.

The two forces met and engaged in a fierce battle, some using spears, some slashing with their battle-axes, while others shot arrows. Many were injured on both sides, blood flowed freely on the battlefield as the Melakan forces launched a ferocious assault.

When Maharaja Jaya and Tun Damang surveyed the battlefield they both mounted an attack on the Melakans. Wherever they attacked, many lay dead—bodies were piled high. Thus, the Melakans fled to the water, except for the Seri Nara al-Diraja, and Ikhtiar Muluk, who were still standing erect, and not moving from their positions. On the other hand, Maharaja Jaya and Tun Damang also stood their ground with the people of Kampar, their arrows falling like rain.

The Seri Nara al-Diraja bowed and addressed Maharaja Jaya, 'My Lord, I would like to ask of you this little piece of ground on which I am standing. However, if you persist, I shall present you with this spear that is a gift of your elder brother.'

Then, Tun Damang stabbed Ikhtiar Muluk with his spear, piercing his shoulder. Ikhtiar Muluk grabbed at Tun Damang's head cloth.

Said he to the Seri Nara al-Diraja, 'My Lord, I am wounded.'

He was soon bandaged by the Seri Nara al-Diraja.

Next, Ikhtiar Muluk, armed with a bow, arrows and shield released an arrow which pierced through Tun Damang's ear. It immediately bled, and he fell under the elephant.

When Maharaja Jaya saw that Tun Damang was slain, His Majesty crashed his elephant, in order to keep the Seri Nara al-Diraja at a safe distance. But the Seri Nara al-Diraja in turn hurled his spear at Maharaja Jaya, piercing his chest, causing him to fall from the elephant. Thus, Maharaja Jaya was overcome.

When it was clear that Maharaja Jaya was dead and so too Tun Damang, the people of Kampar dispersed and were scattered over the battlefield. They were immediately pursued by the Melakans, who killed many of them while they were gathering the bodies of their compatriots and carrying them into the fortress. Shortly, the Melakans broke in, in large numbers. Not long afterwards, the Seri Nara al-Diraja, returned in victory.

In time, they arrived in Melaka. The Seri Nara al-Diraja sought the audience of Sultan 'Alauddin. His Majesty was extremely pleased that Kampar has been defeated and subsequently bestowed gifts on the Seri Nara al-Diraja and Ikhtiar Muluk. It was Ikhtiar Muluk who bore the father of Khoja Bulan, who bore Khoja Muhammad Shah, who was appointed a courtier with all the others, standing by the gallery.

Kampar was then given to the Seri Nara al-Diraja. It was the Seri Nara al-Diraja who was first appointed the Adipati of Kampar. In time, His Majesty instructed that he sail to Kampar to install his son, Raja Munawar Shah as King, and Seri Amar Diraja as his Vizier. The Seri Nara al-Diraja soon departed. Upon his arrival, he crowned the new king, with the title of Sultan Munawar Shah of Kampar. When he completed his assignment, the Seri Nara al-Diraja, returned to Melaka, again to seek His Majesty's audience to report his mission.

After a term of thirty-three years on the throne, the wheel of time turned further. His Majesty fell ill. When he felt that death was imminent, he asked that his son, Raja Mamat, be summoned, along with the senior officers of state. They all came to wait on him. He asked that the maids support him so that he might sit at a recline.[2]

Among those present were five who were asked to wait on him: firstly, the Bendahara; secondly, the Chief of the Treasury; thirdly, the Temenggung; fourthly, the Kadi, Munawar Shah; and fifthly, the Laksamana.

His Majesty began, 'My Lords, I feel that my life is coming to an end. When I am dead, please crown my son, Raja Mat, to succeed me.

---

[2]   *Berbaring*, recline, to rest.

You must care for him to the utmost of your abilities, just as you have shown your great love for me, that should also be your love for him. Should he err or is at fault, please be kind and forgive him, for he is but a boy.'

Listening to His Majesty's words, tears flowed down their cheeks involuntarily.

They approached His Majesty, 'May Allah increase your days, for we are not done being Your Majesty's servants. But should the flower wilts in your clasp, we shall make haste to do as Your Majesty has instructed, for we do not desire to be the subjects of other rajas.'

His Majesty was extremely happy to hear their pledges. He turned to look at his son, Raja Mamat.

Said Sultan 'Alauddin, 'My son, be reminded that this world is not the eternal one. All those who breathe today will, sometime, pass away, only our faith shall last forever. At my departure you must be a devout believer, seize not the possessions and rights that do not belong to you, for the fate of all your subjects is given into your trust. If they are in difficulties, you must quickly help them. If they are made victims, you must quickly and carefully investigate their cases, so that the after-world will not weigh heavy on you. The Prophet, *sallallahu 'alaihi wasallam*, has reminded us that those who tend to their flock will be questioned about the care they give it. That is, all the rajas will be questioned in the hereafter about the management of their subjects. It is for this reason that you must be just and fair, so that in the next world you will be protected by God. Furthermore, you must consult with all the prime ministers and all the chiefs, for though the kings may be wise and knowledgeable, if they do not consult with their officers, they will find no peace, and will not be able to deliver justice to all of their subjects. The rajas are like the fire, all the prime ministers, the firewood, for the fire without wood may not result in a flame. Meaning, your subjects are comparable to the roots of a tree, and the king its trunk, wherever there is no root the tree will not be able to stand upright. That is the metaphor of the king and his subjects. As concerns the Malays, if their sins be great, do not quickly put them to death, except when it is applicable to the laws of Allah, for all the Malays are your subjects, as is pronounced by the words of the Prophets: meaning, the servant is his master, if you slay him when he is innocent, your reign shall be stained. You should rule to earn the blessings of Allah.'

Soon after that, Sultan 'Alauddin was deceased, journeying from this impermanent world to the eternal one. Thus, his son, Raja Mamat, succeeded him on the throne. His title was Sultan Mahmud Shah. Sultan Mahmud Shah was extremely good-looking, no one was his compare.

His royal *keris* was minted in Melaka; it was three spans long, however, it was but a second weapon.

Once the Bendahara Putih said to the Seri Bija al-Diraja, 'My Lord, His Majesty willed that you should replace him.'

Seri Bija al-Diraja replied, 'I heard no such will.'

When Sultan Mahmud Shah heard the Seri Bija al-Diraja's word he remained quiet, but in his heart he bore a grudge against the Seri Bija al-Diraja.

Sultan Mahmud Shah bore three children, the boy was Sultan Ahmad, it was he who would succeed him on the throne, while the other two were girls.

It was related that Seri Rama had died, and his son had succeeded him, also with the title of Seri Rama. He was also the master of the elephants, his status similar to his father's. He had two boys, one with the title of Seri Nata, and another with the title of Tun Aria. Seri Nata fathered Tun Biajit Hitam, while Tun Aria fathered Tun Mamat, and in turn Tun Mamat fathered Tun Ishak Tun Pilu.

One day, the Seri Bija al-Diraja, did not sail down to Melaka from his province in the upper reaches of the river. It was only on the Idilfitri that he did. This caused Sultan Mahmud Shah to be annoyed with him.

Sultan Mahmud Shah enquired, 'Why was the Seri Bija al-Diraja late in coming? Are you ignorant of the customs of the palace?'

The Seri Bija al-Diraja, bowed his head and said, 'I am late in coming for I thought the month had not begun. I have been oblivious, except that Your Majesty will pardon me.'

Sultan Mahmud Shah said, 'We know that the Seri Bija al-Diraja does not like our rule.'

His Majesty soon ordered that Seri Bija al-Diraja be put to death.

Seri Bija al-Diraja said to his executioner, 'What is my sin towards His Majesty? Is it because of this trifle of an error that I am sentenced to death?'

All the words of the Seri Bija al-Diraja were relayed to Sultan Mahmud Shah.

His Majesty replied, 'If the Seri Bija al-Diraja does not know of his sin, show this letter to him. In that letter are listed four or five of them.'

After looking at the letter Seri Bija al-Diraja remained quiet. He was soon executed. After him, it was his son, Sang Setia Bentayan, who was given authority over Singa Pura.

* * *

One dark night, Sultan Mahmud Shah visited the house of a woman, Tun Dewi was her name. He found only Tun 'Ali there. So, Sultan Mahmud Shah returned while looking back at him. He noticed that Datuk Muar's grandfather was in his company. In his village of Kampung Tembaga, he was known as Tun Biajit, and in Kampung Kelang as Tun Isak.

So, Sultan Mahmud Shah took a betel leaf from its container and gave it to Tun Biajit.

In his heart Tun Biajit was puzzled,[3] 'What may be the reason that His Majesty has bestowed me with this betel leaf? In my mind, perhaps it is to command me to slay Tun 'Ali Sandang.'

In the days of old, the betel from the Sultan's container was an honourable gift, and not given to just anyone. So Tun Biajit returned to Tun Dewi's. There he stabbed Tun 'Ali Sandang, on his chest, killing him. After Tun 'Ali had been slain, Tun Biajit came to seek His

---

3   *Bingung,* perplexed, confused.

Majesty's audience. There was an uproar saying that Tun 'Ali Sandang was dead, killed by Tun Biajit.

Seriwa Raja was informed of the murder, for Tun 'Ali Sandang was family to him. He was extremely angry and ordered that Tun Biajit be waylaid and slain. But, in the meantime, Sultan Mahmud Shah asked him to flee and he chose to sail to Pasai.

But Tun Biajit would not make obeisance to the Raja of Pasai.

Said he, 'This Biajit will not make obeisance to anyone other than Sultan Mahmud Shah.'

Tun Biajit then journeyed to Haru; there too he would not bow in obeisance to the Raja of Haru. Subsequently, he was on his way to Berunai, and there too he would not show his allegiance to the Raja of Berunai.

However, before long, Tun Biajit married the Raja's daughter. There he begat children and grandchildren, starting a large family. That was the reason that Datuk Muar had many relatives.

Tun Biajit reasoned. 'Melaka is my homeland; it is there that I shall end my days.'

Therefore, he returned to Melaka. Upon his arrival, he sought the audience of Sultan Mahmud Shah. His Majesty offered him his victuals. When the meal was over, Sultan Mahmud Shah embraced and kissed Tun Biajit; he asked that the head cloth be formally wrapped around Tun Biajit's head and ordered that he be taken to Seriwa Raja, for, in His Majesty reasoning, if we have bound him and sent him to Seriwa Raja, he would not be slain by him.'

It happened that, at that moment, Seriwa Raja was on his elephant. Tun Biajit approached, escorted by the Raja's servant.

He pleaded on his behalf, 'His Majesty said, this is Tun Biajit, if he has committed any sin, His Majesty asks for My Lord's forgiveness.'

On seeing him, Seriwa Raja promptly gouged Tun Biajit's head with his elephant goad, bashing it in and killing him.

The Sultan's servant returned to report Tun Biajit's death, his head bashed in by Seriwa Raja's iron goad.

Sultan Mahmud Shah remained quiet as he listened to the servant's report, for he loved Seriwa Raja very much. In those days, four people were his favourites: firstly, Seriwa Raja; secondly, Tun 'Umar; thirdly, Hang 'Isha; fourthly, Hang Hasan Cengang.

It was narrated that when Sultan Mahmud Shah was to depart to sport at sea, His Majesty would ask that Seriwa Raja be summoned. Sultan Mahmud Shah would wait for him at the harbour, but he would not appear, for it was the habit of Seriwa Raja that, whenever he was summoned by the King's servant, he would ascend the stairs of his house and take a nap.

However, when he was awakened, he would raise himself, attend to his toilet and take a bath. When that was accomplished, he would take his meal, dress himself, twice or thrice changing his clothes. However, if he was not satisfied, he would change them again. When this had been completed, he would put on his headgear. That too went through the same complicated process. If it was not just right, he would put it right. So too with the shawl, going through fourteen or fifteen changes— when it did not satisfy him, he would change it all over again. It was only after that that he would depart, reaching the threshold. However, he would then return to ask his wife's opinion, 'Dear, please remark on the incongruences in my dressing.'

If his wife did not approve of his appearance, he would alter it. Then only would he descend the stairs and proceed to the yard; and once again return to sit on the swing. It was only when he was alerted by the servant, did he depart to pay His Majesty his obeisance.

If His Majesty wanted Seriwa Raja to come quickly, he would ask Tun Isak Berakah to fetch him. When Tun Isak arrived at his house, he would say, 'My Lord is summoned.'

Seriwa Raja replied, 'That's very well.'

So Seriwa Raja would ascend the stairs to the house. As Tun Isak was well acquainted with the habits of Seriwa Raja, he would request for a mat, so he could lie down for a nap in the front gallery.

Then Tun Isak would call out, 'Please tell My Lord that I would like some rice, for I am famished.'

So Tun Isak would then be served.

After his meal, Tun Isak would demand, 'I am thirsty, please make me something to drink.'

Seriwa Raja complained, 'When it is Isak who comes to fetch me, he makes all kinds of demands. Quick, give me my coat and sarong!'

So Seriwa Raja would dress hurriedly, putting on his coat, headgear, *keris* and shawl, and then descend the stairs to seek His Majesty's audience.

All the habits of Seriwa Raja were tolerable to His Majesty, for he treasured him deeply.

It was well known that Seriwa Raja was much loved by the Sultan. One day, His Majesty summoned Seriwa Raja, Tun 'Umar, Hang 'Isa and Hang Hasan Cengang. Soon, all the four of them were in attendance.

His Majesty asked of them, 'What do My Lords wish from us? Ask so that we can bestow them on you. We shall not refrain from presenting anything to you.'

Seriwa Raja was the first to come forward.

These were his words, 'Your Majesty, if it pleases you, I would like to be the Captain of the Elephants.'

Sultan Mahmud Shah agreed, 'We grant your request; however, we are quite helpless as Seri Rama still holds that post. How can we take it away from him? We may not dismiss him for he has done no wrong. When Seri Rama is gone, Seriwa Raja will become the Captain of the Elephants.'

After him came Tun 'Umar, bowing low, 'My Lord, if it pleases you, I would like to be the Admiral.'

Sultan Mahmud Shah replied, 'It's agreed, but the Laksamana still holds that post, thus we are unable to take it away from him. Though, we would like to dismiss him, he has done us no wrong. When he is no longer around, we shall appoint Tun 'Umar to be the Admiral.'

After observing that his two colleagues had not been bestowed any post, Hang 'Isa Pantas and Hang Hasan Cengang considered again what they would request of the Sultan.

Sultan Mahmud Shah addressed Hang 'Isa and Hang Hasan, 'Now, both of you, what would you request of us?'

Hang 'Isa approached His Majesty, 'My Lord, if it pleases Your Majesty, I would ask of you about thirteen *tahils* of gold, four betel containers, a scarlet silk fabric and finally, a chest.'

In a second, he was granted all that he had requested.

Then, it was Hang Hasan Cengang's turn to come forward.

He said, 'Your Majesty, I would like to request for some twelve or thirteen female buffaloes and twelve or thirteen pieces of land to be planted as orchards.'

Those too were bestowed on him.

It came to pass that Sultan Mahmud Shah had an affair with the wife of Tun Biajit, the son of the Laksamana. At that moment, he (Tun Biajit) was not at home, as he was in his quarters. One evening, His Majesty visited Tun Biajit's house. When it was almost morning, he returned to the palace. On his return, he met Tun Biajit, who had just disembarked from his boat, accompanied by his many companions. Although there were not many in His Majesty's company, Tun Biajit realized that Sultan Mahmud Shah had just left his house. If he had wanted to slay him at that moment, it was indeed possible. However, he was a Malay servant, bound by his loyalty to the King and would not alter that loyalty.

He merely trained his spear as a warning, saying, 'Hai, Sultan Mahmud Shah, is this how you treat your servants? It's a pity that you are my King. If you weren't, I would hurl this spear into your chest.'

All the Raja's servants were duly apprehensive.

His Majesty said, 'Do not be angry, for he has spoken the truth. We have erred,[4] he should have slain us. But the Malay servant does not alter his loyalty, thus his behaviour.'

His Majesty returned to the palace. Meanwhile, Tun Biajit divorced his wife and he would not attend to the Sultan or work for His Majesty. The Sultan persuaded Biajit, and sent him his secondary

---

[4] *Bersalah*, err, to make a mistake.

wife, Tun Iram Sundari was her name. Tun Biajit took her, however, he still would not come to the palace.

* * *

The story now turns to the episode of Seriwa Raja, who was preparing to celebrate his wedding to the daughter of Kadi Munawar Shah, the granddaughter of Maulana Yusuf.

In time, Kadi Munawar Shah initiated the celebrations. At a propitious moment, Seriwa Raja approached his betrothed's residence, mounted on Sultan Mahmud Shah's elephant, Balidamesai, in a procession. Tun 'Abdul Karim, the son of Kadi Munawar Shah, sat at the head of the elephant, Tun Zainal 'Abidin shared the howdah, while Seriwa Raja himself sat at the rear. Thus, the procession progressed to Kadi Munawar Shah's, who was waiting in his village with firecrackers and ceremonial bomb throwers. His gate was locked.

Kadi Munawar Shah said, 'If Seriwa Raja is able to enter my village, then I shall marry him to my daughter.'

When he has come to the gates, Kadi Munawar Shah instructed that the firecrackers and fireworks be torched. The din of the fireworks melded with the yells and joyous ovations, and finally into the music. So loud was the ruckus that Balidamesai fled in panic. Not all of Tun 'Abdul Karim's commands could stop him. When Seriwa Raja noticed how chaotic the situation was becoming, he addressed Tun 'Abdul Karim, 'Brother, please move to the rear, and let me come to the front.'

So Tun 'Abdul Karim moved to the middle and allowed Seriwa Raja to come to the fore. At that moment, Balidamesai turned its head and crashed into the gate of Kadi Munawar Shah's fence. Although many threw firecrackers, it still did not heed their warning and lumbered into the yard. Eventually, it halted at Kadi Munawar Shah's gallery and Seriwa Raja duly jumped down on to it.

Thus, Kadi Munawar Shah betrothed his daughter, in the presence of Sultan Mahmud Shah. After the rites were pronounced, a feast followed. Soon after, His Majesty departed for the palace.

It was related that Kadi Munawar Shah was a master of the *beladau*, the tiny curved dagger, as he had studied under the Raja of the Moluccas when the King visited Melaka during the reign of Sultan 'Alauddin.

Kadi Munawar Shah sat before an audience in a veranda covered with trellises.

Kadi Munawar Shah would address those who came to seek his company, 'How many of these trellises do you want me to extract?'

They replied, 'Two pieces, My Lord.'

Kadi Munawar slashed at two of the trellises, cutting them clean. If they had requested three, then he would cut three of them. However numerous their requests were, he would faithfully cut them.

The months passed after Seriwa Raja's marriage to the daughter of Kadi Munawar Shah. They bore a son, Tun 'Umar—he was dubbed Seri Petam, and referred to as Datuk Rambat. Seri Petam had many children, the oldest was Tun Daud; he was the Lord of the Upper Reaches. There was another boy, Tun 'Ali Sandang, who became the father of Datuk Muar. He had another child, a girl, Tun Bentan was her name, she was the mother of Tun Mai; and another still, Tun Hamzah, the father of Munawar; lastly, Tun Tukak who died in Patani. Tun Tukak, was the father of Tun 'Umar. There were indeed many more, however we shall not mention all their names.

It is common knowledge that Seriwa Raja was very knowledgeable in the care and supervision of elephants and horses.

There was once a silvery horse which he owned, that he loved dearly. A part of his veranda was reserved for it, and that was where it would be secured. If anyone wanted to borrow it for a ride in the moonlight, Seriwa Raja would give his consent.

He would ride two or three rounds, and then return it to its stable. Isak Berakah too was allowed to borrow it and take it for two or three rounds around the circuit before it was brought back to its stable.

Tun Isak Berakah said to Seriwa Raja's boys, 'Please tell My Lord that I am thirsty.'

So Seriwa Raja granted his request. When he finished his drink, Tun Isak Berakah said to Seriwa Raja, 'Now I shall take this horse for a spin.'

Seriwa Raja replied, 'As you please.'

Tun Isak Berakah rode it for two or three rounds and then brought it home. Tun Isak said to Seriwa Raja's boys, 'Tell My Lord that I am hungry, and request for some rice.'

So, he was given some rice by Seriwa Raja. When he had finished, he again took the horse for another two or three rounds and brought it back. After that, he requested of Seriwa Raja things not easily obtained or given.

Seriwa Raja complained, 'When Isak comes, so many are his requests. Say to him, "Go ride the horse as long as you wish, the whole night through even." Thus, Tun Isak Berakah rode the horse for all the hours of the night.

One day, it so happened that there came a Pathan, who was very knowledgeable in the breeding and sports of horses. Sultan Mahmud Shah instructed that he be brought to Seriwa Raja. When he arrived at Seriwa Raja's, the servant said, 'My Lord, on the orders of His Majesty, I bring this gentleman who is an expert in equestrian sports.'

Seriwa Raja asked the Pathan, 'Does the khoja know how to ride horses?'

The Pathan replied, 'I do, My Lord.'

Seriwa Raja ordered, 'Then please take a ride on my horse.'

So, the horse was saddled as instructed and he mounted the animal and urged it to move forward.

Said Seriwa Raja, 'Khoja, the whip.'

So, the Pathan whipped it; and immediately he was unceremoniously thrown off its back.

Seriwa Raja asked, 'Hai, khoja, what happened?' Seriwa Raja then called out to his son, 'Umar!'

When Tun 'Umar arrived, Seriwa Raja said to him, 'Whip the horse, my boy.'

When Tun 'Umar whipped the horse, to the astonishment of the Pathan, the horse began to dance.

It was related that 'Umar was much loved by Sultan Mahmud Shah. It had been foretold that he would not die at his enemy's hands, which was the reason why he was very eccentric and fearless of his adversaries.

There was a son of Seri Bija al-Diraja, Datuk Bongkok, who was extremely brave. And there was Hang 'Isa Pantas, who was quick in everything that he did. One day, there was a log in the Melaka River, afloat and continually turning. If one stepped on it, it would sink about fifteen inches deep. However, if Hang 'Isa Pantas walked on it, from the left, it would turn right, and from the right it would turn to the left; thus, he would arrive on the other bank, his feet quite dry.

Now, it was related that Hang Hasan Cengang married the daughter of Hang Usuh. At the end of the ceremony, they sat before each other, consuming their ritual first meal as man and wife. After three handfuls, the rice and the curry were about to be cleared.

But Hang Hasan Cengang restrained the hands of the servant, 'Do not take it away yet, the lady is about to finish, but I still want to continue eating, for I have spent a lot on this marriage!'

All the women who heard him laughed but Hang Hasan Cengang continued to dine. It was only when he had finished that the curry was taken away and he went into the bridal chamber.

It was also related that on one occasion Sultan Mahmud Shah was on his way to study the sciences under Kadi Yusuf. But the Kadi seemed to have been possessed. If someone flew a kite that passed over his roof, he would instruct that it be brought down with a sling. When they had retrieved it, he would ask them to reel it in, saying, 'How disrespectful, passing over my roof.'

Those were the ways of Kadi Yusuf, however, he was no longer the Kadi after that. It was his son, Munawar Shah, who succeeded him. One day, His Majesty rode an elephant to the Maulana's, accompanied by his royal entourage. As he arrived outside his fence the Sultan's servant called out to the Maulana's guard, 'Tell Maulana Yusuf, His Majesty has come.'

The Maulana was duly informed. He replied, 'Close the door! What business has His Majesty that he comes to my humble dwelling?'

When the words of Maulana Yusuf were repeated to Sultan Mahmud Shah, His Majesty returned to the palace. When evening had fallen, His Majesty asked his servant to return to the Maulana's. When there was no one around, His Majesty went by himself, accompanied only by a boy. The Sultan carried his book of scriptures himself.

As he arrived at his outer door, His Majesty said to the guard, 'Tell Maulana Yusuf, Fakir Mahmud has come.'

The door was opened, for it was right that a fakir came to the house of another fakir. Thus, Maulana Yusuf presently greeted the Sultan and invited him to take a seat. That was how Sultan Mahmud Shah studied under Maulana Yusuf.

* * *

After some time, words were related of the good looks of Raja Zainal 'Abidin, the Sultan's brother. No one was his compare in these times. His looks were without blemish, his conduct was extremely commendable—agreeable, sweet, deft and quick. If he wore a sarong, he would wear it at a slant and with its end hanging down, as he wanted it to be of the best of possible styles.

Raja Zainal 'Abidin had a horse that he indulged in extravagantly. Ambangan was its name. He kept it quite close to his bed, making a special room for it. It was there that it was secured. He would wake it up twice or thrice during the night.

When Raja Zainal 'Abidin went riding, it would also be fully decked. After he had completed its dressing, he would rub fragrances onto the horse's hide. Only then did the prince ride her. The townspeople would be full of excitement seeing the prince riding by. All the women, wives and maidens about to be married, all of them rushed forward to catch a glimpse of Raja Zainal 'Abidin. They watched him from their doors, some from the latticework, some from their windows, and yet some others from the gables, some even denting the walls or climbing their fences. Their offerings to

Raja Zainal 'Abidin were so numerous that he could no longer catch them. Ripe betel amounted to tens of containers, that is, besides the lover's betel. There were so many of them. Hundreds of containers of fragrances and perfumes—the prepared incenses that came with bouquets of frangipani would make for many baths. Jasmines that had been picked filled many trays, and so were the posies. However, Raja Zainal 'Abidin would only retain what he liked, the rest he would give to all the young men. Thus, the *negeri* was tainted with sin and evil.

When Sultan Mahmud Shah heard the news of Raja Zainal 'Abidin's conduct, he was enraged. But he kept it to himself alone. His Majesty asked that all the servants whom he trusted be summoned.

He asked of them, 'Who among you is capable of secretly slaying Zainal 'Abidin?'

No one spoke. A guard, Hang Berkat, by name, was the only one willing to undertake the job.

Sultan Mahmud Shah said to him, 'If you are able to do as you say, I shall consider you as family.'

Thus, when evening had fallen and it was all quiet, and everyone was asleep, Hang Berkat went to Raja Zainal's house. When he got there, he climbed into the chamber where the horse was kept. Raja Zainal was asleep. Hang Berkat stabbed him right through his chest. When he felt his wound, he groped for the goad, but could not find it. In pain, his body tossed up and down like a hen slaughtered. Soon Hang Berkat descended and departed.

Raja Zainal was dead. There was an uproar, and the people were saying that Raja Zainal was killed, slain by a thief. Their excitement reached His Majesty's ears.

Sultan Mansur Shah called out, 'I am here under the palace!'

Hang Berkat continued, 'We are all here, Your Majesty, the four or five of us.'

Sultan Mansur Shah enquired, 'What is that clamour out there?'

Hang Berkat replied, 'Your servant has no knowledge of it.'

Sultan Mansur Shah ordered him, 'Go and take a look.'

After he had seen it, he reported to the Sultan, 'It seems your brother, Raja Zainal, has been slain. It's not clear whether a thief has done the deed.'

Sultan Mahmud Shah knew that Hang Berkat had slain Raja Zainal. His Majesty continued, 'Go and gather all of my servants.'

However, all the officers of state came along too.

Soon Sultan Mansur Shah departed to visit Raja Zainal. When it was daylight again, his brother was buried according to the royal rites accorded to a Raja.

After that, His Majesty returned to the palace.

After some time, Hang Berkat was bestowed the title of Sang Sura, he was a favourite of the King.

* * *

It so happened that the wife of Sang Sura desired Sang Guna. Sang Sura came to know of the affair, so Sang Guna was stopped on his way. Sang Guna was known to be a man of good bearing, his body was tough and strong. His voice was manly. However, Sang Sura's was mature, though of slight build. News of the affair came to the Sultan's ears (His Majesty dearly loved Sang Guna as he was no ordinary person, and he was the one who first minted the Melaka *keris* that is two and half spans long). But Sultan Mahmud Shah also favoured Sang Sura. Therefore, he was in a dilemma. He asked that Sang Sura be summoned. When he was present, he took him to a quiet place and said to Sang Sura, 'Is there something you wish from us?'

Sang Sura replied, 'If there is one, I shall ask for it from Your Majesty and shall not detain myself from expressing it. Even this brain inside my head belongs to Your Majesty.'

Sultan Mahmud spoke, 'I heard that you waylaid Guna; if you have any love for me, I request that you desist. I ask repeatedly of you to stay away from him.'

Sang Sura was rolling up his sleeves when he heard Sultan Mahmud's command.

He said, 'My Lord does not feel the shame that I feel. Meanwhile wasn't I the one who removed yours?'

Sultan Mahmud Shah replied, 'Whatever you wish to have, we shall give it to you, but we do not consent that you intercept Sang Guna. We shall not allow him to leave his house to walk freely hither and thither, and sport with all his friends. If we have need of him, we shall summon him and then dismiss him after that.'

Sang Sura replied, 'Very well, My Lord, your words are my command, for I am servant to Your Majesty, and if I do not obey your words then I am no servant of yours.'

Thus, Sang Sura no longer waylaid Sang Guna after that. Meanwhile, Sang Guna was not permitted by His Majesty to freely move here and there and to sport with his young friends. However, if he was ordered to accompany His Majesty, he would be summoned, then he was asked to return home.

One day, when Sultan Mahmud heard that Sang Guna was standing at his door, there came a servant to rebuke him.

Said Sang Guna, 'Rather than be punished in this manner, it's better that I be tied and surrendered to Sang Sura and be killed.'

Allah knows the truth; to Him shall we return.

XVI

The narrative now turns to Sultan Munawar Shah, the Raja of Kampar, who had recently passed away. He had a son by the name of Raja 'Abdullah.

In time, Raja 'Abdullah came to pay homage to Melaka. Upon his arrival, Sultan Mahmud took him as his son-in-law, to be married to his daughter, the sister of Raja Ahmad. His Majesty instructed that Raja 'Abdullah be crowned in Kampar. Thus Sultan 'Abdullah returned home as King.

In time, the Bendahara Putih died. Sultan Mahmud Shah accorded him funeral services as was customary for all the Bendaharas. After the funeral rites were completed, Sultan Mahmud Shah assembled all those who were qualified to be Bendahara: firstly, Tun Zainal 'Abidin; secondly, Tun Telanai; thirdly, Paduka Tuan; fourthly, the Seri Nara al-Diraja; fifthly, Seriwa Raja; sixthly, Seri Maharaja; seventhly, Abu Sa'id; eighthly, Tun 'Abdul; ninthly, Tun Bijaya Maha Menteri; all nine of them stood in a row before Sultan Mahmud.

Sultan Mahmud Shah asked, 'Who among My Lords shall be the Bendahara? Who is the most suitable?'

Paduka Tuan spoke first, 'Your Majesty, all nine of us gathered here are eligible to be the Bendahara; whoever is chosen by His Majesty, he is the one who will be the Bendahara.'

At that moment, His Majesty's mother, who was listening from behind the door, suggested to his son, 'To my mind, it's Tun Mutahir who should be the Bendahara.'

So, Sultan Mahmud Shah repeated her suggestion, 'Uncle Mutahir should assume the post.'

All those present agreed with His Majesty to appoint the Seri Maharaja. This was followed with a ceremony of bestowal of suits of costumes, as was the custom of old, and each of them was also presented with a complete set of *karas bandan*[1] chests. When one was appointed the Bendahara or the Chief of the Treasury or the Temenggung or a minister of the various portfolios, he was bestowed with a complete set of the betel container and accompanying implements, but not the *kobak*[2] container. The Bendahara, however, was presented with a set of the chests and also bottles of ink. However, the Temenggung would be presented with a spear swaddled in yellow cloth.

After Seri Maharaja was appointed the Bendahara, Melaka became even more prosperous and populous, for the Bendahara Seri Maharaja was extremely just and generous. He was also very considerate in the affairs of the merchants and traders, and exemplary in his deportment.

As concerns the departure of vessels from the west—which had Melaka as their destination—when they were about to depart, the captains would praise the Prophet. When this was completed, they would say, 'Greetings to the city of Melaka, the needle bananas, the water of Bukit China and the Bendahara Seri Maharaja.'

And the sailors would respond, 'People in the breeze, old folks in the breeze.'

The Bendahara Seri Maharaja, had many children. The oldest was Tun Hasan, who replaced him as the Temenggung. He was handsome and always cordial.

---

[1] *Karas bandan*, says Wilkinson: possibly a type of betel container made of wood. The context in each case suggests that *karas* was some sort of chest, the upper tray of which housed a betel set, while the lower compartment was used for other valuables.

[2] *Kobak*: most probably a container or a *gobek* 'betel pounder', to pound the leaves and the nuts.

As was the custom of those days, the Temenggung would arrange the seating of guests in the audience hall: his men would sport the sarong at a slant and a shawl along with a headdress called *halaman* adorned with aigrettes and tassels.

He would walk along the length of the audience hall ushering guests to their places, pointing to them with his fan, like a singer dancing. It was related that Tun Hasan Temenggung was the first person to lengthen the Malay ceremonial coat.

Tun Hasan Temenggung had a son, Tun 'Ali was his name.

It happened that once the Bendahara Seri Maharaja was being attended to. He said to all those who had come to seek his presence, 'Who is better, Hasan or I?'

They bowed and said, 'The datuk is better than his son.'

Seri Maharaja rejoined, 'My Lords are all mistaken, for I have glasses over my eyes. Si Hasan is better, for he is young, but I am better-looking!'

So, all of them shouted, 'It is true as the datuk has spoken!'

Seri Maharaja was naturally handsome and also liked to use cosmetics. He would change his clothes seven times a day. He owned a thousand accessories of all shapes, readily-tied headdresses around their blocks, which totalled twenty or thirty—all of which he used. He also had a full-length mirror.

When the Bendahara Seri Maharaja was dressing, after securing the sarong, he would then put on the coat, then the *keris*, then the shawl. After that he would ask his wife's opinion, 'My dear, which headdress would go well with this sarong?'

His ladyship would reply, 'That headdress would suit it well.'

Whatever his wife suggested he would follow to the letter.

There was a son of the Bendahara Seri Maharaja, Tun Biajit Ruqat was his name, and there was also another, named Tun Lela Wangsa. His daughter was Tunggal, titled Tun Lela Wangsa, she was betrothed to the Orang Kaya Tun Abu Sait, the son of Seri Udana, who gave birth to Orang Kaya Tun Hasan.

In the history of Melaka's Bendaharas, Seri Maharaja was most renowned. Whenever he was in the audience hall and being attended to, he would not step down from his dais, even if princes came before him. Instead, he would beckon them with his finger and invite them to ascend and find their seats. The only exception he made was when the crown prince paid him a visit. However, if it was the Raja of Pahang, his highness would ascend to sit beside the Bendahara Seri Maharaja. The Seri Nara al-Diraja, Tun Tahir, the elder brother of the Bendahara, was also the Chief of the Treasury.

The Seri Nara al-Diraja had five children, three boys: Tun 'Ali, Tun Hamzah, and Tun Mahmud; and two girls, Tun Kudu, who was good-looking, and was married to Sultan Mahmud Shah, and was much loved by His Majesty. His Majesty instructed that all of the maids and courtiers address her as 'My lady, the Datuk'; however, all his family members would address her as 'Datuk Putih'.

Tun 'Abdul, the younger brother of the Bendahara Seri Maharaja also bore many children. Some boys and some girls—one of the girls was married to Orang Kaya Tun Rana, and gave birth to Tun Hidup Panjang Datuk Jawa; and another, Tun Minda, was adopted by the Seri Nara al-Diraja.

* * *

It so happened that once the Pangeran of Surabaya, Patih Adam by name, came to pay his obeisance to Melaka. He was bestowed with gifts of fine attire and was invited to take his place on the same level as the ministers. It so happened that one day Patih Adam sat by Seri Maharaja's front veranda. At that time, Tun Minda was but a little girl, just learning to walk. She ran before the Seri Nara al-Diraja.

Said the Seri Nara al-Diraja to Patih Adam, 'Listen to my daughter. She wants to have you as her husband.'

Patih Adam bowed low in obeisance, saying, '*Inggih*, yes.'

In time the season to return to Jawa had come, and Patih Adam respectfully sought leave of Sultan Mahmud Shah.

His Majesty presented him with fine fabrics and other gifts. Patih Adam then bought a slave girl and freed her (she was the same age and size as Tun Minda) and brought her back to Surabaya.

Upon his arrival, he carefully took care of the girl. In time, she grew into an adult of marriageable age.

Soon Patih Adam made preparations to sail to Melaka. He chose forty children from good noble families. When all the preparations were complete, he set sail. Upon his arrival, he went to seek the audience of the Seri Nara al-Diraja.

He said, 'I have come to claim My Lord's promise, to marry me to your daughter.'

Seri Nara al-Diraja replied, 'No, I did not make you a promise, My Lord.'

Patih Adam reminded him, 'Did My Lord not say to me, when your daughter was running in front of you, 'Patih Adam, listen to my daughter, she wants to have My Lord as her husband?'

The Seri Nara al-Diraja, replied, 'It's true that I uttered those words, but I was but jesting with My Lord.'

Patih Adam replied, 'Is it an attribute among the nobility to make fun of people?'

After that Patih Adam returned to his residence.

In his heart he decided he would rape Tun Minda. Tun Minda had grown into an adult, with a house all to herself. Patih Adam bribed all the guards of the Seri Nara al-Diraja, with gold, saying to them, 'Let me and my forty lads enter the residence of Tun Minda.'

The guards allowed him to enter for they were blinded by the glitter of gold, their loyalty had vanished. This is echoed by the words *Ali karramallah wajhahu*, meaning: 'It is useless to be loyal to people who in themselves have no self-respect.'

Thus, one night, Patih Adam and his forty chosen companions ascended the stairs of Tun Minda's residence. There was much uproar.

Presently the Seri Nara al-Diraja was informed; he was extremely angry and ordered that his people be assembled. They came with all their weapons and surrounded Tun Minda's residence. Patih Adam just sat beside Tun Minda; he placed his thigh over hers. Then he loosened his waist cloth and tied a half of it to Tun Minda, and the other half to himself. His *keris* was unsheathed.

Many were those who surrounded the house. Their weapons looked like they were arranged in overlapping circles. Immediately, the Javanese proceeded to defend themselves; however, all forty of them died.

Patih Adam said, '*Punapa karsa andeka dening priyayi purnika kabeh sampun pejah.* What shall my plans be now, now that all my followers have been slain?'[3]

He continued, '*Dimene kang sampun pejah kabeh, ingsun putra dalem iki belane sinpadani.* It does not matter if all of them are killed, I have this maiden, she is all that I want.'[4]

The Melakans were intent on slaying Patih Adam.

He said, 'If you kill me, I will kill the daughter of the Seri Nara al-Diraja.'

His words and conduct were immediately conveyed to her father.

The Seri Nara al-Diraja responded, 'Do not kill him, for fear that my daughter will be slain. In my heart, even if all of Java is killed, it is not equal to my daughter's life.'

Hence, Patih Adam was spared. He was then married to Tun Minda.

It was related that while he was in Melaka, Patih Adam was never separated from Tun Minda, for even the length of a finger. Wherever they went, they went together.

When the season to return to Java came, Patih Adam sought leave of the Seri Nara al-Diraja and asked for permission to take Tun Minda with him. The old minister gave him his consent. Then, Patih Adam sought the audience of Sultan Mahmud Shah. His Majesty bestowed on him a gift of a complete suit of clothes.

Soon after that, Patih Adam sailed to Surabaya. After several days at sea, they arrived in the harbour.

---

[3] *Punapa karsa andeka dening priyayi purnika kabeh sampun pejah.* Meaning, what are your plans now, now that all your followers have been slaind?

[4] *Dimene kang sampun pejah kabeh, ingsun putra dalem iki belane sinpadani.* Meaning, it does not matter if all of them are killed, I have this maiden, she is all that I want.

With Tun Minda, Patih Adam bore a boy, they named him Tun
Husin. He was appointed the Pangeran[5] of Surabaya.

Allah knows the truth; to Him shall we return.

---

[5]   *Pangeran,* prince.

XVII

The narrative now turns to the Raja of Kedah who had journeyed to Melaka to request the installation *nobat*. On his arrival he was given a position comparable to a minster. Numerous were the gifts presented to him.

One day, the Bendahara Seri Maharaja was in his gallery, attended to by his people. Tun Hasan Temenggung and all the ministers were present. Soon, the midday meal was served to the Bendahara Seri Maharaja. As was the custom of the palace, everyone waited for the Bendahara Seri Maharaja to finish his lunch, and only after that did those present dine. That was how it was in the days of old.

It so happened that when the Bendahara Seri Maharaja was at his meal, the Raja of Kedah arrived. The Bendahara invited him to take a seat with Tun Hasan Temenggung. When Seri Maharaja had finished his betel condiments, the remainder of his meal was duly taken by Tun Hasan Temenggung and shared with all the ministers.

Tun Hasan Temenggung invited the Raja of Kedah, 'My Lord, let's dine.'

The Raja agreed, 'Let's.'

The Bendahara said, 'Please do not dine on my leftovers.'

The Raja of Kedah replied, 'It is of no consequence, for My Lord, the Bendahara, is my senior in age.'

So, the Raja of Kedah, Tun Hasan Temenggung and all the ministers consumed the rest of the Bendahara's meal. After that the betel preparations were served and they partook of them.

Time passed. The Raja of Kedah had been in Melaka for some time, so he requested leave of Sultan Mahmud Shah. The Sultan bestowed on him the *nobat*, and along with it a full suit of robes. After which, the Raja of Kedah of returned to his *negeri* and was ceremonially installed there.

There was a minister of His Majesty, Tun Perpatih Hitam, a descendant of the family of Tun Jana Buga Dendang. He in turn had a son, Tun Husin, who was extremely exemplary in his conduct and manners.

Said Tun Husin, 'If anyone speaks evil of my father, I shall run amok.'

On that fateful day, Tun Perpatih Hitam was discussing a matter with a trader. Soon after that he related it to the Bendahara. At that moment, the Laksamana was present, for it was the custom of the court of the Bendahara that whenever the Laksamana was deliberating cases at hand with the Temenggung, he was not separated from the Bendahara. If there was anyone disrespectful towards him, it was the Laksamana who would slay him. If there was anyone who deserved to be put in the stocks, it was the task of the Laksamana to arrest him. Those were the customs of the Melaka of old.

After Tun Perpatih Hitam was summoned by the Bendahara Seri Maharaja, Tun Husin, Tun Perpatih Hitam's son, came to join his father. However, when Tun Perpatih Hitam noticed that Tun Husin had come armed with a long *keris*, in his heart, he thought, 'Might it be true as told of Tun Husin before this?'

Tun Perpatih Hitam then rose, kicking the mat aside and said, 'What kind of a minister puts someone on trial in this manner?'

The Laksamana promptly unsheathed his *keris* and said, 'Why is My Lord showing disrespect by kicking away the mat in the presence of the Bendahara?'

He immediately slashed at him, while those present unsheathed their weapons and stabbed at Tun Perpatih Hitam. Although the

Bendahara repeatedly bade them to desist from violence, it was to no avail, they continued to stab at him. Soon Tun Perpatih Hitam was dead. When Tun Husin saw that his father has been slain, he unsheathed his *keris* to avenge him.

The Laksamana spoke, 'It looks as though you are intent on being treasonous,[1] Tun Husin!' And Tun Husin was also stabbed, he died there. The Laksamana soon sought the audience of Sultan Mahmud Shah and related all that had happened.

His Majesty said, 'If the Laksamana had not slain him at that moment, we would have slain him afterwards, for he was in want of respect in the presence of the Bendahara, and it seems in our presence too.' Sultan Mahmud Shah then bestowed gifts of robes on the Laksamana.

Allah knows the truth; to Him shall we return.

---

[1] *Pengkhianatan*, treason, betrayal.

XVIII

The chronicle turns to the Maharaja of Merlung, who was the Raja of Inderagiri and had just departed this life in Melaka. He had a son, Raja Nara Singa, whose mother was the daughter of the late Raja of Melaka. It was he who was given authority over the people of Inderagiri. In those times, the children of the lords of Inderagiri were often summoned by the lords of Melaka. They were sometimes asked to carry them when they went hither and thither. After one had been carried, another would come to ask that he too be ferried over the muddy patches in the street. Thus, the people of Inderagiri were unhappy with the shabby treatment meted out to them. So they came to seek the audience of Raja Nara Singa.

They said, 'Your Majesty, we come to seek leave to return to Inderagiri, for we cannot endure living here. We are treated like servants.'

Raja Nara Singa agreed, 'Very well.' So Raja Nara Singa approached Sultan Mahmud Shah, who was then being attended to by several people.

When his turn came, Raja Nara Singa bowed, saying, 'Your Majesty, with your blessings we would like to request to return to Inderagiri, which you have bestowed on me, although I am yet to lay eyes on it.'

However, Sultan Mahmud Shah did not give him permission to return. Raja Nara Singa remained quiet hearing His Majesty.

As the wheel of time turned, Raja Nara Singa sailed back to Inderagiri. On his return, he discovered that His Majesty, Maharaja Tuban, the younger brother of Maharaja Merlung had died, leaving only a son, Maharaja Isak. It was he who ruled over Inderagiri. After Maharaja Nara's arrival in Inderagiri, he ordered Tun Kecil and Tun Bali Maharaja Isak, two senior officials of Inderagiri, to do away with Maharaja Isak.

However, Maharaja Isak fled to Lingga and married the daughter of the Raja there. After the Maharaja of Lingga died, Maharaja Isak succeeded to the throne in Lingga. His Majesty had several children. In the meantime, Raja Nara Singa ascended the throne in Inderagiri.

* * *

As time passed, Sultan Mahmud Shah instructed his officers to sail to Benua Keling, to obtain cloths of forty kinds, four to each kind, and to each cloth forty different designs.

It was Hang Nadim who was ordered to sail there. Hang Nadim was originally from Melaka, the son-in-law of the Laksamana, and a descendant of the Bendahara Seri Maharaja.

Thus, Hang Nadim sailed to Benua Keling in Hang Isak's vessel. Before long, they arrived, and presently Hang Nadim sought the audience of the Raja of Keling. To His Majesty he conveyed his Raja's request. Subsequently, the Raja of Keling instructed all his designers to assemble, about five hundred of them. They were then ordered to design as was requested by Hang Nadim. So, the designers set to work. When they had finished, they showed their work to him. However, they were not to Hang Nadim's taste. So, they designed another set— that too did not strike his fancy. Many times did they repeat their sketches—but none of their designs were approved by Hang Nadim.

The designer spoke up, 'Very well, My Lord, but that is all that we have in our inventory. Other than that, we are not able to provide you, My Lord. But do give us an example so that we may follow it.'

Said Hang Nadim: 'Come, bring the paint and the ink.'

Thus, they soon provided the paint and ink, and Hang Nadim began to design the patterns as requested.

When they laid their eyes on Hang Nadim's trembling hands and the way he was designing, they were in awe of his artistic gift.

He showed his work to all the designers, saying, 'These are the designs that His Majesty has requested.'

Among the few hundred, only two could follow those designs sketched by Hang Nadim.

Said all the Keling artists, 'We are not able to draw in Hang Nadim's presence, let's return to finish the task.'

Hang Nadim agreed, 'Very well.'

Thus, the Keling designers returned to their respective homes to draw. After completing them, they duly presented them to Hang Nadim.

In time, the northwest monsoon began to blow and it was time to return to Melaka. Thus, Hang Nadim prepared all the goods he had bought, and loaded them into the boat, this time as a passenger on Hang Isak's boat.

In Hang Isak's boat was also another passenger, who was a *sharif,* a holy man. In the *sharif*'s calculation Hang Isak still had some *tahil*s of gold owed him.

He said to Hang Isak, 'There is still some *tahil*s of my gold with you. Please return them to me.'

Hang Isak replied loudly, 'What else is there with me? What kind of a holy man are you, accusing me thus? A testicle of holy man you are!'

The holy man replied, 'Hai, Hang Isak, I am a servant of Allah, you give me your penis. You will now be destroyed on your return.'

Hang Nadim quickly enjoined, 'Sir, I beg for your forgiveness. Please, let me return in safety.'

Then the holy man patted Hang Nadim's back, saying, 'Nadim, may you return safely.' And the holy man presently returned home.

Hang Isak soon set sail. In the middle of the sea, there descended no rain, no storm, but suddenly the boat sank. Thus, Hang Isak and all his passengers died.

Only Hang Nadim and a few of his men escaped unhurt, in a boat with all their valuable goods, making their way to Selan.

When the Raja of Selan heard of this misfortune, His Majesty summoned Hang Nadim and asked him to fashion an egg lantern. He carved the shell of the egg; it was a fine work of craftsmanship. Soon a candle was lit, enhancing its beauty. After it was tried, it was presented to the Raja of Selan, who bestowed on him various gifts. His Majesty wanted to keep him in Selan, but Hang Nadim was intent on returning, this time a passenger on a vessel sailing to Melaka.

When he arrived in Melaka, he sought to present himself before Sultan Mahmud Shah. The cloths still in his possession were unsewn and four in number. These he presented to His Majesty, and duly recounted all that had happened to him.

Said Sultan Mahmud Shah, 'When you knew that the holy man had put a curse on Hang Isak, why did you still become a passenger on his ship?'

Hang Nadim replied, 'I boarded Hang Isak's because none of the others was going to Melaka. If I had waited for the others, then I would have been late in returning.'

His Majesty was furious with Hang Nadim for his delay.

In time, Laksamana Hang Tuah died. It was his son-in-law, Khoja Husin, who was appointed in his place, for the Laksamana, Hang Tuah, had two wives: one from the clan of Seri Bija al-Diraja Datuk Bongkok, having three children with her—the oldest, a girl, who was betrothed to Khoja Husin, the middle one, a boy, Tun Biajit, and the youngest, a girl, Tun Sirah. She was taken as wife by Sultan Mahmud Shah, begetting Raja Dewi. The other wife of the Laksamana, hailed from the clan of the Bendahara Paduka Raja, who was a relative of Paduka Tuan. She had two children—one was a boy, Guna, the other a girl, who was betrothed to Hang Nadim. Thus, Khoja Husin was appointed the Laksamana, the Admiral, succeeding his father-in-law. Laksamana Khoja Husin had a son, Tun 'Isa.

Allah knows the truth; to Him shall we return.

XIX

The words of the chronicle now turn to Sultan Mahmud Shah, who received news that the old Raja of Pahang was deceased. It was his son who succeeded him on the throne. At that moment, the Bendahara of Pahang was Seri Amar Wangsa al-Diraja. He begot a girl, Tun Teja Ratna Menggala was her name. She was extremely beautiful; in Pahang none was her compare; in all her ways she was sweet and proper. That was the reason that a poem was composed for her:

> *Tun Teja Ratna Menggala,*
> *Pandai membelah lada sulah;*
> *Jika tuan tiada percaya,*
> *Mari bersumpah kalam Allah.*

> Tun Teja Ratna Menggala,
> She's adept at splitting the pepper;
> Let's swear on the book of Allah,
> If you do not believe these words that I utter.

It so happened that Sultan ʿAbdul Jamal desired to make Tun Teja his wife. The Bendahara of Pahang consented, but they had to wait for the right season for the ceremony and the union. Thus Sultan ʿAbdul Jamal ordered Seri Wangsa al-Diraja to journey to Melaka to bring the pall cloth,[1] and news of his father's demise. The letter of was subsequently carried in a procession to the boat, and Seri Wangsa al-Diraja was on his way. After a few days at sea, they arrived in Melaka.

When the letter arrived, Sultan Mahmud Shah was holding court. He ordered that the letter be fetched, and had it read aloud as soon as it arrived in the hall of audience. It said:

> This is the *sembah* of your servant, to the Duli Yang Dipertuan. Your father has departed this earth, returning to the mercy of God.

When His Majesty heard of the news that the Raja of Pahang had died, he did not hold court for seven days. After the mourning was over, he instructed Seriwa Raja to travel to Pahang to crown Sultan 'Abdul Jamal. The royal letter was carried in a procession, and Seri Wangsa al-Diraja was duly presented with a suit of fine clothing.

Soon Seriwa Raja was on his journey to Pahang, along with Seri Wangsa al-Diraja. Sultan 'Abdul Jamal was extremely pleased to hear of the arrival of the Melaka mission. He presently ordered that the letter be fetched, and when it had arrived in the audience hall it was read. This was what it said,

> Prayers and good wishes for my brother. What has happened is in accordance with the law of Allah; who may dispute Him? Thus, I have ordered My Lord, Seriwa Raja, to crown my brother.

Sultan 'Abdul Jamal was elated to hear his brother's words. Soon, His Majesty commenced the ritual of festivities that lasted for seven days and seven nights. After that Sultan 'Abdul Jamal was crowned by Seriwa Raja. When all the ceremonies were completed, Seriwa Raja sought leave of His Majesty to return to Melaka.

---

[1] *Membawa rahap*, to bring the pall cloth.

Sultan 'Abdul Jamal persuaded Seriwa Raja, 'Do wait a bit, let's go snare elephants, for this is the season of the elephants. Great is the entertainment of the sport.'

Seriwa Raja replied, 'My Lord, if Your Majesty would grant me a favour, I would like to request permission to sail back when the winds begin to blow; otherwise I should have to wait, and Your Majesty's brother would be unhappy. However, I am indeed very keen to see elephants being trapped; may we set free the tame elephants and then trap them again?'

Sultan 'Abdul Jamal responded, 'This may be done.'

Shortly, His Majesty ordered that the master mahouts be summoned. In no time, they were all present, and the wishes of the raja were repeated to them.

They put their palms together and replied, 'Even wild elephants may be snared, what more the tame ones?'

Seriwa Raja said to all of them, 'Please try, we wish to see it done.'

So Sultan 'Abdul Jamal ordered that a tame elephant be released. It was soon surrounded by other elephants, and several men held the snare according to the ways of old. The snare caught the foot of the tame elephant that had been set free; it did not only catch its foot but also caught the leg of another elephant and also the neck and leg of a caretaker. All the elephant caretakers were astonished.

Then all of them came forward to beg for His Majesty's forgiveness saying, 'My Lord, we shall never capture the elephant in the sight of Seriwa Raja, for his lordship is very knowledgeable in matters dealing with elephants.'

Sultan 'Abdul Jamal was deeply embarrassed witnessing that unsuccessful attempt, and presently returned to his palace.

And soon, all those who had come to attend to the king returned to their own homes. On the morrow, Sultan 'Abdul Jamal brought out Markapal, the Sultan's favourite elephant, and it was duly oiled but not saddled for the howdah.

As concerns Markapal, its back was extremely sloping, only two could sit on it. The two could stay up there, if they were in a howdah.

Sultan 'Abdul Jamal mounted Markapal and proceeded to Seriwa Raja's residence. When news of His Majesty's imminent arrival was reported to Seriwa Raja, he immediately went into the yard to await His Majesty.

Sultan 'Abdul Jamal addressed Seriwa Raja, 'My Lord, where is your son? We would like to take him for a spin on this elephant.'

Seriwa Raja replied, 'He is here, Your Majesty.'

In his heart he thought, 'The King will kill my son, carrying someone on an elephant with a back so sloping and oiled down, yet without a howdah.'

Seriwa Raja called to his son, 'Come, Awang 'Umar! His Majesty wants to give you a ride.' Soon Tun 'Umar was present before them.

Seriwa Raja then whispered into Tun 'Umar's ear, after which he said, 'Go, ride with His Majesty.'

Sultan 'Abdul Jamal knelt the elephant and Tun 'Umar quickly mounted its rear. Then the animal stood up and began to walk in the direction of Air Hitam. Sultan 'Abdul Jamal brought it up and down the steep cliffs. In his heart he hoped that 'Umar would slip and fall. However, when Tun 'Umar felt he was slipping he would press his legs against the back of the elephant, while giving orders. Thus, however, much it was goaded, it refused to move forward; its front legs were hanging loose. When Tun 'Umar felt that he was once again safely seated he let it go and after being restrained two or three times, only then allowed it to move forward. Sultan 'Abdul Jamal was truly amazed, and presently returned to the palace.

In due time, Seriwa Raja sought leave to return to Melaka. Sultan 'Abdul Jamal instructed that his brother's letter be replied to and a gift of fine clothes was given to Seriwa Raja. The letter was soon carried in a procession to the boat, and they set sail for Melaka.

When they arrived in Melaka, the letter was duly carried in a procession to the audience hall. Sultan Mahmud Shah was very pleased to hear the sound of the letter and with it also Seriwa Raja's capers in Pahang. He heaped praises on him and bestowed presents befitting his accomplishments.

In turn, Seriwa Raja sought His Majesty's audience to describe the incomparable beauty of Tun Teja, the daughter of Datuk Bendahara Pahang. However, at that moment she was engaged to be married to the Raja of Pahang, and the betrothal ceremony was to be held within days. When Sultan Mahmud Shah heard of her description from the lips of Seriwa Raja, His Majesty desired Tun Teja all the more.

Said His Majesty, 'Whoever is able to bring the daughter of the Bendahara of Pahang to Melaka, we shall grant his request. If he wanted half of the fortress, he shall have it.'

At that moment, Hang Nadim was present in the audience. When he heard the Sultan's words, he thought in his heart, 'Let me travel to Pahang, if fortune smiles on me, I shall be able to bring Tun Teja to His Majesty.' After thinking thus, he went to Pahang, as a passenger on a small craft.

After his arrival in Pahang, Hang Nadim befriended a gentleman from Champa, Sidi Ahmad was his name. They became great friends. Said Hang Nadim to Captain Sidi Ahmad, 'Is it true that Tun Teja, the daughter of the Bendahara, is exceptionally beautiful? How I wish to gaze upon her face.'

The captain replied, 'It's true, unfortunately she is already engaged to be married to His Majesty, the Raja of Pahang. How can you ever look upon her, for she is the daughter of a noble lord? Furthermore, we are mere mortals, even the sun and the moon have not looked at her?'

Hang Nadim thought in his heart, 'How shall I find a way to see her?'

At that moment an old lady masseuse[2] happened to come before them. Presently Hang Nadim invited the masseuse into the house and asked that he be given a massage.

Nadim enquired of her, 'Oh, auntie, who is your master?'

The old lady answered, 'I am the servant of My Lord, the Bendahara.'

Hang Nadim, 'Do you ever enter his house?'

---

[2]   *Tukang urut*, Masseuse.

The masseur replied, 'I am used to entering Datuk Bendahara's, as his daughter, Tun Teja, is my customer.'

Hang Nadim replied, 'Is it true what I have heard, that she is very good-looking?'

The masseuse responded, 'There is no one as beautiful as she is and she is engaged to His Majesty. Their wedding shall be in the coming season.'

Hang Nadim whispered to the old lady, 'Can you keep a secret, auntie?'

'God-willing I can, for I am used to being sent on errands.'

In no time, Hang Nadim heaped the woman with gold and many rolls of fabric and clothes. As she looked upon such riches, in her heart she was captivated. Thus, she promised to keep his secret.

Said Hang Nadim, 'If it is possible, find a way to bring Tun Teja here so that I may present her to the Raja of Melaka.' He gave her a potion, 'Brush it on her.'

She replied, 'Very well.' Subsequently, she entered the Bendahara's compound and called out, 'Who wants a massage, I can give you a massage?'

Upon hearing her voice, Tun Teja instructed her maids, 'Bring the masseuse here, I want a massage.'

Thus, the masseuse entered and began to give the young lady a massage. When it was all quiet, the masseuse whispered to Tun Teja, 'It is a pity, you, a princess with such beauty, have to marry this Raja. How much better would it be if you could marry a more famous Raja.'

Tun Teja asked, 'Who is greater than this Raja of Pahang?'

Immediately she replied, 'The Raja of Melaka is greater, and also a handsome monarch.'

Tun Teja was quiet, listening to the masseuse rubbing fragrance over her and persuading her with sweet words.

'There is a servant of the Raja of Melaka here; Hang Nadim is his name, instructed by His Majesty to fetch my lady. If he had directly asked His Majesty, it is possible that the Raja would not consent to it. That was the reason why Hang Nadim has come to take you away. If you agree, he will take you to Melaka, and you will be His Majesty's consort, for he is yet unmarried. My lady will then be the Queen in Melaka. If you were to marry the Raja of Pahang, you will only be his second wife. However, if you are the wife of the Raja of Melaka, it is for certain that the Queen of Pahang will make obeisance to you, my lady.'

Tun Teja was agreeable to the reasoning of the masseuse. There is a saying: *La ta'manunna 'ajuzatan dakhalatu'l-khabail, hal ta' manunna asada m'a 'l-ghanam*, meaning, trust not an old woman into your house; as a lion is to be trusted among goats.

When the old woman was sure of Tun Teja's consent, she immediately informed Hang Nadim. On his part Hang Nadim was well pleased hearing her words, and sought his friend Nakhoda Sidi Ahmad, saying, 'Do you have some love for me?'

Nakhoda Sidi Ahmad was surprised and retorted, 'Why shouldn't I have love for you, My Lord? Even to the point of endangering my life, I shall be with you.'

Thus, Hang Nadim unfolded the whole story of how he had made a promise with Tun Teja. Hang Nadim continued, 'My Lord, if you have some love for me, let me be a passenger in your junk; please wait for me at the estuary, I shall come downstream at dawn to your boat, then we can sail to Melaka, so that you may be rewarded and given titles by His Majesty.'

Nakhoda Sidi Ahmad was in full agreement.

Immediately, Nakhoda Sidi Ahmad ordered, 'Men, hurry to the junk and prepare to set sail; the winds have started to blow.'

Nakhoda Sidi Ahmad himself was no ordinary man, they knew him thus. He soon boarded the vessel and sailed downstream to the estuary of the Pahang River, stopping at the barriers. When night had descended, Hang Nadim called out to the masseuse, asking her to bribe all the Bendahara's guards with gold. Thus, she made her way as instructed, and was ready to assist Hang Nadim. When it was almost dawn and everyone was asleep, the masseuse brought Tun Teja to the guard, who readily opened the gates for them.

Nadim was ready, waiting outside, and the masseuse told Teja to go to Hang Nadim. Subsequently, Hang Nadim wrapped his hand with a piece of cloth and received Tun Teja, bringing her to the cross-river passenger boat, which was already there waiting for them. So, they were rowed, and on their way to the harbour.

In those times the Pahang River had two stages. So, Hang Nadim filled his sleeves with sand, and after that cast it into the water, making a sound as though he was fishing with a throw-net. He subsequently asked that the barrier be lifted. When the guard heard the sound of somebody fishing, he raised it. Thus, Nadim passed through the first. Coming to the second, he again pretended to be fishing. There again, the barrier was lifted. As soon as he passed the second barrier, he rowed with all his might, to reach Nakhoda Ahmad's junk. There Hang Nadim helped Tun Teja board the vessel. Fortunately, the winds began to blow and Nakhoda Sidi Ahmad ordered to hoist anchor and sail for Melaka.

When it was daylight, the maids of the palace came to report to the Bendahara, 'My Lord's daughter cannot be found, we know not where she has gone.'

The Bendahara was astonished. He ordered that a thorough search be carried out, but still she was not found. From the palace they could hear the sound of women weeping.

When Sultan 'Abdul Jamal came to hear of the news His Majesty too was surprised, coupled with a feeling of grief. His Majesty ordered that they explore all the possibilities. It so happened that someone from the Kuala Pahang had seen Hang Nadim at the break of dawn, carrying a woman, magnificent was her countenance, and boarding Nakhoda Sidi Ahmad's junk, sailing for Melaka. Hearing the report, His Majesty was furious and ordered that the boats be prepared. Within a few moments, all the forty boats were ready. Sultan 'Abdul Jamal himself followed Hang Nadim. Along with them came in a great hurry, all the military chiefs. When they arrived at Keban Island they found Nakhoda Sidi Ahmad's junk. Immediately the Pahang people engaged those in the boat in a fight. A Pahang military chief pulled in the junk, but when

Hang Nadim noticed what the man was doing, he shot him; the arrow pierced the military man, slaying him.

His boat withdrew. Then came another, that too withdrew. When two or three of their boats suffered the same fate, none of the Pahang military chiefs wanted to come forward. Surveying the scene, Sultan 'Abdul Jamal decided to bring his vessel to the fore. As soon as it came near, Hang Nadim shot it with an arrow, striking the Raja's umbrella, splitting it into two.

Said Hang Nadim, 'Oh, you people of Pahang, look at me and my arrows. If I were to combat with each one of you, I could easily gouge out your eyes.'

They were truly in awe of Hang Nadim's skill with the bow and arrow, for in those days Hang Nadim was a champion in this art, in fact he could even split logs with his arrows.

The winds began to blow hard, and the junk was directed to the middle of the sea, leaving the Pahang fleet behind, and furthermore, the waves were exceptionally high, while their boats were quite small in size. So, the Pahang fleet returned, following the coastline.

Thus, Nakhoda Sidi Ahmad was on his long journey to Melaka. After several days, he arrived in the harbour. The news of his arrival came to the ears of Sultan Mahmud Shah that Hang Nadim sailed from Pahang, a passenger in Nakhoda Sidi Ahmad's junk, bringing the daughter of the Bendahara of Pahang, Tun Teja. His Majesty was immensely pleased listening to the report.

When night had fallen, Hang Nadim sought His Majesty's audience, bringing Tun Teja, with him. His Majesty was in awe, giving praises to Allah. He heaped praises on Hang Nadim and presented him with full suits of fine costumes. Moreover, he gave a limitless amount of gold and silver. Also, as a sense of gratitude to Hang Nadim, he was betrothed to the sister Paduka Tuan. Nakhoda Sidi Ahmad himself was bestowed the title of Tun Setia Diraja, presented with a sword and given a place by the gallery, on the same status as all the other heralds.

Thus, Sultan Mahmud Shah married Tun Teja, he was full of love for her. In time Sultan Mahmud Shah and Tun Teja bore a girl, Puteri Iram Dewi.

In another anecdote it was related that the Sultan asked Tun Teja, 'How were you brought by Hang Nadim, my dear?'

Tun Teja replied, 'My Lord, he would not even come near me, not even look at me from close quarters. When he was receiving me down into the boat, he would wrap his hand with a piece of cloth.'

His Majesty was extremely delighted listening to her story, and he gave Hang Nadim other gifts of great value.

* * *

It was related that after Nakhoda Sidi Ahmad's junk had sailed away, the Raja of Pahang returned on his royal vessel called Biman Jengkubat. He was full of anger, ordering the Bendahara and all the military chiefs, 'Make all the preparations at this very moment; we want to invade Melaka! Attention all, I swear I will crash this Biman Jengkubat against Melaka's palace!'

He demonstrated it by crashing the elephant against his own palace, which was crushed.

His Majesty reiterated, 'This is what will happen to Melaka's palace, when I crash it with my elephant.'

All the military chiefs stood with their heads bowed down in fear of the furious Sultan. Soon after that, he returned to his palace.

Sultan Mahmud Shah asked his military chiefs, 'Who among you is able to capture Raja Pahang's elephant which will destroy our palace? Speak up, whatever your sin is we shall not slay you.'

Laksamana Khoja Hasan spoke up, 'I am ready, Your Majesty; command me to Pahang, God-willing I shall take the Sultan of Pahang's elephant and bring it back to My Lord.'

Sultan Mahmud Shah was happy, 'Very well,' he replied.

Immediately, His Majesty instructed that a letter be written to the Bendahara Seri Maharaja. When it was concluded it was taken in a procession to the boat, which soon set sail for Pahang.

After a journey of several days, the Laksamana arrived in Pahang. The news of their arrival was reported to His Majesty, 'The

Laksamana has arrived carrying the words of your brother for Your Majesty.'

So, Sultan 'Abdul Jamal came to the audience hall with many in attendance. Melaka's letter was instructed to be fetched and taken in a procession as was the custom in those days.

As it arrived at the palace it was read, it was decent to His Majesty's ears and he was glad. The Laksamana made obeisance and sat above Seri Akar Raja Pahang.

The Laksamana put his palms together in obeisance, 'My Lord, we hear of Your Majesty's anxiety, which is the reason why we have been asked to come before Your Majesty. Your younger brother says: "Why is there discord among brothers? For Melaka and Pahang are like a single state".'

After hearing the Laksamana, His Majesty enquired, 'Who was it who brought the news to Melaka? He is lying. In the Laksamana's opinion, should Pahang go to war with Melaka?'

Within a moment of the discussion, Sultan 'Abdul Jamal departed for his chambers. Those who came to attend to His Majesty returned to their own homes.

In the meantime, the Laksamana cast anchor near a bath for the royal elephants. One day, when the mahouts[3] were taking the elephants to their bath, they were fed and then given gifts of gold. Thus, all the mahouts began to love the Laksamana. Biman Jengkubat was the elephant that was most favoured by the Laksamana. It was lovingly scrubbed and oiled, and a half of his vessel was emptied and prepared. The Laksamana's fleet was composed of only four vessels.

After some days in Pahang, the Laksamana sought leave to return to Melaka.

Subsequently, Sultan 'Abdul Jamal replied to his brother's letter and bestowed a change of fine costume on the Laksamana. Soon the letter was carried in a procession to the vessel, and when it had arrived, those who came to send them returned to the palace. The Laksamana paused

---

[3]   *Pengembala*, mahout, an elephant carer.

for a moment to await the mahout to bring the elephants to their bath. Biman was there too. The Laksamana called out to Biman, and it was soon loaded into the boat. As the mahout so loved the Laksamana, he obeyed all his orders. After the elephant had come aboard, they sailed downstream. Among the Pahang people there was an uproar, saying that Biman had been forced on to the boat.

When Sultan 'Abdul Jamal heard the report, he was extremely annoyed.

Said His Majesty, 'We are treated by the Raja of Melaka like a monkey: its mouth is fed with a banana whilst its rear is pricked with a thorn.'

So, Sultan 'Abdul Jamal ordered all his military chiefs to make preparations to follow the Laksamana, with thirty boats in the fleet. Tun Aria was appointed its commander.

It was in Sedili Besar that the military chiefs of Pahang met the Laksamana and engaged him in a furious battle.

From his vessel, the Laksamana would shoot at anyone within his range. So, the people of Pahang were circumspect in approaching the Laksamana's vessel. Soon, Tun Aria edged closer. Seeing this, the Laksamana shot the top of Tun Aria's mast, splitting it into two. Now his second arrow struck the *payang* boat, cleaving it asunder.

It so happened that Tun Aria was standing by the mast holding his long shield, not realizing that the Laksamana's arrow came like lightning, splitting it in half. Thus, all those with the long shields fell with their shields in hand, and all those with their long shields were also severed along with their shields. Now, the dead were countless.

However, Tun Aria was intent on crashing against the Laksamana's vessel. In the meantime, the Laksamana trained his arrow at Tun Aria's shield. It struck it, penetrating through his chest, wounding him. When his men saw that Tun Aria was wounded, all of the boats in the Pahang fleet retreated in all directions, not knowing where they were going.

Before long, the Laksamana was on his way to Melaka, following the shore line.

In time, he arrived in Melaka. When news of his arrival came to the ears of His Majesty, and that the royal elephant of the Raja of Pahang was also on board, Sultan Mahmud Shah ordered that the Laksamana be welcomed. Soon, the Laksamana was standing before His Majesty making his obeisance. His Majesty heaped upon him gifts as though he were a royal prince. Then the elephant was taken up to the palace and brought into the audience hall. His Majesty was extremely pleased to see the animal. It was later given into the care of Seri Rama, who was the captain of the elephants.

It was narrated that the Pahang fleet that had been pursuing the Laksamana eventually returned and sought the audience of Sultan 'Abdul Jamal. A full report was given to His Majesty, who became extremely angry, like a snake in coils. Before long, Sultan 'Abdul Jamal crowned his son, Sultan Mansur, to replace him on the throne, while he removed to Lubuk Peletang. He went to a place as far away as possible, from where he was unable to hear the *nobat* drums and ensemble. It was there that he chose to live. Sultan 'Abdul Jamal studied under a sheikh, and when he departed for the next world, he came to be known as Marhum Sheikh. However, during Sultan Mansur Shah's reign, Raja Ahmad and Raja Muzaffar deputised on his behalf.

Allah knows the truth; to Him shall we return.

XX

Now the story is narrated of a certain *negeri*, Kota Maligai was its name. Raja Sulaiman Shah was its King. It came to the ears of the Siamese that Kota Maligai was well-endowed.

There was a Siamese prince, Chau Seri Bangsa was his name. He made preparations with all his subjects to invade Kota Maligai. However, Raja Sulaiman was able to expel him and they fought outside his fortress.

Chau Seri Bangsa said, 'If I am able to defeat Raja Sulaiman, I shall convert, and become a Muslim.'

It was fated by Allah *Subhanahu wa Ta`ala*, that Kota Maligai was defeated. Raja Sulaiman Shah died, slain by the Siamese, and Kota Maligai came under the authority of Chau Seri Bangsa.

Chau Seri Bangsa converted to Islam. In time, he sought a good new location for a new *negeri*. In the meantime, it was relayed to His Majesty: 'There is a fisherman living by the sea. Pa' Tani is his name and his place is an ideal location.'

Soon Chau Seri Bangsa departed for Pa' Tani's village. His Majesty discovered that the place was indeed very suitable as was told by the person who brought the news. So, Chau Seri Bangsa built a *negeri* there. He named it Pa' Tani, after the fisherman. Even to this day, it is called Pa' Tani by one and all

His Majesty ordered that a mission be gathered to pay obeisance to Sultan Mahmud Shah. Akun Pal was ordered to journey there. After sailing for several days at sea, he arrived in Melaka, and his arrival was conveyed to Sultan Mahmud Shah. Chau Seri Bangsa's letter was fetched and carried ceremoniously, as would a letter from Pahang.

Thus, when it had arrived in the audience hall it was read. This is how it sounded:

> My obeisance is made before Your Majesty, my father. Our praises and commendations, I have requested Akun Pal to come before Your Majesty in reverence and seek Your Majesty's royal consent to be installed.

Sultan Mahmud Shah was very pleased. He bestowed on Akun Pal a gift of fine costumes as was the custom in those days of old. Furthermore, he was given a seat on the same level as the herald.

* * *

In the meantime, Sultan Mahmud Shah requested that an elucidation be written by Kadi Munawar Shah.

Chau Seri Bangsa was bestowed the title of Sultan Ahmad Shah and presented the installation letter. Akun Pal was again presented with a gift of fine costumes. Soon the letter and the Kadi Munawaf Shah *khitab*[1] were carried in a procession to the boat. Subsequently, Akun Pal sailed back to Patani.

When he arrived in Patani, Akun Pal ordered that His Majesty be formally installed. Thus, Chau Seri Bangsa was crowned, and was known as Seri Sultan Ahmad Shah. He begat Chau Gma, and Chau Gma begat the Kings who ruled Siam.

* * *

---

[1] *Khitab*, religious book.

One day, there came to Melaka a vessel from the west. In the vessel was a religious scholar, Maulana Sadar Jahan, who was extremely pious. Even Sultan Mahmud Shah and his son, Raja Ahmad, studied under his tutorship. In time, Maulana Sadar Jahan came to be known as Makhdum. Many were the chiefs and the members of the royal family who studied with him.

It was related that one day, the Bendahara Seri Maharaja was in a discussion with Makhdum Sadar Jahan. At that moment, Seri Rama, notoriously known to be a drunkard, barged in, quite drunk as usual. He came to make obeisance to Sultan Mahmud Shah.

His Majesty instructed his servant, 'Bring a meal for Seri Rama.'

Soon the food was served on a silver tray, covered with a ritual wrap, and given to Seri Rama. But when the page approached Seri Maharaja, he found him to be deep in conversation with the Makhdum.

Seri Rama said, 'I would like to enrol in the study of the Quran.'

The Bendahara Seri Maharaja, invited Seri Rama, 'Come, My Lord, take a seat.'

When Makhdum Sadar Jahan noticed that Seri Rama was drunk, his mouth smelling of arrack, he said, '*Al-khamru ummu'l-k aba'ith*,' meaning: arrack is the mother of all filth.

Seri Rama replied, '*Al-hamku ummu 'l-khaba'ith*,' meaning: foolishness is indeed the mother of all filth. Why does My Lord come here from above the wind if not to seek riches, from that very foolishness?'

When he heard Seri Rama's rebuke, Makhdum promptly left, although the Bendahara Seri Maharaja implored him to stay.

The Bendahara Seri Maharaja asked Seri Rama, 'What kind of drunkenness is this that you have spoken with such disrespect to the Makhdum? It's fortunate that His Majesty is not around to hear it. If His Majesty were to hear it, he would be very angry with My Lord.'

Seri Rama replied, 'To His Majesty his wishes; what has been spoken may not be unspoken?'

Soon food was served, and all those who were present partook of the meal. When it was over, Seri Rama immediately sought leave of the Bendahara Seri Maharaja, and returned home.

On the morrow, the Bendahara himself proceeded to the Makhdum's. Makhdum Sadar Jahan was overjoyed to see Bendahara Seri Maharaja. In the meantime, Tun Mai Ulat Bulu was also studying with the Makhdum. Tun Mai Ulat Bulu's name was Tun Muhiyuddin, the son of Tun Zainal 'Abidin, and grandson of Bendahara Paduka Raja. Being excessively hirsute, he was nicknamed Tun Mai, the caterpillar.

He was unable to follow Makhdum's teaching for his Malay tongue was unable to pronounce Arabic words. This caused Makhdum Sadar Jahan to be annoyed.

He said, 'Tun Mai Ulat Bulu's tongue is so stiff; whenever I say something, it's always something else that emits from your mouth?'

Tun Mai Ulat Bulu replied, 'I am speaking your language, master; it is difficult for me to pronounce the words, for it is not my language. If you try to pronounce the words in my language, it will produce the same effects.'

Makhdum Sadar Jahan shrugged, 'What difficulty is there in Malay that I am unable to pronounce it?'

Tun Mai Ulat Bulu said, 'Please say "*kunyit*".'

The Makhdum said, '*kun-yit*.'

Tun Mai Ulat Bulu said, 'That is not right, sir. Please say "*nyiru*".'

The Makhdum said, '*niru*.'

Tun Mai Ulat Bulu continued, 'Now, "*kucing*".'

The Makhdum, followed, '*kusing*.'

Tun Mai Ulat Bulu concluded, 'You are unable to pronounce our words, just as we are unable to articulate your language.'

This made Makhdum Sadar Jahan very annoyed, 'I swear that I shall never teach Tun Mai Ulat Bulu again!'

In time, Sultan Mahmud Shah wanted to send a mission to Pasai to enquire about the various views of the scholars known as 'Ulama Mawar al-Nahar, 'Ulama of Khurasan and 'Ulama of Iraq.

Therefore, His Majesty called a meeting with the Bendahara and the chiefs to counsel him; he asked of them, 'What should be the manner in which we ask a mission to bring a scholarly issue to Pasai? If we were to write it down on paper, we will surely lose out, for the Pasaians are champions of misinterpreting letters. If we wrote "greetings" they will read it as "obeisance".'

The Bendahara Seri Maharaja agreed, 'If that is the case, let us not write it down. We shall ask the envoy to memorise our message.'

Sultan Mahmud Shah said, 'It is true, what My Lord has said, and we shall ask My Lord Orang Kaya-kaya Tun Muhammad to be our delegate.'

The Orang Kaya-kaya Tun Muhammad, agreed, 'Very well, Your Majesty.'

Thus, the letter was carried in a procession to the vessel, His Majesty's gift was a sword minted in Pahang, inlaid with gold. The envoy also carried with him two parrots, one of which was purple in colour. So Orang Kaya-kaya Tun Muhammad set sail and throughout the journey, he memorised the letter.

When they reached Pasai, their arrival was reported to the Raja of Pasai, 'Your Majesty, the mission from Melaka has come.'

Immediately, the Raja of Pasai instructed all his chiefs to receive them with a fanfare of drums, flutes and *nagara*, to honour their arrival.

When they met Orang Kaya-kaya Tun Muhammad, they enquired of him, 'Where is the letter? We would like to take it along in the ceremonial procession.'

Orang Kaya-kaya Tun Muhammad replied, 'I am the letter, take me in your procession.'

Therefore, they mounted him on the elephant, and he was taken in a procession. When they arrived at the gallery, Orang Kaya-kaya Tun Muhammad dismounted. He then stood in the place where letters were read. Next, he verbalised the contents of the letter from his mouth. This is how it sounded:

My greetings and prayers for my brother, Seri Sultan al-Muazzam Muluk Mulk al-Mukarram zil Allah fi al-'Alam. My reason for sending Orang Kaya-kaya Tun Muhammad and Tun Bija Wangsa is to consult you on the issue of *Man kala, Inna'llahata'ala khalikun' warazkun fi'l-azali fakad kafara*; meaning: Whoever says that Allah

Ta'ala creates and does not give His creations sustenance since the beginning of time has become a *kafir*.[2] We ask that Your Majesty give us its meaning.

In time, the Raja of Pasai assembled all the scholars in Pasai and asked them to interpret this verse. However, not one of them was able to offer an answer.

So the Raja of Pasai invited the Orang kaya-Kaya Tun Muhammad. When he arrived, it was His Majesty himself who gave the answer.

Next, the Sultan enquired of Orang Kaya-kaya Tun Muhammad, 'Is it the answer that our brother wishes to hear?'

Tun Muhammad was happy with His Majesty's interpretation and replied, 'It's true, as Your Majesty has spoken.'

After that Orang Kaya-kaya Tun Muhammad sought leave to return. So the Raja of Pasai replied to the Raja of Melaka's letter. When it was completed, it was carried in a stately procession to the boat, and then Orang Kaya-kaya Tun Muhammad set sail for Melaka.

Upon their arrival in Melaka, the letter was again carried in a procession, and was read in the audience hall. The Orang Kaya-kaya Tun Muhammad graciously presented all the words of the Raja of Pasai and reported all that happened there. His Majesty was greatly pleased to hear Pasai's reply. Soon, Orang Kaya-kaya Tun Muhammad and Tun Bija Wangsa were duly presented with gifts of costumes, in the fashions of the princes of the land.

Allah knows the truth; to Him shall we return.

---

[2] *Kafir*, a non-believer, infidel.

XXI

Now the words of the narrative turn to the Raja of Ligor, Maharaja Dewa Sura was his name. One day, Maharaja Dewa Sura made preparations to invade Pahang. News of his intention came to the ears of Sultan Munawar Shah, the Raja of the *negeri*. His Majesty ordered that the fortress be mended and his subjects be assembled and remain in the fortress while they readied their weapons. The news that the Raja of Ligor was preparing his soldiers to invade Pahang, as an instrument of the Raja of Benua Siam, also reached Melaka. So Sultan Mahmud Shah asked that the Bendahara Seri Maharaja, and the Seri Bija al-Diraja, and all the chiefs be summoned to deliberate on the Raja of Ligor's plan.

Said the Seri Nara al-Diraja, 'Your Majesty, if we do not request that Pahang be helped, and if anything untoward should happen, would Your Majesty regret it?'

Sultan Mahmud Shah responded, 'In that case, may we instruct the Bendahara and the military chiefs to go to Pahang?'

The Bendahara, bowed, 'Very well, Your Majesty.'

Thus, the Bendahara Seri Maharaja, made the necessary preparations. He was bestowed with costumes of great beauty. When the preparations were complete, the Bendahara Seri Maharaja departed with Seri Amar Bangsa, Seri Utama, Seri Upatam, Seri Nata, Sang Setia, Sang Naya, Sang Guna, Sang Jaya Pikrama and all the military chiefs.

From afar their ships, big and small, seemed innumerable, for in those times, the inhabitants in the *negeri* were ninety thousand in all, not including those in the colonies and dependents. And to them were added the Laksamana, who had an authority over Sungai Raya.

When the Laksamana was ready, he sailed downstream to Melaka. The fleet of Sungai Raya totalled forty three-masted fast boats in all, sailing south to Batu Pahat. There they met the Bendahara Seri Maharaja.

The Laksamana greeted the Bendahara Seri Maharaja, who subsequently instructed him, 'My Lord, let's go to Pahang.'

The Laksamana replied, 'I have not received orders from His Majesty.'

Bendahara Seri Maharaja said, 'If you have not, I have received them from His Majesty.'

The Laksamana responded, 'I have not paid His Majesty my homage.'

The Bendahara Seri Maharaja, said, 'I have done that; let's go.'

The Bendahara shook the Laksamana's hand and he was unable to decline. Thus, he went with the Bendahara. When they arrived at their destination, they noticed that Pahang's fortress was incomplete; now it was the task of the Melakans to finish it. Then the Bendahara Seri Maharaja and all the military officers sought the Raja's audience; Sultan Mansur Shah was very glad.

Said Bendahara Seri Maharaja to His Majesty, 'Your Majesty, the fortress is yet unfinished.'

Sultan Mansur Shah agreed, 'Very well, we shall finish it as soon as possible.'

Thus, the Bendahara ordered all the Melakans to work on the fortress and the Laksamana to lead the assignment. Subsequently, the Laksamana gathered all the Melakans to work on it.

At that time, the Laksamana's hands, feet, eyes, and mouth all went to work to direct his men. His eyes were tasked to see the good and the bad of their workmanship, and his feet took him here and there, his hands were employed to peel the rattan. With Allah's help, it was completed in three days.

In time, the Raja of Ligor arrived in Pahang with his innumerable subjects, and they began to battle with the people of Pahang. With the grace of Allah *Subhanahu wa Ta`ala*, Pahang did not fall, while the people of Ligor suffered much destruction at the hands of the Pahang people; many lay dead. The Raja of Ligor fled in confusion to the upper reaches of the Pahang River, and from there, he walked on to Patani, and finally returned to Ligor.

When they had reassembled, Sultan Mansur bestowed honours and gifts on the Bendahara Seri Maharaja, and all the Melakan military chiefs, and finally bestowed costumes of fine fabric on those who had accompanied them into victory. Before long, Bendahara Seri Maharaja sought leave of His Majesty. The Sultan sent a letter of obeisance to Melaka, and they set sail for home.

When they arrived in Melaka, they sought the audience of Sultan Mahmud Shah. His Majesty was delighted to hear that Pahang was not defeated.

It was narrated that in these times Melaka was densely settled. Merchants would come to trade and reside there. From Air Leleh to the upper reaches of the Muar River there were long rows of shops and markets and so too from Kampung Keling to Kuala Penajuh, back-to-back, their continuous rows were uninterrupted. If one travelled to Jugra, one needed not carry fire, for wherever one went there were houses.

Thus was the greatness of Melaka; in those times, its inhabitants totalled one hundred and ninety thousand, aside from its colonies and dependents.

* * *

In time, there came a Portuguese vessel from Goah. It set itself to trade. It observed that Melaka was tremendously prosperous and its city well populated. Many Melakans gathered to see the Portuguese.

They were amazed looking at them, they said, 'These are white Benggalis.'

Each Portuguese had tens of men crowding around him. Some played with his beard, some touching his head, some inspecting his hat or beret, some holding his hands.

Soon, the captain came to seek audience with the Bendahara Seri Maharaja. On his part the Bendahara Seri Maharaja adopted him as his son and gave him presents of costumes, while the captain gave the Bendahara Seri Maharaja a golden chain.

When the time came for the captain to return, they departed for Goah. In Goah they described to the Viceroy the greatness and prosperity of Melaka and how densely it was inhabited.

The name of the Viceroy was Alfonso d'Albuquerque, and he was moved to visit Melaka and see it with his own eyes. He then ordered that preparations be made: seven vessels, ten long galleons and thirteen fustas.

When all was ready, they were ordered to invade Melaka.

Upon their arrival and meeting the populace, they shot them with cannons. The Melakans were shocked to hear the sound of these cannons. They enquired, 'What are those sounds that explode like thunder?'

Soon the cannons hit many in the city. Some were decapitated, some had their hands blown off, some had their thighs shattered.

The Melakans were surprised at how the cannons worked. 'What is the name of the round weapon that kills with such great precision and brutality?'

On the morrow, the Portuguese landed with their guns, two thousand in all, while the soldiers and sailors were innumerable. However, the Melakans soon expelled them. Tun Hasan Temenggung was their war chief. The two sides met and battled as though in a field of fire, the weapons were like heavy rain. Then Tun Hasan Temenggung and all the Melakans crashed into the clusters of Portuguese, they were left in disarray and subsequently retreated. On their part, the Melakans mounted another attack to the edge of the water, driving them away. The Portuguese clambered on to their vessels and sailed back to Goah.

Upon their arrival in Goah, they reported the progress of the battle to the Viceroy, who was deeply annoyed at their defeat. He asked them to make new preparations to attack Melaka.

Said Captain Mor: 'If the Bendahara Seri Maharaja is still around, Melaka will never be defeated.'

The Viceroy replied, 'In that case, when I am no longer the Viceroy, I shall myself invade Melaka.'

Allah knows the truth; to Him shall we return.

XXII

The chronicle now turns to the incomparable beauty of the daughter of the Bendahara Seri Maharaja; Tun Fatimah was her name. As she began to grow into adulthood her looks likewise bloomed into a greater radiance. All the more so, as she was the daughter of the Bendahara, clothes that were forbidden to other women were allowed her. She was to be betrothed by her father to Tun 'Ali, the son of the Seri Nara al-Diraja. At her engagement, the Raja of the Upper Reaches called upon the Bendahara Seri Maharaja, who was the uncle of Sultan Mahmud Shah, being the eldest brother of Sultan 'Alauddin. He called upon the Bendahara Seri Maharaja before the engagement ceremony and was enchanted by the beauty of Tun Fatimah. He showed the maiden to the Raja, who was enchanted by her beauty.

He asked, 'Has His Majesty seen your daughter?'

The Bendahara Seri Maharaja, replied, 'Not yet, His Majesty has not.'

The Raja of the Upper Reaches said, 'Bendahara, if this does not cause you to be apprehensive, let me take this opportunity to talk to you.'

The Bendahara, replied, 'What is in your heart? Please say it.'

Raja di Baruh said, 'Your daughter is indeed a beautiful maiden. In my heart she should not have a husband not of nobility. If it comes to the ears of His Majesty—do not marry her yet, for the Queen has just passed away. It is the custom among Malay Rajas, when there is no Queen, it is the daughter of the Bendahara who is made Queen. '

Bendahara Seri Maharaja replied, 'I am evil-hearted, therefore my place should be among the evil ones.'

Raja di Baruh said, 'Very well then, as it suits My Lord. I am merely reminding you.'

Soon after that, the Bendahara Seri Maharaja began the wedding celebrations. When it was the appropriate time to invite Sultan Mahmud Shah, the Bendahara Seri Maharaja, sought His Majesty's audience.

The Sultan came to the Bendahara's house to grace their marriage and Tun 'Ali was wedded to Tun Fatimah.

Soon, Sultan Mahmud Shah entered into the inner chamber of the house to show his esteem for the newlyweds. As soon as he set his eyes on Tun Fatimah's countenance, he was in awe of her magnificence; he desired her to have her as his own.

In his heart he said, 'Pa' Mutahir has a wicked heart; he does not show us his daughter's exceptional beauty!'

Thus, Sultan Mahmud Shah nursed a grudge against the Bendahara.

After the betrothal, the Sultan returned to his palace, he did not even take his meal. Tun Fatimah was always in his heart. Each day, he would find fault with the Bendahara. After they had been married several months, Tun Fatimah gave birth to a daughter, she was named Tun Terang, a beautiful baby she was.

* * *

It was related that there was a man from Keling who lived in Melaka and had become the harbour master, Raja Mendeliar was his title; he was the richest in the state at that time. One day, Raja Mendeliar was having an audience with the Bendahara Seri Maharaja.

The Bendahara said, 'Hai, Raja Mendeliar, now tell me the truth, how much gold does My Lord possess?'

Raja Mendeliar replied, 'My Lord, I have just a little gold—only five *baharas.*'

Bendahara Seri Maharaja responded, 'Ah, we have a *bahara* more than My Lord.'

It was related that the Bendahara was avaricious. He would often gather all his clansmen and say, 'Would you like to look upon gold?'

When his young clansmen replied, 'Yes, we would, My Lord.'

The Bendahara would then instruct them, 'Go and fetch the chest from that place.'

The young men would fetch it and he would instruct them to empty its contents on to the mat and measure it with the *gantang*[1] measure.

Said the Bendahara to his kinsfolks, 'Each of you, take a handful as your plaything.'

Thus, each one took a handful of gold, which they then brought to the new house he had just built. The gold was placed in all the chiselled niches on the walls and then the youths returned to their homes.

Soon after, the carpenters returned to their site for work. When they noticed the gold, they took it. However, the young clansmen had not forgotten the gold, and presently ascended into the house to collect the gold to play with it. When they found that it was gone, they wept.

Their weeping was heard by the Bendahara Seri Maharaja, who asked, 'Why are the children weeping?'

They replied, 'The gold is gone, My Lord.'

The Bendahara said, 'Do not weep, tell me the truth, and I shall replace it.'

That was how each was given another handful of gold.

* * *

One day, his clansmen went hunting for wild buffaloes or deer and failed to catch any game. So, they dropped by at the Bendahara's

---

[1] *Gantang*, a measure for rice, cereal and small fruits.

buffalo shed and slaughtered two or three of his animals. They sent the thigh of a buffalo to the Bendahara.

The Bendahara asked, 'What meat is this?'

The man who delivered the meat replied, 'Buffalo meat, My Lord. Your children and grandchildren went hunting this morning but did not get any game, so they stopped at the buffalo shed in Kayu Ara and picked out one of them.'

The Bendahara replied, 'How naughty these children are. It has now become their habit to hunt the buffaloes in my shed if they do not get any game!'

Whenever the Bendahara Seri Maharaja returned from the upper reaches or hinterland he would wear a purple coat, and a rainbow-coloured headdress. Then he would ask his clansmen to take their seats, pretending they were visitors from across the shores. And they would follow his instructions.

The Bendahara Seri Maharaja, would ask, 'Who are you?'

And they would reply, 'I am your servant, the son of so-and-so, and the grandchild of so-and-so.'

The Bendahara would reply, 'If you are the son of so-and-so, go down there and take a seat.'

Those were the eccentric ways of the great Bendahara Seri Maharaja.

It crossed his mind, 'All these riches will last for many generations long.'

* * *

One day, the Bendahara and all the senior statesmen entered the gallery to wait for His Majesty to depart from the audience hall. It happened that Raja Mendeliar sought his lordship's audience and sat with both his hands raised in customary obeisance.

The old minister shoved aside Raja Mendeliar's hands, saying, 'Ah, the ways of the Kelings, who know not the customs of the land! How could you raise your hands to me in obeisance in this royal hall? Shouldn't you come to my house for whatever you should want?'

Thus, Raja Mendeliar became quiet and returned home. After him, there came another merchant, Nina Sura Dewana was his name. He was the chief among all the merchants in the land. One day, Nina Sura Dewana accused Raja Mendeliar of some wrong doing, so they both approached the Bendahara to arbitrate their case.

Said the Bendahara to Raja Mendeliar and Nina Sura Dewana, 'Do return home now, My Lords, the day has already turned into evening. Please come tomorrow.'

So, Raja Mendeliar and Nina Sura Dewana sought leave of the Bendahara and returned to their respective homes.

In his heart, Nina Sura Dewana thought, 'Raja Mendeliar is indeed a rich man. If he bribes the Bendahara, I shall lose my case, let me go to the Bendahara's tonight.'

Night was fast approaching. Nina Sura Dewana took a *bahara* of gold and brought it to the Bendahara's. As soon as he arrived outside the gates, Nina Sura Dewana told the guard, 'Please inform, My Lord, the Datuk Bendahara that Nina Sura Dewana seeks his audience.'

Thus, the guard presently informed the Bendahara Seri Maharaja. The Bendahara presently appeared and Nina Sura raised his hands in obeisance, giving him the *bahara* of gold he had brought with him, saying, 'My Lord, this gold is my gift to your lordship for whatever use you he might find for it.'

Bendahara Seri Maharaja said, 'Very well, My Lord has given it to me, so I'll take it.'

Soon Nina Sura Dewana sought leave of the Bendahara and returned to his home.

There was another Keling man, who was family to Nina Sura Dewana, Kitul was his name. Kitul owed Raja Mendeliar a *kati* of gold. After Nina Sura Dewana had departed from the Bendahara's, Kitul went to Raja Mendeliar's at midnight. He thumped on Raja Mendeliar's door. Raja Mendeliar was disturbed at dinner and said as he opened the door, 'Who is there at my door?'

Kitul asked that the door be opened, and soon it was opened. He entered to find that Raja Mendeliar was entertaining his family.

Kitul said, 'Raja Mendeliar, it is indeed fine that you are entertaining your family tonight, for you know not what awaits you?'

Raja Mendeliar led Kitul into a quiet place and said, 'Hai, Kitul, what news do you bring me? What have you heard?'

Kitul replied, 'Last night, Nina Sura Dewana went to the Bendahara and gave him a gift of one *bahara* of gold, so that you will be killed. Now the Bendahara too thinks just like Nina Sura Dewana; he wants to do you in.'

As soon as Raja Mendeliar heard Kitul's words, he fetched the letter that recorded Kitul's debt and tore it to pieces.

Raja Mendeliar said to Kitul, 'You are forgiven of your debt of one *kati*, now and forever. And you are now family to me.'

So Kitul returned to his own house. On that very night, Raja Mendeliar fetched a *bahara* of gold, glittering jewels and beautiful robes and brought them to the Laksamana; for the Laksamana was very close to Sultan Mahmud Shah.

When he arrived at the gates, he requested they be opened. Thus when the doors were opened, Raja Mendeliar entered to seek the audience of the Laksamana, and subsequently, presented all the valuable gifts to the Laksamana.

Said Raja Mendeliar: 'I am seeking your lordship's audience to prove my innocence. My Lord should present this news to His Majesty so that I am not accused as being of one mind with my chief, for it has come to my knowledge that the Bendahara is planning to rebel, to wrest the throne from His Majesty; his intention is to become King in his place in Melaka.'

After seeing so much riches, the Laksamana was no longer able to think rationally, his sense of judgment has been impaired by the worldly assets.

The Laksamana assured Raja Mendeliar, 'I shall be the one to bring the news to His Majesty.'

Thus, the Laksamana sought the audience of Sultan Mahmud Shah to convey all the words of Raja Mendeliar. After His Majesty heard them, he nursed further his old grudge for the Bendahara Seri

Maharaja, that initially began when his daughter was behrothed to someone else.

Soon, His Majesty commanded Tun Sura Diraja and Tun Indera Segara to slay Seri Maharaja. Thus, the two officers went with all the King's servants to the Bendahara's. However, all of the Bendahara Seri Maharaja's clansmen and family had gathered around him, all armed. Tun Hasan Temenggung, the son of the Bendahara, was ready to defend his father.

The Bendahara reminded him, 'Hai Hasan, are you intending to rebel, to taint the good name of all of our old folks, for it is the custom of the Malays never to rebel against their masters?'

When Tun Hasan Temenggung heard his father's warning, he cast his weapon aside and wrapped his hands around his body. Said the Bendahara to all his clansmen, 'Whoever fights back, I shall charge him in the hereafter.'

So, all who had come armed, cast aside their weapons and returned home. Only the Bendahara and his brother, the Seri Nara al-Diraja, and their clansmen remained. Subsequently, Tun Sura Diraja and Tun Indera Segara entered the compound bearing the *keris* from Sultan Mahmud Shah, placed on a special tray, covered with a fine wrap. It was taken before the Bendahara.

Tun Sura Diraja addressed the Bendahara and Seri Nara al-Diraja, 'My greetings and prayers. On this day the law of Allah is done.'

The Bendahara and Seri Nara al-Diraja replied, 'All that had happened according to Allah's providence we readily accept.'

Thus, Bendahara Seri Maharaja and Seri Nara al-Diraja and all their clansmen were ready to die with them.

At that moment, Sang Sura came running from within the palace to convey the words of the Sultan, 'His Majesty has commanded not to slay all of them; keep some of their offspring for the future.'

Tun Sura Diraja and Indera Segara reported, 'How can we undo what's already done? His Majesty will be enraged with us, for only this small boy has escaped death.'

Indera Segara quickly answered, 'This is Master Hamzah, let us care for him for as long as he lives.'

Tun Hamzah was the son of the Seri Nara al-Diraja, who was already wounded from his neck to his nipples. Thus, Tun Hamzah was brought before His Majesty, who ordered that he be attended to by a physician. By the grace of God, he did not die. He was the one much-loved from then on by Sultan Mahmud Shah.

After the Bendahara's demise, all of his possessions were moved into the inner chambers. When His Majesty discovered that the accusations against the Bendahara were untrue, he was extremely remorseful for commanding the Bendahara Seri Maharaja, to be slain without fully investigating into the matter. Subsequently, Raja Mendeliar was ordered to be killed for crafting a false accusation. After that Kitul, was impaled horizontally on a stake. Then, the Laksamana was ordered by the Sultan to be castrated.

Paduka Tuan, the son of Bendahara Paduka Raja was appointed the harbour master. However, Paduka Tuan was already advanced in age, and moreover showing signs of senility. All his teeth had fallen. When he heard that he had been appointed the Bendahara, he let his body drop from his seat on to the floor and said, 'What kind of Bendahara is this, he is lame and stiff?'

But, His Majesty persevered, and went on to appoint him as the Bendahara. It was he, who was called the Bendahara of Lubuk Batu, who had several children, thirty-two in all, all from a single mother. Of grandchildren and great-grandchildren he had seventy-four.

His eldest was Tun Biazid; however, Tun Biazid was an eccentric.[2] If he went downtown, he would pick up all that he liked, even though they belonged to other people. Soon, this was reported to the Bendahara. Consequently, whenever Tun Biazid went out, he was followed by a servant, carrying with him some gold. At the shop where he stopped, the servant would try to remember what Biazid had taken. After Tun Biazid had left, his servant would return to ask, 'What did the master take from your shop just now?'

So, the shopkeeper would recount what was taken by him.

Then the servant would ask, 'How much do they cost?'

---

[2] *Sasar-sasar bahasa*, eccentric.

And the shopkeeper would name the price, and the servant would pay it.

* * *

There was once an elephant that was a gift of the Bendahara. The animal had been sold several times. When the Bendahara Lubuk Batu, heard that it had been sold again, he would redeem it and give it to somebody else. However, when Tun Biazid happened to see anyone mounted on it, he demanded that the person dismount, 'That's my elephant, a gift from my father.'

And he would repossess the animal. After two or three months in his possession, he would sell it again. When his father heard of it, he would redeem it. That was how it was, over and over again. Tun Biazid had been thrice tied up by his father for hitting a Raja's servant. He instructed Seriwa Raja to tie him up and brought inside the house.

Said the Bendahara, 'Seriwa Raja, please plead with His Majesty to just slay this Biazid. What's the use of such an *orang bunuhan*?[3] I dare not slay him for fear of incurring His Majesty's wrath.'

Seriwa Raja then took him into the palace and he repeated the words of the Bendahara.

Sultan Mahmud Shah said, 'How odd, the Bendahara! Just because of somebody else's servant, he ties up his own son. Set him free!'

So Tun Biazid was set free and the Sultan presented him with a suit of clothes. Then he was asked to return to the Bendahara. And, subsequently, all the instructions of the Sultan were repeated to his father.

The Bendahara responded, 'That's our Sultan. While the young man, Biazid, was bound, he ordered that he be freed and gave gifts of fine clothes, so he becomes all the bolder!'

---

[3] *Orang bunuhan*, irrational.

Behind his father's back, Tun Biazid often said to his young friends,
'I am being bound by my father. To match my purple coat, he bound
me with a fine *chindai*[4] cloth with a green tint!'

All those who heard him laughed aloud.

* * *

There was another son of the Bendahara Lubuk Batu; Khoja Ahmad
was his name. He was titled as Tun Pikrama. He had a son, Tun
Isak Berakah. He held the post of Tun Pikrama and bore Tun Isak
Berakah. A daughter was also born to him, called Tun Pauh. She bore
Tun Jamal, and Tun Jamal had several children—the eldest was Tun
Utusan; another was Tun Bakau; others still were Tun Munawar, Tun
Sulaiman, who was titled as Seri Guna Diraja. His daughter, Tun Seni
was betrothed to Tun Tiram, the son of Sang Setia. Another daughter
was married to Tun Biajit Hitam, who bore Tun Mad 'Ali.

Tun Bakau had three children; they were Tun Biajit Ibrahim, Tun
Bentan, Tun Abu, who was titled Seri Bijaya Pikrama. Meanwhile,
Tun Munawar had four children: Tun Buang, Tun Husin who was
titled Paduka Seri Raja Muda, Tun Hasan, titled as Seri Pikrama Raja;
and another, a daughter, who was married to Tun Bentan.

Likewise, Seri Guna Diraja too had many children: Tun Mat,
Tun Boh, Tun Pekuh and Tun Zaid Boh. Another daughter of the
Bendahara of Lubuk Batu married Tun Perpatih Kasim, who gave
birth to Tun Puteri, who married Tun Iman Diraja, who in turn bore
Tun Zahir. It was he who was bestowed the title of Seri Pikrama Raja,
now residing here in Batu Sawar.

* * *

The chronicle now turns to the daughter of Bendahara Seri Maharaja,
Tun Fatimah, whose beauty was without compare in these times. She

---

4   *Cindai,* a fine exotic fabric.

was taken by Sultan Mahmud Shah as his wife. He was enormously infatuated by her. However, Tun Fatimah missed her father. While she was the wife of Sultan Mahmud Shah, she would not even smile, much less laugh.

His Majesty was concerned and remorseful of his deeds. In time, he abdicated and crowned his son, Sultan Ahmad, and surrendered all the state regalia and officers. Then, Sultan Mahmud Shah removed himself to Kayu Ara, where Sang Sura, his friend, lived.

It was narrated by the author of the chronicle that when Sultan Mahmud Shah sought entertainment in Tanjung Keling, or any other place, he would go riding. It was Sang Sura alone who would accompany His Majesty.

He would bring with him a tray for the betel, a footstool and a bottle of water.

Whenever Sultan Ahmad heard that his father went sporting, he ordered officers to accompany him. However, when Sultan Mahmud Shah noticed that there were people coming to accompany him, he would gallop away, for he preferred to be alone. So, Sang Sura too would run along, not wanting to be separated from his master. While he was running away, Sang Sura would erase the marks of the horse's hooves, so that they would not find them.

With his own hands, he would make the betel preparations for His Majesty. That was how His Majesty conducted himself after abdicating his throne.

While Sultan Ahmad was on the throne, he had little love for the officers of state. He only prized the friendship of Tun 'Ali, Tun Mai Ulat Bulu, Tun Muhammad Rahang and all the thirteen young men and all the servants. They were his friends at his play and entertainment.

Tun Mai Ulat Bulu was the son of Tun Zainal 'Abidin and the grandson of Bendahara Paduka Raja, who resided in Lubuk China, and was known as the Datuk of Lubuk China. Tun Zainal 'Abidin bore four children: three boys—the eldest, Tun Salehuddin, the middle one, Tun Jalaluddin, and the youngest, Tun Muhaiyuddin. The daughter was married to Bendahara Seri Maharaja.

Tun Salehuddin bore Tun Zahiruddin, and Tun Zahiruddin bore Orang Kaya Sogoh and Tun Jalaluddin, who was the father of Tun Sulaiman, who bore Tun Mai—he was the one known as Tun Mai the Caterpillar, very much loved by Sultan Mahmud Shah, and appointed the Temenggung, with the title of Seri Udana.

Sultan Mahmud Shah loved Tun Fatimah to extremes. His Majesty instructed that she be called 'the Queen', but whenever she became with child, she asked that the foetus be aborted. This went on for two or three times.

Eventually, His Majesty said to Tun Fatimah, 'Why does my dear abort every time you are with child? Do you not like to have our children?'

Tun Fatimah replied, 'What business has Your Majesty having children with me, for there is already one on the throne.'

Sultan Mahmud Shah promised, 'Do not terminate your pregnancy. If it is a boy, I shall crown him Sultan.'

After she became pregnant again, she did not terminate it. When the months were due, she gave birth to a beautiful baby girl. Sultan Mahmud Shah kissed her and named her Raja Putih. He loved her to extremes, words may not describe it. Soon Tun Fatimah gave birth to another girl, she was named Raja Hatijah.

It was related that Sultan Mahmud Shah often took religious lessons with the Makhdum Sadar Jahan.

Allah knows the truth; to Him shall we return.

XXIII

The story now turns to Alfonso d'Albuquerque, the Viceroy, who sailed to Portugal,[1] to request the King of Portugal for an armada. He was given four vessels and five long galleons. On his return, in Goah, he made preparations for war, with three vessels, eight galleons, and in addition four long galleons, fifteen fustas, in all totalling forty. Thus, they sailed to Melaka.

Upon their arrival in Melaka, there was tumult in the city. It was reported to Sultan Ahmad that the Portuguese were approaching with seven ships, eight galleons and ten large galleys, besides the fifteen trading ships and five fustas. Sultan Ahmad promptly ordered that all his subjects be gathered and armed.

So, the Portuguese battled the Melakans. They fired from their ships, their cannon balls falling like rain, and sounding like thunder in the skies. Flashes of light seemed like lightning, and the guns shots were like nuts being fried. None of the Melakans could stand by the beach, for the volleys were relentless. The galleys and fustas crashed from the end of the Melaka bridge.

Soon Sultan Ahmad appeared on an elephant, Jituji was its name. Seri Udana was at its head, sharing the howdah with His Majesty, for

---

[1]   Portugal, however all Europeans were classed as French in the 12-16th centuries.

he had studied metaphysics with Makhdum Sadar Jahan. Tun 'Ali Hati was at its rear, heading for the bridge, standing in the path of the volleys that were falling like a downpour.

Makhdum Sadar Jahan had both his hands on the howdah.

The Makhdum said to Sultan Ahmad Shah, 'Hai, My Lord, this is no place for metaphysics! Let's return.'

Sultan Ahmad smiled and returned to his palace.

The Portuguese then called from their ships, 'Hai Melakans, remember, tomorrow we will land.'

The Melakans shouted back, 'We will be waiting for you!'

Thus, Sultan Ahmad Shah ordered that his subjects be summoned and assembled. When it was nightfall, all the warriors and the sons of the lords entered into the audience hall, with their heads bowed as a mark of respect for their King.

The sons of the lords said, 'Why are we sitting idle here? Let's read the narrative *hikayat*[2] of old, so that it will be of some benefit to us.'

Tun Muhammad Unta agreed, 'It's true what My Lord has said. Let's request the *Hikayat Muhammad Hanafiah*.'

The sons of the lords said to Tun Aria, 'If it pleases, My Lord, we would like to request the *Hikayat Muhammad Hanafiah*, hoping that we may gain some benefit from its reading, for the Portuguese will be invading tomorrow.'

Soon, Tun Aria sought Sultan Ahmad's audience, bringing all the words of his companions to His Majesty. Thus, Sultan Ahmad Shah bestowed on him the *Hikayat Hamzah*.

Sultan Ahmad continued, 'Though we would like to bestow on My Lord the *Hikayat Muhammad Hanafiah*, we are afraid My Lords would not be as courageous as he was. However, if you all are like Hamzah, you are indeed the brave sons of your fathers. That is the reason why we are giving you the *Hikayat Hamzah*.'

---

[2]   *Hikayat*, an extended prose narrative.

Thus, Tun Aria departed, carrying the *Hikayat Hamzah*. Soon, all the words of Sultan Ahmad were conveyed to the sons of the lords. All of them said not a word.

Tun Isak Berakah spoke up, replying to Tun Aria, 'Please present to His Majesty that his orders are less than perfect. If His Majesty wants us to be like Muhammad Hanafiah, we will all be like the warriors of Bania. If His Majesty's courage is like Muhammad Hanafiah's then ours is like that of the warriors of Bania.'

Soon Tuan Aria conveyed all the words of Tun Isak Berakah to Sultan Ahmad. His Majesty smiled. Thus, he bestowed on him the *Hikayat Muhammad Hanafiah*.

* * *

On the morrow, the Portuguese landed and battled with the Melakans. Sultan Ahmad was on his elephant, Juru Demang, with Seri Udana at its head, and Tun 'Ali Hati sharing the howdah with him.

Thus the Portuguese battled the Melakans—so numerous were they on the battlefield. As the Portuguese onslaught was so fierce the Melakans dispersed, except for His Majesty, isolated on his elephant from his people. Soon His Majesty was engaged in a duel of spears with the Portuguese, he was slightly hurt on his hand.

He then turned his hand to show the wound, saying, 'Look here, all you Malays!'

When they saw that Sultan Ahmad was wounded, the warriors advanced and combatted with the Portuguese. Tun Salehuddin wished that Orang Kaya Sogoh would stab his spears at the enemy. But unfortunately, he himself was hit in the chest, and Tun Salehuddin subsequently died. And soon all the twenty warriors who were separated from the group also died. In the meantime, Seri Udana was wounded in his groin. Thus, Sultan Ahmad ordered that the elephant kneel down and Seri Udana be taken to the doctor. He was treated using the tail end of the betel leaf.

The healer said, 'It is all right, he may be cured; however, if it had entered even half the length of a rice grain deeper, then Seri Udana would have been dead.'

Thus, Melaka was defeated, ambushed by the Portuguese. The Melakans fled. The Bendahara Lubuk Batu himself was carried on a stretcher and rushed to safety. It was Si Selamat the Strong who carried him.

The Portuguese came in consecutive stages. The Bendahara said to the man who was carrying him, 'Crash me into the Portuguese.' But his children would not let him.

The Bendahara said, 'I challenge you all young men, if I were young as you are, I would have given my life for Melaka.'

Before long, Sultan Ahmad retreated to the upper reaches of Muar and then on to Pagoh. His father, Sultan Mahmud Shah stayed on in Batu Hampar. Sultan Ahmad himself built a fortress in Bentayan.

Thus, the Portuguese occupied Melaka. And the stones from the enclosure of the palace were used to erect a fortress—it is still there even now. Then the Portuguese came to Muar to attack Pagoh. There they battled, but after a few days, Pagoh was defeated and Sang Setia was killed.

It was related that Sultan Ahmad Shah retreated to the hinterland of Muar. And the Bendahara died there, buried in Lubuk Batu—that is the reason why he was called the Lord of Lubuk Batu.

After that Sultan Ahmad Shah and His Majesty's father, Sultan Mahmud Shah, trudged up the hills into the hinterland of Muar and then crossed over to Pahang. There they were welcomed by the Raja of Pahang.

There the daughter of Sultan Mahmud Shah and the Queen of Kelantan was given in marriage to the Raja of Pahang, Sultan Mansur Shah. From Pahang they sailed to Bentan. Sultan Ahmad established a *negeri* in Kopak.

It was related that Sultan Ahmad had no love for all the officers and chiefs, but only to all those mentioned before this. Only after the young men ate a feast of turmeric rice and ghee in the palace, would the officers of state and chiefs seek an audience with Sultan Ahmad.

The young men would then ask, 'Where is the turmeric rice and the remainder of the chicken soup that we ate?'

Sultan Mahmud Shah was not happy hearing the antics of his son, so he ordered that Sultan Ahmad be slain. When he died, His Majesty returned to the throne. He then assembled all the sons of chiefs, dignitaries and servants who were loyal to Sultan Ahmad.

Sultan Mahmud Shah addressed them, 'You do not have to be apprehensive about us. As it is to Si Ahmad, so is it to us.'

They bowed in obeisance, 'Very well, Your Majesty, your words are our command. We are with Your Majesty.'

Then Tun 'Ali Hati was summoned by Sultan Mahmud Shah. But he would not come.

He said, 'It is your royal son who improved me. If your son were to die at the hands of enemies, then I would want to die with him. But now it seems the hand of Your Majesty lies on my fate, I am helpless, the sky falls on the earth, and the Malay servant shall never rebel against his King. I ask that I too be slain.'

All the words of Tun 'Ali Hati were brought to His Majesty.

Sultan Mahmud Shah said, 'Say to 'Ali if we improve Ahmad, we will improve him too. Why does he speak in such a manner, for I do not want to slay him?'

Presently the words of the Sultan were relayed to Tun 'Ali Hati.

Tun Ali Hati replied, 'If His Majesty would grant me a favour, your servant wants to be slain, for he does not want to look upon faces other than his master's.'

So numerous were the persuasions, so that he would not follow the path of his master. But they were not heeded, for he earnestly wanted to follow him.

Thus, Sultan Mahmud Shah ordered Tun 'Ali Hati to be slain.

* * *

Sultan Mahmud Shah thus began to rule his new kingdom. Tun Pikrama, the Bendahara's son, was appointed the Bendahara with the title of Paduka Raja. Seri Amar Bangsa, the grandson of the Bendahara Putih, was made Prime Minister, who sat across from the Bendahara.

It was related that Seri Amar Bangsa had a son, Tun Abu Ishak, who bore Tun Abu Bakar, who was titled as Seri Amar Bangsa during the Johor period; his brother was called Orang Kaya-kaya Tun Muhammad. It was he who had two sons, called Orang Kaya-kaya Tun Undan and Orang Kaya-kaya Tun Sulat. Tun Abu Ishak was bestowed the title of Paduka Tuan. And Tun Hamzah, the Seri Nara al-Diraja's son, was appointed Chief of the Treasury with the title of Seri Nara al-Diraja. He was a favourite of Sultan Mahmud Shah.

In the meantime, Tun Biajit Rupa, the son of Bendahara Seri Maharaja, was made a minister, and known as Seri Utama. And Seri Utama had a son, Tun Dolah. In the meanwhile, Tun 'Umar, the son of Seri Maharaja, was also made a minister with the title of Seri Petam. Tun Muhammad, the brother of Seri Nara al-Raja, became the Chief of the Heralds, and given the title of Tun Nara Wangsa, while the son of Paduka Tuan, Tun Mat, held the title of Tun Pikrama Wira.

It was related that the Laksamana had a son, Khoja Hasan was his name; Khoja Hasan had died in grief and was buried on Bukit Pantau; it was he who was known as the Laksamana of (Bukit) Pantau.

After him Hang Nadim was made the Laksamana, he was the warrior renowned for his strength and courage, and was bathed in blood in thirty-two battles.

The Laksamana married *orang peraturan bonda*,[3] a relative, a cousin of Bendahara Lubuk Batu, on the mother's side, and bore a boy, Tun Mat 'Ali.

As the wheel of time turned, Sultan Mahmud Shah's son, Raja Muzaffar Shah, was preparing to succeed him on the throne. He was betrothed to Tun Terang, the granddaughter of Bendahara Seri Maharaja, and the daughter of Tun Fatimah and Tun 'Ali.

---

[3]   *Orang peraturan bonda*, a relative from one's mother's side.

In the hall, where Raja Muzaffar Shah held his audience, it was the convention of the court to first spread three mats—at the base was a mat of five layers, and on it another mat, on the top of them the royal carpet, upon which the Sultan sat.

Tun Fatimah was soon with child again. When her days were complete, she bore a boy, who was extremely good-looking. His Majesty named him Raja Alauddin Shah. When he was born, the carpet where Raja Muzaffar Shah sat was taken away. After seven days when Sultan 'Alauddin Shah was brought outside and his head shaved by His Majesty, the next layer of carpet was taken away, leaving the ordinary mat for commoners. After forty days, he was brought out of the palace. Sultan 'Alauddin was crowned Sultan, succeeding his father. He was called the 'Young Sultan' or 'Sultan Muda'. In due time, the Young Sultan grew into an adult, and a very handsome prince he was.

Allah knows the truth; to Him shall we return.

XXIV

Now the narrative of the chronicle turns to Sultan 'Abdullah, the Raja of Kampar. He was rebellious and refused to show his allegiance or pay his obeisance to Bentan. On the other hand, he sent a mission to Melaka, requesting assistance from Kapitan Melaka. A poem was composed to describe this new predicament, its words were thus:

Dihela-hela diretak sehasta
Kandis dipenggalkan
Alangkah gila Raja Kecil
Manggusta manis ditinggalkan
Melihat buah hartal masak.

A cloth is spread and cut to a span
The *kandis* fruit is cut
Raja kecil is indeed mad
For the sweet mangosteen he's abandoned
When he spotted the toxic fruit ripening.

When Sultan Mahmud Shah heard the news regarding Sultan 'Abdullah, he was extremely angry. So, His Majesty commanded that a fleet be prepared to attack Kampar. He ordered four ministers, firstly,

Seri Amar Bangsa; secondly, Seri Utama; thirdly, Seri Petam; fourthly, Seri Nata; and with them were fifty others. Tun Biajit, the son of Laksamana Hang Tuah, was appointed their military chief. When the preparations were complete, they sailed for Sumatra; Seri Amar Bangsa was its commander.

When they arrived in Kerumutan, the Portuguese too had reached there to assist Kampar, with ten fustas, five two-masted *banting*[1] vessels.

The Malay fleet then came into contact with the Portuguese boats and began to battle. However, the Malay boats were soon wrecked; and all their crew dived into the river at Kerumutan, and then proceeded to Inderagiri.

At this point of the battle, the concubine of Tun Biajit could not retrieve anything, except for his cockspur. There were those who brought their concubines—when they were about to depart, their concubines would be rolled in a mat, and then the slaves were ordered to carry them on their shoulders. It was only when they reached their destinations that the mats were unfolded.

After a few days of trudging, they arrived in Inderagiri. There Seri Amar Bangsa, Seri Utama and Seri Petam, Seri Nata and Tun Biajit and all those who had escaped, entered the palace to seek the audience of Sultan Nara Singa. On his part, Sultan Nara Singa gave gifts to all of them, each according to his status.

In Inderagiri, with only the resources he had left, Tun Biajit sought a cock, which he tended. He used it in a competition. When the Minangkabau clansmen noticed that Tun Biajit was partaking in cockfights, they too entered the contest to challenge him in the arena. Sometimes Tun Biajit won, but at others he lost, although mostly he won against them. Finally, all of the Minangkabau came together to defeat Tun Biajit.

There was a fighting cock owned by Raja Nara Singa, brought from Minangkabau. It was told that the cock had seen competition in thirty arenas. No one dared to challenge it. It was also ten *tahils* in weight.

---

[1] *Banting*, a Malay boat, with two masts.

Says the narrator of the chronicle, the owner of the fowl said, 'Whoever fights my fowl, its weight is its very stake.'

Raja Nara Singa encouraged Tun Biajit to try his luck.

Tun Biajit, 'Very well, Your Majesty.'

Soon Tun Biajit was seeking a fowl to champion his contests in the various villages. When he found one according to his choice, he began to carefully raise it. As soon as he was ready, he released it into the ring to challenge the Minangkabauans.

Raja Nara Singa said, 'Let us fight for ten *tahils* each and the weight of their cockerel is the stake. These are all the stakes, making one *kati* of gold, in all.'

Some of the gamers on the outside, placed a bet of ten *tahils,* making them thirty in all. Those who came with Tun Biajit, all placed their bets on his fowl. When the bets were considered sufficient, the fowls were released into the arena. Presently, Tun Biajit put on his special coat, which was made of potent with words from the *Quran.*

Tun Biajit said, 'Bet on me.' Thus, the Minangkabauans began to bet on his fowl. Some placed a *tahil,* some two, some three. When the bets totalled thirty *tahils,* Tun Biajit divided the gold: some in groups of two *tahils,* some in one, some in half a *tahil.* After all the *tahils* had been divided among his friends, the rest were tied up securely by Tun Biajit.

Then the cocks were freed. As soon as they began to combat, Raja Nara Singa's was stabbed at its side by Tun Biajit's, it tumbled at that very spot. The applause of the Bentan people was thunderous. From then on, all the Minangkabauans vowed never to challenge Tun Biajit again.

After they had been for some time in Inderagiri, Raja Nara Singa ordered that his men accompany them to return to Bentan.

* * *

It was related that the Portuguese fleet that had defeated the Bentan boats had sailed upriver, to seek the audience of Sultan 'Abdullah.

Sultan 'Abdullah bestowed gifts of clothes on Kapitan Mor.² Soon Raja 'Abdullah boarded the Portuguese fusta to inspect it. However, on board, he was bound by them, and the vessel sailed back downstream and taken to Melaka.

Upon their arrival, His Majesty was soon taken to Goah. And from there he was carried to Portugal. A *pantun* was composed to reflect on the incident:

> *Ke sana-sana raja duduk,*
> *Jangan ditimpa oleh papan;*
> *Diketahui ganja serbuk,*
> *Mengapa maka dimakan?*

> The raja sits far in the distance,
> Hoping that he's safe from falling planks;
> Why did he take it in the first instance,
> When he knew that marijuana intoxicates?

When Sultan Mahmud Shah heard of the news that Sultan 'Abdullah was captured by the Portuguese, he was deeply saddened. Promptly he ordered that they sail to Kampar to summon all the officers of Sultan 'Abdullah. Soon all of them arrived and sought His Majesty. Sultan Mahmud was full of wrath at all of them.

Sultan Mahmud Shah enquired, 'Is it true that all of you have chosen to die along with my son?'

All of them had their heads bowed, not even one of them dared to raise his head. The Bendahara of Kampar was Paduka Tuan; he was demoted and now only known as Seri Amar al-Diraja.

Allah knows the truth; to Him shall we return.

---

² *Kapitan Mor*, Portuguese 'great captain'

XXV

The narrative now turns to the passing of the old Maharaja of Lingga. Maharaja Isak succeeded him to the throne. Soon, he fitted vessels to seek the audience of the Sultan in Bentan. Upon his arrival, he sailed upstream to pay his homage. Sultan Mahmud Shah honoured him as was the custom of the land.

He was further looked upon with esteem, and placed under the Laksamana, for it was the arrangement from times of old that the Maharaja of Lingga was in rank lower than the Laksamana. Should he go anywhere, he was required to pause and praise the Laksamana. Those were the customs of old, and especially so when the Laksamana was an older relative to Maharaja Isak.

In the meanwhile, Raja Nara Singa, the Raja of Inderagiri, was preparing his ships in order to seek the audience of the Sultan in Bentan.

When His Majesty, learnt that Lingga was not paying him homage, he sailed to the island and sacked it. The wives and children of those who were captured were brought to Inderagiri as Raja Nara Singa was ready to do battle with the Raja of Lingga.

Soon Raja Nara Singa, who was much loved by Sultan Mahmud Shah, sailed to Bentan to pay Sultan Mahmud Shah his homage. But

he soon discovered that the Maharaja of Lingga had returned home
to Lingga.

* * *

In time, news of the death of Sultan Mansur Shah, the Raja of Pahang,
was heard in Bentan. His Majesty was slain by his father for adultery
with His Majesty's wife. Thus, Sultan Mahmud Shah invited to Bentan
his daughter, whom he then betrothed to Raja Nara Singa. He was
given a seat beside Sultan Mahmud Shah, and bestowed the title of
Sultan 'Abdul Jalil, complete with the *nobat* music in accompaniment.
Sultan Mahmud Shah had a great affection for Sultan 'Abdul Jalil,
more than his other sons-in-law.

Sultan 'Abdul Jalil and his Queen bore two boys—Raja Ahmad
and his younger brother, Raja Muhammad (nicknamed Raja Pang).

In time, Maharaja Isak arrived in Lingga. He soon discovered
that his *negeri* had been destroyed, and his wife and children captured
by the people of Inderagiri. So, Maharaja Isak returned to Bentan,
his intention was to report the incident to Sultan Mahmud Shah.
However, when he arrived, he discovered that Sultan Mahmud
Shah had taken Sultan 'Abdul Jalil as his son-in-law. Maharaja Isak
felt bereft.

As the months progressed, Sultan Mahmud Shah initiated an
accord between Maharaja Isak and Sultan 'Abdul Jalil, and thus his
children and wife were returned to him. However, Maharaja Isak
noticed that in the eyes of Sultan Mahmud Shah there was a great
difference in treatment of him against that of Sultan 'Abdul Jalil, for
Sultan 'Abdul Jalil was already Sultan Mahmud Shah's son-in-law.
Therefore, Maharaja Isak soon sought leave of Sultan Mahmud Shah
to return to Lingga.

When he arrived in Lingga and was giving an audience to all his
officers, he painted his face black with charcoal or white with chalk.

When they noticed it, they said, 'Your Majesty, there's charcoal or
chalk marks on your face!'

Then Maharaja Isak would wipe it. When he went outside the palace too, he would mark his face—this he did more than twice or thrice.

One day, Maharaja Isak was in court being attended to in the audience hall—there too he painted his face with charcoal.

All the officers commented, 'Why do we all see charcoal marks on Your Majesty's face?'

Maharaja Isak replied, 'Do you not know that my face has been smeared?'

They replied, 'No, Your Majesty, we do not know.'

Maharaja Isak continued, 'If you are able to wash this smear off my face, I shall tell all of you.'

The officers replied, 'Why would we not want to do it? Should it be to the point of sacrificing our lives that we would still venture to do it?'

Maharaja Isak enquired, 'Do you not know that my wife and children have been captured by the Inderagiri attackers? Now we wish to attack Inderagiri. Do you want to accompany us in this venture?'

The officers replied, 'Very well, My Lord. We pledge you our word.'

Soon the Maharaja began to make preparations. When all was ready, he moved against Inderagiri, and destroyed the *negeri*. The people of Inderagiri were not able to defend themselves, for all their military chiefs had journeyed to Bentan to accompany Sultan 'Abdul Jalil. Thus, all of their wives and children, who had been left in Inderagiri were seized.

In due time, Maharaja Isak returned to Lingga. There, he could not help but be apprehensive of the possibility that he would be attacked. So, Maharaja Isak sent a letter to Melaka to request for assistance. He was given three galleons, two fustas, and eight *banting* boats, besides twenty other vessels.

In the meantime, the Inderagiri officers sailed to Bentan to bring the news to Sultan 'Abdul Jalil. Sultan 'Abdul Jalil immediately sought the audience of Sultan Mahmud Shah, requesting leave to return to Inderagiri for his *negeri* had been destroyed by Maharaja Isak.

Sultan Mahmud Shah was enraged, and immediately ordered that a fleet be equipped to attack Lingga. The mission was to be led by the Laksamana. However, the Laksamana begged that he be excused from the task.

The Laksamana bowed in obeisance, 'Please My Lord, include me not in the mission to Lingga, for Maharaja Isak is a relative of mine. Should Lingga be undefeated, I would be accused as deceiving Your Majesty. Let me go to Melaka instead, My Lord.'

So, the Laksamana gathered a fleet of twenty large vessels and twelve smaller praos.

In the meantime, Sang Setia was commanded to lead the attack on Lingga. All of the military chiefs came along on the mission. As they arrived, they met with the Portuguese who were coming to assist Lingga. Their boats were anchored in the port of Dendang. The two sides were soon engaged in a battle, with Sang Setia fighting the Portuguese, in a great clatter of weapons. They could not land in Lingga as the waters were obstructed by the Portuguese. But Sang Setia rammed his boats against the Portuguese fleet. Thus, many of his men were hit and wounded by the cannons of the enemies.

Standing on the deck of his ship, Sang Jaya Pikrama was also hit, his arm smashed, and his muscles and veins dangling. The boat was not overcome; on the other hand, Lingga remained unbeaten. So, Sang Setia returned to Bentan to seek Sultan Mahmud Shah's audience.

In court, he related to His Majesty all that had happened in the battle. His Majesty was furious. So, he ordered that Sang Jaya Pikrama find a doctor to treat his wound and stop the bleeding.

Sang Jaya Pikrama cried out in agony.

Sang Guna addressed Sang Jaya Pikrama, 'Why are you crying? Aren't you a brave man?'

When he heard Sang Guna chiding him, he kept quiet. Many healers tried their hands, and he still said not a word. After a few days Sang Jaya Pikrama died.

* * *

It was narrated that the Laksamana and Sang Naya sailed to Melaka in twelve vessels. Upon arriving in Melaka, the Laksamana berthed his boat for three days in the estuary. The Portuguese did not appear, as all their boats had sailed to Lingga, and only two fustas were left. A Portuguese man by the name of Gongsalo was recently appointed captain.

He spoke to the old Kapitan Melaka, 'If you sail out with these two fustas you will not be attacked by the Malays.'

Kapitan Melaka responded, 'If I sail in these two fustas, the Laksamana will crash into me, for he is like no other warrior.'

Hearing this response, Gongsalo took a shallow dish and asked that it be taken to the bridge, saying, 'Whoever wants to accompany me to the bridge to pursue the Laksamana, do partake in this betel leaf.'

Soon all the soldiers assembled together. Then Gongsalo went to the bank of the river to prepare his boats. Subsequently both the fustas were rowed out, the soldiers no longer rowing him—all of them Portuguese, all of them white Caucasians.

When the Laksamana noticed the two fustas approaching, he said to Sang Naya, 'My Lord, you in six boats, are to crash against the single fusta, and I, in another six, will crash into the other.'

After they had apportioned their tasks, the Laksamana and Sang Naya rowed away. Soon, they met the Portuguese boats and began to battle. The Laksamana's crashed against Gongsalo's fusta and came alongside it. A huge battle broke out. In Gongsalo's, many were those who died or were wounded, their blood flooded into the Laksamana's, rising as high as the knees.

From the rugs and *kasang*[1] that were hung to dry, blood showered down like rain. The scene was the same in the Portuguese fusta. As they battled, their boats were drifted away from the estuary, in the direction of Punggur.

In the meantime, Sang Naya crashed his boat against the other fusta. The Portuguese opened fire, hitting Sang Naya, wounding him

---

[1]   *Kasang*, according to Wilkinson, is a type of curtain that is hung.

grievously. Soon after that Sang Naya was adrift and no one was left in his boat.

Help came to Gongsalo, in the form of assistance to fire on the Laksamana. If it had not received this help, perhaps the Portuguese would have been defeated. At that moment, the people battling each other were dispersed and the Portuguese retreated to Hujung Pasir. There they were delayed, unable to return to the Melaka River.

However, soon the Portuguese from the fort came to assist them. That was the reason why a homily was composed by the Melakans, here is what it sounds like:

Gongsalo namanya Kapitan Melaka,
Malunya rasanya kedapatan kata.

Gongsalo is the Kapitan of Melaka,
It's a shame that he was found out.

Soon after that, the Laksamana and Sang Naya returned to Bentan, to seek the audience of Sultan Mahmud Shah. His Majesty was angry with the Laksamana for having refused to go to Lingga, but His Majesty bestowed upon Sang Naya fine costumes and along with them his concubine, Tun Sadah.

In time, he married her, and they had two children, one a boy named Tun Dolah, another a girl, Tun Munah, who was betrothed to Tun Bilang, the son of Tun 'Abdul, grandson of the old Laksamana, Hang Tuah, and he begot Tun Merak.

In time, Sultan Mahmud Shah ordered that preparations be made to attack Melaka. Paduka Tuan was commanded to lead it. Tun Nara Wangsa, Tun Pikrama, the Laksamana, Sang Setia, Sang Naya, Sang Rana, Sang Seri Setia and all the military chiefs came along. Sultan 'Abdul Jalil, the Raja of Inderagiri, came as their scout. When all the preparations were complete, Paduka Tuan and Sultan 'Abdul Jalil departed with all the warriors, except for all the ministers who remained to mind the *negeri*.

As they approached the Sea of Sawang, they came across a junk from Berunai that was sailing for Melaka. Paduka Tuan called out to the captain of the junk. So, the captain came to pay his homage to Paduka Tuan. In the meantime, Sang Setia drew alongside the junk, along with Tun Kerah, Tun Munawar and Tun Dolah. Sang Setia and the young men boarded the junk and ransacked it. When the captain of the junk noticed that his junk was being ransacked, he requested permission to return. When Sang Setia noticed what was happening to the junk, he boarded his prao. When the captain had boarded, he ran amok amongst all those who ransacked his boat, causing them to jump into the water. Soon, he was on his way, but much was looted from his boat.

Said the Laksamana to Paduka Tuan, 'In my opinion it would be good for My Lord to probe to find out who has kept the loot because His Majesty is sure to enquire later.'

Paduka Tuan agreed, 'What My Lord has suggested is true. My Lord, Laksamana, please go and probe.'

The Laksamana answered, 'Very well, I shall go and begin the investigations into those captured. If two men are seized, then he takes one, if four are captured, then he takes two.'

Soon the Laksamana came to Tun Kerah's vessel. At that moment, Tun Kerah was issuing lunch to his slaves. The slaves were gathered at the helm. When the Laksamana noticed that Tun Kerah's vessel was heavier at the helm, he decided Kerah had not gained any booty. So, the Laksamana went to Tun Dolah's vessel, who had seized two women, one fair and the other dark.

The Laksamana ordered Tun Dolah, 'Tun Dolah, choose one according to your preference, and keep her.'

Tun Dolah replied, 'I have only captured the two; although I have taken so few, yet you are taking one from me. If you want, take all then!'

The Laksamana shouted, 'Do not behave so! It's fair to choose one and keep her.'

Tun Dolah replied, 'I do not want to, you take all.'

The Laksamana shouted back, 'Very well, if Tun Dolah does not want to, you can disembark now.'

It was only when the Laksamana took both of them that Tun Dolah called out, 'Leave the dark one with me.'

The Laksamana smiled, leaving the dark woman. Then, the Laksamana rowed to Sang Setia's. By then, Sang Setia had gathered all the boats in the expedition.

Sang Setia said, 'If the Laksamana investigates into my dealings, I shall fight him, for it has never been the custom among warriors to enquire into each other's takings. If you're a great military chief, so am I!'

The Laksamana said, 'Brother, I have been commanded by his lordship, Orang Kaya-kay Paduka Tuan to start the enquiry, and not to start a quarrel. If my brother agrees to it, I shall examine; if not, I shall return to report to his lordship.'

So, the Laksamana returned to Paduka Tuan and relayed all the words of Sang Setia. Subsequently, Paduka Tuan ordered his clansman to examine Sang Setia.

Upon his arrival, Sang Setia said, 'If the clansmen of Orang Kaya-kaya Paduka Tuan are agreeable, please go ahead and do your job, for the Laksamana may not examine me, as I am also a military chief.'

From there, Paduka Tuan sailed to Sawang. After a few days at sea, he arrived in Melaka, and dropped anchor in Sabat Island. Sultan 'Abdul Jalil, Paduka Tuan and all those who accompanied them came ashore to amuse themselves. The day wore on and the Inderagiri men brought out their *nobat* drums.

Sultan 'Abdul Jalil interceded, 'Do not beat on the *nobat* drums, for his lordship is still here.'

Paduka Tuan replied, 'Go ahead, beat your *nobat* drums, for we are about to confront the enemy.'

Sultan 'Abdul Jalil agreed, 'Very well, if it is with Paduka Tuan's permission.'

Subsequently, the musicians began to beat a roll on the *nobat*. After that Paduka Tuan returned to his boat.

Sultan 'Abdul Jalil said, 'I have been shamed by Paduka Tuan. He knew that he shall not be able to face the royal ensemble, that's why he asked that the *nobat* be beaten and he returned to his vessels; isn't it not to embarrass me?'

Sultan 'Abdul Jalil's words were heard by Paduka Tuan.

Paduka Tuan retorted, 'Is it possible that I meet the requirements and am qualified to play on the *nobat* of the Raja of Inderagiri?'

And his words were likewise relayed to the ears of Sultan 'Abdul Jalil.

Sultan 'Abdul Jalil replied, 'I was afraid that Paduka Tuan would not face the *nobat* drums, that was the reason why I forbade them to be beaten. Why did he ask them to go ahead?'

After some time, they crossed into Melakan waters. They agreed that the attack should be launched on Thursday evening, Sang Setia would come from the sea, while Paduka Tuan and the Laksamana with all their warriors, by river, from Air Leleh. However, that evening a violent storm descended, with heavy rain pouring down. So, the onshore attack had to be postponed, but Sang Setia crashed into one of the Portuguese ships, destroying it.

On Friday night, Paduka Tuan was prepared for the attack. It so happened that Sultan Mahmud Shah's elephant, Bidam Setia, was left behind in Muar. Paduka Tuan ordered that it be fetched. During the expedition, Paduka Tuan rode on Bidam Setia. The mahout at the head of the elephant was Maharaja Kunjara. In the meantime, Paduka Tuan had asked his son, Tun Mahmud, to accompany him on Bidam Setia. Tun Mahmud was known as Datuk Ligor, the chief of Ligor.

Thus, the Laksamana and all the military chiefs walked under the elephant of Paduka Tuan. From the top of the fort, the Portuguese fired their cannons, the shots came as heavy as rain. Many died. No one was willing to carry lanterns except two of the young clansmen of Paduka Tuan. One was Hang Hasan, the other, Hang Husin. Those on foot did not dare to walk far from the elephant, which they used as a shield from the shots.

They all reminded each other, 'Be wary of Bidam Setia, it is extremely naughty: while we are dodging the cannon fire, the elephant may trample on us.' Maharaja Kunjara called out, 'Do not fear. Should the trunk move even an inch, I shall kick at it.'

They then approached the fortress of Melaka. Paduka Tuan subsequently crashed Bidam Setia against it, breaking its right tusk. In the meantime, many had died of wounds caused by the cannons and shots fired from the fortress above. When daylight came, they retreated to the hill. Soon after that, Sultan 'Abdul Jalil sent a letter to Bentan, describing the progress of the war. Sang Setia was highly praised by His Majesty. But of Paduka Tuan evil words were spoken.

When the letter arrived in Bentan, Sultan Mahmud Shah was enraged. His Majesty ordered Tun Bijaya Sura to recall Paduka Tuan. Two letters were sent, one to Sang Setia, here is how it sounded:

Greetings and prayers to my brother Sang Setia.

Another was to Paduka Tuan, although no name was mentioned till the end, this is what it said:

If you compare yourself to the warriors of Prophet Muhammad, Hamzah and 'Ali, if you consider yourself more knowledgeable than Imam Ghazali, if it is not so, than you are a greater liar than Saiyid al-Haq.

Tun Bijaya Sura departed. Upon his arrival in Melaka, the words of His Majesty were relayed by Bijaya Sura to Paduka Tuan and the letter was read before the whole assembly. When Paduka Tuan heard the contents of the letter, he knew that it was himself that the letter referred to. Immediately Paduka Tuan, Sultan 'Abdul Jalil and all the military chiefs returned, and Bidam Setia was also taken back to Bentan.

After a while, they arrived back in Bentan. Every member of the expedition sought His Majesty's audience. At the time, His Majesty was holding court, so Raja 'Abdul Jalil, Paduka Tuan and the rest of them made obeisance and took their respective places. Sultan Mahmud Shah presently enquired of Sultan 'Abdul Jalil of the progress of the war. So, Sultan 'Abdul Jalil narrated to His Majesty all that had happened in the battle.

Sultan 'Abdul Jalil bowed and said, 'If Paduka Tuan wanted to attack on Thursday night when Sang Setia did attack, it would probably have been dangerous for the Melakans.'

When His Majesty heard Sultan 'Abdul Jalil's words he was very annoyed with Paduka Tuan. Paduka Tuan bowed low with his hands between his legs.

Then he raised his hands in homage and, while turning to face 'Abdul Jalil, he said, 'Your servant, oh Sultan 'Abdul Jalil, has come to do obeisance. My Lord has narrated with words untrue. Though I had promised to launch the attack on Thursday night, on that very night a storm descended on us. What could we old folks do? Going to war when even to pull up my blanket is a difficult task for me. Did not My Lord see that on Friday night Bidam Setia broke his tusk while ramming against the fort? What you meant to say, Sultan 'Abdul Jalil, "I am a favourite son-in-law of His Majesty, so I can say anything I like." Let me say this, I fear you not; I fear not your words that denounce me. I only fear His Majesty. My Lord, my very head is like Raja Inderagiri, whatever your wishes may be, I am ready to oppose them!'

Sultan 'Abdul Jalil bowed his head as he silently listened to Paduka Tuan. After His Majesty had been in the audience hall for a while, he departed. All those in the hall also returned to their respective homes.

Allah knows the truth; to Him shall we return.

XXVI

Now, the words of the narration turn to Sultan Ibrahim, the Raja of Siak who was deceased. His son, Raja 'Abdul, the husband of the Raja of Melaka's daughter, succeeded him on the throne. When he had ascended the throne, Raja 'Abdul prepared his vessels to seek the audience of Sultan Mahmud Shah in Bentan. When all the preparations were complete, he departed.

After a few days into the journey, they arrived in Bentan and duly sought the audience of Sultan Mahmud Shah. His Majesty was extremely pleased to see Raja 'Abdul, and duly bestowed on him the *nobat* and bestowed on him the title of Sultan Khoja Ahmad Shah and married him to his daughter.

In due time, Sultan Khoja Ahmad Shah and the Princess bore two boys, Jamal and Biajit.

In the meantime, Sultan Khoja Ahmad Shah had a brother, Raja Sami'un. He married the daughter of Raja Muara Kinta, and they had three daughters and two boys. The boys were Raja Isak and Raja Kudrat.

It so happened that one night, Sultan Mahmud Shah was recalling the list of all the *negeris* to the west that owed him allegiance but had not sought his audience, like Beruas and Manjung. And also, Tun Aria Bija Diraja, who have not come to pay him homage since the defeat of Melaka. That very night, Sultan Mahmud Shah asked that the Bendahara be bidden. So, the Bendahara presently arrived.

Sultan Mahmud Shah enquired of him, 'My Lord, the Bendahara, what is My Lord's view on this matter —for all our territories to the west have become no longer attached to us?'

The Bendahara replied, 'My Lord, in my opinion it is proper that Paduka Tuan be sent to the west to invite Tun Aria Diraja, for he is his in-law.'

Sultan Mahmud Shah agreed, 'It is true what My Lord has said. Convey our wishes to Paduka Tuan.'

The Bendahara replied, 'Very well, My Lord,' and presently returned home. He ordered that Paduka Tuan be called. When Paduka Tuan arrived, he repeated all the orders of Sultan Mahmud Shah. Paduka Tuan agreed to go. On the morrow, Sultan Mahmud Shah was in court, with all the rajas and the prime minister, courtiers and war chiefs. The Bendahara and Paduka Tuan came into the audience hall and took their respective places.

The Bendahara raised his hands and spoke, 'My Lord, I have relayed to Paduka Tuan all that Your Majesty had ordered yesterday. He has promised to make the journey.'

Sultan Mahmud Shah was greatly pleased to hear the Bendahara's words. His Majesty said, 'Very well, if Paduka Tuan has agreed to go, then we shall command him.'

Paduka Tuan spoke, 'Very well, Your Majesty. I am your servant, and it is not possible that I shall go against your words. If I cannot persuade him to come, then I shall stress to him the need to come before Your Majesty.'

Soon Paduka Tuan fitted twenty vessels. When all the preparations were complete, he sailed, taking along his wife and his son, Tun Mahmud Shah, who was also known as Datuk Ligor. It was related that Paduka Tuan's wife was called Tun Sabtu, and she had a brother by the name of Tun Aria Bija al-Diraja.

After a few days at sea, Paduka Tuan arrived from the west. Tun Aria Bija al-Diraja came to the harbour to welcome Paduka Tuan. When they met, they embraced each other.

'I have brought your sister with me.'

Tun Aria Bija Diraja asked, as though not believing his ears, 'Have you brought my sister, Sabtu, with you?'

Presently he took them all to his house.

Tun Aria Bija al-Diraja said to Paduka Tuan, 'What is your assignment here this time?'

Paduka Tuan replied, 'I come at the command of His Majesty to invite you.'

Tun Aria Bija al-Diraja replied, 'Even if I am not invited, I am ever ready to seek an audience with His Majesty, for who else shall be my master and My Lord other than Sultan Mahmud Shah? However, with just an invitation I shall not come to court. Even if with but a small prao, it is still considered a mission. If I come to court this time, then people will conclude that I come without my real intention, as though required by My Lord.'

Paduka Tuan agreed, 'It is true what My Lord has spoken, but let us betroth your daughter, Tun Mah, to Mahmud.'

Tun Aria Bija al-Diraja responded, 'Very well.'

On an auspicious day, Tun Mahmud was married to Tun Mah. Soon after that Paduka Tuan sailed to Bentan. In the meanwhile, Tun Mahmud remained with Tun Aria Bija al-Diraja. Furthermore, the authority over Selangor was given by Paduka Tuan to Tun Mahmud.

Soon after that, Paduka Tuan returned. Upon their arrival in Bentan, Paduka Tuan proceeded to court to seek the audience of Sultan Mahmud Shah. He repeated all the words of Tun Aria Bija al-Diraja to His Majesty, who was greatly pleased to hear them.

It was narrated that, as soon as Paduka Tuan departed for Bentan, Tun Aria Bija al-Diraja made preparations to sail. Thirty vessels were fitted. When all the preparations were completed, they set sail in the southward direction.

As soon as they arrived in Bentan, Tun Aria Bija al-Diraja proceeded to the audience hall. His Majesty was greatly delighted to see that the Raja of the West has come.

His Majesty presented him with a complete change of the finest costume and bestowed the *nobat* on him, so that he be crowned in the west. In response, Tun Aria Bija al-Diraja promised to bring the people of Manjung and all those from the territories to invade Melaka.

In due time, Sultan Mahmud Shah requested Tun Aria Bija al-Diraja to return home. Presently, His Majesty removed a ring from his finger and gifted it to him.

Said His Majesty, 'Tun Aria Bija al-Diraja is like our ring; if we cast it into the sea, and if our fortune is good, it shall rise to the surface.'

Subsequently, Tun Aria Bija al-Diraja bowed low and raised his hands in homage. Again he was bestowed with gifts of fine clothes, after which he departed.

After a journey of a few days at sea, he arrived in the west. There he was installed in a coronation, complete with the *nobat*. Along with him, all his officers and courtiers sat facing the *nobat* ensemble. When the ceremony was complete, they raised their hands in homage to Tun Aria Bija al-Diraja.

In turn, Tun Aria Bija al-Diraja raised his hands in homage, facing Bentan, saying, '*Daulat* Sultan Mahmud Shah.'

It was related that Tun Aria Bija al-Diraja had three boys: one was titled Raja Lela; the second, Tun Rana; and the third, Tun Sayid.

Soon after that, Sultan 'Abdul Jalil sought the permission of Sultan Mahmud Shah to return to Inderagiri. In due time, he arrived safely home.

Allah knows the truth; to Him shall we return.

XXVII

Now the words of the story turn to the Raja of Haru, Sultan Husin was his name. He was extremely good-looking and gracious in his ways, and furthermore was resolute and brave.

He once said, 'If I am on my elephants, with Dasinang and Si Tambang in the rear, and Si Pikang under it, I will defeat all the Javanese, all the Chinese and also all the Portuguese from the mainland.'

When news of the beauty of Raja Putih, the daughter of Sultan Mahmud Shah, reached his ears, His Majesty became enamoured of her. Therefore, Sultan Husin intended to sail to Bentan, to seek the hand of Raja Putih, for he had heard of her beauty and how she was much loved by her father.

Sultan Husin's mother advised him against it, 'Do not travel to Hujung Tanah, for it is our enemy.'

Sultan Husin replied, 'Even though I could be killed by the great rajas, I would still want to seek the audience of His Majesty, the Raja of Hujung Tanah.'

Though he was dissuaded by his mother, he still intended to sail there. Soon, he set sail to Bentan in two junks, one passenger vessel and another carrying only male passengers.

After a few days in the Straits, he arrived in Layam. Sultan Mahmud Shah ordered the Bendahara and all the officers to welcome him. And the crown prince was asked to be taken on to the Bendahara's laps.

So, they set out to greet them in numerous vessels, both sides gathering in Tekulai. Sultan Husin's vessel drew up alongside the crown prince, Sultan Muda's. Presently Sultan Husin came from under the awning and stood erect. Then the Bendahara came from under the awning, bringing along the crown prince with him.

Sultan Husin suggested 'Let me come over to My Lord's vessel.'

Said the Bendahara: 'Let me come over to your vessel instead.'

Said Sultan Husin: 'I would like to be rowed by the slaves.'

The Bendahara replied, 'In that case, please do come to our boat.'

So, Sultan Husin boarded the Bendahara's vessel. The Sultan, Muda, was taken on to Sultan Husin's laps. When the slaves began to row Sultan Husin's boat was left far behind. When they arrived at Kota Kara, the Bendahara commanded, 'Wait here.'

Sultan Husin asked, 'What need is there to wait?'

The Bendahara said, 'My Lord's vessel is yet to arrive.'

Sultan Husin replied, 'Hai, Bendahara, great is our longing for Your Majesty, the King of Haru. We have now come in two vessels. Let's proceed so that we may pay our homage to His Majesty.'

So, he bowed, and his boat was promptly rowed away.

Upon arriving at Jambu Air, Sultan Mahmud Shah himself came on an elephant to welcome Sultan Husin. Promptly Sultan Husin bowed and made obeisance. Sultan Mahmud Shah embraced and kissed him, taking him up on the elephant, and giving him a seat beside him in the howdah, along with Sultan Muda in his lap.

When they arrived and entered the audience hall, Sultan Mahmud Shah invited Sultan Husin to sit by him. Soon a meal was served, and Sultan Mahmud Shah dined with Sultan Husin.

It was said that Sultan Husin brought along a herald, Seri Indera was his name. He stood close to his master. There was a cock fight in the yard of the court and there was much riotous applause, Sultan Husin was enthralled by the competition. He leant involuntarily towards His Majesty, pointed to the cocks and said, 'Put this on for me!'

On seeing this, Seri Indera squeezed Sultan Husin's leg, 'My Lord, my beloved father,'

Soon, Sultan Husin paid homage and bowed low—that was the way he conducted himself.

There was a warrior of Sultan Husin, Din was his name. Whenever Sultan Husin was inebriated, he would praise the warrior, 'This Din has a brave father, his courage has been inherited. Is it ever possible for a cowardly father to beget a brave son?'

Thus he continued to praise Si Din. He praised all and sundry but especially Din.

It was rumoured that Sultan Husin was not well received by Sultan Mahmud Shah as a prospective son-in-law.

When he heard of the news, he said, 'If this Husin is not received well by the people, I shall invade Bentan!'

His Highness ripped off his shirt. Then he pushed hard at his *keris* and forcibly split its sheath.

It was told that in these times Sultan Husin changed his clothes seven times a day. Then Sultan Mahmud Shah had a change of heart, and accepted him as a prospective son-in-law. Sultan Husin was greatly pleased. Soon, all Sultan Husin's warriors from Haru came to greet him. On each day, a boat or two would berth in the port. Finally, all of them had gathered—there were a hundred in all.

So, Sultan Mahmud Shah began to initiate the wedding ceremony between Sultan Husin with Raja Putih; the festivities lasted for three months, after which, Sultan Husin was married to Raja Putih. However, after the wedding Raja Putih did not love Sultan Husin and returned to her father. As a replacement, Sultan Mahmud Shah bestowed on him another daughter.

Sultan Husin was unwilling to accept her, saying, 'She is my relative, my sister-in-law, how can I accept her? I want my own wife!'

The Bendahara said to Sultan Mahmud Shah, 'Your Majesty, why does My Lord listen to your daughter's wishes? If My Lord allows her to have her ways, how then would it be perceived by those who hear about it?'

Sultan Mahmud Shah replied, 'It is true what My Lord has said.' Soon he persuaded Raja Putih to return to Sultan Husin. In due time, Raja Putih returned Sultan Husin. His Majesty was extremely happy. Eventually, Sultan Husin and Raja Putih became very loving towards each other.

After a while, Sultan Husin was homesick for Haru. Sultan Husin said, 'I cannot be long in Bentan for three reasons: firstly, the whispers of Hang Embung; secondly, the salutations of Tun Rana; thirdly, the swaying of Tun Bija Sura. As for the whispers of Hang Embung, if a word was spoken, be it good or evil, it would be said in whispers, for a whisper has within it a secret, those who hear it will harbour a suspicion. As for the salutations of Tun Rana, even if the place is crowded and the people sit cross-legged with their thighs overlapping Tun Rana will still be trying to make his way in, saying, 'Excuse me, excuse,' and he would walk over them with discourtesy. And as for the swaying of Tun Bija Sura, when he is swaying his body, as long as nobody paid him any attention, he would go ahead with his *latah*,[1] causing tears in his sarongs. These were the three people who dissuaded Sultan Husin from wanting to remain long in Bentan.

So, His Highness sought leave of Sultan Mahmud Shah to return to Haru. Sultan Mahmud Shah agreed, 'Very well.'

Thus, Sultan Husin made preparations and when they were ready, he came with his wife, Raja Putih, into the audience hall to pay homage. Sultan Mahmud Shah embraced and kissed both his children. The sound of the weeping in the palace sounded as though they were at a wake. Then Sultan Mahmud Shah gave the royal costumes and instruments of state to Raja Putih, they were numerous indeed, innumerable. To this was added a *bahara* of gold.

Moreover, he bestowed all his costumes that he was dressed in to Raja Putih. Only a brass bowl, called 'Adimona Sari Air' was given to Sultan Muda and a sword of state decorated with a dragon.

---

[1] *Latah*, 'a peculiar nervous paroxysmal disease.'

The Bendahara bowed in obeisance towards Sultan Mahmud Shah, 'My Lord, your son the prince, Sultan Muda, shall be installed as monarch, however, Your Majesty has given all to your daughter who is departing for Haru, and nothing is left to your son.'

Sultan Mahmud Shah replied, 'If there is a sword of state with Sultan Muda, there is also gold, meaning, when there is a kingdom, there shall also be gold.'

Additionally, His Majesty bestowed on the forty men and forty women who would accompany them to Haru—some bringing their wives along, some leaving their fathers and others as fathers leaving their children behind.

Soon Sultan Husin sailed downstream. Sultan Mahmud Shah accompanied them up to Dada Air. When Sultan Husin's vessel was no longer visible, His Majesty disembarked and returned to his palace.

In due time, Sultan Husin arrived in Haru. His Majesty entered the palace, bringing along his consort, and then sought his mother, who kissed and embraced both her children. Thus, ended his mother's longing for them.

She asked of him, 'What are the memorable things that you have seen?'

Sultan Husin replied, 'Many are the beautiful things that I have seen, but none more than two occasions.'

His mother enquired, 'What are these two occasions?'

Sultan Husin Shah replied, 'When the King gave a feast, there were twenty or thirty tables of food, sixteen or seventeen servings, but were they loud? Not even the creaking of the floor could be heard; suddenly one finds one is served. How big were the servings? Four times our servings. And furthermore, all their plates, bowls and trays were of gold and silver or brass.'

Sultan Husin's mother was in awe of the description articulated by her son.

Allah knows the truth; to Him shall we return.

XXVIII

The words of the narrative now turn to the Sultan of Pahang coming to pay homage to Sultan Mahmud Shah. Upon his arrival, he was subsequently chosen as the Sultan's son-in-law, to wed His Majesty's daughter, Raja Hatijah, and they were both bestowed the *nobat* during the ceremony. After some time, in Bentan all the rajas who had come to do obeisance sought permission to return to their respective *negeris*.

In the meantime, it was reported to His Majesty, 'A fleet from Goah had laid anchor in Melaka, with thirty vessels, four galleons, five long galleons, eight fustas and two *banting*, and they will strike at us.'

So, Sultan Mahmud Shah ordered the Bendahara to repair the fortress and assemble the subjects. Subsequently, His Majesty commanded Seri Udana, for he was the Temenggung, to direct the workers who would repair and strengthen the fortress.

From Seri Udana's own initiative, all the servants were given notice in writing, ordering them to come to work. Here is how it reads:

I, Seri Udana, and another, Si Tanda is his name, and Pertanda, the
spear-bearer, and another still, Si Selamat, are navigating our vessel,
and carrying the betel bowl; another, Si Tuha who is a rower, bearing

a sword. Another still, Si Teki, an attendant and also a bearer of the water vase.[1]

This letter was written in honour of Sultan Mahmud Shah. After His Majesty had seen the contents of the letter, he became extremely angry.

He said, 'When it comes to Seri Udana's turn to become Bendahara, let Allah kill us all before then!'

Soon the fortress was completed. In the meantime, Sang Setia agreed to guard it.

Sang Setia said, 'If the fortress is breached or defeated, then I am dead. If the Portuguese attack what shall we do? We shall shoot at them with these two cannons. Their shots are as big as pomelos—one is called Naga Ombak, the Dragon of the Waves, the other Katak Berenang, the Swimming Frog. Those are our strength.'

In due time, the Portuguese came. Patih Suradara was commanded by the Sultan to spy on their plans and movements. He met them and rowed by in a hurry. When asked by the people, 'Patih Suradara, what is the latest news?'

He replied, 'Their boats are in Lubuk, while their warships are roaming around in Tengkilu.'

He had witnessed the latest incidents, when he returned to Kopak, he could describe them all to His Majesty.

Soon His Majesty relayed the message to Paduka Tuan, 'The Portuguese are now in Kuala Tebing Tinggi!'

Seri Nara al-Diraja was rowed to Paduka Tuan's vessel for a consultation. In the meantime, the Portuguese had sailed upstream in four galleys. Thus, Paduka Tuan's vessel was flanked by the Portuguese, two on the right and two on the left. It seemed like all the other vessels in the expedition were also approaching.

His men asked of Paduka Tuan, 'What do you think, My Lord, now that there are so many Portuguese vessels arriving?'

---

[1]   *Kemendalam*, water vase.

Paduka Tuan was quiet, taking his time to think, and in his heart saying, 'If I were to attack at the time the Seri Nara al-Diraja was here, he would be easily recognised, for he is a favourite of Yang Dipertuan.'

So Paduka Tuan summoned Hang Aji Maris, for he was the captain of the Paduka Tuan's vessel, and whispered to him. Subsequently, Hang Aji Maris moved to the bows.

Said the Seri Nara al-Diraja, 'Paduka Tuan, My Lord, let's crash against these Portuguese.'

Paduka Tuan replied, 'Very well.'

From the bows Hang Aji Maris shouted, 'Our boat has run aground.'

Paduka Tuan called back, 'If our boat is aground, then retreat.'

Thus, Hang Aji Maris ordered his men to row upstream, and they followed his instruction, rowing upstream.

When the tide was low the Portuguese returned to attack. They secured their galley to the fort. However, when it was high tide, all the stakes came loose. From land, volleys were fired incessantly, striking the ship.

Next, Sang Setia's fortress was attacked. And the two sides were soon involved in a real combat, many were those in the fray, and many died or were wounded. Sang Setia asked for help from those on the other side of the bank.

Sultan Mahmud Shah ordered Tun Nara Wangsa, 'Assist Sang Setia!'

Tun Nara Wangsa bowed and went to help. Paduka Tuan witnessed that those who went were, if not dead, naked and swimming towards the bank.

Paduka Tuan came to Sultan Mahmud Shah, saying, 'My Lord, I would like to ask the assistance of my son-in-law, for the enemy is indeed numerous. Who will assist me, if not him?'

Sultan Mahmud Shah agreed, 'Very well, Tun Nara Wangsa.' So, Nara Wangsa returned.

The war had spread. Sang Setia had died. The Laksamana was wounded. The Bentan side broke and the soldiers fled. However,

Sultan Mahmud Shah did not move from his palace. In his mind, 'If the Portuguese arrive, I shall run amok from this place.'

The Seri Nara al-Diraja said, 'My Lord, it's wise that you retreat for the *negeri* is defeated.'

Sultan Mahmud Shah replied, 'Hai Seri Nara al-Diraja, we have long known that Bentan is an island state. In our mind we shall not retreat, that is why we choose to live here. If it is in our plans to retreat it would have been better to live on the mainland, for it is the custom on land that when it is lost, the King dies.'

Seri Nara al-Diraja said, 'My Lord, your words are incorrect, for there are Kings all around. If Your Majesty is granted long life, then more *negeris* can be established.'

Sultan Mahmud Shah said, 'Say no more, Seri Nara al-Diraja, we shall never retreat from here.'

Then the Seri Nara al-Diraja took Sultan Mahmud Shah's hands and helped him down to walk away with him.

Sultan Mahmud Shah said, 'Seri Nara al-Diraja shall die as a martyr taking me to safety.'

The Seri Nara al-Diraja, replied, 'I am ever ready to take Your Majesty away.'

Sultan Mahmud Shah then said, 'We are leaving behind much possession and gold, what shall we do?'

The Seri Nara al-Diraja, replied, 'In my opinion we will still save the assets and the gold.'

The Seri Nara al-Diraja, then ordered the Bendahara, 'Save His Majesty's assets and belongings in the palace.'

The Bendahara replied, 'Very well.'

The Bendahara then stopped all those who were about to flee. And all the properties and gold were divided among them in smaller quantities and he instructed them to carry them all. All were saved, not even one was left behind. Soon, the Portuguese came and looted the place; the inhabitants ran helter-skelter to save themselves.

Sultan Mahmud Shah then trudged through the forest; many were the women in their company, but Seri Nara al-Diraja was the only man, as he would not be parted from His Majesty. At an appointed place, they met Tun Nara Wangsa who was searching for his wife and children.

When the Seri Nara al-Diraja, recognised him he called out, 'Brother Mahmud, where are you off to?'

Nara Wangsa answered, 'I am searching for my wife.'

Seri Nara al-Diraja responded, 'Come, My Lord, for this is in His Majesty's service.'

Tun Nara Wangsa answered, 'His Majesty is already here. My wife and children—what would happen if they were captured by the Portuguese?'

The Seri Nara al-Diraja, replied, 'So says My Lord, for is it not the custom of the Malays to want their wives and children. Is it possible that they are lying to their masters? Especially our father, who would kill them? Not this Raja! Now is the time we repay his sacrifices for us. Is it not also true that you are my relative, how could you leave me in such a predicament?'

When he heard Seri Nara-al Diraja's words, he returned to attend to the Sultan, who was walking through the forest, his feet sprained, and not able to continue as he was quite weak.

When his feet were bandaged, he could start to walk again. Sultan Mahmud Shah said to Seri Nara al-Diraja, 'We have not eaten since early this morning.'

When the Seri Nara al-Diraja, heard his words he said to Tun Nara Wangsa, 'My Lord, please go and find some rice for His Majesty.'

So, Tun Nara Wangsa went; after some time, he met a woman carrying rice in a basket.

He said to her, 'Dear auntie mother, please give me some rice.'

Said the woman, 'Please take it, My Lord.'

So Tun Nara Wangsa plucked a few large *dedap* leaves and wrapped the rice in them. Then he took it to Sultan Mahmud Shah, who promptly ate it.

After he had eaten, His Majesty asked, 'What says you, My Lord; I have not even a cent of gold with me?'

Then the Seri Nara al-Diraja, ordered Tun Nara Wangsa, 'Go and find His Majesty's gold for me.'

Tun Nara Wangsa replied, 'Very well.' So, he went to the palace. There he saw someone carrying a chest, about two *katies*[2] in weight. Tun Nara Wangsa took it from him and carried it away.'

Those who saw him said, 'See, Tun Nara Wangsa is stealing!'

The accusation did not register with him. So, he covered the chest and carried it to the Sultan.

The Sultan said, 'It's enough.'

They then proceeded on foot to Dompok.

It was related that the Bendahara followed His Majesty from behind. In the meantime, Paduka Tuan and all his family departed from the other side of Bentan, to proceed to Sayung.

Said Paduka Tuan to his son, Tun Pikrama, 'You row out to the sea, and gather all His Majesty's subjects there. Then let's receive His Majesty there.'

Thus, Tun Pikrama rowed to gather all the slaves, who all came at his command.

Tun Mahmud, the son of Paduka Tuan, came from Selangor in twenty boats, and met Tun Pikrama on the island of Buru.

Said Tun Pikrama to Tun Mahmud, 'Let us go and invite His Majesty.'

Tun Mahmud agreed, 'Very well.'

Soon, Tun Pikrama and Tun Mahmud sailed to welcome Sultan Mahmud Shah in Dompak. It was related that the Portuguese had retreated fifteen days since. His Majesty was delighted to see Tun Mahmud come from afar. They brought a special boat for His Majesty, on which he embarked.

The Sultan said to the Bendahara, 'What says My Lord now, where shall we go?'

The Bendahara replied, 'I heard it told by my father that if anything should happen to the *negeri*, the Raja should be taken to Kampar.'

---

[2] *Kati*, a measurement of weight.

Said Sultan Mahmud Shah, 'If that is so, then let's go to Kampar.'

So, His Majesty departed for Kampar. Upon his arrival, His Majesty made it his chosen abode. Furthermore, he wanted to reward Tun Mahmud for coming promptly to seek his audience.

Thus, Sultan Mahmud Shah ordered the Bendahara, 'Choose from among these titles that is most fitting for Tun Mahmud Shah: firstly, Tun Telani; secondly, Tun Bijaya Maha Menteri; thirdly, Tun Aria Bija al-Diraja; fourthly, Seri Nara al-Diraja. Pick the one My Lord thinks is most appropriate.'

The Bendahara bowed, 'The title of Tun Telani, though an ancient one from our ancestors, sounds archaic, originating from life in the forest. As for Tun Bijaya, though a ministerial title, it is inappropriate for Tun Mahmud Shah. And as for Tun Aria Bija al-Diraja, though a title bestowed on his father-in-law, is a title used in Hujung Karang. And as for the Seri Nara al-Diraja, though it is a great title, it is too ancient.'

He soon came to seek His Majesty's audience, advising, 'Bestow on him the title of Seri Akar Raja.'

So, His Majesty bestowed on Tun Mahmud, the title of Seri Akar Raja. Soon after that, Paduka Tuan and all the chiefs and officers came to the audience hall.

When the news that Bentan had been defeated reached Haru, Sultan Husin sailed to Kampar to pay his obeisance. His Majesty was truly delighted to see Sultan Husin. Sultan Husin's Vizier, Raja Pahlawan, accompanied His Highness. Raja Pahlawan was the Raja of Seri Benyaman, a great King in Haru. It was the custom in Haru that, during a reception, the highest of the chiefs dined at a higher level in the hall, and whoever was known for his courage was also invited to dine at this level. As for Raja Pahlawan, he dined at a higher level and also took his drinks at this level for he was a great and brave chief.

After some time in Kampar, Sultan Husin sought leave of His Majesty, to return to Haru.

In due time, the Bendahara returned to the mercy of Allah. He was buried in Tambak, that is reason why he is known as the Bendahara of

Tambak. Paduka Tuan succeeded him as Bendahara. It was also related then that Seri Udana had passed on and Tun Nara Wangsa became the Temenggung.

Sultan Mahmud Shah said to the Seri Nara al-Diraja, 'Great is Seri Nara al-Diraja's service to us, we could never repay you. If Seri Nara al-Diraja wishes to marry my daughter, I shall take you as my son-in-law.'

Seri Nara al-Diraja bowed low, 'Forgive me, Your Majesty, I am but a servant, and your daughter is my mistress.'

Sultan Mahmud Shah enquires, 'Why does Seri Nara al-Diraja say so, if we thought that you are not suitable, we would not want to take Seri Nara al-Diraja as our son-in-law.'

Seri Nara al-Diraja raised his hands in obeisance, 'It is true what Your Majesty has said, we human beings are but children of the Prophet Adam *'alaihissalam*, not one is from another species, some are Muslims, some non-believers. This is the situation we find ourselves in, for my ancestors were servants to the ancestors of the rajas of old. If I marry Your Majesty's daughter, then the name of the Malays of old who preceded us will be tainted.'

Sultan Mahmud Shah said, 'If Seri Nara al-Diraja does not obey our orders, then My Lord commits treason.'

Seri Nara al-Diraja bowed, 'My Lord, forgive me; let me be cursed with a good name but not commit treason towards Your Majesty.'

Sultan Mahmud Shah approved, 'If it's true that My Lord, Seri Nara al-Diraja, does not want to marry my daughter, and then we may give her to another?'

Seri Nara al-Diraja said, 'Very well, My Lord, it is my wish that Your Majesty gives your daughter to another.'

So, Sultan Mahmud Shah gave his daughter, the princess, to marry the son of the Raja of Pahang, who was also from the original line of kings.

In due time, Sultan Mahmud Shah became ill. He asked that the Bendahara, Paduka Tuan, Seri Nara al-Diraja and two or three of the senior chiefs be fetched. His Majesty leaned his forehead on the Seri Nara al-Diraja's shoulder.

Sultan Mahmud Shah said, 'We feel that this illness shall bring our life to a conclusion. We leave as *petaruh*[3], entrust Sultan Muda into your care, for he is yet a small boy.'

The Bendahara and all the chiefs said, 'My Lord, may Allah protect and keep all evil from Your Majesty. However, should the grass wither in Your Majesty's meadow, we shall never go against your instructions.'

His Majesty was truly delighted to hear the words of his chiefs. Within a few days, Sultan Mahmud Shah returned to his Lord, the Creator, going from this transient world to the eternal one. Sultan Mahmud Shah was buried according to the royal rites of the land. He was known as Marhum di Kampar.

His Majesty was on the throne of Melaka for thirty years, and then Melaka was defeated. After a year in Muar he went to Pahang, His Majesty was in Bentan for twelve years and in Kampar for five years. Thus, His Majesty was on the throne for forty-eight years in all.

After the Marhum di Kampar had died, His Majesty Sultan Muda became King, his title on the throne was Sultan 'Alauddin Ri'ayat Shah. However, the Crown Princess was expelled by the Bendahara and all the chiefs. Raja Muda Perempuan asked, 'Why am I forbidden? It is not possible that I would want to wrest the throne from the Sultan Muda?'

They all replied, 'Let the Raja Muda be gone from this *negeri*!'

Raja Muda replied, 'Wait a moment, my rice is still on the boil.'

Said all the chiefs, 'Why wait? Leave now!'

So, the Raja Muda descended from the palace with his wife, Tun Terang, and his son, Raja Mansur.

The Raja Muda said, 'Send word to Encik Leman, if I were to die, Mansur Shah should be investigated by Encik Leman.'

The chiefs replied, 'Very well.'

The Raja Muda found a place on his boat to Siak. From Siak he journeyed to Kelang. There was a gentleman from Manjung, Sik Mi was his name. He was a merchant who traded between Perak and Kelang.

---

[3] *Petaruh*, entrust, ward.

When he found the Raja Muda in Kelang, he took him to Perak, and crowned him in Perak. His title in the state was Sultan Muzaffar Shah.

As was reported, Seri Akar Raja had been earlier asked by the Bendahara, Paduka Tuan, as though the Bendahara had an authority over Selangor.

* * *

In the meantime, the Sultan of Kedah begot a girl, Raja Siti was her name. After many years, Seri Akar Raja travelled to Kedah to marry Raja Siti and took her to Selangor.

In the intervening time, Sultan Muzaffar Shah ordered that his daughter and her husband be fetched. When Seri Akar Diraja arrived in Perak, he was appointed the Bendahara.

Meanwhile, Sultan Muzaffar Shah begot a girl, Raja Dewi was her name; and then another, Raja Ahmad, then another, Raja 'Abdul Jalil, then Raja Fatimah, then Raja Hatijah, then another, Raja Tengah. With his wife, Tun Terang, he bore sixteen children. However, with his concubine he had a boy, Raja Muhammad was his name.

Allah knows the truth; to Him shall we return.

XXIX

The narrative now turns to the episode of Sultan 'Alauddin Ri'ayat Shah. After some time on the throne, His Majesty sought a wife in Pahang. He ordered the Bendahara Paduka Tuan, to make the necessary preparations for the journey. Thus, the Bendahara Paduka Tuan, got busy making the arrangements, and when they were complete, Sultan 'Alauddin Ri'ayat Shah journeyed to Pahang.

After some time, they arrived at their destination. Sultan Mahmud Shah was the Raja of Pahang then. As soon as he heard of the arrival of Sultan 'Alauddin Ri'ayat Shah, His Majesty promptly came to welcome him. When they met, Sultan Mahmud Shah bowed low in obeisance, and was soon taken into the *negeri* and given a seat of honour on the throne. His Majesty shared some pleasurable times with Sultan Mahmud. At an auspicious moment His Majesty was wedded to a sister of Sultan Mahmud.

After some time has passed, it was time for the Raja of Pahang to deliver the golden and silver flowers to Siam as an acknowledgement of its authority over Pahang. His Majesty ordered that preparations be made. When they were complete, His Majesty ordered that a letter be written to the Raja of Siam and Berakelang. The letter of Pahang to the Berakelang was a '*sembah*', an obeisance. At that moment the Bendahara Paduka Tuan, was present.

Sultan Mahmud enquired of the Bendahara Paduka Tuan, 'Does Pahang send a letter of obeisance to the Berakelang?'

The Bendahara Paduka Tuan, replied, 'Not just your good self, even I sent him no obeisance.'

Tun Derahman enquired, 'What type of letter do the Pahang folks write in Kelang, My Lord?'

The Bendahara Paduka Tuan, replied, 'I would like to write a letter, but my epistle contains nothing.'

Sultan Mahmud interjected, 'Let us send greetings.'

The Bendahara replied, 'Very well.' So, the Bendahara drafted a letter to the Berakelang, and here is how it read:

A letter of affection from the Bendahara, addressed to the Adi Berakelang.

After that other words followed. In the meantime, Sultan Mahmud added, also just conveying his affection. When the mission was ready, it departed for Siam. As it arrived, news of its coming was relayed to the Berakelang, that it was carrying an epistle from the Raja of Pahang and the Bendahara of Hujung Tanah.

The Berakelang enquired, 'What does the letter from the Bendahara and the Raja of Pahang say?'

The envoy replied, 'It says—from the Bendahara, a letter of love and affection; and also the same greetings from the Raja of Pahang.'

The Berakelang commanded, 'Bring the letter from the Bendahara of Hujung Tanah in, and as for the letter from the Raja of Pahang, return it, for it is not the custom of the Raja of Pahang to send his love and affection to the Berakelang of Ayodia!'

The envoy replied, 'Why is the letter of the Bendahara Hujung Tanah accepted, while that of the Raja of Pahang is rejected? Is it because the Raja of Pahang is master to the Bendahara?'

Said the Berakelang, 'He who is there understands not? In this palace it is recognised that the Bendahara Hujung Tanah, is of a higher status than that of the Raja of Pahang. If you are uncertain go and examine the *tambera*, the genealogy. Order that the letter be changed so that we can receive it.'

Thus, the envoy copied the epistle and replaced it with the word '*sembah*', homage, and it was duly accepted by the Berakelang. Soon the Pahang mission returned. Upon its arrival, the episode in Siam was related to His Majesty, Sultan Mahmud.

After spending some time in Pahang, Sultan 'Alauddin Ri'ayat Shah departed for Hujung Tanah. There he built a palace and a protective wall in the upper reaches of Talar River.

In time, news that Seri Akar Raja had been installed as the Bendahara in Perak arrived in Hujung Tanah. Sultan 'Alauddin was infuriated. And when the Bendahara Paduka Tuan heard of the news, he cast away his ceremonial headgear in anger.

Said the Bendahara, 'If I had not brought Seri Akar Raja for an audience with His Majesty, it is as though I have come without my headgear.'

So, the Bendahara Paduka Tuan entered the audience hall without his headgear, only with the *keris* and coat.

The Bendahara bowed before Sultan 'Alauddin Ri'ayat Shah, saying, 'My Lord, I seek leave to travel to Perak to summon Seri Akar Raja.'

His Majesty said, 'Let not the Bendahara go, let Tun Nara Wangsa travel to Perak.'

Sultan 'Alauddin Ri'ayat Shah enquired of Tun Nara Wangsa, 'Does My Lord consent to go to Perak to summon Seri Akar Raja?'

Tun Nara Wangsa bowed, 'Even though Your Majesty commands me to defeat Perak I am willing to go. But to summon him, I beg for your forgiveness, for the Queen of Perak is my niece.'

The Sultan continued, 'In that case we shall order Tun Pikrama to summon Seri Akar Raja.'

Tun Pikrama bowed, 'Very well, My Lord.'

Thus, Tun Pikrama made the necessary preparations, and when they were complete, he departed for Perak. After a few days, he arrived and sailed upstream to Labuhan Jong. Soon, it was heard that Tun

Pikrama had arrived to summon Bendahara Seri Akar Raja. As a response, the Bendahara asked that the rice and its pot, along with curry in the bamboo be brought to him.

When Tun Pikrama saw this, he was enraged at the Bendahara's haughtiness. Promptly Tun Pikrama returned to Hujung Tanah.

As soon as he had arrived, he went to the palace to seek His Majesty's audience. At that moment, His Majesty was holding court, with his chiefs and subjects in attendance. Promptly Tun Pikrama paid obeisance and took his seat. Next, he began to describe to His Majesty all that had happened in Perak.

When the Bendahara Paduka Tuan heard of the news he bowed and said, 'My Lord, if Your Majesty ordered somebody else rather than I to Perak, Seri Akar Raja will not come. Let me go to Perak. As soon as I arrive there, I will grasp his hands and take him to the boat. If he refuses, I shall draw my *keris* and stab him; if he falls to the left I shall fall to the right.'

Sultan 'Alauddin Ri'ayat Shah agreed, 'Very well, see to it as My Lord thinks fit.'

Soon the Bendahara departed for Perak.

Upon his arrival, it was ordered by Sultan Muzaffar Shah that he be welcomed. He was taken to the palace directly and served a meal.

Sultan Muzaffar Shah said to the Bendahara, 'Let's dine.'

The Bendahara Paduka Tuan, replied, 'I beg Your Majesty's forgiveness, do please dine, let me have your leftovers, Your Majesty.'

Sultan Muzaffar Shah enquired, 'Why is the Bendahara acting thus? In our opinion, if it is not fitting that we invite My Lord to dine with us, why should we do so?'

Bendahara Paduka Tuan replied, 'It is indeed fitting that I dine with Your Majesty, that is the very reason that I refused, for many are those who are not fitting, dining with the princes for the distinction. For me, it would not be distinctive as it is customary for a Bendahara to dine with the Raja. Please dine, My Lord. Let me find another place.'

Sultan Muzaffar Shah insisted, 'Do come and dine with us, Bendahara, for we have been apart for too long; we miss My Lord very much.'

The Bendahara continued, 'Why does Your Majesty insist that I dine with you. I know what Your Majesty means, "When I invited him to dine with me, he will be generous towards me." I hope this thought doesn't not cross your mind. If there is still Sultan 'Alauddin Ri'ayat Shah as King of Hujung Tanah, I shall never bow before another master.'

Sultan Muzaffar Shah, 'That is not what is in my mind, the Bendahara supposes incorrectly,' and he pulled the Bendahara's hand and placed it on the rice.

The Sultan said, 'Do not say any more, Bendahara; now let's eat.'

Thus the Bendahara took a little rice and placed it on the betel leaf.

The Bendahara said, 'Please dine, My Lord.'

Presently Sultan Muzaffar Shah began to dine and the Bendahara Paduka Tuan ate with him. When he had finished the rice on the betel leaf, he added another bit of the meat. When the meal was over, the Bendahara Paduka Tuan sought leave of Sultan Muzaffar Shah, and proceeded directly to Seri Akar Raja's residence.

Soon Seri Akar Raja was standing before the Bendahara. He promptly held Seri Akar Raja's hand and brought him to his vessel. When they were safely on board, the vessel weighed anchor and sailed downstream and then on to Hujung Tanah. Sultan 'Alauddin Ri'ayat Shah was extremely delighted that Seri Akar Raja had been brought back by the Bendahara.

In the meantime, the Adipati of Kampar arrived to bring his tribute as was the custom of old. The adipati soon sought the audience of the Seri Nara al-Diraja for it was the custom that when it was about the Adipati of Kampar, the Raja of Tunggak and the Mandulika of Kelang and all those who had authority over the districts of the *negeri* which had products of their own, to present them first to the Chief of the Treasury and it was the Chief of the Treasury who carried them into the palace.

At that moment, the Adipati of Kampar came in to meet the Seri Nara al-Diraja, for he held the post of Chief of the Treasury. However, the Seri Nara al-Diraja was ill.

So, the Seri Nara al-Diraja said to the Adipati of Kampar, 'If it pleases My Lord, do seek an audience with Sang Bijaya Ratnap, for I am now unwell.'

Thus, the Adipati, accompanied by Sang Bijaya Ratna, who was the harbour master of Kampar, presented all the gifts as their tribute. At that moment, Sultan 'Alauddin Ri'ayat Shah was holding court, attended by all the chiefs who had gathered in Hujung Tanah.

When His Majesty noticed the Adipati coming, and bringing in with him the tributes, Sultan 'Alauddin Ri'ayat Shah enquired, 'Where is My Lord, Orang Kaya-kaya Seri Nara al-Diraja, that the Adipati of Kampar and Sang Bijaya Ratna have come to the palace on their own?'

So the Adipati of Kampar and Sang Bijaya Ratna bowed and replied, 'Your Majesty, My Lord is unwell and is unable to come and pay Your Majesty obeisance. It was with his lordship's consent that we have come in his place.'

Sultan 'Alauddin Ri'ayat Shah said, 'Take back all the tributes. If My Lord is unwell why should the tributes be brought without him. Do you not know the customs of the palace? Is it from a need to talk to us?'

Thus, the Adipati of Kampar and Sang Bijaya Ratna brought all the gifts back to the Seri Nara al-Diraja. They reported to him His Majesty's words.

The Seri Nara al-Diraja said, 'In that case, let us all go to the audience hall.'

He took all the gifts from the Adipati of Kampar. As soon as he arrived, the Seri Nara al-Diraja, raised his hands in obeisance, 'My Lord, I was not able to come earlier for I have been ill.'

Said Sultan 'Alauddin Ri'ayat Shah: 'It is nothing serious, it is just the custom of the palace. If My Lord does not accompany the gifts, then the customs are stained.'

Thus, the tributes from each of the chiefs were handed over to the Bendahara.

After some time, Sultan 'Alauddin Ri'ayat Shah ordered Tun Pikrama to invade Merbedang. Soon, Tun Pikrama departed with sixty vessels in his fleet. Upon their arrival they presently went to war for several days. Merbedang was defeated; much was the plunder.

After that, Tun Pikrama returned to Hujung Tanah in triumph. He then sailed upstream to Pekan Tuha to seek the audience of Sultan 'Alauddin Ri'ayat Shah. His Majesty was greatly pleased, and bestowed gifts on Tun Pikrama.

Allah knows the truth; to Him shall we return.

XXX

The words of the narrative now turn to Sang Naya, who had been resident in Melaka from times of old. He was married in Melaka, for in those days there were many Malays there.

Sang Naya planned to run amok with all the Malays at the time when the Portuguese were about to enter the church for their service. In those days, when they entered the church, they would leave their weapons outside. So those who had agreed to join in gave their *kerises* to Sang Naya. These were then placed by Sang Naya under the chest.

One day, a Portuguese came to ask him for a betel preparation. In the meantime, Sang Naya quickly pushed the chest. Soon, the Portuguese took a bite of the betel. After he had finished, he lifted the wedge of the chest and saw an enormous number of *kerises* beneath it.

The Portuguese duly reported his discovery to the captain, 'Senhor, Sang Naya has hidden a great many *kerises*. Whatever was his intention?'

As soon as the captain heard the man's report, he ordered that Sang Naya be summoned. He soon came; the *keris* on Sang Naya's hip was removed.

The captain asked, 'Why does Sang Naya keep so many *kerises* under the chest?'

Sang Naya said, 'In preparation to kill all of you.'

When he heard Sang Naya's reply, he took him to the highest point of the fortress and pushed him off it. Sang Naya fell on his legs, then tumbled down and died.

Soon afterwards, the Portuguese sent a messenger to Pekan Tuha to bring news of Sang Naya's death as he was planning to run amok in Melaka. However, Sultan 'Alauddin Ri'ayat Shah ordered that the Portuguese envoy be arrested. He was then carried to a tall tree and from there he was pushed down. So, the Portuguese envoy died.

When word reached Melaka that their messenger was dead, killed by Sultan 'Alauddin Ri'ayat Shah in Pekan Tuha, the captain was enraged. He ordered that preparations be made to attack—three galleys, two long ghalias, ten *fustas* and thirty native *banting*s of medium sizes were equipped. When all the preparations were completed, they set sail for Hujung Tanah.

News of the imminent attack was heard in Pekan Tuha. Promptly, Sultan 'Alauddin Ri'ayat Shah ordered that the fortress be manned. Tun Nara Wangsa and Tun Pikrama were to be the war chiefs. Soon, Tun Nara Wangsa and Tun Pikrama proceeded to mend the fortress and secure the twelve guns in their appropriate places. Their shots were the size of the Chinese sweet lime.

Soon, the Portuguese arrived; their galleys anchored before the fortress. Both sides began to fire their cannons in long, unending volleys, in a great din of clamour. However, the Portuguese were unable to overrun it. So, they landed and secured a place to build their defences at a bend of the river. They only had a few guns, but they fired them endlessly.

The Laksamana came to confer with Tun Nara Wangsa and Tun Pikrama for the Laksamana was at that moment under the wrath of His Majesty, he was not in the palace's employment, wearing a green coat and a black sarong, while his headgear was likewise black.

Said the Laksamana to Tun Nara Wangsa, 'It is on account of My Lord that I have come here.'

After that Tun Nara Wangsa presented a suit of new clothes to the Laksamana.

Said the Laksamana, 'It has been three years since His Majesty was annoyed with me, my costume has remained unchanged. It is only now that I have new clothes.'

The Portuguese guns were firing incessantly, and the cannon balls came heavy like rain. Those who were hit suffered dreadfully. Some lost their arms, some, their legs, some, their heads. So, it was no longer possible to stand guard on the fortress.

Tun Pikrama confronted Tun Nara Wangsa, 'What thinks you, My Lord? Let us fell this tall *kempas* tree and fashion shields out of it, and thereby defend our stand.'

Tun Nara Wangsa replied, 'If we were to fell it on to the bank, how can we retrieve it? However, if it is into the water, we could easily recover it.'

The Laksamana offered a way out, 'Let's use our arrows.'

So, he tied the arrow to a fine fishing line. Then he tied it to the notch of the arrow which was then drawn upward and to that was fastened some fine braid. Then, the Laksamana shot it in the direction of the *kempas* tree. It wound around a branch. Then the string of the hook was hauled up. Subsequently, he looped it again with a fine wicker work.

Presently, the *kempas* tree fell in the direction of the river, as it was intended. When it was down, they cut its trunk into three parts, and made them into shields. As the *kempas* was thick the guards could be put to stand up on the fortress; in no other place could they do this. In the meantime, the Portuguese fired at the fortress continuously for three days and three nights. Many were the dead, countless.

The Bendahara Paduka Tuan was with the Seri Nara al-Diraja and Sultan 'Alaudddin Ri'ayat Shah.

Said the Bendahara to the Sultan: 'My Lord, I seek Your Majesty's permission to go upstream to inspect those fighting there.'

So, he was rowed upstream from the fortress and soon enough, found out that the war had spread far and wide.

In his heart the Bendahara thought, 'If the fortress falls and is overrun, Tun Nara Wangsa and Tun Pikrama are dead.' Therefore, he immediately returned.

Upon his arrival he reported to His Majesty, 'My Lord, in my opinion the fortress will soon be overrun. And if the fortress is overrun, Tun Nara Wangsa and Tun Pikrama will be killed. It is indeed almost impossible to have servants as extraordinary as they are. Let us order that they return.'

Sultan 'Alauddin Ri'ayat Shah instructed Hang 'Alamat, 'Go summon Tun Nara Wangsa and Tun Pikrama.'

So, Hang 'Alamat departed.

When he arrived at the fortress, Hang 'Alamat called out to Tun Nara Wangsa and Tun Pikrama, 'My Lords are summoned.'

When they heard his words, the noise of the people felling the trees could also be heard, no one could stop them.

Tun Nara Wangsa asked Tun Pikrama, 'What is My Lord's view of the situation, for there are yet many weapons belonging to His Majesty out there? If we go upstream all the weapons will be lost.'

Tun Pikrama suggested, 'Let's throw them into the water.' So, all the guns and weapons were thrown into the river. Then Tun Nara Wangsa and Tun Pikrama went downstream to seek Sultan 'Alauddin Ri'ayat Shah.

The Bendahara Paduka Tuan said, 'My Lord, it is best that Your Majesty depart for Sayung.'

Sultan 'Alauddin Ri'ayat Shah said, 'Our boat, Lancang Medang Serai, that is planked with the wide-stemmed *karah* bamboo, we fear it might be taken by the Portuguese.'

Tun Nara Wangsa said, 'Please depart, My Lord. Let me free the boat.'

Thus, His Majesty was rowed upstream to Sayung. The Bendahara and all the chiefs followed suit. The Portuguese pursued them. Then Tun Nara Wangsa brought twenty men from Sukal into his *lancang* boat, and ordered them to row; with twenty men holding their large axes waiting at the source of Batu Belah River.

Soon Tun Nara Wangsa followed, bringing His Majesty's *lancang*, as though in a sequence, with the Portuguese. When they arrived at Batu Belah, a tree was felled by Orang Kaya-kaya Perembat. That is how the place got its name to this day—Rembat it was called. In the meantime, the Portuguese had sailed upstream to Pekan Tuha, in two galleys.

Soon after that, Sultan 'Alauddin Ri'ayat Shah requested that a letter be written and brought to Kapitan Mor, the Portuguese captain. However, this order could not be carried out because whoever was sent, returned immediately; the fusillade from the guns from the Portuguese galleys came as heavy as rain. Tun Amat 'Ali, the son of the Laksamana, was asked to carry the letter. When they sighted the galley, they fired at it; their volley, likewise, came as heavy as rain.

Said the slaves: 'Sir, let us return, for the guns are indeed heavy.'

'But what would become to the name of a son of a Laksamana if I cannot deliver a letter? Row on, so that I may reach it.'

So, the slaves rowed on, but the Portuguese guns kept firing. All the slaves jumped into the water, only Tun Amat 'Ali stood alone in the boat, in a hail of bullets.

Tun Amat 'Ali's boat drifted close to the Portuguese's. Kapitan Mor ordered that a fine *chindai* cloth be lowered. Tun Amat 'Ali was hoisted into the vessel and was given a place on a carpet and, furthermore, shown much respect and honour. Kapitan Mor then ordered that the letter be taken to Melaka. Upon its arrival in Melaka, it was duly read. When the contents of the letter had been understood, the captain of Melaka ordered Kapitan Mor to accept the peace arrangement.

When, in turn, it arrived at Pekan Tuha, Kapitan Mor presented Tun Amat 'Ali with a suit of fine clothes as was the custom of the times. He was then asked to return with a letter of peace.

In Sayung, he had an audience with Sultan 'Alauddin Ri'ayat Shah, recounting all that had taken place. His Majesty was very pleased, and promptly presented Tun Amat 'Ali with a gift of a fine suit. Thus, there was peace at that time and the Portuguese subsequently returned to Melaka.

In due course, the Seri Nara al-Diraja, returned to the mercy of Allah. He was buried in Sayung, according to the customs of great chiefs, and came to be known as the Chief with the Great Tombstone.

In time, Tun Nara Wangsa was appointed the Chief of the Treasury and Tun Pikrama, the Temenggung. Tun Amat 'Ali, the son of Hassan Temenggung, was made the chief herald. Tun Amat 'Ali was particularly distinguished in his deportment. It was related that he was handsome beyond compare in these times. In his habits too he was outstanding.

Allah knows the truth; to Him shall we return.

XXXI

The words of the chronicle now turn to the tribal Chief of Singapura, Patih Ludang was his name. He had committed a wrong against Sang Setia; thus, Sang Setia wanted to have him slain. On his part, Patih Ludang fled to Pahang with every member of his community. At this time, Sultan Muhammad Shah, the Raja of Pahang, had just died. His brother, Raja Jainad succeeded him on the throne and intended soon to pay his homage to Hujung Tanah. Thus, His Majesty made preparations; Ludang was taken as the row master, for in his mind, 'If I bring him as my row master, he will eventually be presented into my keeping.'

When they had arrived, His Majesty's boat was rowed upstream to Sayung, and there they were duly welcomed by Sultan 'Alauddin Ri'ayat Shah. Soon Raja Jainad paid obeisance, in a most courteous manner. His Majesty bestowed on Raja Jainad the title of Sultan Muzaffar Shah.

Subsequently, Patih Ludang was summoned. Patih Ludang soon came, for in his mind, 'Sang Setia shall not want to slay me, for I am come on Sultan Muzaffar Shah's vessel.'

When he arrived before Sang Setia, he was duly slain. And when Sultan Muzaffar Shah heard that Patih Ludang has been slain by Sang Setia, His Majesty was infuriated.

His Majesty said, 'That is indeed a vile deed. In our opinion, as we come to pay homage it will also bring goodness, but to His Majesty's officers, this is not the case. Is it true that Patih Ludang was forced down from our vessel, and killed by Sang Setia? If he had any intention to do so, could it not wait for tomorrow or any day after that?'

The incident in which Patih Ludang was taken from Sultan Muzaffar Shah's vessel and slain by Sang Setia came to the ears of Sultan 'Alauddin Ri'ayat Shah, and he was soon summoned. Now His Majesty was enraged and wanted to return to Pahang.

Sultan 'Alauddin Ri'ayat Shah spoke to the Laksamana, 'Please go, Laksamana, tie Sang Setia up, and bring him to me.'

The Laksamana bowed, 'Very well, My Lord.'

Promptly, the Laksamana departed for Sang Setia's house. When Sang Setia heard that the Laksamana had come to seize him, he asked that his gates be closed.

The Laksamana called, 'Unlock the gates, I have come on His Majesty's orders.'

Sang Setia answered, 'If the Laksamana is ordered to slay me, I shall open the gates. If it is to tie me up, the doors shall remain shut. Though I consent to His Majesty's orders, you are now my adversary, for it is not the custom among warriors to tie each other up.'

The Laksamana answered, 'My dear brother, I am not instructed to argue with you, merely to tie you up. If you give your consent, I shall tie you up, if not, I shall return and report to His Majesty.'

Sang Setia responded, 'I do not consent to the Laksamana to tie me up, for you're a great warrior, and so am I.'

Hence the Laksamana returned to seek the Sultan, repeating Sang Setia's words to His Majesty.

After hearing the Laksmana's report, His Majesty was infuriated. Sultan 'Alauddin Ri'ayat Shah subsequently commanded the Bendahara, 'Go and tie up Sang Setia.'

The Bendahara bowed, 'Very well, My Lord.'

Presently the Bendahara arrived at Sang Setia's. When Sang Setia heard that the Bendahara had come, he promptly descended and prostrated before his feet, saying, 'If the Bendahara wishes to tie me up I am ready, for you are my chief, it is proper, not you alone, but also your clansmen. If it is the Laksamana, then I do not agree.'

Thus the Bendahara brought Sang Setia before Sultan 'Alauddin Ri'ayat Shah.

His Majesty ordered, 'Please bring him to us.'

The Bendahara said, 'Very well, My Lord.'

Sultan 'Alauddin Ri'ayat Shah addressed the Laksamana and all the warriors, 'Go you all, My Lords, escort the Bendahara.'

The Bendahara ordered that Sang Setia be tied with the cloth of the *destar*[1] headdress.

Sang Setia said to Sang Jaya Pikrama, 'Tie me loose, for Sang Guna stands so close to me that his *keris* stabs at me. If the Pahang people seem hostile, signal to me with your eyes. Only His Majesty is My Lord. Is it possible that the other rajas are also my masters?'

Soon after that, the Bendahara departed to bring Sang Setia to the court.

As he came in, he stood on the lawn before Sultan Muzaffar Shah, with all the other warriors. The Bendahara Paduka Tuan too ascended to receive His Majesty's instructions.

The Bendahara Paduka Tuan bowed and said, 'My greetings, I have brought Sang Setia before Your Majesty, for your lordship to command as he is an officer under Your Majesty's authority.'

Sultan Muzaffar Shah was quiet, his head was bent downwards, he was full of wrath.

Said the Bendahara, 'Free Sang Setia.'

Thus, Sang Setia was freed.

The Bendahara ordered Sang Setia, 'Go pay your obeisance.'

Hence Sang Setia came up to bow low with his hand clasped together and he subsequently took his seat. And all the warriors took theirs.

Said the Bendahara to Sultan Muzaffar Shah, 'Why did My Lord remain quiet, for Your Majesty had ordered that Sang Setia be tied up, and I was asked to accompany him, is this not true? Furthermore, My

---

[1] *Destar*, a head cloth

Lord, Sang Setia is a warrior, and sentenced by His Majesty according to the law, while I was in a faraway place. As soon as His Majesty heard that I came bringing Sang Setia, he immediately stepped down, and ordered that the bond be loosened. If I did not ask that he be freed, His Majesty would not have done so. Is it right, Your Majesty, what I have done?'

Sultan Muzaffar Shah replied, 'A servant never goes against the wishes of his master, even in the matter of evil intent. How much more so in matters of noble intentions.'

The Bendahara replied, 'It is true what My Lord has said, so that the mouth does not dispute with the heart.'

The Bendahara continued, addressing Sang Setia, 'All the more so, for the Sultan of Pahang and the Sultan Perak are different from Yang Dipertuan. But all are our masters, however, in times of good or bad, the Yang Dipertuan is our only master.'

After hearing the words of Bendahara Paduka Tuan, Sultan Muzaffar Shah said, 'We would like to take our leave, now. What message shall I take to his lordship, your brother?'

Bendahara Paduka Tuan replied, 'Say to His Majesty that I bow to him in obeisance. However, if His Majesty would ask me to care for all the indigenous Sakais of Patih Ludang, that instruction must come from His Majesty.'

Thus the Bendahara requested the Sultan.

When Sultan 'Alauddin Ri'ayat Shah had arrived, all the requests of Sultan Muzaffar Shah were repeated to His Majesty.

Sultan 'Alauddin Ri'ayat Shah said, 'Very well, we bestow all the Sakais on him.'

After some time in Sayung, Sultan Muzaffar Shah sought leave to return to Pahang. He was bestowed with fine costumes, according to the customs among Kings. Soon Sultan Muzaffar Shah returned to Pahang. And after a journey of a few days he arrived there.

Allah knows the truth; to Him shall we return.
Wa kitabuhu Raja Bongsu.[2]

---

[2]   *Wa kitabuhu Raja Bongsu*: And the Author is Raja Bongsu.

BIBLIOGRAPHY

A. Samad Ahmad (ed.). 1975. *Sulalatus Salatin.* Kuala Lumpur: Dewan Bahasa dan Pustaka.

Abdullah bin Abdul Kadir (Munsyi). 1884. *Sulalatus Salatin, yaitu Sejarah Melayu.* Leiden: Verlag Nicht Ermittelbar.

Abdullah Samad (ed.). 1975. Abu Mansor Asha'ry, et al. *Kamus Am Bahasa Melayu.* Pulau Pinang: Bingkisan Pujangga.

Abdullah Yusoff. 1979. *Kamus Sinonim.* Kota Bharu: Dian.

Albert, Robert S. (ed.). 1992. *Genius and Eminence.* Ed. ke-2. Oxford: Pergamon.

Ali Ahmad. 1987. *Karya-karya Sastera Bercorak.* Kuala Lumpur: Dewan Bahasa dan Pustaka.

Andaya, Leonard. 2008. *Leaves of the Same Tree.* Honolulu: University of Hawaii Press.

Asmah Haji Omar. 1991. *Bahasa Melayu Abad ke-16 – Satu Analisis Berdasarkan Teks Melayu 'Aqaid al-Nasafi.* Kuala Lumpur: Dewan Bahasa dan Pustaka.

Asmah Haji Omar. (ed.). 2003. *The Genius of Malay Civilisation.* Tanjong Malim: Institute of Malay Civilisation, Universiti Pendidikan Sultan Idris.

Barron, F. 1992. "Creative Writers". In Robert S Albert, (ed.). *Genius and Eminence*. Edisi ke-2. Oxford: Pergamon. Blagden, C.O. 1909. Notes on Malay History. *JSBRAS*. No.53.

Blagden, C.O. 1925. "Sejarah Melayu: An Unpublished Variant Version of the Malay Annals". *JMBRAS*. 3: 1. 10-52.

Bloom, Harold. 2002. *Genius: A Mosaic of One Hundred Exemplary Creative Minds*. New York: Warner.

Bowrey, Thomas. 1701. *Dictionary, English and Malayo, Malayo and English*. London: Printed by Sam Bridge for Author.

Braginsky, Vladimir. 1990. "*Hikayat Hang Tuah*: Malay Epic and Muslim Mirror; Some Considerations on its Date, Meaning and Structure". *BKI*, Vol. 146.

Brown, C.C. 1970. *Sejarah Melayu or Malay Annals*. Kuala Lumpur: Oxford University Press.

Brown, C.C. (trans.). 1976. *Sulalat al-Salatin* (*Sejarah Melayu*) *or Malay Annals*. Kuala Lumpur: Oxford University Press.

Buyong Adil. 1973. *Sejarah Melaka dalam Zaman Kerajaan Melayu*. Kuala Lumpur: Dewan Bahasa dan Pustaka.

Cockshut, A.O.J. 1977. *Man and Woman: A Study of Love and the Novel*. London: Collins University Press.

De Beauvior, Simone, 2018. "The Second Sex: Quotable Quotes". https://www.goodreads.com/quotes/5366-one-is-not-born-a-genius-one-becomes-a-genius (Accessed on 8 August, 2018).

de Jong, Josselin P.E. 1961. "The Character of the Malay Annals". In John Bastin and R. Roolvink (ed.), *Malayan and Indonesian Studies*. Kuala Lumpur: Oxford University Press.

Dedring, Juergen. 1976. *Recent Advances in Peace and Conflicted Research*. Beverly Hills: Sage.

Drakard, Jane. 1988. *Sejarah Raja-raja Barus*. Bandung: Angkasa-Ecole Francaise d'Extreme-Orient.

Dulaurier, Edouard. 1948. *Collection de Principales Chroniques Malayes*. Paris: Imperimeric Nationale.

Epstein, Joseph. (ed.). 2007. *Literary Genius: 25 Classic Writers Who Define English and American* Literature. London: Haus.

Fau, Nathalie. February 2011. "The Strait of Malacca: An Inland Sea". http://www.gis-reseau-asie.org/monthly-articles/strait-malacca-nathalie-fau (Accessed on 5 December, 2018).

Fennigan, Ruth. 1977. *Oral Poetry*. Cambridge: Cambridge University Press.

Foucault, M. 1977. *Discipline and Punishment*. London: Tavistock.

Foucault, M. 1980. *Power/Knowledge*: *Selected Interviews and Other Writings, 1972-1977*. Brighton: Harvester.

Gibson-Hill, C.A. 1956. "The Malay Annals: the History Brought From Goa". *JMBRAS*. 29: 1, 185-188.

Haron Daud. 1989. *Sejarah Melayu: Satu Kajian daripada Aspek Pensejarahan Budaya*. Kuala Lumpur: Dewan Bahasa dan Pustaka.

Hikayat Hang Tuah. Mss KL 4. Leiden University Library.

Hooykaas, C. 1937. *Over Maleische Literatuur*. Leiden: Brill.

Hooykaas, C. 1940. "Recension: The Malay Annals or Sejarah Melayu". By R.O. Winstedt (ed.). *TBG* 80, 301-303.

Iskandar, T. 1964. *Tun Seri Lanang, Pengarang Sejarah Melayu*. Dewan Bahasa dan Pustaka. Vol. III, No. 11 November. Dewan Bahasa dan Pustaka. , 1997.

Iskandar, T. 1995. *Kesusasteraan Klasik Melayu Sepanjang Abad*. Bandar Seri Begawan: privately published.n.

Hale, Carl S. 1995. "Psychological Characteristics of the Literary Genius". *Journal of Humanistic Psychology* (jhpsagepub.com/contact/35/3/113.s) (Accessed on 8 August, 2018).

Jelani Harun. 2009. *Bustan al-Salatin*: *A Malay Mirror for Kings*. Pulau Pinang: Penerbit Universiti Sains Malaysia.

Jelani Harun. 2008. *Undang-undang Kesultanan Melayu dalam Perbandingan*. Pulau Pinang: PUSM.

Jones, Russell (ed.). 1999. *Hikayat Raja Pasai*. Kuala Lumpur: Karya Agung.

Jong, P.E. de Josselin de. 1965. "The Rise and Fall of a National Hero". *JMBRAS*. 38.2: 140-55.

Kamus Dewan (Edisi Keempat). 2005. Kuala Lumpur: Dewan Bahasa dan Pustaka.

Kang Kyong Seock. 1995. *Gaya Bahasa Sejarah Melayu*. Kuala Lumpur: Dewan Bahasa dan Pustaka.

Kasetsiri, Charnvit. 1976. *The Rise of Ayudhya*. Kuala Lumpur: Oxford University Press.

Kassim Ahmad. 1968. *Perwatakan dalam Hikayat Hang Tuah*. Kuala Lumpur: Dewan Bahasa dan Pustaka.

Kassim Ahmad (ed.). 1975. *Hikayat Hang Tuah*. Kuala Lumpur: Dewan Bahasa dan Pustaka.

Khalid Hussain. 1964. "Menempatkan *Sejarah Melayu* dalam Kesusasteraan Melayu Klasik dan Sejarah". *Dewan Bahasa*. 8: 6, 266-272.

Khoo Kay Kim. 1976. *Panji-panji Gemerlapan: Satu Pebicaraan Pensejarahan Melayu*. Kuala Lumpur: Penerbit Universiti Malaya.

Leyden, J. 1821. *Sejarah Melayu, 'Malay Annals': Translated from the Malay Language*. Raffles (ed.), London.

Liaw Yock Fang. 1982. *Sejarah Kesusasteraan Melayu Klasik*. Singapura: Pustaka Nasional.

Linehan, W. 1947. 'The Sources of the Shellabear Text of the Malay Annals". *JMBRAS*. 20: 2, 107.

Maier, H.M.J. 1999. "Tales of Hang Tuah. In Search of Wisdom and Good Behaviour". *Bijdragen tot de Taal-, Land-en Volkenkunde*.

Maier, Henk M.J. 2004. "An epik that never was an epic – the Malay *Hikayat Hang Tuah*", in Jan Jansen and Henk M.J. Maier, *Epic Adventures: Heroic Narrative in the Oral Performance Traditions of Four Continents*. Literatur: Forschung und Wissenschaft, Band 3. Munster: Lit Verlag.

Marrison, G.E. 1949. The Siamese Wars with Malacca During the Reign of Muzaffar Shah. Royal Asiatic Society, Malayan Branch. Vol.XXII,Pt.l

Marsden, W. 1812. *A Dictionary and Grammar of the Malayan Language*. Singapore: Oxford University Press.

Milner, Anthony. 1982. *Kerajaan: Malay Political Culture on the eve of Colonial Rule*. Tucson, Ariz: Published for the Association for Asian Studies by the University of Arizona Press.

Md. Salleh Yaapar. 2008. "Another Place, Another Form: Hang Tuah in the Netherlands of the Nineteenth Century". In Lalita Sinha, (ed.) *Exploring Spaces*. Cambridge: Cambridge Academic Publication.

Mohd Said Haji Sulaiman. 1939. *Buku Katan Kamus Melayu*. Kuala Lumpur: Dewan Bahasa dan Pustaka.

Mohd Taib Osman. 1974. *Kesusasteraan Melayu Lama*. Kuala Lumpur: Federal.

Muhammad Haji Salleh. 1981. *Sajak-sajak Sejarah Melayu*. Kuala Lumpur: Dewan Bahasa dan Pustaka.

Muhammad Haji Salleh. 1988. "Unsur-unsur Teori dalam Kesusasteraan Melayu dan Nusantara". *Monograf* No. 3. FSSK, Bangi: Universiti Kebangsaan Malaysia.

Muhammad Haji Salleh. 1989. Interviews in Medan, Terengganu and Kelantan.

Muhammad Haji Salleh. 1990. "Malay Ethno- Poetics: Looking at Literature with Our Own Eyes". Solidarity, No. 26. April-June, 1990.

Muhammad Haji Salleh. 1991. *The Mind of the Malay Author*. Kuala Lumpur: Dewan Bahasa dan Pustaka.

Muhammad Haji Salleh. 2002. "Hang Tuah dalam Budaya Alam Melayu". *Warisan Manuskrip Melayu*. Kuala Lumpur: Perpustakaan Negara Malaysia. 95-107.

Muhammad Haji Salleh. 2008. "*Sulalatus Salatin: Adikarya Akal Budi Melayu*". In Muhammad Haji Salleh, Permata di Rumput Gilang: Sastera sebagai Ruang Bangsa, hlm. 3-35. Kuala Lumpur: Dewan Bahasa dan Pustaka.

Muhammad Haji Salleh. 2009. "Pekerjaan dan Ilmu di Pusat Masyarakat". Kertas Kerja, Majlis Ilmu, Bandar Seri Begawan, Negara Brunei Darussalam.

Muhammad Haji Salleh. 2013. "Hang Tuah dalam Hayat Lisan di Air dan Daratan". In Halimah Mohamed Ali and Mohamad Luthfi Abdul Rahman, *Sastera dalam Budaya dan Media*. Pulau Pinang: Penerbit Universiti Sains Malaysia.

Muhammad Haji Salleh (ed.). 1997. Tun Seri Lanang. *Sulalat al-Salatin*. Kuala Lumpur: Karya Agung.

Mustafa Muhammad. 1973. *Perwatakan dalam Sejarah Melayu*. Kuala Lumpur: Adabi.

New World Encyclopedia. 2017. "Genius". http://web. newworldencyclopedia.org/entry/Genius (Accessed on 17 August, 2018).

New World Encyclopedia. 2018. "Malacca Sultanate". http://web. newworldencyclopedia.org/entry/Malacca_Sultanate (Accessed on 17 August, 2018).

Noriah Taslim, et al. 2010. *Naratif Baru Sastera Melayu Tradisional*. Kuala Lumpur: Dewan Bahasa dan Pustaka.

Noriah Taslim. 2010. Protagonis dalam Era Pascakolonial: Perubahan Ideologi dan Naratif Baru. In Noriah Taslim et al, *Naratif Baru Sastera Melayu Tradisional*. Kuala Lumpur: Dewan Bahasa dan Pustaka.

Overbeck, Hans. 1938. *Malaiische Chronik*. Dusseldoft: Diederichs.

Padover, Saul K. 1960. *The Genius of America*. 1960. New York: MC Graw Hill.

Parnikel, R.B. 1976. "An Epic Hero and an Epic Traitor". In *Hikayat Hang Tuah. BKI*. 132, 4: 403-17. *Warisan Manuskrip Melayu*. 2002. Kuala Lumpur: Perpustakaan Negara Malaysia.

Raja Ali Haji. (Dikarang 1275 Hijrah = 1858). In *Pengetahuan Bahasa, Kamus Loghat Melayu Johor, Pahang, Riau dan Lingga*.

Rajatheran, M. 1999. *Kesan Hubungan Kebudayaan Melayu dan India*. Kuala Lumpur: Dewan Bahasa dan Pustaka.

Reiss, Timothy J. 1992. *The Meaning of Literature*. Ithaca: Cornell University Press.

Roolvink, R. 1967. "The Variant Versions of the Malay Annals". Published in C.C. Brown, 1970, *Sejarah Melayu or the Malay Annals*. Kuala Lumpur: Oxford University Press.

Sacks, Sheldon (ed.) 1979. *On Metaphor*. Chicago: Chicago University Press.

Shellabear, W.G. (ed.). 1961. *Sejarah Melayu*. Singapura: Malaya Publishing House.

Simatupang, T.D. & A. Teeuw. 1952. *Sedjarah Melayu*. Jakarta: Jambatan.

Siti Aisah Murad (ed.). 1993. *Konsep Wira dalam Sastera Melayu*. Kuala Lumpur: Dewan Bahasa dan Pustaka.

Skeat, William. 1967. *Malay Magic*. New York: Dover.

Sulalat al-Salatin (Manuscript). 1812. Raffles Malay 18. London: Royal Asiatic Society.

Sutrisno, Sulastin. 1983. *Hikayat Hang Tuah: Analisa Struktur dan Fungsi*. Yogyakarta: Gadjah Mada University Press.

Suwannathat-Pian, Kobkua. 1988. *Thai-Malay Relations*. Singapore: Oxford University Press.

Sweeney, Amin 1972. *The Ramayana and the Malay Shadow-Play*. Kuala Lumpur: Penerbit Universiti Kebangsaan Malaysia.

Syed Zulfida. April 1976. "Wit dan Humor dalam Sejarah Melayu". *Dewan Bahasa*. 197-218.

T. Iskandar, "Tun Seri Lanang, Panggong *Sejarah Melayu*". *Dewan Bahasa*. Vol. III, No. 11 November 1964.

Tambling, Jeremy. 1988. *What is Literary Language?* Milton Keynes: Open A.O. J.

Teuku Iskandar. 1995. *Catalogue of Malay, Minangkabau, and South Sumatran Manuscripts in the Netherlands*. Leiden: Documentatiebureau Islam-Christendom.

Teuku Iskandar. 1995. *Kesusasteraan Klasik Melayu Sepanjang Abad*. Brunei Darussalam: privately published.n.

Tun Seri Lanang. 1997. *Sulalat al-Salatin*. Muhammad Haji Salleh (pnyt.). Kuala Lumpur: Yayasan Karyawan.

Voorhoeve, P. 1964. "A Malay Scriptorium". In John Bastin dan R. Roolvink (ed.). *Malayan and Indonesian Studies. Essays Presented to Sir Richard Winstedt on His Eighty-Fifth Birthday*. Oxford: Clarendon Press. 256-66.

Wahyunah Hj. Abd. Ghani. 1991. *Panduan Kosa Kata Sastera Klasik*. Kuala Lumpur: Dewan Bahasa dan Pustaka, Kementerian Pendidikan Malaysia.

Wang Gungwu. Julai 1968. "The First Three Rulers of Malacca." *JMBRAS*. 4: 1.

Willkinson, R. J. 1903. *A Malay-English Dictionary*. Singapore: Kelly and Walsh.

Wilkinson, R. J. 1907. "The Malacca Sultanate". *JMBRAS*. 13 (ii), 22-97. Papers on Malay Subjects, Kuala Lumpur.

Winstedt, R.O. 1920. "The Genealogy of Malacca's Kings From a Copy of *Bustanu's Salatin*". *JSBRAS*. 91, 39-47.

Winstedt, R.O. 1938. "The Malay Annals or Sejarah Melayu". *JMBRAS* 26 (iii), 1-226.

Winstedt, R.O. 1940. "Alexander the Great and the Mount Meru and Chula Legends". *JMBRAS*. 18: 2.

Winstedt, R.O. 1958. *A History of Classical Malay Literature. JMBRAS*. Vol. 31. pt.3

Winstedt, R.O. 1969. *A History of Classical Malay Literature*. Kuala Lumpur: Oxford University Press.

Wyatt, K David. 1984. *Thailand: A Short History*. New Haven: Yale University Press.

Yusoff Iskandar. February 1977. "*Sejarah Melayu* – Edisi Shellabear dan Edisi Winstedt: Beberapa Perbezaan". *Dewan Bahasa*. 21: 2, 110-121.

Yusoff Iskandar dan Abdul Rahman Kaeh. 1985. *Sejarah Melayu Satu Perbincangan Kritis dari Pelbagai Bidang*. Kuala Lumpur: Heinemann Educational Books (Asia).

Zalila Abidin Abdul Wahid. May 1983. "*Sejarah Melayu*". *Dewan Bahasa*. 18: 5, 2017-215.

Zalila Sharif and Jamilah Haji Ahmad (ed.). 1993. *Kesusasteraan Melayu Traditional*. Kuala Lumpur: Dewan Bahasa dan Pustaka.

Zoetmulder. 1974. *Kalangwan: A Survey of Old Javanese Literature*. The Hague: Martinus Nijhoff.

INDEX

Abdullah Munshi, xii

Abu Bakar bin al-Siddik, 46

Aceh, vi, ix, 151

Adipati of Kampar, 168, 279–280

Adiraja Rama Mendeliar, 17, 34

Air Hitam, 201

Air Leleh, 219, 253

Akun Pal, 212

Alfonso d'Albuquerque, 220, 234

Ambangan, 180

Amir Hamzah, 12

Andalas, 18, 20

Apung, 115

Arab, vii, 132

Aria Bokala, 25–26

Awi Cakri, 79

Awi Dichu, 51–52, 84–85

Badang, 36–43

Balidamesai, 176

Bania, 236

Barsam, 15

Bat, 21, 23–24

Batu Belah, 285

Batu Pahat, 84–85, 218

Batu Sawar, 231

Bawa Kaya, 48

Bemayam, 26

Bemban, 26

Bencha Nagara, 12, 17, 34

Bendahara Lubuk Batu, 230–231, 237, 239

Bendahara Paduka Raja, 84–87, 96, 112, 114–116, 120, 122, 124, 131, 142–146, 151–156, 158, 161–162, 164, 197, 214, 229, 232

Bendahara Paduka Tuan, 272, 274–279, 284–285, 290–291

Bendahara Seri Akar Raja, 278

Bendahara Seri Amar Diraja, 72–73, 129

Bendahara Seri Maharaja, 185–187, 191–192, 195, 207, 213–226, 228–229, 231–232, 239

Bendahara Seriwa Raja, 74, 77–78, 83

Bendarang, 40–43

Bentan, vi–vii, 25, 28–29, 32, 112, 177, 231, 237, 241, 243, 245–248, 250, 254, 256, 258–260, 262–263, 265, 267–268, 270–271, 273

Bentan Karangan, 115

Bentara, 35

Bentiris, 16

Benua Keling, 12, 17, 34–35, 39, 71–72, 195

Benua Siam, 86, 217

Berakelang, 275–277

Bertam, 60

Beruas, 70, 256

Beruas Ujung, 70

Berunai, 119–120, 172, 251

Besisik River, 36

Biajit, 171

Bia Suri, 149

Biawak Busuk, 60

Bidam Setia, 253–255

Biman Jengkubat, 207–208

Bubunnya, 79, 85, 87–89, 120

Bukit Cina, 119

Bukit Pantau, 239

Bukit Seguntang Mahameru, 95

Bunguran, 57

Buru, 43, 115, 147, 270

Champa, 65, 148–151, 202

Chau Gma, 212

Chau Pandan, 85–86

Chau Seri Bangsa, 211–212

Chenderagiri Nagara, 13

Dada Air, 264

Dam Raja, 36, 43

Dang Biba, 136

Dang Bunga, 136

Dang Raya Rani, 140

Dasinang, 260

Datuk Bongkok, 84, 179, 197

Datuk Darat, 162

Datuk Ligor, 253, 257

Datuk Muar, 171–172, 177

Datuk Putih, 187

Datuk Rambat, 177

Datuuk Lubuk Batu, 229

Demang Lebar Daun, 18, 20–24, 28–29

Demi Puteri, 36

Dewan Bahasa dan Pustaka, vii

Dika, 15

Din, 262

Dompak, 270

Dur 'al-Manzum, 135–136

Fansuri, 47

Faras al-Bahri, 16

Gangga Shah Nagara, 9–10

Goa, vii

Goah, 219–221, 234, 244, 265

Gong Pengerah, 117

Gongsalo, 249–250

Guna, 182, 197

Hamzah, 228

Hang 'Alamat, 285

Hang 'Isa Pantas, 174, 179
Hang Aji Maris, 267
Hang Berkat, 181–182
Hang Embung, 263
Hang Hamzah, 144–145
Hang Hasan, 175, 253
Hang Hasan Cengang, 173–175, 179
Hang Husin, 253
Hang Isak, 155–156, 195–197
Hang Iskandar, 96
Hang Jebat, 96, 99
Hang Kasturi, 96, 99, 109–112
Hang Lekir, 96
Hang Lekiu, 96
Hang Nadim, 195–197, 202–207, 239
Hang Tuah, vii, 96–97, 99, 106–112, 197, 242, 250
Hang Usuh, 179
Haru, 47, 90, 132, 163–164, 166, 172, 260–264, 271
Hasan Temenggung, 186, 191–192, 220, 228
Hikayat Hamzah, 235–236
Hikayat Iskandar, 2n3, 3
Hikayat Isma Yatim, xi
Hikayat Muhammad Hanafiah, 235–236
Hikayat Raja-Raja Barus, 45
Hindi, 9, 13, 17
Hindustan, 6, 17
Hujung Karang, 271
Hujung Pasir, 250
Hujung Tanah, 133–134, 260, 276–281, 283, 288

Ikhtiar Muluk, 166–168

Imam Ghazali, 254
Indera Bokala, 25–28
Inderagiri, 97, 106–107, 140, 194–195, 242–243, 245–247, 250, 252–253, 255, 259
India, 2n3, 3, 7
Islam, 46–48, 211
Iyu Dikenyang, 122

Jamal, 256
Jambi, 97
Jambu Air, 49, 55–56, 72, 145, 261
Jawa, 187
Jepara, 149
Jituj, 234
Johor, vi–vii, ix, 38, 239
Jugra, 164, 219
Juru Demang, 75, 236

Kadi Munawar Shah, 168, 176–177, 212
Kadi Yusuf, 138–139, 179
Kampar, vi, 184, 241
Kampung Kelang, 171, 219
Kampung Tembaga, 171
Kanchanchi, 123
Kapitan Melaka, 241, 249–250
Kapitan Mor, 244, 286
Karaeng Ditandering Jikinik, 133
Karaeng Mejokok, 133
Karaeng Semerluki, 133–135
Katak Berenang, 266
Kayu Ara, 225, 232
Keban Island, 205
Kedah, 191–192, 274

Kelang, 78, 80–82, 107, 273–274, 276, 279
Kelangkui, 10
Keling, 9, 11–12, 14, 17, 34–35, 39–40, 69, 71–72, 195–196, 223, 226
Kerangkang, 144
Kerumutan, 242
Khoja Ahmad, 231, 256
Khoja 'Ali, 72
Khoja Baba, 129–130
Khoja Bulan, 168
Khoja Hasan, 207, 239
Khoja Muhammad Shah, 168
Khurasan, 214
Ki Mas Jiwa, 92
King of Bencha Negara, 17, 34
King of Champa, 148
King of Chenderagiri Nagara, 13
King of China, 126–127
King of Fatani, 1
King of Heaven, 116
King of Hindustan, 17
King of Maja Pahit, 92
King of Melaka, 74, 88, 127, 142
King of Mengkasar, 133
King of Portugal, 234
King of Samudera, 50
King of Siam, 79
King of Singa Pura, 39
King of Tanjung Pura, 20, 91
Kini Mertam, 151
Kitul, 226–227, 229
Kopak, 237, 266
Kota Buruk, 60
Kota Maligai, 211

Kuala Paya, 56
Kuala Penajuh, 219
Kudar Shah Jahan, 8, 17

Labuhan Jong, 277
Laksamana Bukit Pantau, 239
Laksamana Hang Tuah, 197, 242
Laksamana Khoja Hasan, 207
Laksamana Khoja Husin, 197
Lancang Medang Serai, 285
Langkawi, 10, 58
Layam, 260
Ledang Mountain, 140
Lingga, 97, 115n16, 195, 245–250
Li Po, 116–118
Lubuk Batu, 229–231, 237, 239
Lubuk China, 232
Lubuk Peletang, 210

Ma'abri, 46–47
Maha Indera Bahukala, 34–35, 41
Maharaja al-Diraja, 163–165
Maharaja Dewa Sura, 217
Maharaja Isak, 195, 245–248
Maharaja Jaya, 166–168
Maharaja Kunjara, 253–254
Maharaja Peri Sura, 129–130
Maharaja Sura, 120–123
Maja Pahit, 31–33, 59–60, 84, 91–99, 101–106, 149
Makhdum Sadar Jahan, 213–214, 233, 235
Makhdum Sayid (Sidi) 'Abdul' Aziz, 138
Makkah, 46, 48
Malapatata, 148

Malay Archipelago, v, x, 2n3
Mancitram, 19
Mandulika Kelang, 279
Mani Purindan, 71–73, 82
Manjung, 56, 256, 259, 273
Maqaduniah, 2n3
Marah Jaga, 45
Marah Silu, 45–48
Marhum di Kampar, 273
Marhum Sheikh, 210
Markapal, 200–201
Maulana Abu Bakar, 135–136,
    138–139
Maulana Jalaluddin, 74
Maulana Yusuf, 176, 179–180
Mawar al-Nahar, 214
Megat Kudu, 130
Melaka, vi–vii, 61, 70–74, 79–81,
    84–86, 88–90, 96–98, 100–
    101, 103, 105–107, 116–120,
    122, 126–127, 129–130, 132,
    134–139, 141–143, 145–146,
    151–152, 154, 156–161, 164–
    166, 168, 170, 172, 177, 182,
    184–189, 191–192, 194–197,
    199, 201–210, 212–213,
    215–221, 223, 227, 234, 237,
    241, 244, 247–249, 251–257,
    259, 265, 273, 282–283, 286
Melaka River, 179, 250
Melayu, 18, 100
Mengkasar, 133–136
Menteri Jana Putera, 86–90,
    119–120
Merbau, 115, 129
Merbedang, 280–281

Merlung, 97, 107, 194–195
Merlung Inderagiri, 107
Mi Duzul, 165–166
Minangkabau, 20, 45n2, 242–243
Muar, 60, 81, 115, 136, 219, 237,
    253, 273
Muara Tatang, 18
Muhammad, 1, 62, 130, 132, 246,
    254, 274
Muhammad Haji Salleh, ix–x
Muhammad Hanafiah, 235–236
Muhammadiyah, 145
Muhammad Sulaiman, ix

Naga Ombak, 266
Naga Patam, 9, 13
Nakhoda Jemu, 65
Nakhoda Sidi Ahmad, 204–207
Nila Tanam, 19
Nina Madi, 72, 82
Nina Sahak, 144–145
Nina Sura Dewana, 226–227
Nizam al-Muluk, 71

Orang Kaya Hitam, 83
Orang Kaya Raja Kenayan, 84
Orang Kaya Sogoh, 233, 236
Orang Kaya Tun Abu Sait, 162, 186
Orang Kaya Tun Adan, 162
Orang Kaya Tun Hasan, 129, 186
Orang Kaya Tun Muhammad, 162
Orang Kaya Tun Rana, 187
Orang Kaya Tun Sulat, 162

Pa' Si Bendul, 153–154
Pa' Tani, 211

Padang Gelang-Gelang, 45

Padang Maya, 56–57

Paduka Isap, 119

Paduka Mimat, 119

Paduka Seri China, 119

Paduka Seri Maharaja, 44, 58–59

Paduka Seri Pikrama Wira, 29–32,
    34–36

Paduka Seri Raja Muda, 231

Paduka Seri Sultan, 1

Paduka Tuan, 147, 164, 166, 184,
    206, 229, 239, 244, 250–255,
    257–258, 266–267, 270–272,
    274–279, 284–285, 290–291

Pagar Ruyung Pekan Tuha, 166

Pagoh, 237

Pahang, vii, 79, 120–122, 132, 157–
    160, 187, 198–199, 201–210,
    212, 215, 217–219, 237, 246,
    265, 272–273, 275–277,
    288–291

Pahili, 71

Paladutani, 19

Palembang, vi–vii, 2n3, 18, 20,
    24–25, 97, 106, 150–151

Pancar Serapung, 115

Parmada Buana, 49

Pasai, 45–46, 50–52, 54, 57, 65,
    72, 80, 84, 132, 134, 136–138,
    142–147, 163–165, 172,
    214–216

Pasangan, 45

Pasir Raja, ix, 1

Patani, 177, 212, 219

Patih Adam, 187–190

Patih Aria Gajah Mada, 91–95

Patih Ludang, 288–289, 291

Patih Semedar, 80, 266

Pau Bia, 149

Pau Gama, 149–150

Pau Glang, 148–149

Pau Kubah, 150

Pau Mechat, 150

Pau Tri, 149

Pekan Tuha, 166, 281, 283, 286

Penghulu Bujang Kari, 138

Perak, 10, 80, 273–274, 277–278,
    291

Perbata, 163

Perlak, 40, 48–49

Permain Island, 92

Perpatih Sandang, 73

Phra Chau, 89

Portugal, 234, 244

Portuguese, xi, 219–220, 234–237,
    242–244, 248–250, 253, 260,
    266–270, 282–286

Princess Bakal, 90, 107

Princess Cenandi Wasis, 13

Princess Genggang, 48–49

Princess Gunung Ledang, 141

Princess Hang Liu, 118–119

Princess Iram Dewi, 206

Princess Mathab al-Bahri, 16

Princess Naya Kesuma, 92–94, 96

Princess Onangkiau, 12–13

Princess Ratna Sundari, 63

Princess Rokan, 73

Princess Semangangrat, 31

Princess Shahr al-Bariyah, 5–7

Princess Talla Punchadi, 34–36

Princess Uwan Sundari, 21, 23–24

Pu Ji Bat Ji, 150
Punggur, 249
Pustar, 31

Queen of Kelantan, 237
Quran, 47–48, 213, 243

Raden Anum, 61, 77
Raden Bagus, 61
Raden Galuh, 103, 105
Raden Galuh Ajeng, 149–150
Raden Galuh Awi Kesuma, 91
Raden Galuh Cendera Kirana, 96,
    102, 105, 107
Raden Perlangu, 91–92
Raffles, vii, ix, xii
Raja Abdullah, vii
Raja Afdhus, 7–8
Raja Aftab al-Ard, 15–16
Raja Ahmad, 55, 124, 130–131,
    184, 210, 213, 246, 274
Raja Akbar Muluk Padshah, 71
Raja Alauddin Shah, 240
Raja Amtabus, 7–8
Raja Arashthun Shah, 7
Raja Arusiribikan, 8
Raja Ashkainat, 7
Raja Bongsu, vii, 291
Raja Chiran, 13
Raja Chulan, 13–19, 34
Raja Chulin, 10–13
Raja Dariya Nusa, 8
Raja Dewa Pahlawan, 143
Raja Dewi, 197, 274
Raja di Baruh, 222–223
Raja Fatimah, 274

Raja Ibrahim, 73
Raja Indera Pahlawan, 143
Raja Isak, 256
Raja Jainad, 288
Raja Jikanak, 149–150
Raja Kasdas, 7
Raja Kasim, 73–76
Raja Kastih, 8
Raja Kecil, 241
Raja Kecil Bambang, 61
Raja Kecil Besar, 59, 61
Raja Kedah, 191–192, 274
Raja Kharuaskainat, 7
Raja Kida Hindi, 3–7, 19
Raja Kobad Shahriar, 9
Raja Kofi Kudar, 8
Raja Kudar Shah, 17
Raja of China, 14, 116–119, 127
Raja of Daha, 97–98
Raja of Perlak, 40–41, 43, 48–49
Raja Pagar Ruyung, 166
Raja Putih, 233, 260, 262–263
Raja Raden, 151–152
Raja Ramji, 8
Raja Sabur, 8
Raja Sami'un, 256
Raja Seri Benyaman, 271
Raja Shahi Tarsi, 8
Raja Shahr Nuwi, 51–54
Raja Shah Taramsi, 8
Raja Shulan, 9–13
Raja Siti, 274
Raja Sulaiman, 19, 211
Raja Sulaiman Shah, 211
Raja Suran Padshah, 8, 13
Raja Tarsi Bardaras, 8

Raja Teja, 8
Raja Tengah, 61–63, 274
Raja Turkistan, 7
Raja Uramzad, 8
Raja Zainal, 154, 181–182
Raja Zainal 'Abidin, 180–181
Raya River, 218
Rokan, 73–74, 76–77, 156
Rotan Siam, 81

Sabat Island, 252
Sakidar Shah, 25
Sambar Straits, 25
Samudera, 46–48, 50–57
Sang Aji Ningrat, 94
Sang Aria, 121, 143
Sang Bentan, 32
Sang Bijaya Ratna, 280
Sang Guna, 65, 120–121, 143, 166,
    182–183, 217, 248, 290
Sanggung Mountain, 45
Sang Jaya Pikrama, 120–121, 129,
    143, 217, 248, 290
Sangkaningrat, 102
Sang Maniaka, 20, 91
Sang Naya, 120–121, 143, 166,
    217, 249–250, 282–283
Sang Raden, 121
Sang Rajuna Tapa, 59–60
Sang Rana, 143, 250
Sang Seperba, 20, 129
Sang Setia, 65, 120–121, 139–141,
    166, 217, 231, 237, 248,
    250–255, 266–267, 288–291
Sang Setia Bentayan, 171
Sang Setia Pahlawan, 143

Sang Sura, 121, 182–183, 228, 232
Sang Surana, 121, 129, 143
Sang Sura Pahlawan, 121, 143
Sang Uratama, 20
Sanskrit, 21n1
Sawang, 115, 251–252
Sayung, 36, 38, 115, 270, 285–286,
    288, 291
Sedili Besar, 132, 209
Sejarah Melayu, v
Selan, 197
Selangor, 57, 258, 270, 274
Sepat Straits, 25
Seri Agar King of Fatani, 1
Seri Akar Raja, 121, 157–159, 208,
    271, 274, 277
Seri Amar al-Diraja, 244
Seri Amar Bangsa, 162, 217, 239,
    242
Seri Amar Diraja, 63, 72–73, 129,
    168
Seri Amar Wangsa al-Diraja, 198
Seri Awadana, 129–130
Seri Bija al-Diraja, 65, 68, 84–85,
    112, 121–123, 132, 142, 145,
    164–166, 170–171, 179, 197,
    217
Seri Bijaya Pikrama, 231
Seri Guna Diraja, 231
Seri Indera, 164, 261–262
Seri Kaya, 48
Seri Maharaja, 44, 58–59, 121, 124,
    154–156, 184–187, 191–192,
    195, 207, 213–215, 217–226,
    228–229, 231–232, 239
Seri Maharaja Mutahir, 161

Seri Nara al-Diraja, 63, 72–77,
    82–84, 96, 108–110, 115–116,
    122–125, 132, 154, 161,
    166–168, 184, 187–189, 217,
    222, 228–229, 239, 266–272,
    279–280, 284, 286
Seri Nara Wangsa, 1
Seri Nata, 170, 217, 242
Seri Petam, 177, 239, 242
Seri Pikrama Raja, 231
Seri Pikrama Raja Pahlawan, 158
Seri Pikrama Wira, 29, 31–32, 34–36
Seri Raja Pahlawan, 143
Seri Rama, 123–124, 170, 174, 210,
    213
Seri Rana Wikrama, 36, 38–39,
    41–43
Seri Teri Buana, 21–29
Seri Udana, 186, 233–234, 236–
    237, 265–266, 272
Seri Upatam, 217
Seri Utama, 217, 239, 242
Seri Wangsa al-Diraja, 199
Seriwa Raja, 73–74, 77–78, 83,
    172–174, 176–178, 184,
    199–202, 230
Setang Ujung, 60
Shah Indera Berma, 151
Shah Johan, 10
Shahmura, 114
Shah Palembang, 150–151
Shahr Nuwi, 51–55, 79, 85
Siak, vi, 129–130, 155–156, 160,
    256, 273
Siam, 79, 81, 84, 86–90, 120, 212,
    217, 275–276

Siamese, 81, 84–85, 88, 90, 211
Siantan, 106–107
Si Betung, 165
Sidi 'Ali Ghiatuddin, 52–55
Sidi Samayuddin, 48–50, 54–57
Sindi, 9, 13
Singa Pura, 28–35, 38–40, 57–61,
    85, 96, 171
Si Pikang, 260
Si Selamat, 237, 265
Si Tambang, 260
Si Tanda, 265
Si Teki, 266
Si Tuha, 265
Sudar, 115
Sukal, 285
Sulalat al-Salatin, v–vii, ix, xi–xiii, 2
Sulawesi, vii
Sultan 'Abdul Jalil Shah, 107
Sultan 'Abdul Jamal, 154, 198–201,
    205–206, 208–210
Sultan 'Alauddin Ri'ayat Shah,
    152, 273, 275, 277–281, 283,
    285–286, 288–291
Sultan Abu Shahid, 74–76
Sultan Ahmad, 55–57, 154, 170,
    212, 232, 234–238
Sultan Alauddin Ri'ayat Shah, 1
Sultan Husin, 260–264, 271
Sultan Ibrahim, 130, 160, 256
Sultan Iskandar Shah, 59–61
Sultan Iskandar Zulkarnain, 44
Sultan Khoja Ahmad Syah, 256
Sultan Mahmud Shah, 170–176,
    178–185, 187–189, 192–195,
    197–199, 201–202, 206–207,

210, 212–215, 217, 219,
    222–223, 227–230, 232–233,
    237–239, 241, 244–248, 250,
    253–273, 275
Sultan Makota, 61
Sultan Malik al-Mansur, 49, 51,
    54–57
Sultan Malik al-Salleh, 48–50
Sultan Malik al-Zahir, 49–51,
    54–57
Sultan Mansur Shah, 90–97,
    102–110, 112–116, 118–120,
    122–124, 127, 129–132, 134–
    136, 138–141, 146, 151–152,
    181–182, 210, 218, 237, 246
Sultan Muda, 240, 261, 263–264,
    273
Sultan Muhammad, 46, 132, 152,
    157–158
Sultan Muhammad Shah, 63–64,
    70, 73, 152, 288
Sultan Munawar Shah, 168, 184,
    217
Sultan Muzaffar Shah, 76–88, 90,
    274, 278–279, 288–291
Sultan Sujak, 163
Sultan Zainal 'Abidin, 142, 145–
    146
Sumatra, vi–vii, 45n1, 46–47, 72,
    97, 242
Sumatranese, vii
Surabaya, 187, 189–190
Syoyar, 87

Talar River, 277
Tandil Muhammad, 72

Tanjung Batu, 135
Tanjung Buras, 35
Tanjung Keling, 232
Tanjung Pura, 20, 31, 92, 95–98
Tanjung Tuan, 164
Tebing Tinggi, 266
Tekulai, 261
Telanai Terengganu, 156–157
Teluk Belanga, 27
Teluk Terli, 134
Temasik, vi–vii, 14, 27–28, 32
Tengkilu, 266
Tentai, 115
Terengganu, 132, 157–159
Terengganu Ujung Karang, 70
Terli, 134
Thobri, 47
Tirubalam, 156
Tuban, 195
Tun 'Abdul, 116, 125, 184, 187, 250
Tun 'Abdul Karim, 176
Tun 'Ali, 72–73, 171, 186–187,
    222–223, 232, 239
Tun 'Ali Haru, 90
Tun 'Ali Hati, 235–236, 238
Tun 'Ali Sandang, 171–172, 177
Tun 'Umar, 84–85, 173–174,
    177–178, 201, 239
Tun Abu, 162, 231
Tun Abu Bakar, 239
Tun Abu Ishak, 239
Tun Abu Saban, 129
Tun Ahmad, 129, 147
Tun Amat 'Ali, 286–287
Tun Aria, 170, 209, 235–236,
    256–258

Tun Aria Bija al-Diraja, 257–259, 271

Tun Bakau, 231

Tun Bali, 195

Tun Bambang, 1

Tun Bentan, 177, 231

Tun Biajit, 171–172, 175–176, 197, 242–243

Tun Biajit Hitam, 170, 231

Tun Biajit Ibrahim, 231

Tun Biajit Rupa, 239

Tun Biajit Ruqat, 186

Tun Biazid, 229–231

Tun Bija al-Diraja, 120, 166

Tun Bija Sura, 263

Tun Bija Wangsa, 136–138, 215–216

Tun Bijaya, 271

Tun Bijaya Maha Menteri, 82, 184, 271

Tun Bijaya Sura, 96, 98, 103–106, 143, 254

Tun Bilang, 250

Tun Boh, 231

Tun Buang, 231

Tun Bulan, 83

Tun Damang, 167–168

Tun Daud, 177

Tun Derahman, 276

Tun Dewi, 171

Tun Dolah, 239, 250–252

Tun Esah, 129

Tun Fatimah, 222–223, 231–233, 239–240

Tungkal, 97, 115

Tun Hamzah, 129, 147, 162, 177, 187, 229, 239

Tun Hasan, 137–138, 185, 231

Tun Hasan Temenggung, 186, 191–192, 220, 228

Tun Hidup Panjang Datuk Jawa, 187

Tun Husin, 190, 192–193, 231

Tun Iman Diraja, 231

Tun Indera Segara, 113–114, 228

Tun Isak, 162, 164–165, 171, 173–174, 178

Tun Isak Berakah, 164, 173, 177–178, 231, 236

Tun Ishak, 170

Tun Jalaluddin, 232–233

Tun Jamal, 231

Tun Jana Buga Dendang, 29, 41, 192

Tun Jana Khatib, 57–58

Tun Jana Makhluk Biri-biri, 138

Tun Jana Muka Bebal, 129–130

Tun Jana Pakibul, 160

Tun Jana Putera, 29

Tun Kecil, 195

Tun Kerah, 251

Tun Kudu, 78, 83, 115, 166, 187

Tun Kumala, 83

Tun Lela Wangsa, 186

Tun Mah, 187, 253, 258, 270–271

Tun Maha Menteri, 143

Tun Mahmud Shah, 257, 271

Tun Mai Ulat Bulu, 214, 232

Tun Makhdum Mua, 137–138

Tun Mamad, 140–141

Tun Mamat, 170

Tun Mat, 231, 239

Tun Merak, 250

Tun Minda, 187–190
Tun Muhaiyuddin, 232
Tun Muhammad, 114–115,
    215–216, 239
Tun Muhammad Rahang, 232
Tun Muhammad Unta, 235
Tun Muhiyuddin, 214
Tun Munah, 250
Tun Munawar, 231, 251
Tun Mutahir, 115, 124, 185
Tun Naja, 116, 154
Tun Nara Wangsa, 239, 250, 267,
    269–270, 272, 277, 283–285,
    287
Tun Pauh, 161, 231
Tun Pekuh, 231
Tun Pematakan, 136
Tun Perak, 78–82, 129
Tun Perpatih Besar, 63
Tun Perpatih Hitam, 192–193
Tun Perpatih Kasim, 147, 231
Tun Perpatih Muka Berjajar, 61
Tun Perpatih Pandak, 40–43, 49
Tun Perpatih Permuka Berjajar, 29,
    36
Tun Perpatih Permuka Sekalar, 29
Tun Perpatih Putih, 43, 78,
    116–118, 126, 162
Tun Perpatih Putih Permuka
    Berjajar, 29
Tun Perpatih Tulus, 36, 59, 61
Tun Perpatih Tulus Tukang Segara,
    55
Tun Pikrama, 65, 143–144, 147,
    231, 239, 250, 270, 277–278,
    280–281, 283–285, 287

Tun Pikrama Wira, 147, 164,
    239
Tun Puteri, 231
Tun Rana, 259, 263
Tun Ratna Sundari, 72
Tun Ratna Wati, 72–73
Tun Sabtu, 257
Tun Sadah, 250
Tun Salehuddin, 232–233, 236
Tun Sayid, 259
Tun Sebab, 96
Tun Seni, 231
Tun Seri Lanang, vii, ix, xiii
Tun Setia, 140
Tun Setia Diraja, 206
Tun Shah, 115
Tun Shahid Madi, 82
Tun Sirah, 197
Tun Sulaiman, 231, 233
Tun Sura Diraja, 228
Tun Tahir, 115, 124, 187
Tun Teja Ratna Menggala, 198
Tun Telanai, 86–90, 119–120, 143,
    157, 184
Tun Tempurung Gemeratukan,
    29
Tun Terang, 223, 239, 273–274
Tun Tiram, 231
Tun Tukak, 177
Tun Tunggal, 186
Tun Utusan, 147, 231
Tun Zahir, 231
Tun Zahiruddin, 233
Tun Zaid Boh, 231
Tun Zainal 'Abidin, 161, 176, 184,
    214, 232

Tun Zainal Naina, 96

Ulu Sepantai, 107
Ungaran, 115, 135
Utang Minang, 89–90
Uwan Empuk, 18–20

Uwan Malini, 18–20
Uwan Seri Bini, 25–26, 28–29

Yak, 149–150
Yang Dipertuan, 22, 146, 199, 267, 291